Pra
THE SON OF A

"There is more fabulous writing in just the first chapter of *The Son of a Certain Woman* by Wayne Johnston thaň in most entire books." Linwood Barclay

"Religion, sex, incest—all receive Johnston's incredible treatment, the mixture of comedy and pathos that has made him a best-seller. . . . Percy . . . has a captivating voice that won't be soon forgotten in Canadian literature." *Salon* magazine

"Extraordinary writing." *Telegraph-Journal*

"Johnston is the kind of storyteller who can go well past the point of believability with his tale, yet still give the reader a true sense of the history and flavour of his hometown of St. John's, and say something essential about human nature while he's at it." *The Gazette*

"Obsessed by sex, [Percy's] a Canuck version of the *schlemiels* (somewhat lovable inveterate losers) in American Jewish '60s novels by the likes of Philip Roth and Bruce Jay Friedman. . . . Instead of the earnest, put-upon heroine we might expect, [Penelope's] exuberantly foul-mouthed and erudite, defending her freedom with inspired irony and rapier-like repartee." *Maclean's*

"A surprising turn for the celebrated author of such CanLit staples as *The Colony of Unrequited Dreams*. . . . As elsewhere in his work, St. John's is here brought wonderfully to life."

The Globe and Mail (Best Book)

"The family, the city, the crisis: these are compacted myths, even characters' names—Percy, Penelope—are packed with resonance and archetype that Johnston then unwinds and refurls and twists. . . . *The Son of a Certain Woman* is constructed with layers of authority and fable [and] builds to an aptly Joyce-ean finish."

The Telegram

"Well-written, witty and hilarious. . . . Brilliant novel."

Literary Review of Canada

"Wayne Johnston seduces us from Page One."

Ottawa Magazine

the

SON

THE SON
OF A
CERTAIN WOMAN

WAYNE JOHNSTON

VINTAGE CANADA

VINTAGE CANADA EDITION, 2014

Copyright © 2013 1310945 Ontario Inc.

Published in Canada by Vintage Canada, a division of Random House of Canada
Limited, Toronto, in 2014. Originally published in hardcover in Canada by
Alfred A. Knopf Canada, a division of Random House of Canada Limited, in 2013.
Distributed by Random House of Canada Limited.

Vintage Canada with colophon is a registered trademark.

www.randomhouse.ca

Grateful acknowledgement is made for permission to reprint from the following:
"Leda and the Swan," "The Second Coming" and "A Prayer for My Daughter"
by W.B. Yeats, from *The Collected Works of W.B. Yeats* (Scribner, an imprint of
Simon & Schuster, Inc., New York, 2 Sub edition October 1, 1997).

Library and Archives Canada Cataloguing in Publication

Johnston, Wayne
The son of a certain woman / Wayne Johnston.

ISBN 978-0-345-80790-8

I. Title.

PS8569.O3918S66 2014   C813'.54   C2013-901562-0

Text and cover design by Terri Nimmo
Cover image: Roderick Field/Trevillion Images

Printed and bound in the United States of America

2 4 6 8 9 7 5 3 1

certain

For my friend Kevin Kenneally,
citizen of Canada, Ireland, the World

PART I

FSS

MOST of the people who knew my mother either slept with her or wished they had, including me, my aunt Medina and a man who boarded with us; though he was neither old nor someone's father, he went by the name of "Pops." I know that's ambiguous, but it's better left ambiguous for now. As for me wanting to sleep with my mother, if you disapprove, try spending your childhood with a face that looks long past its prime, with hands and feet like the paws of some prehuman that foraged on all fours—and then get back to me. Or better yet, read on.

It's hard to describe what your own face looks like. It's hard to be honest, but it's also hard, period, because most faces defy description. Mine *inspires* description. They used to say that the Inuit had a hundred words for snow. That's about as many ways as my face has been described. Someone once told me it looked as if it had been worked on by an abstract tattoo artist. A boy asked me if my mother had eaten more than the medically recommended amount of beets on the day she had me. Another said that I should wear a mask three hundred and sixty-four days of the year and go outside *without* one only on Halloween.

You may have seen people with birthmarks like mine. Something like mine, anyway, for mine are at the far worst end of the spectrum. Doctors call them "port wine stains" even though no one, when they see one, thinks of port. They're also described as strawberry-coloured, even though they're not. My mother said they call them "strawberry" to "put the best face on it," then apologized for what she said was an unintended pun.

When asked, I would try to explain that my birthmark was called a birthmark because it was discovered at birth, not because my face was marked *by* birth, but most people couldn't let go of the idea that something must have gone wrong *as* I was being born. My mother said they didn't like the idea of a fetus that was beet-faced, just lurking there in her womb, waiting to come out and spoil everything, because it made my birthmark seem more like God's mistake than hers. She added that people didn't like the idea of fetuses at all, so it was doubtful that one with a face that could stop a clock would change their minds.

For my first two weeks I was thought to have some kind of rare congenital syndrome. What I in fact had was the "benign" version of that syndrome which mimics the real thing for a short while after birth until the most sinister features simply fade away and all that remain are port wine stains and, in my case, oversized hands and feet. The false syndrome is even rarer than the real thing. It's called False Someone Syndrome. FSS. The "Someone" stands for three someones, three doctors with hyphen-joined last names who convinced my mother and the doctors at St. Clare's that I was doomed. The more names in front of a syndrome, the worse it is—two hyphens, three names, a syndrome that took three doctors to discover—or invent, as it's often seemed to me.

The doctors warned of possible "complications" that might manifest as I grew older. The stains, the ones on my face especially, might darken, spread, swell, blister, become infected, require tending to by dermatologists, the nearest of whom was in Halifax, five hundred miles of the North Atlantic away, to the west of St. John's, which itself is at the far eastern end of the island of Newfoundland.

People like me are apparently just one gene away from some major disability, and we so closely resemble those who *have* that disability that we are often mistaken at birth as having it. The only way to be sure is to wait to see if the sinister symptoms go away in a couple of weeks.

My mother's doctor didn't wait two weeks. He told her I had Someone's Syndrome, told her I was unlikely to make it through my teens and would have to live in a special home of some kind. But two weeks later—two weeks I spent in hospital—he told her that I had FSS, a kind of "watered-down version" of the syndrome. I had an overabundance of blood-engorged capillaries that, luckily for me, stayed clear of my brain. She told me that when he gave her word of what she called my "reprieve," she cried more than when she thought I was as good as gone, then sought him out and told him he was a watered-down version of a doctor. She said it wasn't like finding out that I'd been healthy all along, but as if I'd been dead and had come back to life merely because someone had changed his mind. "I was *so* happy, Perse," she said. The doctor seemed oblivious to the change in my mother's mood, so thrown off was he by her attractiveness. A couple of weeks after having a baby and she looked, he said, like Elizabeth Taylor. My mother pointed to his wedding ring with the finger on which she wore her engagement ring.

Flustered, the doctor then said that he was "thrown off" in his diagnosis of me by the "local gigantism" that was almost always a symptom of the real syndrome—"local gigantism" not meaning that you grow to eight or nine feet tall, but that parts of you are oversized, most often the extremities. In my case, as I said, my hands and feet were—in addition to being stained like my face—larger, which was better than having just one or two toes or fingers that were oversized, as is sometimes the case, and which would have made it necessary for me to have custom-made, and very odd-looking, gloves and shoes.

I know you're wondering if a certain other part of me was oversized. It wasn't, but that didn't stop people from assuming that it was, or speculating, or gossiping about it, and of course it didn't stop me, once I reached a certain age, from *claiming* it was oversized.

My large hands looked as though they were stained with blood, front and back, and flopped about—or so it seemed to me—on the ends of my wrists like empty gloves attached by a string lest I lose them. Hairless hands the size of a grown man's, a butcher's begrimed and exfoliated by his profession, they might as well have been grafted onto me. They barely fit into the pockets of my slacks and my blazer, and when I withdrew them, my pockets turned almost completely inside out. I always looked as if I were wearing shoes or boots that were far too big for me, boots handed down from a father or much older brother because my parents couldn't afford to buy me ones that fit. Hands and feet like fins I had, except there was no webbing between the fingers and the toes. My red feet made it look as if I'd stood for far too long in ankle-deep, scalding water. I had a swollen lower lip of the sort associated with a lack of intelligence and that made me speak as if there was still some freezing left from a trip to the dentist's. What did the people of St. John's see when they looked at me? A slobbering, jabbering aberration, I suppose, whose mind, character and personality must likewise be aberrant, altered for the worse by whatever "something" had marred me from the moment of my conception, some God-willed conflux of mishaps in my makeup, in the chaos that attended my creation.

That my mother named me before the good news has always made me feel a little as though I bear someone else's name, that of the poor infant who "lived" for just a few weeks and whose "death" was not mourned but celebrated. Sometimes, perverse though it seems, I've found myself feeling sorry, even guilty, about that other, helpless Percy whom I supplanted, Percy the First, whose reign was brief, illusory.

My mother told me she had chosen the name "Percy" before I was born. "Percy" in case of a boy. "I named you after the poet, Percy Bysshe Shelley," she said. "You came this close to going through life named Bysshe."

So I missed total catastrophe by a genetic whisker—and wound up with a "watered down" catastrophe. Despite countless reassurances, I worried that this "whisker" in my makeup would wither or be worn away and the real version of the syndrome would be activated. I told my mother I had heard someone say "there's a first time for everything."

"It's just an expression, Perse," she said. "There isn't a first time for everything. Most things have never happened and never will."

"But what if it happens?"

"It can't happen. It won't happen. It has never happened and it never will."

During the first two weeks I'd spent in hospital after I was born, my mother believed that she would never take me home, that I would never speak, that I would be blind, and that my other senses would be almost as badly compromised. She believed that she would visit me in a home as often as she could stand to for however long I had on earth.

And the prospect of all this hit her, she said, just seven months after my father had lit out for what he must have thought was greener grass.

My mother still wore her engagement ring. "Call me Miss Havisham," she often said, though at the time I didn't know what she meant.

My father ran off when my mother was two months pregnant, making me the bastard child of Penny Joyce. Born out of wedlock, though my parents were engaged. My mother changed her last name, which had been Murphy, to Joyce. It was wrongly assumed she did this because, even though her fiancé Jim Joyce had left her, she still loved him and wanted their child to bear his name. "I like to wear the engagement ring," she said. "It has a discouraging effect on men, those who know me and those who'd like to."

The boys at school said it was because my parents couldn't "wait" for marriage that I was born beet-faced. Some said that it was because my *mother* couldn't wait, a woman who wouldn't take no for an answer from her fiancé. They had planned to marry on the one-year anniversary of their engagement. Although it was the general opinion that making your fiancée pregnant would not be held against you in the long run, it being so common, the widely repeated version of the story was that Jim Joyce had run off out of shame for what he'd done. But the most widely held belief was that there must be something more to the story, that perhaps I was not Jim Joyce's son, which he would have been certain of if he and my mother had never "done it" or had done it at a time that did not jive with that of her pregnancy. My mother, if not exactly regarded with suspicion, was the subject of many wink-and-nudge jokes and much skeptical speculation. The truth is that Jim Joyce is, or was—he might be long gone—my father. There will be no surprise revelations to the contrary.

The eternally engaged Penelope Joyce, a fiancée forever.

She had a Gallic complexion, was said to be descended from the Black Irish, the children supposedly born from the mingling of those who survived the sinking of the Spanish Armada with Irish women who took them in after the British blew their fleet to smithereens, Spaniards who crawled, swam, thrashed and washed ashore on the east coast of Ireland and were hidden by the English-loathing Irish. There was not a single authenticated instance of this having happened and therefore no recorded instances of Black Irish emigrating to the New World, but about one in ten Newfoundlanders was Latin-looking for no other even half-convincing reason that anyone could name. My mother was one of the ten percent, or rather one of the five percent of exotic, hot-blooded, passionate, reputedly fuck-loving women.

The Catholic Black Irish were known as Black Micks to Protestants, and even to those who lived on the Mount. I was not a Black Mick. Jim Joyce wasn't one. Genetically speaking, having a Black Mick mother didn't make you more likely to be a Black Mick than anyone else. That portion of me that was not port wine coloured did not bear the complexion of someone long tanned by the sun. It bore the complexion of someone who, like most Newfoundlanders, was long deprived of sunlight. My hair was not as slick and black as my mother's, nor my eyes as dark as hers. Many people on the Mount who didn't know, or pretended not to know, what Black Irish meant took it to mean that blacks from Africa perched somewhere, somehow, in the family tree, that my mother was "coloured," that her being coloured had something to do with my being miscoloured; how much mixing of races could there be before the result was a calamity like Percy Joyce? Priests, nuns and other missionaries were dying in Africa in an effort to convert the pagans of that continent to Christianity, and here at home were the Joyces, unconverted blacks or coloureds of *some* kind, my mother a recalcitrant, non-churchgoing maverick and me an unbaptized, non-denominational renegade, walking therefore the high wire above the abyss of damnation, liable to fall at any time yet allowed to go on working without the net that others (including my mother) had—the safety net of baptism by which the fallen are caught far short of Hell.

The thing about rumours, half-truths, misconceptions, is that people believe them all, so it doesn't matter if one contradicts the other—you are credited and blamed as if all of them are true.

I was black. I was a Mick. I was a Black Mick whose face just happened to be purple. I was a Catholic because my mother was one—the whole "not being baptized" thing was just a technicality. But my mother was a lapsed Catholic, which was worse than being non-Catholic. There was hope for ·non-Catholics—they might someday be converted—whereas someone who had been shown the truth and had turned away from it, well, that was what rebel angels such as Satan and Lucifer had done. My mother was looked down on by some for being a Black Mick, a sexual animal, a descendant of the same people as the Spanish fishermen who, smoking their foul-smelling cigarettes, prowled the St. John's waterfront in search of whores. She was lusted after by most men for having that little bit of Spanish blood that supposedly made her such a fire-fuck.

I often compared myself to my mother.

The facial stain extended from my scalp to within about an inch of my Adam's apple, which made it look as if every other inch of my torso must be thus discoloured, even though I have no other stains on it except a small one that has my belly button at the centre. My mother was relieved that I had no stains on my backside or on what she said might be considered the worst possible place. I sometimes complained of the unfairness of the stain on my face, which could just as easily have been discreetly located on the soles of my feet or in my armpits, but my mother reminded me of how close I had come to a life in which the location of my stain would have been the least of my problems.

And my mother? My mother was five-eight, big-breasted, wide-hipped, bust and waist in perfect proportion, full-lipped, high-cheekboned, the Sophia Loren of the Mount. I can only faintly remember a time when my ardour for her was not at least equal to the most Penny Joyce–pining, Black Irish cunt–coveting, balls-aching adolescent on the Mount, the name for the hill on which St. John's is built. And forget Freud. If Mrs. Clancy next door had been my mother, I wouldn't have, couldn't have, thought of her in *that way*.

"I'd be happy to trade my looks for yours," Medina said to my mother.

"Would you be happy to trade your looks for mine?" I asked my mother.

"Sure I would, squirt," she said, and kissed me on top of the head.

"You're afraid to kiss my cheek," I said. And suddenly she was stamping my face all over with kisses as if it were a well-travelled passport. Kiss, kiss, kiss, kiss.

Medina, my aunt, Jim Joyce's sister, had a kind of Betty Boop look: short, tightly curled black hair, round, dark, lashy eyes. She was more attractive than she gave herself credit for—tall, large-boned, with long, lanky legs that were a touch too thick just below her bum.

I was first known throughout the neighbourhood as the Joyce Baby, a euphemism that stood both for my stain and for my father being "on the lam"—the expression used until it was clear he wasn't coming back. When I was old enough to walk with my mother about the neighbourhood, I became known as the Joyce boy. My mother said people made too big a deal of my birthmark. She said they probably thought that if Helen Keller had been given the added burden of my limbs and face, she'd never have amounted to anything. Some thought that physically manifested within me were the qualities of the sort of man who would desert his pregnant fiancée—and so I would forever be a reminder to the world, as well as to my mother and myself, of his inexplicable offence—though my mother also thought that people believed she was somehow to blame.

ST. JOHN'S DAY, JUNE 24

I WAS born on June 24, which was known as St. John's Day after the city, which itself was named after Saint John the Baptist because the site of it was supposedly discovered on June 24, 1497, the feast day of the Baptist. My mother often said that St. John's was "my city." On my fourth birthday, my mother, Medina and I went out for an evening walk in my city; at my mother's insistence, Pops, our boarder and a chemistry teacher at Brother Rice High School across the street from our house, never went anywhere with us. It was a familiar sight, my mother and her not-quite sister-in-law walking about the neighbourhood, my mother and the woman who was regarded as the last vestige of her delinquent husband—and between them, holding their hands, me. On this evening, filled to near bursting with birthday cake, I plodded along, wishing that a tour of "my city" wasn't one of my birthday presents.

The eyes of every man we passed were on my mother. Motorists honked their horns, hastily rolled down their windows to whistle or shout something about her, or me, that they would not have dared say to her face.

"Nothing like a nice inconspicuous walk around St. John's," my mother said.

"You'd be less conspicuous if you tied down or covered up those tits of yours," Medina said. "I swear that the colder it is, the less you wear."

Between those who ogled my mother and those who gaped at me, almost no one, driving or on foot, passed us without some acknowledgement. Many of them guessed her name because she was with me. "Percy Joyce's mother" was known of even by those who had never set eyes on either one of us. She was known to be an eye-popping voluptuary, so when people saw my face and realized that I was "Percy Joyce," they knew the name of the better-looking of the two women who held my hands, knew it was "Penny and Percy" they had sighted, Beauty and the Beast, and they acted accordingly.

"They see you two, but they don't see me," Medina said one evening. "I might as well be invisible."

"I wish I was invisible," I said.

"Don't mind me," Medina said. "I'm just jealous of your mother."

We walked through narrow stone alleyways and down long sets of stairs in our descent from the Mount. On every landing there was at least one open doorway leading to a bar, sometimes two or three. These narrow passages reeked of beer and cigarette smoke, and the hubbub from within was sometimes such that it sounded to me as if a mass argument was taking place among the patrons. An old man in a sod cap came out, looked at me, said, "Oh, sweet Jesus, I gotta stay off the London Dock," laughed loudly, and hurried back inside.

"Toothless fucker," my mother shouted. "Next time I'll shove a pool ball down your throat."

"Nice bangers, Penny. How's your mash?" "How's your shrimp dick, Dick?" "I'd love a clam sandwich." "Your wife is famous for hers."

A group of boys on the other side of the street—they seemed to be not altogether unfriendly—called out to me, "HEY PERCY," almost in unison, as one would at the sight of the sort of city mascot my mother feared I would become. Being but four years old, I had no better sense than to say hello and wave—which the boys found hilarious. "What's *your* name?" I said, more or less to all the boys. It seemed odd that people I'd never seen before knew my name, but I was tickled by it. They laughed, but none of them offered up a name, as if asking strangers to reveal their names was something that Little Percy Joyce was famous for. A middle-aged woman on their side of the street told the boys to leave me alone, at which they laughed yet again and protested that all they'd done was say hello. "Oh, they're not doing any harm," my mother said to the woman, who gave her a look of rebuke, shook her fist at the boys and said: "That poor little fella is just as much God's child as any of you. The Good Lord made him as he is so you crowd should leave him alone." This, my mother later told Medina, who'd remained silent throughout the exchange, was about the last thing you wanted anyone to do in your son's defence, to loudly proclaim in public that the Good Lord had made him what he was, that all appearances and opinions to the contrary, he was as much "a child of God" as anyone. What did it say about someone that you felt you had to remind people he was a child of God? "You'd think he had scuttled onto the street on seven arms and legs," my mother said, and Medina laughed.

Medina said she didn't mind the boys as much as the men. "Frig off," she shouted that evening at a man who said that, judging by the look of me, my mother had never been laid properly. "He botched *that* job," the man said. "I said frig off," Medina shouted. He was standing in the doorway of a house across the street, wearing an undershirt, his pants tightly buckled beneath the bulge of his belly. "I wasn't talking to you, ugly duckie," he said. "I bet your you-know-what looks like that youngster's face. I'd rather eat a plate of chips."

"Leave him alone or I'll come over there and smack *your* face."

"You'll have to forgive her," my mother intervened. "She's not used to meeting men whose daughters double as their sisters." The man laughed, threw his cigarette butt on the sidewalk and went inside.

"You talk to them the way they talk to you," Medina said.

"No, I don't."

"You do."

"It was the politest way I could think of to call him a mother-fucker. He did say 'you-know-what' instead of what he might have said. I thought one euphemism deserved another."

"You shouldn't talk like you do in front of Perse."

"Things will be even worse for him if I shield him from what's coming."

"I could have used a bit of shielding. So could you."

"It's not the same. I beat them at their own game. That's why they laugh and go away. It's more effective than 'frig off.'"

"I'll stick with 'frig off.'"

We went past the corner beer bars with their ever-open doors, but in spite of that, they were too dark to see a thing inside. Accordion music blasted out into the streets, the siren call to patrons who couldn't stand to stay at home. We walked through Rabbit Town, past the haphazardly built houses of the very poor, each with a single concrete block to serve as its front steps. There were no front yards, just sidewalk-overlooking windows with closed sheer curtains that allowed both privacy and light. I caught glimpses of tiny front rooms unlit but for television screens that flickered in the early evening gloom. We went to Jackman's Grocery Store, on the windows of which prices were scrawled in whitewash. Rabbits hung upside down like talismans in the doorway. My mother bought from Mrs. Jackman three squares of chocolate and vanilla fudge sprinkled with coconut, pure sugar blocks that I bolted down while my mother looked at me and grimaced even as she smiled.

We walked through the richer neighbourhoods where grand, many-storeyed wooden houses blocked most of what little light was left. We didn't go by Medina's neighbourhood, which she said was "crawling with saucy crackies" who would descend upon someone of my "unique features"—a phrase she borrowed from my mother—like wild dogs. They were brought up outdoors, she said, and knew a hundred ways to steal a nickel. "You don't want to see my room," she said, though I protested that I did. "It's just a room, a table, a hot plate, a bed. A few other things. St. John's is full of rooms just like it, so I'm not ashamed of it." My mother winked at me and I fought back the urge to scrutinize Medina to see if she looked ashamed.

Always, as we turned a corner, a gale blowing uphill from the harbour hit us full in the face, smelling of the sea, of the bilge from foreign ships, of everything that lay between the water's edge and us: grass, birchbark, deep-fried chips, cigarette smoke, chimney smoke, beer, tar, pitch, asphalt, creosote, the exhaust of cars and trucks, the impossible-to-isolate, indefinable something that was the smell of the wind itself. The wind blew through the upper levels of the largest trees, which shimmered and crackled cease-lessly. Subdued into silence by the onset of night and by the bite of a new chill that betokened fog, we headed home.

"The old, sad city of St. John's," my mother called it when we were back home and sitting around the kitchen, saying that it looked sad and its history was sad. She said it looked as though it had been under water or under ice for centuries, the sea or glacier having just recently withdrawn, leaving everything in a state of rust, the paint peeling, the wood rotting, the stunted trees sag-ging windward, the green metal street signs wind-warped, bent, corkscrewed, the buildings stained with salt, the pavement pot-holed beyond repair, the earth cracked and strewn with streams that ever-widened or overflowed with the least bit of rain. My mother read Poe's "The City in the Sea" to me, a poem about a city that, although it didn't look like St. John's, made me think of it, for it *felt* the same, gloomily submerged in time itself, slumping under the weight of its own history.

My mother called St. John's a lot of things. She called it The City of Percy. A City Upon a Hill, which she said was from the Biblical parable of Salt and Light. She called it The City Without Pity and The Glorified Town. The City of Chaotic Traffic because of the number of purposeless one-way streets, dead ends, sharp turns, all-but-vertical cul-de-sacs, intersections that were rem-nants of streetcar lines that criss-crossed in ways so random they could keep you going in a circle or a square for minutes with no clue from a road sign as to how you might escape. The City of Salt. The City of Wind, The Anemopolis. The City of Aeolus Who Was the God of Wind. The City of Water. The City of Eros and Erosion. The City of Aphrodite. The City of Fog. The City of Fire. The City of Winter. The City of Ice. The City on the Eastern Edge, the Fringe, the Rim. The Little City. The City of Fish. The City of Well-Attended Churches and Overflowing Bars. The City of Big Boys and Girls Heading Home in a Hurry with Grease-Stained Brown Paper Bags. The City of Eccentrics. The City of the Sane, the Half Cracked and the Unmistakably Demented. The City of the Open-Hearted, the Broken-Hearted, the Half-Hearted. The City of Gossip and Unimpeachable Discretion. The City of Piety and Blasphemy. The City of Night and Day. The City of Abstinence and Revelry. The City That Thrice Went Up in Smoke. The City of Milkmen, Meat Men, Cod-Tongue-Hawking, Bucket-Lugging Boys from the Battery and Brow. The City of Shut-ins. Of Homesick Sailors and Too Many Men. The City of Hilarity. The City of Storm-Scorning, Weather-Oblivious,

Bar-Bound Pedestrians. The City of Unwarranted Optimism and Entirely Justified Despair.

The boys of Bonaventure lusted after my mother. A boy with the unlikely name of Squire Coffin would grab his crotch and say to me: "Give my love to Miss Juice." Some, to my mystification, called her Miss Joy Juice, some simply Miss Joyce, "Miss" being the most important part, invoking older but still young, a single mother, forbidden, illicit, not widowed but without a man, without one through no choice of hers and therefore surely craving what she hadn't had in years. Some simply seemed to savour her first name, shouting it as they went past our house: "*Penelopeee.*" "*Elope with me, Penelope.*"

I saw my mother pause at her typewriter to listen to them, to the primal ritual of school-day afternoons below the Mount, the bellowing of the boys who could see our house from the windows of their classroom, the house of the beautiful, lonely Miss Joyce who was longing for it from the sort of boy who in her youth had pleasured her as her long-absent husband never could. My mother would laugh even as Pops, the chemistry teacher, clad in his white lab coat, shouted at the boys from the steps, telling them to shut their mouths, shaking his fist.

My aunt Medina couldn't afford bus fare, so she walked everywhere. She had a full-body yellow oilskin that she'd bought second-hand from the Canadian Coast Guard. It was too big for her, so she was able to wear underneath it a parka that she had bought at the Goodwill. She had a pair of black workboots that laced tightly up her shins. In rain, snow, wind, cold, she would arrive at our house after her mile walk from her room like a crew member who had just stepped off a stormbound ship in the harbour, her yellow raincoat glistening with water or coated on the windward side with melting snow, wearing a black watch cap inside her hood, and leather-palmed mittens.

Once she was out of her oilskin and parka, Medina was bone-dry. In the coldest weather she would come in with her hands tucked into her armpits, stamping her feet, which she said felt as if they were being stuck with pins and needles. "I'm cold to the very core," she'd say. "There's a ball of ice in my belly that only a beer can melt."

She'd spend the next half-hour defrosting by the stove, sipping on her beer, or rather Pops' beer, which she took from the fridge without asking, while the smell of her mittens drying on the radiator spread throughout the house.

"I thought I would perish this time, Pen, I really did," she'd say.

She smoked Matinée cigarettes; the top of the yellow package always protruded from the side pocket of her hospital uniform or the pocket of whatever blouse she was wearing, because she didn't have a purse, didn't want one, never saw the need for one, eschewed one. She believed she was looked at, the rare times she'd carried one, as if she'd stolen it, though her coat pockets were always crammed with chewing gum, Kleenex, lipstick—her only form of makeup—as well as bills and coins and gloves. "Some women, like Pen, look good with a purse," she said. "Some, like me, don't. I don't like accessories, I like necessities." She was quoting my mother, who had said she liked to feel she could get by no matter what her world was reduced to.

One day, I strayed away from the front yard just as a snowstorm was about to start. By the time I crested Bonaventure, I couldn't see a thing, so I turned back.

As I was heading down Bonaventure to our house at 44, the wind blew the breath down my throat and I wondered if I should run. Then I saw Medina coming toward me, barely visible in the storm, all her clothing flattened at the front and flapping and wagging behind her in the wind, one hand on her hood as, head down, she struggled up the slope, her face turned to avoid the sting of slantwise-driven snow. When she drew near me, she was as frantic-looking as if I had been missing in the storm for hours. It strikes me now how alone and vulnerable she looked, as if her being out in such weather was due to some emergency that she could find no one else to help her with. A woman on her own when the balance of the city was indoors and the outdoors looked deserted but for that yellow raincoat. "PERCY!" she shouted, her voice just audible above the wind and sifting snow. When she reached me, she shielded my face with her hand and hugged me to her with her free arm. When we got to 44 and stood in the shelter of the porch, she put her hands on my shoulders and kissed me several times, kissed me on the forehead, on the cheeks and once right on the lips. "You're a real little bugger," she said, "you know that? A real little bugger." For my mother and her to stamp me with kisses until I coyly protested became our game.

That night, lying in bed, I overheard my mother and Medina playing cards and drinking beer in the kitchen. The more they drank, the louder they spoke.

"I've seen children at the hospital who don't have any kind of syndrome who make Percy look like Rock Hudson," Medina said. My mother said she couldn't help but wonder what adulthood held in store for me. "Not to mention young adulthood. Jesus."

"Any girl or woman would be lucky to get him," Medina said. "He's a good boy. He's smarter than all the other boys. The day will come when they'll wish they hadn't been so mean to him."

But she eventually reached the point of making my mother laugh away her troubles by predicting that her very worst fears would be realized. It wasn't long before my mother joined in. "Future-wise," Medina said, "his best bet is to get his hermit's licence."

"Or he'll have to be a Christian Brother or a priest," my mother said. "In which case he'll be known as Cleric the Red."

"Whatever that means," Medina said.

I laughed along with them and hoped that, in their tipsy condition, they didn't abruptly switch tone as they sometimes did. "If he grew a beard thick enough, you might not even see the stain on his face," Medina stage-whispered.

"Oh Christ," my mother said, again sounding sad, "maybe he could learn to type like me and never have to leave the house." But then they began to enumerate television and movie roles for which my facial stain would not disqualify me: Helmet-Wearing Deep Sea Diver; Coal-Dust-Covered Miner; Masked Surgeon; Bandaged Burn Victim; Mummy; Hooded Ku Klux Klansman.

I got up and went out to the kitchen, passing Pops, who was drinking beer in the sunroom. He gave me a little wave and I waved back.

"Hope we didn't wake you up, Perse," Medina said.

I shook my head and sat at the table with them. I sat up late with them. They played Crazy Eights, Cribbage and Auction Forty-fives. They drank brown stubbies of Dominion Ale, poured it into glasses that, when you bought them, were filled with peanut butter, "bonus" glasses on the sides of which were hearts, diamonds, clubs and spades. (Pops always drank his straight from the bottle, saying that he wouldn't stoop to drinking "peanut butter beer.")

My eyes watering from cigarette smoke, I stared at the enormous green glass ashtray that had six grooves for holding cigarettes. It was filled with ashes, stabbed with lipstick-smudged cigarette butts, some of them still smouldering, smoke rising in columns as if from a pincushion that would soon ignite.

"He came out for the food, like always, not for the conversation, right Perse?" my mother said. I nodded.

We—mostly Medina and I—made our way through a bag of salt-encrusted pretzel sticks and a bag of potato chips. "Your mother's watching her figure," Medina teased.

"You wouldn't think I'd need to with so many other people watching it," my mother said, winking at Medina.

"See if Pops is gone to bed, Perse," my mother said. I got up from the table and peeked into the sunroom. Pops' chair was empty, surrounded by what looked to be a dozen beer bottles. I ventured out to the living room, where I saw that the door of Pops' room was closed and the light was off. I went back to the kitchen.

"He's gone to bed," I said.

"Good," my mother said. "Your turn now."

"I haven't had anything to drink. I'm thirsty."

My mother quickly made up some Freshie, adding water to a pouch of powder that she poured into a jug. I drank it all, guzzled it greedily.

"Now, off to bed," my mother said.

I needed no further urging. I reached out my hands to her to signal that I wanted her to carry me to bed. I was almost asleep by the time we got to my room. I heard Medina giggling and my mother telling her to stop.

"The men are asleep," Medina said.

"Thank Christ," my mother said.

My mother and Medina were sleeping with each other on the sly as often as they could. A woman in love with her brother's fiancée, a woman in love with her fiancé's sister—you wouldn't want that to be common knowledge *now* let alone back then, back there, in the late fifties. I didn't find out about my mother and Medina until I was in grade four at St. Bon's School, not long after I also found out that, in exchange for help with the mortgage, my mother, with Medina's knowledge but not her approval, was sleeping on the sly with the obscurely named Pops, the chemistry teacher who taught in the school across the street and rented a room in our house. He didn't know about Medina and my mother, and didn't know that Medina knew about *him* and my mother. It was not a good time or place for anyone to be known to be sleeping with anyone they weren't at least engaged to. A woman caught with a woman or known to be in love with one would likely be sent to jail or deemed to be insane and committed until she was "cured." For certain I'd have been taken away from my mother.

In St. John's, there was, as my mother put it, no separation between Church and Fate. We lived in a neighbourhood known as the Mount, which I'd be willing to bet was the most intensely and exclusively Catholic neighbourhood in North America. St. John's consisted of a patchwork of neighbourhoods, each neighbourhood at war with all the others for reasons either long forgotten or non-existent unless they had to do with religious denominations, of which there seemed to be no end, each one with its own school board, bus fleet, churches and schools, even the Salvation Army, which was known as The Lowest Common Denomination.

Catholicism Central. It was a kind of smaller-scale Vatican City. There were seven Christian Brothers-and-nuns-run schools within a stone's throw of each other: St. Pat's and St. Bon's, rival junior all-boys schools run by the CBs, as the Irish Christian Brothers were called; Brother Rice, an all-boys high school run by CBs; Holy Heart of Mary, an all-girls high school run by some Mercy but mostly Presentation nuns; the Mercy Convent girls' school on Barnes Road; the Presentation Convent girls' school; and Belvedere, an all-girls, junior school–aged orphanage that was also run by nuns.

These were known as The Seven Schools of the Mount.

There were also, at various elevations on the Mount, convents, rectories, dormitories for the CBs, Catholic graveyards, monasteries and the Basilica, the largest cathedral east of Montreal, home of the Archbishop.

If you started from our house and climbed Bonaventure toward the Basilica atop the Mount, there were four schools on the right: Brother Rice, where I would eventually go to high school, Belvedere, Holy Heart and St. Pat's. St. Bon's, which would be my junior school, was on the left, directly across the street from St. Pat's. Past St. Bon's, Bonaventure sloped down the other side of the Mount and became Garrison Hill. The Basilica was on your immediate left, the Mercy Convent School just slightly to the left of that, and the Presentation Convent School was on the right, the two convent schools flanking the Basilica. The Seven Schools and the Basilica formed an imperfect ring, of which the Basilica was the city-and-sea-facing centre jewel, the Big B on a Calvary-like peak, its Roman wings protectively outspread. The whole structure seemed situated and built so as best to repel some Protestant invasion force that would have had to scale the ramparts of the city just to reach the outskirts of its Catholic castle.

There were ascetic, severe-looking Jesuits and nuns, and "normal" priests swishing about in their stark black frocks. There were brown-robed and hooded Capuchin monks who always ventured out in pairs, as if thereby to make themselves look less odd.

Deacons, final-year seminarians who served as assistants to the Archbishop and the basilica priests, were everywhere, pale, intense, zealous-looking young men for whom the Basilica was their first posting in the outside world, soon-to-be priests, champing at the bit as the day of their ordination by a bishop fast approached and for whom every sighting of Penny Joyce must have been a tor-ment. They each had a prominent Adam's apple that bobbed all the more, going up and down like an air-blown bingo ball, as they looked at her.

School blazers of various colours were everywhere. There were maroon blazers, green blazers, blue blazers, grey blazers, and tunics of just as many colours, though the blouse and legs of every girl were white.

And Pops of Brother Rice went about among their black and brown frocks in his conspicuous white lab coat like some obscure official of the Church. The Vatican Chemist, my mother called him.

When I was on the way, my father went away. It was hard not to see this as cause and effect. Jim Joyce. We'd never set eyes on each other, so he didn't know what I looked like, maybe didn't know about my having False Someone Syndrome, but still.

"Why did he go away?" I said. I was not in school yet or even worried about what going to school would be like.

"Don't know," my mother said, cracking her spearmint gum. "Forgot to tell me, I guess. He was very forgetful. All he took from me was the car and a hundred dollars, which was every cent I had. If he could have towed the house away, he would have."

There were no photographs of him in the house, which made me suspect that Jim Joyce had been disfigured too, that I'd inherited my disfigurement from him, but my mother assured me that Jim Joyce had left me with nothing.

She was already living at 44 Bonaventure when Jim Joyce ran off, having inherited from her mother, the second of her parents to die, the house and a mortgage that was larger than the purchase price because her mother was in arrears in payments. The plan had been for Jim Joyce to move in with her after they were married. When he ran off, my mother expected she would lose the house and likely would have if not for Pops, who answered her Room Available ad in the *Telegram*.

Our house was the only bungalow on Bonaventure. The other houses were two-storey or three-storey Victorian mansions: Bonaventure was one of the more affluent streets in the city, not much affected by the fire of 1892 that burned most of the city to the ground. On the north side of the street, however, none of the mansions remained. Schools, churches, graveyards, all Catholic, had replaced the burnt-out hulks. As a result, the value and prestige of the south side had declined. Bonaventure was, literally and figuratively, over the hill, past its heyday, and located on the far side of the Mount that was crowned by the Basilica.

Our house had gone up after a derelict mansion on the same site was torn down in the early fifties, and was not nearly as large as the house that it succeeded. On much of our lot, at the sides and back of the house, trees had grown up, incongruous urban patches of deciduous forest that, except in winter, blocked our view of our immediate neighbours and vice versa. There being little more than two sidewalks and a street separating our front yard and the city's largest school, Brother Rice High School, with its red brick, fortress-like facade, the undeveloped part of our property was all but worthless. Our house was snugly hemmed in by bamboo-thin poplar and birch trees, our front walkway forever buried in leaves, some newly fallen, some so old they crumbled beneath our feet into dust that blew away. Our leaf-strewn concrete walkway led up to a likewise leaf-strewn veranda that was unfurnished and never used. The house was three-toned; the vertical siding that flanked the windows was dark green while the horizontal clapboard beneath them was a rusty red, and the cement foundation was painted with white lime in a vain attempt to discourage cracks. It was, as my mother said, a Plain Jane of a house, unremarkable and easy to overlook.

Our furnishings looked like the temporary, make-do ones of a family that had arrived far in advance of its belongings. Though cramped, the adjoining living room and dining room seemed all but empty as so much of the shag-carpeted floor was left exposed. There was a compact, rickety dining-room table that was never used for dining, a faded brown corduroy sofa and matching chair in the living room, and a faux leather recliner in the gabled outcrop that was called the sunroom. The kitchen, my mother said, was a "chrome-linoleum-Formica masterpiece" with a waist-high fridge and flat-topped stove complete with removable dampers, and Gyproc cupboards. "Home sweet home," my mother would say wryly as she surveyed the rooms. But I think that, even had she been able to afford it, she would not have changed a thing, perhaps because she was as incongruous-looking in the house as our house was on the street. Almost any surroundings would have set my mother off to best advantage, but these made her look, as Pops once said, quoting Ezra Pound, "like a petal on a wet black bough."

There were two bedrooms on the east side of the house, mine and my mother's. Pops' bedroom was on the west side, an afterthought of an extension that jutted out from the house like an extra porch and lay directly opposite the sunroom.

Medina had a very low-paying, part-time job as an orderly at the Catholic hospital, St. Clare's. Pops would often say, "Medina, why are you wearing that bedpan expression?" Medina would tell him that one of these days he would wind up as a patient at St. Clare's and then what would he do, confined to a hospital bed with no one to protect him from her?

Pops was from St. Anthony, but he seemed to have no contact with anyone there or elsewhere on the island. He had inexplicably inconsistent quirks of pronunciation that Medina put down to his being from such a remote outport as St. Anthony. "There *is* no outport that remote," my mother said. "He must have been the only one who lived there, because no one else on earth sounds like *that*."

Pops always called my mother Penelope, but he pronounced *Pen* like *Pay*. Paynelope. He had long ago taught biology at Brother Rice and in one class had famously pronounced *vagina* with a hard *g*, a short *i* and the stress on the first syllable: *vagana*, like *wagon* with an *a* stuck on the end. He said he couldn't help the way that he pronounced some words—he said them as he'd been taught to say them. "Who teaches *anyone* how to pronounce *vagina*?" my mother said.

"At the dawn of time the sky was red, Percy," he told me. "A bad omen. That's why things have been fouled up ever since."

He had a kind of teaching manifesto that he would sometimes recite: "I will consider neither my time nor theirs to have been wasted if, as they look back over their years at Brother Rice, my students are unable to recall me teaching them anything but that death is not only inevitable but could come at any moment. And I should be doubly gratified if they were able also to recall the motto with which I strove to prepare them for the future: Don't bother starting today something you might not live to see the end of tomorrow."

"Did you ever think that you might not be entirely suited to teaching, Pops?" my mother said. "If you had written *Das Kapital*, the course of world history would be very different: 'Workers of the world, disband. Any way you look at it, we all die in the end.'"

The pocket of his lab coat read "Mr. MacDougal." From a distance, it looked like "Dr. MacDougal." He walked with his hands in the pockets of his lab coat, thumbs out in a way that seemed doctorly. All that was needed to complete his "look" was a stethoscope, which the strap of his safety goggles protruding from his lab coat pocket were often mistaken for by those who didn't know him.

He was so common and conspicuous a sight crossing Bonaventure at exactly the same time every morning in his white lab coat that passersby said, "Morning, Pops," and motorists honked their horns, in a partly fond, partly ironic way. Pops would answer with a perfunctory nod of his head and hurry up the steps of Brother Rice, his lips drawn in a tight line as if to humbly emphasize the importance of the work that awaited him, like some celebrity who is concerned that too effusive an acknowledgement of adulation will end with him being swarmed by fans.

In spite of his daily six-pack or so of beer, Pops was quite thin. He didn't eat much, seemed not to relish food or prefer one meal over another. My mother said he ate little more than was necessary to maintain a heartbeat. He spent a great deal of time grooming himself; the extension to the house that contained his room also contained a small bathroom for his exclusive use. He had a barber's kit, which he used to cut his own hair and trim his narrow, Hitleresque moustache. He shaved himself with a straight razor. His hair was as thick as the bristles of the thickest brush and he trimmed it daily with electric clippers. Though he was in his early forties, he didn't have so much as a thin patch, let alone a bald spot. He had the slender, dapper look of a dancer. He sometimes left the door of his room open and I saw him polishing his shoes with a cloth as vigorously as any sailor ever buffed his boots. He would have been the very picture of coiffed and sartorial splendour if not for The Coat of Many Colours. He had but one of them, and in spite of the efforts of my mother and a host of drycleaners, it bore a trace of every chemical that had ever stained it. "What would be the point of having more than one coat?" he said. "They'd all look alike in no time."

I watched his comings and goings, knowing that it wouldn't be long before I was going to the sort of place where he worked. I formed my notions about a "school" from things he said. I watched him drink beer and listened to him ramble on. My mother said his "people" either were deceased or had long ago fallen out of touch. He sat in an armchair in the little sunroom that faced away from Brother Rice, the street, the traffic, the rest of the house, the world. It overlooked the backyard and the house behind us. He drank and drank and seemed to stare at his reflection in the window.

"I live from paycheque to paycheque," Pops said to Medina. "I'm not able to put a cent away. I don't mind doing anything I can for Paynelope, I pay her far more than she asks me to. I do it for her and Percy, but why am I paying for you?"

"You don't give me money, Penny does."

"Which I give to Paynelope. Which means that I'm giving it to you."

"I'm not stealing it from you, Pops. Penny can do what she likes with her money. If you don't want me getting any, give her less than she asks for."

"I don't want to."

"The point is that you *could*."

"You're nothing but a freeloader. I don't care how you try to make it seem, that's what you are."

"And what are you, Pops? Remind me why you're giving Penny extra money. Oh, I remember. Because you have a crush on her."

When Medina was around, my mother had a way of laughing that made *me* laugh even if I didn't get the joke. She opened her mouth so wide you could see her back teeth, but no sound came at first. She'd look around, open-mouthed, until she locked eyes with Medina and then she'd tip her head back even farther and let loose a high-pitched shriek. Pops hated it when Medina made my mother laugh.

The one thing that Pops and Medina didn't fight about was God. My mother, Pops and Medina were all agnostics who had been born Catholic. Our house, my mother said, was "secretly a nest of agnostics." Medina went to church but said she wouldn't have anything to do with it if she didn't work at a Catholic hospital and have to keep up appearances to keep her job. Pops said he wouldn't go except that it was required of everyone who taught at Brother Rice. Even though he dismissed the Bible as "a book of fairy tales," Pops went to Mass in the Catholic chapel at Brother Rice. Pops was vice-principal of Brother Rice, a position he achieved by an automatic line of ascendancy. A Christian Brother always held the position of principal at Brother Rice, and the longest-serving male lay teacher always held the position of vice-principal, a purely titular one because, were the principal to resign or be removed, another Christian Brother would take his place.

In the first few months after I was born, my mother stopped taking the sacraments but still went to church, partly to keep

Medina company, and partly in the hope of mollifying the priests. While I stood at her knee with my hands held in hers, she told me in gleeful detail of the exhortations to have me baptized that often took place in the church doorway as she was leaving Mass with me in her arms. In front of others who paused to listen and those who, passing by, pretended not to listen, my mother was berated by a succession of priests in a succession of churches for being everything from irresponsible to "a wicked woman" for withholding baptism from me. "You are yourself baptized and therefore saved, yet you spitefully refuse to allow your disfigured little child entrance into the Church of God."

"He's not disfigured."

Sometimes they objected to my mother being single.

"Engagement is not a sacrament," a priest said to her after I was born. "You're free to marry."

"Or not to marry."

"Don't you want what's best for Percy?"

"The two of us are looked upon as damaged goods. The men who come sniffing around aren't looking for marriage."

"I don't think everyone regards you as damaged goods. There *are* men—"

"Yes, I'm sure there are, but I don't share your opinion that any husband is better than none at all."

"I was thinking of someone in particular—"

"A widower from the Holy Name Society?"

"As a matter of fact, yes. A good man. You should resume the sacraments."

My mother grew so weary of these weekly chastisements that she stopped going to church altogether. Eventually the priests stopped coming to 44. I knew early in life that Penelope Joyce was more or less universally regarded as a lost cause.

———•———

Pops tried to cheer me up by enumerating people from history and literature who had overcome disfigurements and physical limitations to accomplish great things. My mother told Pops she doubted that telling me my stain was "nothing" next to the disfigurements of others—real or fictional—would do me any good. She said that surely there were greater things I could aspire to than not being Quasimodo.

My mother, because she said this sort of thing in public and was seen arriving home laden with library books, was looked upon as a know-it-all, which is to say someone who not only put on airs by conspicuously pretending to know it all but also—never mind the contradiction—*did* know it all. Educated men were held in high esteem if their education was put to some practical, money-making, family-supportive use, whereas educated women, especially ones who looked like my mother, were said not to know their place and were not to be associated with by those who did. No amount of reading books or pretending to read them could make up for being an unmarried mother or being rewarded for promiscuity by having a child who looked like me, as if the sacrament of marriage would have healed me in her womb. "It doesn't matter how many books I read," my mother told me. "You'll still be seen as a bastard and an eyesore and I'll still be a woman whose big tits predetermined her to be a slut."

As you may have deduced by now, my mother was an autodidact. Though a grade ten dropout, she could probably have overseen the studies of graduate students in half a dozen disciplines.

Second-hand books, library books, hardcover, paperback and pocket editions lay haphazardly scattered on almost every flat surface—floors, tables, countertops, chairs, even beds. Our house looked as if whatever else went on in 44 was incidental to the reading of books. There were books whose covers had been scorched by cigarettes, mementoes of near-miss house fires, books stained with the bottoms of cups and beer bottles, smeared with ashes, sweat-stained with handprints, fingerprints. It looked as if we were not so much readers as we were hoarders of books. Pops and Medina nudged them aside to make room for their ashtrays, beer bottles, dinner plates and elbows as if the books were nuisances to which they were trying to adapt for my mother's sake, for she was the only one who read them. (Pops said that he had once been a "great reader" but no longer had the "inclination" for it.) She owed a fortune in library fines, but no one else ever asked to borrow the kinds of books she liked, so the librarians forever deferred payment. I went with her to the Gosling Library on Duckworth Street where the librarians always smiled at me, so I may have been another reason that they more or less let her keep her books indefinitely.

Pops won her over to what she called the "look-what-Percy's-peers-have-accomplished" strategy of consoling me for my face and hands and feet. She helped me bone up on the freaks of life and literature—Helen Keller, the Elephant Man, countless circus sideshow geeks, the "long-conked" Cyrano de Bergerac who, she told me years later, tried to fuck women to ecstasy with the very nose that prevented him from going down on them. As if she had not chastised Pops for doing so, she invoked the hunchbacked, bell-ringing Quasimodo of Notre-Dame, as well as the limping, lisping, far-too-slowly-dying Tiny Tim Cratchit, and Shakespeare's misshapen murderer of twin princelings, Richard III. And Mary Shelley's Frankenstein, who, at the end of the book, lit out for some Arctic place that sounded much like Newfoundland.

"Books, books and more books," Pops said as he surveyed the house. "A teacher dismayed at the sight of books," my mother said, looking at Medina, hoping to coax a laugh from her, but it never worked, for Medina, who couldn't read or write, regarded my mother's books much as Pops did—as other people would a rival lover. My mother said she placed as many of the books face up as she could because it made them easier to find. Pops complained of the treacherously cluttered floors, books that slid beneath your feet on the once-white shag carpet, and offered to buy her some bookshelves, but my mother declined. She would go about at bed-time in her bathrobe, which she held together at the throat and at the waist as, bent over, she peered to make out the titles, often picking up more books than she could hold in one hand, her robe falling open as she did so, revealing cleavage and brown thighs. I think she kept Medina and Pops at bay with books, kept them from her bed with this conspicuous show of book browsing, which as good as said she planned to read straight through the night. She said she was doing little more than what other people did with church prayer books, merely "following along," but Pops said it seemed she meant to "follow along" from start to finish every book ever written.

My mother read late at night in bed, sitting up, chain-smoking Rothmans. When my door was open, I could hear her striking matches, exhaling cigarette smoke with a kind of sigh, turning the pages of the book that lay open on her lap. I'd fall asleep and, waking up hours later, would hear the same sounds, only by now they'd be punctuated with a cough.

I hopscotched from book to book, trying to see if I could cross a room without touching the floor. I always did it in bare feet, which stuck better to the books than shoes or slippers.

Medina, who had dropped out of school halfway through third grade, glanced at me when the subject of her illiteracy came up. I could see that she felt especially ashamed in front of me. During her two and a half years in school, she had only gone to school about sixty days. "I spent most of my time at home taking care of my sick parents and Jim Joyce," she said.

"An urbane threesome, to be sure," Pops muttered.

I tried to imagine what it would be like, living in a place where I could speak the language, *my* language, but couldn't read a word of it. Words were everywhere. Simple things, like street signs, shop windows, phone books, might as well have been written in Chinese.

Medina had managed to master playing cards because they consisted of pictures and numbers. She had "picked up" rudimentary arithmetic so she could get by with groceries, denominations of bills and coins. Pops said she often didn't know before opening the can what she was having for dinner because stores were forever altering the pictureless labels. "You don't know what you're having for dinner until Penny puts it in front of you," Medina retorted. My mother functioned as a kind of telephone operator for Medina, who would call her to ask her to look up numbers she didn't want to ask the operator for lest she be asked to spell someone's name or that of a street. Also, Medina often came by with her mail so that my mother could sort through it for her, write answers when they were needed, fill out various official forms and applications, address envelopes. She brought her pill bottles so my mother could read the labels for her. "Penny knows more about me than I do," she often said.

"The world is anxiously awaiting her biography of you," Pops quipped.

My mother practically read the newspaper to Medina, the obits, the classifieds, advertisements—she clipped coupons. She scanned the entire paper every day to see if there was something in it that might be of interest or value to Medina. She was her personal interpreter, her tour guide through the foreign country of the printed word.

But one evening, Medina told me that not being able to read didn't mean she wasn't smart. "If the two of us were in China," she said, "I'd be leading you around by the hand." She claimed to have learned to get by using tricks that Pops and my mother knew nothing about. "I might come in handy someday when you're in real trouble, Pops."

"You're right, Medina." Pops was sitting, beer in hand, his back to the kitchen as usual. "Better to be illiterate than ill-prepared for a sudden relocation to China."

"Whatever you say, Pops."

"There's no excuse in this day and age for not knowing how to read and write," Pops said.

"What excuse is there in this day and age for not knowing how to wash your underwear?" my mother asked. "For not knowing how to iron your clothes without setting them on fire? For not knowing how many slices of bread it takes to make a sandwich? You're a man, Pops. It's a permanent disability that half the world is born with."

"I was once as frequent a patron of the Gosling Library as you, Paynelope."

"Like patron *saint*?" Medina said.

"No," my mother corrected her, "not like patron saint. It has a different meaning. It means someone who frequents a particular place."

"Patron. I'm not calling anyone a *patron*," Medina said. "No one says the *patron* is always right. They line up like customers, just like at Woolworth's. That old buzzard who works there checks them out like customers. So Pen, did you wake up one morning with the urge to be a patron of the Gosling Library? It would be a lot more fun to be a patron of the East End Club. Jesus. Eight books a week."

"Tomes," my mother said. "That's what big books are called."

"It must be nice to know what things that people never talk about are called," Medina countered. "What are small books called?"

"There's not really one word for them. Slim volumes, I suppose."

"Slim volumes. Hmmm. What good do you think reading all these books will do you? I never hear anyone who works at the hospital saying, 'Oh my, Medina, it's been a long day. I can't wait to get home to my tome.' Or, 'What are you doing this weekend, Mary?' 'Well, my dear, there's a slim volume with my name on it just waiting for me on the kitchen table.' At work they never stop going on about it, the Gosling this, the Gosling that. It's crazy on Fridays, everybody trying to get off early before the lineup at the Gosling starts. In the morning all you can hear is people talking about how they polished off too many tomes and what time they got to bed. Some of them can't get through a day without a straightener, a few pages of a slim volume on the sly. You pick the hardest-looking books, Pen. Your books really look like *books*." She picked up a large, thick, black book from the floor. "You could kill someone with a book this heavy. Look, it's got a ribbon like a prayer book."

"It's to mark your page," my mother said, tugging gently on the ribbon. "It's a book of poetry. A lot of the books are poetry anthologies. Or the collected works of one poet. Tennyson, for instance. This one is an anthology of nineteenth-century English poetry. I never liked poetry when I was in school, but I do now."

"Poetry? Like Valentine's cards?"

"More like . . . Shakespeare."

"Oh, Shakespeare. At work there's no better way to start an argument than to mention Shakespeare. Pen, you'd be better off getting a good night's sleep than staying up till dawn reading books."

"Some people go to university for ten years or more after they finish high school," my mother said.

"Yeah, doctors. I see them every day. They don't see me."

"Not just doctors," my mother said. "Professors who teach and write books about the books they read."

Medina sniffed. "Jesus, if you start writing books *about* books. . . ."

"She's merely trying to better herself," Pops spoke up again from the sunroom.

"Who will she be better than when she's finished?"

"She's got a good head start on you."

"I never see you reading books, Pops," Medina said. "What are you trying to do, worsen yourself?"

"I've had my fill of books."

"So you've bettered yourself to the hilt, is that it?" Medina quipped. "You could read another thousand books and still show no improvement."

"The time comes when one gives up on books."

"I've often wondered what one does when the time comes."

"You haven't forgotten the books you read, Pops," my mother said. "You even quote them from time to time. And you almost always get my allusions." She smiled at him. Medina's colour rose and I watched her eyes dart back and forth between Pops and my mother.

"He gets your what?" Medina asked.

"Allusions," Pops said. "Literary allusions."

"What the fuck are they supposed to be?"

"Remarks about particular books," my mother offered. "The characters in particular books. Lines from poems."

"It's true," Pops said. "I do get you, don't I, Paynelope?"

"You *get* her?"

"I get her meaning."

"Well, I get her too, Pops. A lot."

"You're secretly erudite?"

"I'm secretly something, Pops. You can be sure of that."

"You're the Abbott to my Costello. And I'm the Abbott to Paynelope's Costello."

"I've heard of Abbott and Costello."

"Would you like to know who's on first, what's on second—"

"What the fuck are you—"

"Ceasefire!" my mother yelled.

"See. She doesn't even understand TV," Pops protested.

"I watch it when I'm here," Medina said. "I haven't got a TV. Don't want one."

"That's it," my mother fumed. "Enough, enough, *enough*."

The three of them were silent for a while. I wondered if it would help if I said something.

"So what happens when you run out of books, Pen?" Medina asked. "Do you get a Girl Guide's medal or something?"

"There are more books in the world than anyone has time to

read. In university they keep track of what you read and write and give out what are called degrees. You can get a bachelor's degree, a master's degree or a PhD."

"Pops, you're a bachelor." Medina grinned at him. "Whoever taught you how to be one must have really known their stuff."

"I spent one year at university," Pops said. "That's all you needed back then to be a high school teacher. Brother Rice's principal, Brother McHugh, has a master's degree in theology."

"Religion," my mother said to Medina.

"Oh my," Medina said, "a master of religion, what does that mean now? He must have spent a long time bettering himself. What's he better at than other people? My great-uncle was a master mariner. Never went to school in his life. All he could do was sail a ship across an ocean of ice without getting himself or other people drowned. But who would you rather have around in a storm at sea, a master mariner or a master of religion?"

"You're not a master of anything," Pops said.

"I'm better than you at talking. I can *talk* the arse off you."

"Whereas I must confess that, often though I've wished that I had seen the last of it, I could not with the help of ten men remove your arse from this house by *any* method, least of all talking, even though I pay for the beer you drink." Pops went to his bedroom and closed the door.

Medina sighed. "I don't suppose you'll ever give up on books, Pen."

"No. But I could teach you to read. You're so smart. You'd learn quickly."

"So you keep saying. I'm not good enough the way I am, that's what you think. I don't want to know how to read and write. That's what *I* keep saying." She started to cry. She leaned her head on my mother's shoulder. "Would you rather have a friend you could talk about books with?"

"No, sweetheart," my mother said, tenderly stroking her cheek and smiling reassuringly at me.

"I can't put things into words like you. Or even Pops."

"It's not always bad to be lost for words. Besides, you have your own way with them."

"Oh fuck, look at me and look at you—"

"Don't you think Medina's pretty, Perse?" My mother raised her eyebrows at me.

"She's really pretty," I said quickly.

And she was, in a way I see now but didn't then. I haven't done her justice yet. She had large brown eyes and the kind of ski-jump nose that these days some women pay plastic surgeons for; frank, lively, smart eyes that made her seem ever-vigilant, never at ease. She was big-boned but not fat, each of the features of her face and her body slightly out of proportion with the others, so that whatever she wore never suited more than part of her. A sweater that fit at the shoulders was too long at the hem. A skirt that was tight and flat at the front sagged in wrinkles at the back. It was as if her body had been well designed but badly made. Her chin moved from centre to left, centre to left, when she was nervous or upset. On a man such a chin would have been dismissed as weak, as pointing to some profound lack of assertiveness, self-confidence. But it made her seem endearingly genuine, incapable of swagger or feigned poise. By not trying to create an impression, she created a sweet one. She was exactly what, at first glance, she seemed to be.

"She should be paying you for all you do for her," Pops said when he came out of his room after the front door had banged shut behind Medina. "She takes advantage of you. You should charge her admission every time she comes to visit. Does she ever bring her own beer or thank me when she's drinking one of mine? She treats the house as if it's hers. I've never seen such disgraceful ingratitude. And you're her only friend—"

"She's *my* only friend," my mother said.

"You have Percy, a family, a purpose, structure—"

"Medina's part of all that, part of my family."

"Well, I'd like to think that I'm your friend. Haven't I been your friend?"

"You've been good to us, to Percy and me," my mother said. "But there's no need to put a label on your place in this household. You're Pops. Our Pops. No one else has one."

Pops smiled at her and then at me. I wondered what it meant, that smile.

I was at least blessed with a *mind* like my mother's. "Hey, Perse," she said, "shouldn't you be solving something? A math problem? Differential calculus? Einstein's beef with quantum physics?"

"I'm not as smart as you."

"You will be. You'll be smarter. Imagine how pleased your teachers would be if you could speak Latin by the time you start school next year."

Not yet five, I was reading at the grade five level, had memorized the multiplication tables into the highest double digits, was adept at long division of numbers up to ten digits, could identify every country in the world on a map Pops brought home from Brother Rice that showed nothing but borders. I wasn't especially interested in any of it, but Pops said that eventually my mind would find its focus. "Maybe not," my mother said. "He might be like me, a jack of all things and a genius of none."

"He's his mother's boy," Pops said. "He's smarter than anyone else his age I've come across. But he'll have to progress through school like everybody else. Skipping grades isn't allowed."

"He'll be bored."

"It can't be helped."

Pops said that Brother Rice's principal, Brother McHugh—who already seemed to be planning my future because, Pops said, he often spoke of me to him—guessed that I would, like my mother, turn out to be not a true genius but merely someone who could easily absorb the work of others. Like her, I would never discover, deduce, figure out, invent anything wholly new. Pops informed us that Brother McHugh—or Director McHugh, as he always called him—said that at best I would be a receptacle for knowledge but not a finder of new knowledge. That he foresaw me as a parrot, a perfect register, a regurgitator of facts, an ever-expanding encyclopedia, a data repository, a potential quiz show prodigy, a human archive who would barely have enough sense to come in from the rain. He told Pops that he attributed my precocious knowledge to my having so much time to study, there being little else a boy like me could do. What else, he said, but precociousness would you expect from a friendless freak holed up in his house, whose hands and feet prevented him from playing any sport or game that required the least bit of athleticism?

"Who the fuck is this McHugh?" my mother said. Who the fuck indeed—but it's too soon to bring him out.

My mother found books for me at the Gosling Library, classic English novels mostly, books by Defoe, Dickens, Thackeray, the Brontës, Sir Walter Scott. She read them aloud to me. She read to me a biography of Toulouse-Lautrec, a dwarf of a man the book told us, that was enlivened for me by the artist's addiction to the services of prostitutes. "It's so stupid," my mother said as she pressed *Ivanhoe* upon me. "You really should wind up in some sort of class for gifted children. But what can we do? There are no such classes in Newfoundland. There wouldn't be much point in you graduating from high school at the age of ten, anyway." But I was glad. It was a prospect I dreaded, being pushed even further from the centre of normalcy—both gifted *and* disfigured, a student body of one.

I'd say that, all in all, it's to my credit that I didn't turn out to be an arsonist.

UNCLE PADDY AND THE
SERMON ON THE MOUNT

ARCHBISHOP P.J. Scanlon, Patrick James Scanlon, was known to many on the Mount as "Uncle Paddy." The Archbishop's limousine was called the Paddy Wagon. It went up Bonaventure at exactly four o'clock every afternoon, bound for the Basilica—coming from where I didn't know, though every afternoon I knelt on the old sofa beneath our front room window to watch it pass.

I was under the Archbishop's protection—under Uncle Paddy's wing, people said, as if he had assigned me a bodyguard or let me live in the Basilica. But the only thing he did publicly for me was preach a sermon when I was four. He said in his sermon that he hoped it would not get back to him that anyone had been teasing or mistreating me. He said, "Hereby I say unto you, inasmuch as you have done it to one of these the least of my brethren, ye have done it unto me." He was quoting Christ's words as recorded by Matthew in the Gospels, but he was taken to mean that anyone who interfered with Percy Joyce interfered with *him*.

"Percy is a special boy born on a special day, June 24, the feast day of Saint John the Baptist, after whom the Basilica is named, to whom it is dedicated and by whom it is blessed and watched over, and the day that the site of this city, which bears his name, was discovered by John Cabot in 1497."

He said that for anyone June 24 was an "auspicious" day on which to be born, but especially for a person from St. John's.

Many pointed out that, as there were 365 days in the year and about sixty thousand people in the city, it was likely that about 150 people of St. John's had been born on June 24, so what made Little Percy so unique? His face, his hands, his feet? If those were the price of a Sermon on the Mount, I was welcome to all the sermons and blessings the Archbishop wanted to bestow upon me.

The sermon earned my mother and me a lot of resentment. People didn't think it was right that the Archbishop should remove me from the daily school of hard knocks just because of my disfigurements, or be so obvious about playing favourites. There were several other unfortunates among the children of the Mount: a boy confined to a wheelchair because of polio, an epileptic girl, a boy with Down's syndrome, a boy who had to gimp about with his legs spread-eagled by a pair of hip-high plaster casts connected at the ankles by a metal rod.

My mother was not on hand to hear the sermon, but Medina was. Medina, who told my mother that the Archbishop had several times referred to me in his sermon as The Little Joyce Boy, one word away from The Little Drummer Boy. The Archbishop's sermon, Medina said, was not about me, Perse, per se. He merely used me as an example of the kind of person Christ was speaking of when he exhorted his listeners to treat even the supposedly lowest of the low no differently than they treated Him, for the low were *of* Him, *part* of Him, as deserving of respect and kindness as

His other children. But the Archbishop did, Medina said, spend a lot of time talking about me, me whom he said he had glimpsed one day from the back seat of his limousine as he was passing 44 and I was sitting on the steps on my mother's lap. "The poor little lad," the Archbishop called me, saying that he had a brother who now lived on the Mainland who had been born with a cleft palate and so he knew all too well what was waiting for me, unless everyone pulled together to prevent it.

Soon after seeing me, he directed his assistants to find out everything they could about me and my family. In his sermon, he portrayed my mother as someone who had turned away from God and the Church because she wrongly believed that God, by allowing her fiancé to abandon her when she was pregnant, and by disfiguring her child when it was in her womb, had turned away from her. But he predicted, even seemed to prophesy, that Penelope Joyce, the Prodigal Daughter, would one day return to her Father, and with her would bring Percy, whom he knew was not baptized and whose eternal soul was therefore imperilled with every passing moment. "The sooner their return comes to pass, the better," he said, as if he was instructing the congregation to hurry near the day of our salvation.

For a child to flout the Archbishop's wishes meant that his or her entire family would earn his ire, which might lead to being snubbed or ostracized, not being invited to Church events or to join Church clubs such as the Knights of Columbus or the Holy Name Society. Boys were warned by their parents not to do anything to me that would land them and their families in Uncle Paddy's bad books. There was no telling what opportunities a boy who provoked the Archbishop might be denied by the Christian Brothers and the nuns. The most devout on the Mount were concerned about earning the ire of God Himself, and warned their children that to disobey the Archbishop was to disobey God and there was no telling what would come of that.

I was regarded by many as if I had somehow obtained my clemency through the sexual conniving of my mother. "What do they think," she wondered, "that I slept with the Archbishop?" She wished Uncle Paddy hadn't referred to me as the least of his brethren, but she also said that it was good to know that a person of such power and influence was in my corner. But having warranted a Sermon on the Mount eventually drew me to the primary attention of Brother McHugh—Director/Principal McHugh—who might otherwise have ignored me.

Not long after the Sermon on the Mount, Pops convinced my mother that it would do no harm to accede to the Archbishop's request to meet us privately at the Basilica at Christmas. The Archbishop lived in the Basilica Residence, a three-storey stone house behind the Basilica and forever in its shadow.

When my mother took me there, we were shown to a private room in the Archbishop's private quarters, one as cluttered with antiques as a museum. The Basilica Residence was as ornately designed and decorated as the Basilica itself. There was a wooden sculpture of the Baby Jesus done by some famous nineteenth-century Irish artist. Under glass, there was the Cappa Magna, an ermine cape worn by one of the first archbishops of St. John's. My mother said later she hardly moved or let me move for fear that we would break something priceless. The Archbishop sat in a throne-backed chair in front of which two chairs were placed side by side for us. Uncle Paddy wore a black soutane with a middle row of brass buttons, and a red skullcap. Two young deacons, who might have been twins, both dark-haired, pale, ascetic, Jesuitical, wearing glasses with thick black rims, flanked him like a pair of Swiss guards.

His Grace put his left hand on my head, seemed to improvise some sort of benediction and with his right hand made the sign of the cross very close to my face, referring to me always as "Little Percy."

"Born on the feast day of Saint John the Baptist. We may say that in a sense he is *your* patron saint." He patted or stroked my cheek several times as he spoke to my mother, held me by my overlarge hands, telling her that God had made me as I was for a purpose that might not seem apparent to us for a long time. He said that although my childhood might be difficult for both of us, we should not despair, and added that he hoped her own troubles would not prevent her from returning to the Church and raising her son "in the religion in which his parents were baptized." My mother made no promises but thanked him for taking the time to see me. She said that he seemed not at all put off by my appearance but, on the contrary, "took a real shine to you," constantly smiling at me as if he knew that one day I would come to see my affliction as being of no great consequence, as if he was so certain of my future happiness that he saw it as clearly as something that had already come to pass.

Before we left, Uncle Paddy offered my mother a job as secretary in the Basilica. Since my birth, she had been a freelance typist who worked at home. When my mother, saying that I needed her at 44, declined his offer, he said he understood, but added that she could do the job of basilica secretary at home. She would be his typist—a part-time position: deacons would deliver to her home whatever needed to be typed, such as letters dictated to and written in shorthand by "busy" stenographers, which would need to be transcribed. The deacons would come to collect them when my mother was finished. She knew this arrangement would only complicate the running of the basilica office and make it more expensive, since any of the "busy" stenographers could have typed, more easily than her, what they wrote in their own shorthand. But she told Medina afterward that she understood he wanted it to seem that he was doing her a favour, making the lives of his staff a touch more difficult for the sake of Little Percy Joyce and his mother. She knew that his real purpose was to maintain daily contact of a sort with us. He had—each visit by a deacon would remind us—made us a public project and could not be seen as merely paying lip service to the notion that we were as worthy of salvation as anyone else.

So my mother accepted the position of basilica secretary. Salary-wise, she said, he had thrown us a not-very-juicy bone, but she would make more money than she had before. So the acolyte deacons came by 44 at random intervals, always on foot for the Basilica was just a few hundred feet away, sometimes delivering mere envelopes or folders, sometimes whole boxes of documents, the originals of which my mother would return to them when she was done, along with her typed facsimiles that always bore the Basilica's official letterhead and stamp. She'd phone the basilica office to inform them that a pickup was needed at 44, and soon after, no matter what the weather, a deacon would turn up on the doorstep, often dripping wet, or his cassock soaked or rimed with snow, the lenses of his inevitable glasses fogged up, rain-splattered, snow-coated, looking like twin windshields through which the young man peered at the apparition of Penny Joyce.

She'd invite them in, but they'd politely decline, standing on the steps beneath the overhang until she came back with whatever parcel they'd been sent to fetch, which they would stow away inside one of the duffle bags they carried on their shoulders.

"They'd throw themselves under a bus if Uncle Paddy asked them to," my mother said.

"Or if *you* asked them to," Medina shot back.

Whenever Medina's hospital work hours were cut back—which happened frequently, unemployment being so high—she'd spend some or all of the day with us at 44. "You should see how disappointed they look"—Medina laughed—"when *I* answer the door." I often went to the door with my mother to greet the deacons, whom I came to know by name. "Hello, Martin," I'd say, and

Martin, transfixed by the sight of my mother, eyes locked on her over my head, would say, "Hello, Percy."

I imagine them now, looking back on their deaconship as the time when they were daily tested by the sight of Penny Joyce, those poor young basilican celibates, now young priests trying not to recall with longing that fleeting year when they were *required* to gaze upon her every day, required to complete with Penny Joyce a wholly legitimate, respectably justified transaction that did not constitute any sort of breach of their soon-to-be-set-in-stone vows of chastity. They came and went, like a succession of rejected suitors. Day after day, year after year, the drove of drones sent out from the hive of the Big B came to 44, cookie-cut deacons who never aged, as if the same forever-to-be-on-the-verge-of-ordination acolytes were doomed to an eternity of bearing gifts to the soul-destroying sorceress of 44.

They slept in a rear annex to the Basilica Residence, a kind of dormitory where, it's easy to imagine, they were all simultaneously kept awake by the image of my mother framed by the doorway of the porch at 44, dressed in a belted bathrobe that, though it showed less of her than her skirts and blouses did, was—they were certain—*all* that she wore, easy to imagine my mother as the common goad of their desire as they lay there on their bunks on their backs, trying to resist doing what they would have to admit to having done at their next confession. *Dear Lord, keep the Evil One away, and keep my hand away from his Minion in my underwear, the little serpent that is modelled after him, the part of my very body which Thou made in his image and attached to me and which I am forbidden to use except to pee.*

"One of those basilica boys is coming down the hill," Medina would say as she stood at the window, keeping watch for them. She said they looked as if their parents had talked them into being priests, or their teachers had, or *someone*. She hated to think what they'd let themselves be driven to ten years from now.

Some of them had declared as early as grade seven that they had heard the call of the priesthood. They either believed that to be a priest was to be heroic in the way that other boys believed that to be one of the few good men of the Marines was to be heroic, or else it was the opposite and they knew even as early as twelve years old that they'd never make it in the outside world. Medina said she was sick of the sight of them on the doorstep, gaping at my mother as if they'd never seen a woman who was not a nun before. They were acne-ridden youngsters who thought it was a mortal sin to obey their bodies, who wished they didn't *have* bodies even as they jerked off in their beds at night and wondered, as they would until they died or did it with a boy, what they were missing.

I thought Medina said these things because she was jealous of my mother's beauty. I didn't yet know that it was the worshippers of Penny Joyce that she was jealous of, which is to say just about every man who ever set eyes on my mother, not to mention a good many women. "Bedroom eyes," Medina remarked. "They look at you like you're wearing nothing but a watch."

Why, she asked my mother once, did she ask the basilica boys to come in when she knew they'd say no? Why did she lead them on and flirt with them? My mother said she never led them on or flirted with them. Medina said that if answering the door in your bathrobe wasn't flirting, there was no such thing. My mother said that one of the perks of working at home was working in your bathrobe. Why did she have to smile at them the way she did? My mother said she didn't even know she was smiling, but she guessed that was just her way of being polite, friendly, nice, whatever. Medina said she liked to lead boys and men on, whether they were seminarians, priests, single, engaged, married, my mother didn't care. And then Medina's voice rose unhappily though I didn't understand why. Why, she said, didn't she take that stupid engagement ring off and put her money where her come-hither mouth was? Men didn't just get it into their heads that she was asking for it, so why didn't she just say yes to one she liked and get on with it and finish what she'd started with Jim Joyce? It wasn't like she had a *reputation* to protect, an unmarried mother, a woman who answered the door wearing next to nothing. It wasn't fair, especially to celibate cocks, to be a cockteaser. Why didn't she just see if she could get one of them to throw off his vocation? She shouldn't let self-respect get in the way!

So they argued on and on, not really shouting, merely picking at each other, throughout most of which my mother smiled and Medina frowned and pouted, arms folded across her chest. My mother laughed. Medina laughed. Medina talked herself out. I could tell that my mother knew she would. She didn't get upset. She seemed to assume that I too knew Medina didn't mean a word of it, for she paid me no mind as they were jousting. They wound up, after Pops came home from Brother Rice and took up his place in the armchair in the sunroom, drinking beer and playing cards in the kitchen until late at night, laughing as if the point of an argument was to joke about it afterward.

My mother, to my disappointment, did relent and stopped wearing her bathrobe while working, switching to skirts and blouses and high-heeled shoes as if she were a receptionist.

I can't remember not knowing what "it" was. My mother and Medina swore I always knew, never bothering to explain how innate knowledge of anything was possible. They both said they never told me, so I suppose it's possible that I always knew. My mother said that I was "gaping" at girls and women by the time I was five. She said she doubted that my "condition" had anything to do with it, but I was as hyper-sexed as some people thought my condition fated me to be, precocious in the extreme when it came to maturation. She *knew*, she said; she did the laundry and never overlooked or ceased to be amazed by what she called a "crusty crotch." She didn't know that, even then, the object of my desire, the object of my dreams both dry and wet was Penny Joyce.

The Archbishop began to send me special occasion cards:

Merry Christmas, Percy. May God bless you and watch over you on His special day. I want you and your mother to know that I remember both of you each day in my prayers. May I humbly ask that both of you remember me in yours? Yours in Christ, P.J. Scanlon, CJM, Archbishop of St. John's.

Sometimes he referred to me in writing as Little Percy and wrote to me as though to a colleague whose job was as important and difficult as his.

Well Little Percy, Merry Christmas to you and your mother. Isn't this a busy time of year for people like us? But we must not forget the importance of Christmas, which celebrates the birthday of our Saviour, The Lord Jesus Christ, who loves us and watches over us always. Well, I must get back to my duties as you must get back to yours. Again Little Percy, Merry Christmas and my best wishes to you and your mother, Penelope, for the New Year: Yours in Christ, Archbishop P.J. Scanlon, CJM, December 12, 1961.

"I'm surprised he doesn't sign the cards 'Your pal, Paddy,'" my mother said, though she always helped me reply to the Archbishop's card with one of my own.

Merry Christmas, Your Grace. I had a cold but now I'm fine. I hope you don't get a cold. My mother is fine too. Happy New Year: Percy Joyce, ESQ., December 17, 1961.

"I guess it's good to have friends in high places," my mother said. I took her words literally and imagined my friend the Archbishop writing to me from high up in the Basilica. "He never forgets to send you a card. Easter, your birthday, St. Patrick's Day, even Valentine's. I think he's using the soft-sell approach to bring us back to the Church. I hope that when he realizes it won't work, we don't have an *enemy* in high places."

Pops said he was sure that the Archbishop was just being nice and had no ulterior motive. But priests from the Basilica who *didn't* use the soft-sell approach and were sent to our house by His Grace exhorted—in some cases ordered—my mother to have me baptized. "Round number two of the basilica missionaries," my mother called them, remembering the priests who had tried in vain to convince her to have me baptized just after I was born. My mother never let them in, even though they roared so loudly the neighbours came out on their steps to watch and listen to them. Father Wallis, the tallest, brawniest priest I had ever seen and the only person I had ever seen who was completely bald, beat on the locked door as he roared: "That boy must be baptized. His very soul depends on it. What if he should perish in his bed tonight? What then, Miss Joyce? What would happen to his soul?"

"Go away," my mother said to him through the front door. "We have all the guilt we need right here in this house."

"What a sacrilege it is that a boy born on the feast day of Saint John the Baptist has yet to be baptized."

JIM JOYCE

FOR a while I believed that my father was killed in a car crash when he missed the turn at the bottom of the Curve of Bonaventure, which was as steep, and in the winter often as icy, as a bobsled run. We lived halfway down the hill where the street turned sharply across from Brother Rice. Instead of a front yard fence, we had, courtesy of the city, a concrete traffic barrier, the Block, that was meant to stop any vehicle that didn't make the turn. I was as unconvinced of the need for it as my mother was that it could stop a car until the winter night a Vauxhall crashed into it long after we had gone to bed, not budging it an inch, the crumpled car pointed straight at the front of our house, its drunk driver having fallen asleep behind the wheel.

The explosion and vibrations of the crash shook the windows of the house, rattled dishes in the cupboards, upended lamps. Shards of glass and metal flew up and over the Block, clattered like shrapnel against our windows, embedded themselves in the clapboard.

It seemed like just the sort of dramatic, spectacular re-entrance into our lives that Jim Joyce should make.

According to Pops—the only one from 44 who joined the neighbours when they went out to investigate—the driver was all but unmarked. I watched everything from the front room window, the crowd, the police, the ambulance, the flashing lights, the stretcher bearing the man whose every inch but for his face was covered by blue blankets. A face, I noted, that wasn't the colour of mine, but then neither was my mother's. I watched until all that was left were a few people standing around, staring at the Block, talking and smoking cigarettes and stamping their feet to keep them warm.

"Cars," Pops said for days afterward, chuckling as if in scorn of newfangled contraptions that would never catch on.

"Yes, Pops, cars," my mother said. "You'd have one if you weren't such a cheapskate."

"I don't have a driver's licence," Pops said.

"It's not something you're either born with or you're not," my mother said. "You can *get* one. *I* have one."

"I have a perfectly good pair of legs."

"You're not still living in that godforsaken outport where everything is close to everything else."

The Block. Whatever reassurance I had gained from its success was more than undone by the fact that I now knew the Block *was* necessary, that it really was all that stood between us and out-of-control cars. That the Block had worked once was no proof that it would work again. For many nights afterward, I knelt on the front room sofa and watched the headlights of every car that came down Bonaventure, in part keeping vigil for Jim Joyce, who I believed was the dead-looking man beneath the blankets, and in part dreading that another car would ram the Block that, for all I knew, would not hold up a second time. The lights of the cars shone straight into the house, getting brighter and brighter until, just short of the Curve, they swerved and disappeared. Each car seemed certain to continue straight into the Block. I let out a gasp each time a car seemed late in turning. One night I stayed up so late that my mother came out and knelt beside me on the sofa.

"He's only been gone a few years. That's what you said."

"Percy," she said, "Jim Joyce was not of woman born."

"How old is he?" I said.

"Twenty-eight. But not in human years. Jim Joyce was so unique that even time had no effect on him."

In daytime, I often stood outside by the Block, from the safe side of which it became my habit to watch cars and pedestrians go by. Other boys my age, four or so, curious to see me close up, came by then. I told them my father had been killed in a car crash but his death had been hushed up for reasons I was not allowed to talk about. At other times I told them that, like the driver, my father had survived the crash without a scratch but, for reasons I was not allowed to talk about, had been whisked away from the scene before anyone noticed he was in the car. I kept a mental dossier of lies about Jim Joyce. That these lies were contradictory did not deter me from telling both to the same people. For me the point was that the stories brought me attention and brought me company—they drew the other children to me with stories that they knew were lies but pretended to believe in order to entice me into telling more—such as that my father had not been in the car at all but in the one behind it that was chasing it and sped away when it crashed. I told them that by his absence he was helping the Church, the police, the army. I said he had broken off his engagement to my pregnant mother because she heroically insisted that he put his secret responsibilities above all others. Someday he'd be back, but not even then, I said, would I be allowed to tell them why he'd left.

SISTER MARY AGGIE

and

THE PATRON SAINT OF
UNATTRACTIVE PEOPLE

STANDING beside the Block, at the foot of the Mount, a tiny
sentinel in front of 44, my face and hands as distantly visible
as red flags, I became a neighbourhood fixture, the little Joyce
boy in his oversized shoes, with large hands that flapped about on
the ends of his wrists like the ears of a rabbit. I stayed close where
my mother could see me from the kitchen window. I obeyed her
order not to venture onto Bonaventure and simply stood by the
Block, hoping to be noticed and spoken to. There was no better
place to meet what Pops called "the vermin on the Mount."

Most of the clerics waved to me as they went by or stopped
to ask me how I was, even the spooky Capuchins whose faces I
couldn't make out and who walked with each of their hands in the
opposite sleeve, each of them one scythe short of being the Grim
Reaper. Some people thought my stained face to be an attendant
symptom of retardation. Others, because of my oversized hands
and feet, mistook me for a dwarf, doubly damned. Most grown-ups

were quite friendly and called me by name. "Hello, Percy, how are you today?" "I'm fine, thank you." "That's good. You're so polite." I was sometimes given candy treats and was always hoping for one. "Poor little thing," I heard a woman say to her husband after they had gone by. Poor little cheerful, attention-craving, candy-deprived, friendless son of a certain woman who already regarded with suspicion every face that turned his way lest he see in it a look of revulsion or be gawked at by someone who thought that no one with such a face would notice. Poor little boy whose innocence would not hold up much longer against what lay in store for him.

On the cusp of what I thought would be my first year of school, in the warm summer months, I kept watch at the Block. One day, a woman whose age I couldn't guess and who was dressed like a nun came by and gave me a Mass card and told me to give it to my mother and have her teach me the prayer on the back that asked the Patron Saint of Unattractive People, Saint Drogo, to intercede with God on my behalf. She told me that, compared to Saint Drogo, who voluntarily hid himself for life inside a cell attached to his church lest his ugliness scare people into mistaking him for Satan, I was "a handsome young man." She spoke slowly, deliberately, in a way that seemed meant to convey serenity, a fear-less, God-conferred reconciliation to all possible happenstance and fates.

On the card there was a cartoon-like depiction of Saint Drogo, his grossly misshapen face more comical than otherwise as he stared out the window of his cell. On the back of the card was a prayer: "Let them not be judged, O Lord, by their earthly appear-ance, but let Your glorious Light shine upon them that all may see the everlasting Beauty of their Souls." Beneath this, in smaller letters, the card read: "A small contribution would be appreciated. May God bless you and keep you, forever and ever. Amen."

"Is this how she gets by, handing out prayer cards to children whose parents she expects will pay for them?" my mother said. "Saint Drogo. I'm sure there was no such person. Drogre is probably how they came up with it. Drogre. Dr. Ogre. I think I know where his office is." She turned to me. "I don't think you should keep this card." She put it on the windowsill above the sink, and in the morning it was gone.

Medina said she knew the woman. They'd never met, but she'd seen her on the street a few times. She went by the name of Sister Mary Aggie, from Mary Agnes. Medina didn't know her last name. "She's harmless—she used to be a nun, or she thinks she still is one, or something." She said Sister Mary Aggie was a kind of self-ordained missionary but was known to run a one-woman brothel out of the single room in which she lived. "A missionary prostitute," my mother sighed. "Wonderful."

Sister Mary Aggie made up a clerical order of one. She wore a headdress much like the one worn by the nuns of the Mount—a black veil and white cowl that completely hid her hair. It was not winged like those of the Presentation nuns, nor as high and narrow as those of the Mercy nuns. Instead of a frock, she wore a belted, tattered grey dress. Her shoes must once have looked like nun's shoes, but they were encrusted with mud and dust and lacked laces so that she had to scuff along to keep them from falling off.

Medina told us she'd been at one time a patient of the Mental, but hadn't been hospitalized in more than a year, having somehow got to the point where her eccentricities were indulged by the various local authorities, even the Church, which had not been amused by her nun-aping caricature. She now lived in the basement of a nearby house on Garrison Hill. One evening, when my mother, Medina and I went out for an evening walk, each of them taking turns holding me in her arms when I got tired, we went to Garrison Hill and saw that in the window of Sister Mary Aggie's room was a picture of the Sacred Heart, the garish heart lit from within by a red Christmas light that blinked at heartbeat intervals. Above and below the Sacred Heart, the window read:

SISTER MARY AGGIE'S HOME FOR WAYWARD SOULS

Sister Mary Aggie returned to the Block one afternoon, talking loudly although she was alone. She looked at me and wiped her face on her coat sleeve as if wiping away a port wine stain of her own.

"Do you have something for me?" she said.

I shook my head.

She said, "That face is your mother's fault. When she carried you, she went outside during an eclipse. That's why you have that face. Now your face is stuck like that. Even if you go to Heaven, your face will still be stuck like that and people who earned their way into Heaven will have to put up with the sight of you. You'll spoil Heaven for everyone else." Her words stung but I could think of no reply.

She gave me another Saint Drogo Mass card. "Give this to your mother," she said.

"She wants me to pay her for the card," I said to my mother.

"No," my mother said. "She wants *me* to pay for it. If you give her a cent, she'll never stop coming back for more. Perhaps you shouldn't stand out by the Block. God knows what hurtful nonsense someone will spout to you next."

I protested but she did not relent until Medina pleaded my cause, saying it was good for me not to hole up in the house, good for me to get used to people and for people to get used to me. "I don't think I'll ever get used to people telling him such vicious things," my mother said, and Pops, who'd been listening silently in the sunroom, piped up that no one ever got used to anyone. My mother said that anyone who stayed out by the Block long enough would meet all kinds. "So let him meet all kinds," Medina said, smoothing the hair at the back of my head.

Sister Mary Aggie came back again. "Do you have something for me this time?"

I shook my head.

She gave me a third card. "You're not baptized and you and your mother never go to church," she said. "You might not even have a middle name."

"I don't," I said.

"Well, things can't be left like that. I'll baptize you." She took from the pocket of her frayed grey coat a small glass vial. "Holy water," she said, "from the Shrine of Sainte Anne de Beaupré. You're going to need more than a patron saint looking out for you." She sprinkled the sign of the cross on me and sprinkled my face, saying: "I baptize you, Percy Patrick Joyce, in the name of the Father, and of the Son, and of the Holy Spirit. Nothing on earth will fix your face. Remember, no matter what happens, no matter what people say or do, God is always with you, Percy Patrick Joyce."

And then she continued on her way down Bonaventure, talking loudly as if conversing with someone who was nearly deaf. I told my mother what the woman had done and gave her the third card.

"She can't just go around throwing water on people," my mother protested. "Or baptizing them or giving them names or handing out these cards as if they're redeemable coupons. Anyway, Percy, your middle name is not Patrick, do you hear me?" I nodded. "And don't tell anyone it is. She named you after the Archbishop. Especially don't tell them that. Don't tell them anything about the old woman."

"Come on, Pen," Medina said.

"Come on nothing! She's fastened onto Percy as if she thinks they have something in common. I should have a word with her. What if it hadn't been water in that vial? You can't have a crazy woman going around sprinkling children with what might or might not be holy water. There could have been anything in that bottle. Even if it *was* water, it could have been water from a ditch."

"Percy looks okay to me," Medina murmured.

"Did you get any in your mouth? Did you swallow any?" my mother demanded of me.

"I got some on my lips." I put out my tongue to lick them tentatively. "It tasted just like water."

"Jesus," my mother said. She announced she would have a word with Sister Mary Aggie the next time she came down the Curve of Bonaventure. She told me I should come inside and let her know if I saw Sister Mary Aggie coming down the hill. "And you *stay* inside," she said.

I did as she told me, running inside the next time I spotted Sister Mary Aggie at the top of Bonaventure. It was seven in the evening in July, Pops was in his sunroom, and Medina and my mother were playing cards. "Here she comes," I shouted, running into the kitchen. "Stay here," my mother ordered. I stayed inside for as long as it took Sister Mary Aggie to reach the Block, then went outside and stood beside my mother and Medina. My mother looked down at me, shook her head with exasperation, then pointed at Sister Mary Aggie.

"You," she said. "Sister Mary Aggie. Leave Percy alone. Use the other side of the street from now on."

"You're the boy's mother. A Jezebel. Women like you used to work for me. Back in the days of the Empire."

"She means Empire Avenue," Medina said. "There was a whorehouse on Empire Avenue. But she was never in charge of it or anything like that."

"Another Jezebel. Two of them. Going at it like a brace of rabbits. It takes one to know two."

My mother gaped open-mouthed at Sister Mary Aggie and then Medina, who ever so slightly shook her head.

"Shut up," my mother hissed, looking around at the houses on either side of ours. "Shut up unless you liked the Mental more than I think you did."

"Pardon *me*, Your Highness," Sister Mary Aggie said, raising her eyebrows.

"I want you to stay away from my boy, Percy, from now on. I don't want you giving him Mass cards or pretending you can baptize him or perform some other sacrament. I don't want him to come indoors and tell me that he's been confirmed or married or just went to confession or is doomed to Goddamn Hell. I don't want you talking to him at all, do you understand?"

"Nothing I did was against the law. If you call the police, all they'll do is talk to me. They like me. I know all of them by name."

"I won't call the police. I'll call His Grace the Archbishop. *He* likes Percy."

Sister Mary Aggie looked momentarily perturbed but quickly recovered. "I like the boy too," she said.

"Here"—my mother extended the three Mass cards to Sister Mary Aggie—"I'm not paying for these."

"I gave them to the boy. They belong to him."

"He doesn't want them."

Sister Mary Aggie looked at me. "I think he does," she said. "He accepted them. Besides, it's bad luck to refuse a Mass card. To refuse three, well. Three is a very important number. Three blessings or three curses, as the case may be."

"First it's blackmail," my mother whispered. "Pay me for my cards or else. . . . You speak of curses and gossip in front of Percy once more and—"

"And what? If you're really not afraid of curses and don't want any blessings for your boy, you can tear up the cards and throw them on the ground right here in front of him."

"We don't want them." She whispered again: "Say whatever you want to whomever you want. You're as mad as a hatter and no one will believe a word of it."

I wanted the cards, would have wanted them even if she hadn't offered the choice of blessings or curses, but now I especially wanted them.

"Mom, can I have the cards?" I said.

"Out of the mouths of babes," said Sister Mary Aggie.

My mother thrust the cards at me and wagged her finger at Sister Mary Aggie.

"Not one cent. That's what you're getting for your cards."

"Jezebel. Slut," Sister Mary Aggie said. "They're not my cards. They belong to the boy now. He looks like he would pay me if he could."

"You're nothing but a common peddler," my mother said. "You peddle superstition in the streets. I'm sure you have a card for every occasion and ailment."

"The Holy Father sends them to me." Sister Mary Aggie smirked.

My mother took a step toward her. "I think you're a beggar. More lazy than crazy. Too lazy to work."

Sister Mary Aggie faintly nodded. "In My name shall ye be persecuted. Scorn, torment and martyrdom shall be your lot if ye follow Me. But ye shall thereby enter into the Kingdom of God."

"Now she thinks she's God Almighty." Medina laughed.

Sister Mary Aggie, without the slightest motion of her head, shifted her eyes to Medina. "I remember Mr. Joyce, your brother. Sometimes he gave me loaves of bread. He got away while the getting was good, didn't he? He wasn't getting any at home."

"Where did he go?" I asked her, but she merely looked up at the sky.

"You wouldn't happen to know who the Patron Saint of Hangovers is, would you?" Medina said, but she sounded nervous.

"Jezebels," Sister Mary Aggie said, her voice as serene as ever. "A brace of Jezebels. A tandem of tarts. I know. It takes one to know two. Back at the Empire, your kind was in great demand. You could wind up in jail. Or worse. A lot worse. I know what goes on in the Mental. You'd be fried like fish on Friday. Or maybe have an operation. Two scars apiece. I made a lot of money during the war, from the Yanks and the British and the Canadians too. I know what's going on. The bats are in the belfry and the rats are in the basement, mark my words."

"Here, Pen," Medina said, "here's two dimes," cocking her head at me and winking as she held the two coins out to my mother. My mother took the coins but put them in her pocket.

"Not one cent," she said, making a sudden lunge at Sister Mary Aggie, who all but ran away, gesticulating with her hands above her head as if she were fending off things falling from the sky.

My mother grabbed my shoulder. "This is why I told *you* to stay inside. Don't say a word to Pops about what Mary Aggie said. She's out of her mind, but Pops might try to make something out of nothing." She turned me briskly about and the three of us went indoors.

But Pops had been watching from the front window and wanted to know what had happened. When Medina told him as much as she safely could, he said, "You did the right thing, Paynelope. Percy doesn't believe in curses, do you, Percy?" I shook my head without conviction. "You should burn those cards, Paynelope. Just so the boy doesn't dwell on them."

"No," I put my hand behind my back quickly. "Mom gave the cards to me."

"That's right," my mother said. "Sister Mary Aggie didn't give them to you, I did. There's no such thing as a curse, but if there was, the three of them would be on my head, not yours. Oh, what am I saying? Now you're going to think I'm cursed."

"No, I'm not."

I taped the cards to the wall above the upper of the two bunks of my bed, two with Saint Drogo facing out, the other between them with the prayer side facing out: "Let them not be judged, O Lord, by their earthly appearance, but let Your glorious Light shine upon them that all may see the everlasting Beauty of their Souls. . . . A small contribution would be appreciated. May God bless you and keep you, forever and ever. Amen."

When my mother saw them taped to the wall, she said, "Jesus, Percy, wouldn't you rather collect hockey cards or something?"

"Well, Pen," Medina said, "you told him you'd let him make up his own mind about religion."

"Religion?" my mother said. "That's not religion. It's worse. Those cards won't change anything, Percy. They won't make anything better. You know that, right?"

I nodded. "They're just for fun."

"And whatever you do," she said, "stay away from Sister Mary Aggie from now on. Not one more piece of her merchandise will come into this house, understand?"

I nodded.

She dropped her voice. "It's important, Perse, to stay away from her, important for all of us. When you're older, you'll understand, okay?"

"Okay."

I probably would have disobeyed her, but Sister Mary Aggie stopped coming by the Block, as if, having done what she could for me, she had moved on to some other part of the Mount, some other boy. My mother, Medina and I—I had nagged them into it by telling them I was worried she was back in the Mental—went up the Curve of Bonaventure, past St. Bon's to Sister Mary Aggie's room on Garrison Hill. And perhaps she was back in the Mental: the pulsing red Sacred Heart was gone and there were no curtains on the window. The room looked empty, but my mother let me knock on the door anyway. No one came.

ONE YEAR'S GRACE

MY mother decided to hold me back from school until I was six, saying that "an extra year might make a lot of difference." I knew what she meant but pretended not to. I didn't mind staying at home. It was fun at 44, watching the weird interactions of the grown-ups and soaking up from them as much "forbidden" knowledge as I could.

"Why does everyone call him Jim Joyce?" Pops asked.

"So as not to confuse him with Joe Blow," Medina said.

"Do you have to be so mean?" Pops snapped. He never, when directly addressing her, used her name, and only rarely used it otherwise.

"Do you *have* to be so nice, Pops? I'm related to Jim Joyce by an accident of birth. What's your excuse?"

"Everyone called him Jim Joyce," my mother said. "'Jim' was insufficient for some reason."

Medina sniffed. "I used to ask him, 'Jim, what would you like to be if you grow up?'"

"What was Jim Joyce, really?" I said. "What was his job?" My mother told me he was a brain surgeon. An admiral in the navy. A big tycoon. "Tell me the truth."

"I've told you before. He was a van driver. He delivered trays of bread to corner stores."

"Really?"

"Really. He had a wallet that was connected to his back pocket by a silver chain. He wore an olive-coloured uniform with his first name on it. Jim. The cock of the walk. He had a white undershirt and a pair of worn-out boots. But the Foreign Legion convinced him to leave all that behind."

"The sky's the limit on the Mainland," Medina said. "I'm sure he's gone on to bigger and better things. Probably drives a bigger and better bread van in some place like New York."

"Was he smart like you?" I asked my mother.

"He was smart like *me*," Medina said. "Not book smart, but smart." She sounded contrite.

My mother sometimes used the initials D.O.D. when speaking about Jim Joyce in front of me. She went on using it long after I knew that it stood for Dear Old Dad. Pops said she shouldn't call him D.O.D. "He's my fiancé," she replied, blowing cigarette smoke at the ceiling. "He never did tell me he was breaking off our engagement. I can call him anything I want. Percy's my son and this is my house. And you're a boarder from the bottom of the bay. So I guess I can call D.O.D. anything I want."

Pops always backed down when my mother spoke to him like that. He shrugged as if to say, "Fine. If you want to make fun of a man who can't defend himself in front of his son, go ahead."

Though she was on less than half a secretary's salary, my mother typed almost incessantly throughout the day, in the evening after supper, on the weekends, always puffing on a cigarette, squinting through the smoke, wincing, blinking, tears running from her red-rimmed eyes. I became so accustomed to the clatter of her typewriter, the dinging of the bell, that they became like the automatic noises of the house, the noises of the furnace, the water pipes, the washer and dryer. Occasionally I would notice a change in the frequency of the dinging of the bell, which was the measure of how fast she was going. Ding, ding, ding, ding, each ding a line, the dinging and the lines accelerating as if the Remington were self-propelled, each line a few more pennies in our pockets, courtesy of Uncle Paddy. Ding, ding, ding, like coins dropped into a piggy bank.

She typed on an expansive but flimsy, thin-topped office table that wobbled more the faster she typed and always looked on the verge of collapsing and dumping the Remington into her lap. With my mother typing so fast amid so much smoke, the table looked like some sort of vehicle that she was trying to coax into motion, the typewriter like some sort of engine or steering apparatus.

"Still at the Helm, Paynelope?" Pops would quip when he came home.

"Still at it, Pops," my mother would answer without removing her cigarette from her mouth.

"All that work and you haven't budged an inch."

She stayed at the Helm for hours without a break. Sometimes drops of sweat ran down her forehead and her cheeks. When she got up from her chair, the back of her dress was damp, sometimes visibly so, depending on its colour.

"Don't you even have to stop to pee?" Medina said when she dropped by.

My mother's typing posture was perfect, her back straight, her high-heeled shoes disposed just so on the floor. Except for the cigarette, she might have been posing for the cover of a typewriting textbook. She had been required to wear high-heeled shoes when she was learning to type and said that she didn't feel right typing without them, even when she wore her bathrobe. When she was done for the day, she slipped out of her shoes and left them under the table. She soaked her fingertips every night in some sort of blister-preventing solution, saying that we were always one blister away from falling behind on the mortgage. "I can always tide you over, Paynelope," Pops said, but my mother ignored him.

While my mother sat in the kitchen after dinner, a beer in front of her, Medina would stand behind her chair and massage her shoulders. "You're nothing but knots, sweetie," she said.

"Mmmmm," my mother said.

DIRECTOR McHUGH

SOMETIMES, when she had no choice, my mother would leave me with Pops, telling him all sorts of things to do and not do, the latter including not to drink beer until she was back and not to take me outdoors. Pops complied, following me about the house, abstaining from beer, until one day when my mother had worked later than usual and said she could get to the grocery store and back faster if she went by herself. She had no sooner boarded the bus than Pops said, "Would you like to go across the street and visit Brother Rice? All this time it's been just across the street, and I go there every day, but you've never been inside."

"Mom said not to take me outdoors."

"She meant not to take you too far from home. We'll only be outdoors for a minute. Then we'll be indoors again. And we'll get back long before she does. We can go out just as we are."

It was April, but there was still some snow here and there and it got quite cold after sunset. He was wearing his lab coat, I a sweater and a T-shirt. "We don't need overcoats," he said. "It's just across the street."

I had often wondered what Brother Rice was like and very much wanted to see it. I was five, so it would be nine years before I went there, but it was always *there* when I looked out the window, the very definition for me of the word "school," a massive block of brick overlooking 44. I decided not to ask Pops what we would say to my mother when she got back. I knew she'd be able to tell just by looking at me and Pops that something had happened and that I would tell her exactly what before she even asked. I didn't say so to Pops, however, in case he changed his mind.

Pops said Brother Rice was the biggest school in the province. It was the hub school that led the way in everything—sports, scholastics—and was run by the highest-ranking Christian Brother on the island. Pops said that Director McHugh was looked upon as the Christian Brothers' equivalent of the Archbishop, which my mother said was like being looked upon as the infantryman equivalent of a four-star general.

Pops took me across the street, holding my hand, waving at motorists who honked and pedestrians who waved back. I waved and smiled as well. He led me to the front door of the school, which he unlocked with one of about a dozen keys he carried on a ring that was wound around his thumb. The vestibule was dark until Pops turned on one of the lights and a world that was entirely new to me burst into life. The floor and the stairs that led up to the night-lit lobby were made of gleaming black marble that caused our footsteps to echo in the empty school. Pops took me by the hand. "By day you can't hear yourself think in here, there's such a din," he said. "It's hard to believe it's the same place." We went up the stairs and into the lobby. I gaped at the large glass-encased sports trophies that were everywhere, on free-standing pedestals, on tables against the wall. Pops flipped another light.

"Brother Rice wins just about everything," he said. "Director

McHugh makes sure of that." He pointed to a floor-to-ceiling wooden scroll, about half of which was blank. "The honour roll," he said with some sarcasm, pointing to the names etched into the wood. "From the year the school started up to last year. If your average is between seventy-five and eighty-five you get second class, eighty-five and up first class. Your name will be on this scroll someday, in the first-class list. When you're old enough to go to high school. You're probably smart enough to go now, but rules are rules. You're going to be as smart as your mother."

He pointed up to a large photograph of a smiling, vestment-laden old man wearing a skullcap. "The Pope. He's in charge of the Church."

"I know."

"Some of the boys call me Pope Pops the First." I laughed because I thought he wanted me to, but he frowned. "You wouldn't believe how stupid most of these boys are. The average student is a dunce with a brain the size of a subatomic particle." He pointed at the honour roll. "Even most of *them* are stupid. Why is it considered necessary for children to want to be something when they grow up? *I* never wanted to be anything." He sounded as if he was living proof that childhood apathy was no deterrent to success.

"Like everything else, stupidity runs in families. When I see the family resemblance, when I see a boy whose brother or father was my student, I know exactly what to expect. There should be signs in front of houses all over the city: 'Murphy and Sons—Makers of Idiots since 1823'; 'Crocker and Sons—Proudly providing St. John's with yahoos and buffoons since 1882.'"

To the right of the scroll, the walls were made of glass. "Principal's Office," a sign on the door read, and below that, "Director G.M. McHugh," followed by a long line of initials, commas and periods. I dimly made out a desk behind the glass.

"Sometimes Director McHugh works late," Pops murmured. "Even in the summer, but not tonight."

"Where's your office?" I asked.

"I guess the chem lab's my office," Pops sniffed. "McHugh has the only real office."

He led me to the right, down a long dark hallway flanked by rows of lockers. About the midpoint of the hallway, there was a gap on the left side. A short flight of stairs led down to a window-less, heavy-looking black door that bore no plate or words.

"That door leads to the tunnel that leads to the Brothers' Quarters," Pops said, "where they live and sleep. I see them coming and going by that door, but I've never been inside the tunnel. The boys McHugh straps are taken to him through the tunnels." I had an image of the Brothers living underground in a catacomb-like maze of torchlit cells, a dungeon-dim place from which they emerged each morning to join the throng of boys in the hallway. And another image of a boy being "taken to" McHugh through the tunnels like a condemned prisoner.

Pops said they had rooms with a toilet and sink but no bath or shower. There was a shared shower like the one used by students after gym class. The Christian Brothers took vows of poverty and chastity. They could drink and smoke but only in their quarters; most did both, though it was said that Director McHugh, who had a suite of rooms and his own shower, did neither.

A beer truck filled to the brim pulled up to the back of the Brothers' Quarters every Friday afternoon at four and was empty when it left. "No one begrudges them a beer and a smoke," Pops said. "It's not as if they have much else. I suppose I live much like they do, even to the point of having just a room to myself which is within feet of the school where I teach."

He showed me the cafeteria. "The Brothers call it the Mess Hall. I call it the Trough. The boys snuffle through their lunches like a herd of swine."

We went to the gym. As he turned on each light, there was a thudding sound and then a loud buzzing that echoed from wall to wall. "Basketball, volleyball," he muttered, surveying the gym from the doorway. "I never heard of them when I was growing up. I still don't know what the rules are. Don't want to know. All we had to skate on was a frozen pond."

He showed me the little library, the tiny music room. He saved the chem lab, which was just outside the gym, for last. He unlocked the door, which had one narrow rectangular window criss-crossed with wire. When he switched the lights on, we faced a raised dais with a desk and chair on top of it, books, papers and pens scattered about the desk.

"My throne, you might say. It can be Percy's throne for now. Sit in the chair." A makeshift set of wooden steps led up to the level of the desk. I climbed up, sat in the chair and looked out across horizontally arranged rows of countertops and sinks.

"Lab stations," he said. "Each one has a gas valve. The last thing I do every day is make sure that all of them have been turned off. So I sit up there and preside over the boys as they conduct experiments that I assign. Everyone, including me, wears safety goggles. Someone always blows something up. The boys also call me Mr. Clean because I dress in this white lab coat. I believe some irony is intended, because my coat is never clean—there are stains which will never come out. But attributing irony to that tribe of trilobites may be giving them too much credit. I see it all from where you're sitting, Percy, row upon row of nose-picking, cretinous, never-to-evolve baboons, and here and there among them a star—a star because the number of letters in some of the words he says exceeds four and because he doesn't always join in when the other boys light up wind from their behinds with Bunsen burners." Pops' room at home, which I caught only occasional glimpses of through his partly open door, was full of chemistry "props," likely one of everything that was in his lab: a petri dish for growing what he called "baketerial cultures," a Bunsen burner, a broken microscope, a beaker, a pipette, a large brown bottle stoppered with a cork.

He fell silent and put his hands in the pockets of his lab coat, his thumbs outside. "Does your mother ever mention me, Percy?" He dropped his chin onto his chest as if he had fallen asleep.

"What do you mean?"

"Has she ever said, I don't know, something nice or something bad about me when I wasn't around?"

"Sometimes. But she's just joking with Medina. They joke about everyone: They joke about me."

"Yes, I know—I'm sure it's all in fun, but your mother, she never mentions me to you, when the other one is not around I mean?"

"I guess so. I'm not sure."

"So—she's never taken you aside to tell you something about me?"

"Like a secret?"

"Something like one, I suppose. You tell me. What does she say?"

"She never tells me secrets."

"That's why they're secrets, I suppose."

"I suppose."

"Does she ever speak about Medina when I'm not around?"

"Not really."

"They're as thick as thieves, the two of them. If you ever hear anything that sounds like a secret, let me know. We're the men of the house. We have to stick together, right?"

"I suppose."

"All right. Well, never mind. Don't tell them I asked you any questions. Okay? *That* can be our secret."

"Okay."

"Here"—Pops reached into the desk drawer and took out a pair of safety goggles—"put these on." He helped me, adjusting the back strap until it was tight. Then he put on his own. "You're goggle-eyed. Look at your reflection in the window." I looked like a snorkeller who had lost his breathing tube. "You look funny too," I said, and we both laughed.

Next he took out what he called "a model of a molecule," balls of various colours connected by wooden pegs. "This is a good one," he said, "magnesium tetra dioxide." He handed it to me. "You can keep it," he said. "There are no labs in junior school, but you'll take chemistry when you get to grade ten. Probably from me." I thought of it, being taught chemistry at school by Pops who boarded with us. "Do you like the molecule?" he asked. "Yes, thanks." But I wasn't sure what to do with it. "You can make different shapes with it," he said. "Different molecules. The sticks are the bonds that hold the atoms together. A bundle of atoms makes up a molecule. Atoms and molecules are too small for us to see. But they are what we are made of, nothing else."

"Medina said that invisible atoms are going for sixty cents a bundle at the grocery store."

"Ignorance. Blissful ignorance. And this from a woman who works in a hospital surrounded by science. Her knowledge of science, her notion of how things work, is on a par with that of some raw-meat-eating savage from the paleolithic age. We are millions of molecules, Percy. That's all we are. One person"—he pointed at me—"gets a big mind. Another, like Medina, gets a small mind. You deserve no credit. She deserves no blame. We are what matter made us, and that cannot be planned or changed. Atoms don't bind because they love each other or even because they hate each other. Or even because of animal attraction. They bind because of inanimate attraction. Like magnets. Medina, being single and having no chance of ever being otherwise, is a non-binding entity. Subatomic. Sub everything. You know—"

The lab door opened and in walked Director McHugh. I had never seen him before, but I had no doubt that it was him. Had he been wearing a wide-brimmed black hat, he could easily have been mistaken, in spite of his frock, for a priest. He had the deliberate, authoritative air of one, of a man who could say Mass, administer the sacraments, forgive sins or withhold forgiveness, marry people, perform last rites. But a Christian Brother, even *the* Christian Brother, could do none of these. He could only teach and preside over other Brothers, other teachers. Yet he had the air of someone accustomed to having his arrival received with silence, someone whose entrance interrupted conversation and commanded the attention of all who were in the room. He wore a pin identifying him as Director G.M. McHugh. His hair was longer than that of any of the other Brothers, thick and white. It made him look younger than his eyes and his complexion told me he must be.

I laid the model molecule on the desk.

"Director McHugh!" Pops gasped, extending his arms to me and hastily lifting me down from the dais, removing my safety goggles then his own, and standing me square in front of McHugh, whom I expected to crouch down to my height or put his hands on my shoulders as other grown-ups did.

"I didn't see you in your office," Pops said, "or I would have stopped by. I was just showing Percy where I work." He was so nervous he all but swallowed the last half of the sentence.

"No harm done," McHugh said, leaving me to wonder if, when we arrived, he *had* been in his office, in the dark, looking out at us, knowing we could not see him.

"He'll be a pupil here one day." He spoke in a sonorous, modulated voice.

"Yes, that's right," Pops said. "I thought we could spare one of our model molecules, so I gave him one. It's right there on the desk—as a souvenir—"

"A memento," McHugh said, "to remind him of the day when he'll return."

"Exactly," Pops said. "Percy, this is Director McHugh."

"Hello, Brother," I said, uncertain if I should have said "director." I looked up at him. He said nothing. Slowly, very slowly chewing gum with his front teeth, his pursed lips moving slightly as if he was contemplating some difficult decision, he faintly, appraisingly, smiled. Gum, I would learn in time, was his only "vice."

"So this is the little Joyce boy who won't be starting school until he's six," he said, putting his index finger under my chin and raising my face, which he examined at length, his eyes moving slowly about as if he was memorizing my every feature. My heart thumped and I felt myself deeply flushing from head to toe, stained and unstained parts alike. My arms at my sides, I was barely able to resist turning my face away. I suspected that I had last been as closely scrutinized by a doctor as an infant. I felt that my self-consciousness was for the first time being entirely discounted, as if Brother McHugh had a purpose for thus examining me that over-rode any considerations of embarrassment or privacy. He might well have *been* a doctor who was judging how well the face on which he had recently operated was healing, staring at me as if he had just removed a set of bandages. "Hmm," he said, lowering his hand but looking me straight in the eye. His eyes were blue, as blue as the sky on a cold winter's day. "Little Percy, Little Percy. It's not all that bad, is it, Vice-Principal MacDougal, not as bad as His Grace thinks it is and Little Percy and his mother *like* to think it is. And his hands and his feet, they don't seem so oversized to me. Lobster-coloured hands. Not the worst fate in the world."

"Oh no, it's not all that bad. Percy has grown used to his— I think— It's just a question—"

"Be certain that every door is locked before you leave, Vice-Principal MacDougal," McHugh said, turning away from us and walking out without closing the chem lab door behind him. He had not once addressed me directly, not with a single word, but had only spoken *of* me to Pops as if I were inanimate, insensate. He had not even asked me a single question of the sort that the few other clerics I had met had asked, simple questions that more or less instructed you how to answer them, such as "Do you like ice cream?" or "You live at 44, don't you?"

Pops, averting his eyes, put the goggles away. I heard McHugh's receding footsteps, then a door opening and closing.

"He's gone into the tunnel," Pops said. "At least, I think he has. I suppose he wasn't following us around the whole time. I hope he didn't hear any of those things I said about the boys. Some Rice boys come from very influential families. Lawyers, doctors, judges, politicians. How they rose to influence God only knows, because they're as thick as their children."

"I think we should go home," I said. "It's pretty dark outside. It must be late."

Pops looked at his watch. "Christ," he said. "Paynelope must be back by now. She'll be worried sick. And angry." I hurried after Pops as he turned off all the lights and checked that all the doors were locked. "She's going to hang me," Pops said, fidgeting wildly with the keys as he tried to lock the door to the cafeteria.

We ran hand in hand across Bonaventure in the dark, me with my model molecule in my free hand. There were lights on in the house, but there had been lights on when we left, so I wasn't sure if my mother was home. Pops was just about to turn the doorknob when my mother yanked open the door.

"Thank God," she gasped. "Where have you been? I've been going half out of my mind with worry."

"You knew he was with me," Pops said.

"How could I know *anything*? I come home and find the house empty, the door unlocked. I didn't know what to think. Why didn't you leave a goddamn note? And even if I'd been sure he was with you, Pops, what comfort would that have been? Oh, he's with Pops, then nothing could possibly be wrong. You better have a good reason for going outside with Percy, Pops. What was the emergency? Because if there was anything less than one, you're in big trouble."

"I took him to see Brother Rice," Pops said.

"Why?"

"Because he's never been inside there in his life."

"Neither have I and I still somehow manage to make it from one day to the next. What do you have there, Percy?"

"A model of a molecule," I said. "Pops gave it to me when we were in the chemistry lab."

She pulled me away from him and told me to go to my room. I did as she said but then crept back out and watched from the hallway, to which my mother's back was turned.

"You were counting on getting back here before me and me coming home to find that the deed was done, that Percy was safe and content and eager to tell me all about his field trip to Brother Rice, and that because he'd had such a good time, I wouldn't have the heart to spoil things for him by getting upset with you."

"I'm sorry. I should have asked for your permission."

"You didn't ask because you knew you wouldn't get it."

"You make it sound as if I had some ulterior motive for wanting to show Percy Brother Rice. I wanted him to see where I go every day, where I work, that's all."

"You will never worm your way into this family. Remember that. You stay here on certain terms. Don't try to change them. I allow you certain privileges. Don't try to expand upon them."

"I wouldn't. Of course I wouldn't do that."

"So what was it like, your field trip to Brother Rice?"

"We met McHugh."

"You mean you *took* him to meet McHugh."

"No. We were in the chem lab. McHugh just walked in."

"*Percy!*" my mother shouted. I went out to the kitchen.

"So you met the mighty McHugh?"

I nodded.

"What was *that* like?"

"He touched my face."

"What? How?"

When I showed her, she glared at Pops. "What did he say, Pops? Did he touch Percy's hands too?"

"No. He just said it—the stain on Percy's face—he said it didn't look so bad."

"Is that what he said, Percy?"

I nodded. "He said it didn't look as bad as we thought it was, you and me and Uncle Paddy. He didn't really say it to me, he said it to Pops. He didn't really say anything to me. He called me Little Percy."

My mother stood closer to Pops, her face about an inch from his.

"What happened, Pops?"

"It's just as Percy says."

"Little Percy. Whose face McHugh thinks he's free to do with as he pleases, touch it, size it up. *Jesus.*"

"I didn't know he'd be there," Pops said.

"I'm sure you didn't. Are you all right, Percy?"

I nodded. I shook my head when she asked if I'd been scared. I thought of describing how I'd felt but couldn't find the words. I thought of the feel of McHugh's finger on my chin.

"Holy cards and curses from Sister Mary Aggie. McHugh sizing him up as if he were a horse. What next? What did you say, Pops, when McHugh said that Percy's face didn't look so bad?"

"I agreed with him. I don't think it looks that bad. I tried to tell McHugh it was a question of how Percy would be treated by the other boys—"

"You said it wasn't that bad? Is there anything McHugh could have said that you wouldn't have agreed with?"

"I'm sorry—"

"Have you been drinking?" my mother said.

"No," Pops said.

"Then what's your excuse?"

"I told you. I asked him if he'd like to see the chem lab."

"You asked *him*? Since when do you ask *him*? I told you not to take him outdoors. Now listen to me, Pops. There is no 'Pops and Percy,' do you understand? Pops and Percy do not walk hand in hand across Bonaventure. They do not appear in public together, even with me. There is Miss Joyce and Percy Joyce. People do not say 'There go Pops and Percy.' Miss Joyce and Percy Joyce, Penny and Percy, fine. But Pops is not in the picture. There is no Pops and Percy, there is no Pops and Penny. Do you and I go out in public? No. People do not say 'There go Pops and Penny.'"

"No, they say 'There go Percy and the two Miss Joyces.'"

"Leave Medina out of this. You are our boarder. Not our avuncular boarder. Not our good-with-children boarder. Not our pitches-in-to-help-when-he-can boarder. Not our almost-like-one-of-the-family boarder. Not our unexpected boon of a boarder. Not our godsend-to-the-Joyces boarder. I do not need you and Percy skipping back and forth to Brother Rice in front of everyone. You are our boarder, the Joyces' boarder. Otherwise, you are Pops, period. And if from now on you so much as take Percy out on the steps, you will be known as the Joyces' former boarder. The erstwhile boarder. The long-since-replaced boarder. The boarder in search of a new situation. The boarder more abruptly expelled than any other in the history of room and board. The boarder in search of a forwarding address. The boarder they call Mariah—like the wind."

Pops tried to walk away, but she took him by the arm.

"Imagine that someone drew a picture of the two of you on a blackboard. Imagine it, and then erase yourself."

"I just thought he'd like to see where I spend my days, where I work, where I teach, where my students sit, and what the lab equipment looks like. He said he would."

"I told you, it doesn't matter what he says. Percy would say yes if a cab driver he had never seen before walked into the house and asked him if he'd like a ride to Port aux Basques. Percy is *five*."

"Do you plan to carry on all night at my expense?"

"Once more, Pops, just once more and you'll be ideally suited to write a book. You could call it *A View Without a Room*."

I looked at Pops and felt very sorry for him, being dressed down in front of me like that.

GIVE ME MYTH
OR GIVE ME DEATH

P ops returned home from Brother Rice one afternoon
a couple of weeks before my first day of school and
announced that Director McHugh had told him that His
Grace had decreed that Percy Joyce, Little Percy, was to be exempt
from any and all forms of physical discipline or corporal punishment at school. My mother was so happy and relieved I wondered
what exactly I had been exempted from, but she merely said it was
something I needn't worry myself about, now that His Grace had
intervened. "He knows how it would look," I overheard her say
later to Medina. She didn't finish the sentence, but I now know
what she meant. It wouldn't look good if the little Joyce boy were
strapped, what with His Grace having preached a sermon from the
Mount on my behalf, what with my overly large hands that would
make such easy and conspicuous targets for a strap. It wouldn't
look good if, after having been strapped, the little Joyce boy put
those hands beneath his armpits in a vain attempt to put out the

fire in them. It wouldn't look good if, thus disposed, the little Joyce boy, eyes streaming tears, walked forlornly down Bonaventure, his big feet flapping like a pair of codfish.

The night before my first day of school, my mother and Medina drank a lot of beer. Pops kept storming out of his room to complain about the noise they were making, saying that even if they didn't care about him, they ought to remember that they were keeping *me* awake on the night before such an important day in my life. His complaints did not deter them—not that it would have mattered to me if they had for even if the house had been silent I couldn't have slept, what with being so wrought up with anticipation and anxiety. I joined them in the kitchen, drank Crush and watched them drinking beer and, when they abandoned their card playing, watched TV with them as they loudly made fun of a Barnum & Bailey circus programme. My mother asked Medina: Who, at some point in their life, has not longed to throttle a ventriloquist or beat some sense into someone who was forever plucking quarters from the ears of strangers? Who hasn't prayed that some flaming sword swallower would extract from his throat a shish kebab of his vital organs? Who hasn't pictured an acrobat emerge from a somersault with a noose of rigging ropes around his neck? Who hasn't wished that the tuxedo-wearing, unicycle-riding balancer of twenty spinning plates would slip and go down in a clattering tangle of sticks and spokes and broken china?

My mother kissed Medina on the cheek, then kissed me on the cheek. They stopped watching TV and played "What If?" In this case, what if the Church hired cheerleaders to tell its story and promote its cause? Tight-fitting-short-sleeved-blouse-and-short-skirt-wearing cheerleaders. My mother had been a cheerleader at Holy Heart. She stood up and began doing jumping jacks. When my mother nodded at us, Medina and I clapped our hands in time to what she was chanting.

There go the Pagans, there they go.
There go the Pagans, there they go.
How do you spell *victory*?
How do you spell *victory*?
Split that *V*
Dot that *i*
Shake that *c–t–o–r–y*
VICTORY
YEEAHHH PAPISTS!

Come on, Papists, pump it up
Let them Muslims know what's up
We have a team, we have a yell
A team that fights like bloody Hell
How do you spell DESTROY?
D–E–S–T–R–O–Y
Cleave those breastplates
Throw those spears
Kill those darned char-i-o-teers
YEEAHHHH PAPISTS

Come on, prove that you have dicks,
Go out and kill some heretics
YEEAAHHH CHRISTIANS, YEEAAHHH CHRISTIANS

They may be the infidels
But we have better cheers and yells.
What is better for the soul
Than Muslim heads upon a pole?

Put his head upon a stick—
Mohammed is a lunatic!
YEEAAHHH CHRISTIANS

Here we go, Fascists, here we go!
Here we go, Fascists, here we go!

Big noses only make big sneezes
We'll get you back for killing Jesus
We'll stomp your faces, break your bones
Annihilate your chromosomes!

The Krauts may be the craziest
But Communists are atheists!
We've got Hitler, yes we do
We've got Mussolini too
Now don't complain, don't make a fuss
They'll do our dirty work for us.
YEAHHHH FASCISTS

Kill the commie, kill the Jew
We're worth more than ten of you
On your feet, let's hear you stamp!
Can *you* spell *concentration camp*?
YEAAAAHHHH PAPISTS

You know the Papists are the best
We're much better than the rest.
Let's hear that cheer, you know it well
All Protestants will go to Hell
YEAAAAHHHH PAPISTS

Pops came out this time to protest what my mother was saying in front of me. "He doesn't understand a word of it, Pops," my mother said. "We're just having some fun, that's all. Throwing a coming-out party for Perse. Tomorrow's his first day of school, and the last one of life as he knows it."

"He's only six! Barely six! You're biting the hand that protects your son."

"It's not as if we're doing it in front of Uncle Paddy."

"Soon Percy will be talking about His Grace like that. In front of someone who'll tattle to McHugh."

"Old Gloomy Gus McHugh." She put her hand on my head. "Don't call the Archbishop Uncle Paddy, not even in this house, okay?"

I nodded.

"We're just letting off some steam, Pops. Feel free to leave us to it. If you must complain, phone the police and tell them your landlady is making too much noise."

Pops went back to his room.

My mother sat on the sofa with her thigh against Medina's, one arm around her shoulder. She kissed her again. I stood on the sofa and kissed my mother on the cheek. Medina got up and put on a record by Patsy Cline. She and my mother danced to "I Fall to Pieces." Medina kissed her briefly on the lips and slipped one hand between the buttons of her blouse. My mother shook her head, pulled away and rejoined me on the couch. "She was just trying to tickle me," she said. Medina came over and sat me on her lap and tickled me.

Then my mother began to cry. "Oh fuck, Medina. Fuck, fuck, fuck, fuck, fuck. I can't let *them* have him, can I? I can't just send him off like a lamb to the slaughter."

Medina smiled at me but she looked upset. "You'll be fine, won't you, Perse?"

She kissed my mother on the cheek and pulled her head onto her shoulder, stroking her nylon-covered leg. My mother shook free of her again.

"They're not even allowed to *think* about sex. You might as well let loose a pack of dogs upon a flock of sheep. The last thing they're suited for is teaching. Christian Brothers. Jesus. More like a riot squad. They even *look* like their specialty is crowd control. And *nuns*. Nuns attacking with picks and shovels a vein of coal a mile underground would be ideally employed."

Medina told her she was doing a wonderful job of preparing me for my first day of school. "I'm sure he's not at all nervous about what to expect," she said.

My mother cried that she didn't want me going "out there" by myself. Medina held me with one hand and rubbed my mother's back in soothing circles with the other, murmuring something I couldn't make out. She kissed my mother on the lips again. I kissed my mother on the lips, but she laughed and pulled away. "Why don't you go to bed, Perse?" Medina said, stroking a thick strand of my mother's hair. "Go on, now, go to bed. Big day tomorrow."

So, the next morning, I went to St. Bon's, short for St. Bonaventure, the junior school at the top of Bonaventure Avenue, across from the Fort Townsend Fire Station whose trucks, flashing lights and screaming sirens I remember as the seemingly ceaseless accompaniment to the voices of my teachers. The smooth grey stone of St. Bon's looked as if, fifty years after the school's construction, it was still awaiting some sort of cosmetic surfacing—paint, imitation brick, stucco, clapboard, something that would make the place look finished. The school was as unadorned, as monastery-like inside as out—long rows of lockers the same grey colour as the cement floor, which itself was the same colour as the outer walls.

My mother wanted to walk me up the hill to St. Bon's on my first day of school, only, she said, because she was worried about the traffic. She crouched down in front of me and tugged at the shoulders and cuffs of my navy blue St. Bon's blazer. I insisted on going by myself. "I'm six. I'll be the oldest in grade one," I said.

"Don't be too sure," Pops said. "A lot of my students failed grade one."

"He'll have the last laugh," Medina said. "You know what they say about men with big feet."

"What do they say?" I said.

"They say," my mother said, "that they have an unfair advantage in kangaroo look-alike contests." I shook my head. "Never mind Medina," she said. "She should mind what they say about aunts with big mouths."

"What do they say?" I said.

"Jesus, Percy," my mother said. She stifled a sob, her hand over her mouth. "Okay, then. Out you go, I guess. Out the door into the big bad world." She crouched down, took me in her arms and hugged me so hard I felt something snap in my back. Medina reached out a hand toward her but let it drop when my mother stood up quickly, folding her arms.

"Now you'll be here all by yourself," I said. "Will you be lonely, Mom?"

"Yes," she said, dabbing her nose with the back of her hand. "So don't be a stranger, okay, Perse? Some Joyce men have a habit of never coming back."

"I'll come back," I said. "Do I look anything like Jim Joyce?"

"No," she said. "Now don't tell anyone in school that you have False Someone Syndrome. They might treat it as a joke."

"Okay."

Walking up the hill to St. Bon's that first day no one laid a finger on me. But when I got into my new classroom it began. I was called Joyce Face. I was asked why, being six years old, I had yet to wash my face. Nigger Lips. "Jesus, Joyce," one boy said, "you must have come out through your mother's arse."

After school, the indoor part of which lasted less than an hour the first day, I reported it all to my mother, who started to cry. "Little *bastards!*" I know now that she was worried that one of these taunts would stick, become my permanent nickname, the kind of name that stuck to local "characters," that forever kept them from being taken seriously and earned for them a kind of fondly ironic mockery, which in order to survive I would give in to, even encourage, and wind up playing the fool's role that I had been assigned. She told me fiercely that I should ignore people who called me names and do my best to make friends and not become a loner. But I already sensed that not even one of the other misfits of the school would want to further devalue his currency by chumming up with me. That night, I imagined a world beyond the Mount in which, by a string of extraordinary accomplishments, I would earn respect, and the onus would be on others to put *me* at ease.

The second day, I was surrounded in the schoolyard by boys, and by girls who wandered up the street from Belvedere, children my age, most of whom had seen me for the first time the day before and, so far, were merely curious.

"What happened to your hands and face?" a girl named Nancy asked.

I said my father and I were in a car that crashed into the Block. He was killed and I was scarred for life. There were still bits of windshield beneath the skin around my eyes. She could feel them if she liked. She shook her head.

Most of the boys and girls looked scared, a few scornful but envious.

Over the next few days, I kept changing my story, making up all sorts of lies. It was the beginning of "give me myth or give me death."

I suffered a syndrome when I was born.

My face turned scarlet when I had scarlet fever.

My sister went aboard of me with a box of Brillo pads.

I said I was part "Red Indian" as the "supposedly extinct" Beothuk Indians were. I was the only living person with Beothuk blood and there was a great deal of pressure on me from scientists and museums to reproduce so as to keep the Beothuk from dying out altogether. None of the children had heard of the Beothuk.

My father was in charge of wild elephants in a circus on the Mainland.

My mother might take me to Lourdes.

My father was killed in the war. My mother was so sad she almost died and that was why I had a stain.

John the Baptist had his head cut off. I might get mine cut off someday. It might end up like his did, on a plate for doctors to look at.

The stain started after I was born and one day might cover me from head to toe. I would smother if it covered all of me. I just had to wait and see. I used to be afraid but my mother told me it was in God's hands.

I was stained all over, but it would all be gone when I was eight. A doctor was going to fix the stain. I could pick any kind of face I wanted. I would look like everyone else.

I can still see the scared, bemused expressions on the faces of my fellow grade one students, expressions that said, So this is what going to school is like, this is the sort of thing you see when you venture out into the world without your mother for the first time, a boy whose face is purple and whose lower lip is three times fatter than the upper one, which itself is twice as fat as normal, whose hands and feet are the size of a grown man's, and who holds forth about these things to anyone who asks about them, or anyone who'll listen. They must have been wondering what else they would encounter as the first days of their expulsion from their lifelong homes went by. What was out here that the grown-up strangers in whose care they had been left would not shelter or protect them from?

As I told each lie, the grade ones who had heard any of the previous versions of my story drifted away and the older ones mocked me for lying. But it was the few seconds or minutes or days of awestruck, dumbstruck credulity that egged me on. Eventually, there were not even any among the grade ones left for me to try to hoodwink or win over. I was seen by all to be some sort of myth-weaving, odd-looking crank who was better left ignored.

My mother found out about my lies from Pops, who found out about them from Brother McHugh, whose source could have been just about anyone.

"Why did you make up all those stories?" she said. "I told you not to mention FSS."

"I didn't."

"They asked him what happened to his face," Pops said. "He had to say *something*."

"*He didn't have to say everything*. He didn't have to contradict himself with every word. Now they all think he tells lies. About everything." I wanted so badly to describe to her how impressed some of the children had seemed, how in awe of someone so oddly afflicted, someone doomed, someone blessed, someone who had survived a car crash in which his father died, who had been so near to, so intimate with, mystery, who had been to the Mainland, whose future depended on a Lourdes miracle, who had suffered a syndrome and whose father was in charge of elephants.

"You *are* like Jim Joyce," she shouted. "If you must tell lies, can't you be consistent so it isn't so obvious you're lying?"

"*Pen*," Medina said, which sent my mother into tears. She took me in her arms.

"I'm sorry, Perse," she said. "I really wish you'd let me walk you up that hill."

But I shook my head.

I got more or less perfect grades by doing little more than pay attention in class. I didn't bring home school work or even books if I could help it. I assumed it was somehow because of my FSS that I was smarter than the others, but Pops said, as he had when we went to Brother Rice, that I took after my mother. "How do you do it, Perse?" Medina said. "I look at a page and nothing happens. You look at one and you remember everything." I shrugged, though what she said was true. I sponged up words and numbers without effort. I could probably have completed the year's work in a week—but that was just more evidence, it seemed to me, of my freakishness. I sensed it would do me no good to show off what one boy called my "brains" in class, but I was so bored trying to keep pace with the others that I couldn't help finishing my every assignment in seconds. The Brothers started sending me to the "library," telling me I should "read something" until they came back to get me. The library consisted of little more than rotatable trees of paperbacks, a grove of them that Mrs. Crowley, the only woman in the school, watched over as she made up questions for the school TV quiz show that she coached. It was called *Reach for the Top*. Her team of boys, all twelve-year-olds, would come to the library sometimes and Mrs. Crowley would fire questions at them that I almost always knew the answers to. "What is a waiting line of people called? The word can also be used as a verb." "Queue," I said, but they all ignored me and Mrs. Crowley went on to another question. I often sat alone in the library, at one of the long tables, for hours, still bored because the library books at St. Bon's were less interesting than the ones my mother read to me. I stared out of the window at the trees that obscured my view of St. Pat's, at drifting snow or gusting rain, and often fell asleep, my head on my arms.

The teasing and name-calling continued. My mother asked Pops to speak to Brother McHugh about my treatment at school, which, she said, seemed to fly in the face of at least the spirit of Uncle Paddy's Sermon on the Mount. Soon, the boys of all the schools on the Mount had it made known to them that to say an unkind word to Percy Joyce, on or off school property, would earn them the legendary wrath of Brother Rice Principal McHugh. It was said the Archbishop had intervened again and had personally charged Brother McHugh with looking out for the little Joyce boy. Pops said that every boy at Rice and at the other schools on the Mount was justifiably terrified of Brother McHugh. No one wanted to be caught staring at me or even looking at me lest I *think* they were staring at me. I wondered if it would have been better just to get beat up from time to time.

"Thank God for Uncle Paddy," my mother said. "I mean His Grace."

Pops said it was common knowledge that, at a word from Brother McHugh, boys from any of the schools could be called to his office. He said there were boys who stayed home for months after a session with McHugh, waiting for the broken bones in their hands to heal. So it was under the aegis of His Grace/Pops/ Brother McHugh that I would flourish. Hopefully.

"Pops is exaggerating," my mother assured me, but Pops shook his head. "I'm not exaggerating in the least." He said that the Director's strap was actually a "strop," a piece of leather on which barbers sharpened their straight-blade razors.

Brother McHugh, by his own edict, was the only Brother allowed to mete out corporal punishment to boys from any of the schools on the Mount. The other Brothers sent misbehaving boys to him. It was said that he kept a record of all the boys who were sent to his office and meticulously kept track of the number of straps or other kinds of blows that they received, the repeat offenders, those who had been suspended and expelled, those who had cried, those who had vowed not to and had kept their vow, those who had vowed not to but had broken down. And so McHugh was what my mother called "the one-man retribution show," the lone "corrections officer" who shouldered the entire load, primarily, he said, because he wished to spare his fellow Brothers the unpleasantness of punishing young boys, was willing to sacrifice himself for the sake of those who worked beneath him.

But I alone, of all the boys, past and present on the Mount, had a free pass.

I learned at school that, as a child, McHugh had gone by the name of Gus and still did to those who knew him personally, and that Gloomy Gus was his nickname among the students. McHugh was said to have hated the short form of his name all his life. As with Saint Augustine's mother, McHugh's mother's name was Monica. Saint Monica. My son the saint. He takes after me. "I actually like the name Gus," my mother said. "But he doesn't seem like a Gus, does he? What's Gus short for? Angus? Surely not. I don't think that man's parents would name him after a breed of cattle. Augustine, more likely. Saint Augustine. One of the super saints. So McHugh's name is Augustine. A very august name. Augustine McHugh. I can just see little Augustine on his tricycle. A hard name to live up to. A name for a boy for whom his parents had high hopes."

My mother asked Pops what he knew about McHugh's background. Pops said he was from Grand Falls, had three sisters, all of them Presentation nuns who taught school in various places on the Mainland. His working-class parents were still living in Grand Falls.

"The only boy," my mother said. "The hope of the family." She wondered how his parents felt about having no grandchildren. The end of their bloodline. To his parents, my mother speculated, McHugh not getting married was a gamble that they may have hoped would have a bigger payoff. Their son the priest. Instead, it was their son the Brother. *The* Brother, but still. "I might be way wide of the mark," my mother said. "Maybe the only person disappointed in Gus is Gus. Or maybe he's come further than he ever dreamed."

Students overheard using the name Gus by a nun, Brother, teacher, staff member or student tattletale were soon, if they were boys, sent to Gus for punishment, or if they were girls, to Sister Celestine of Holy Heart. Sister C, the use of whose nickname was permitted because she was fond of it, also had a monopoly on discipline, being the sole punisher of all students who misbehaved in the girls' schools of the Mount.

Of course, the extreme ban on the use of "Gus" made the boys all the more inclined to use it, to gleefully, often blasphemously, defy the ban. "You'll be called before Gus" if you do this or that, boys would warn each other. Gus will get you for that. Gus will smite you down for that. Gus knows all your secret thoughts, words and deeds. Almighty Gus; Holy Mary, Mother of Gus; Gus the Father, Gus the Son and Gus the Holy Gust.

My mother said she was not sure she wanted to be beholden to such a man. But she soon stopped voicing her worries when the teasing and taunting all but disappeared.

"He'll be fine," Medina said. "He'll probably be the first boy on the Mount to get to grade seven without a black eye. Even if a bit of name-calling was the worst he had to put up with, he'd be luckier than most."

But that's what I was afraid of, being perceived as being luckier than most, an undeservedly special boy, a pet who, because of the Archbishop, Gus and Pops, was spared even what trials the most popular of boys endured—and who rubbed all that in their faces with his effortless perfection in academics. They mocked me as if I fancied I was Uncle Paddy, as if I was His Grace. "Your Face," boys said to me, and fell to one knee as if to kiss my ring.

I was excused from religion class. I was deemed to be physically "too frail" for gym class but about that I didn't care—I knew I'd be the weak link in any sport because of my oversized hands and feet and didn't want there to be yet one more thing for which I alone could be excused. And I was relieved that I wouldn't have to shower with the other boys, wouldn't have to let them see what was hidden by my clothes. I had an "evaluation" session with the guidance counsellor, a well-meaning but painfully embarrassed young woman who divided her time between all the schools on the Mount. Reading from a laminated list, she asked me about various things having to do with what she referred to as my "specialness."

"Is there anything you want to ask about your specialness? Have you ever been teased about your specialness? What words do other students use when referring to your specialness? Do you sometimes wish that your specialness would go away? Do you feel that your teachers understand your specialness? Have you ever felt embarrassed by your specialness? I stared at the desk and said I didn't mind my specialness. My evaluation session ended when she got to the bottom of the list. I never set eyes on her again.

I told my mother about my appointment when I got home. She began to refer to me as "Your Specialness." "What would Your Specialness like for dinner? Is the macaroni to the liking of Your Specialness?"

During my mother and Medina's card game that night, every other word was "specialness." "So tell me, Penelope," Medina said, "how do you feel about your specialness?"

"How do you feel about yours?" my mother said.

"Do you feel that I understand your specialness?" Medina said.

"Have you ever thought about playing with your specialness?" my mother said.

"I believe I have thoroughly explored my specialness."

"There aren't many sports that require you to cover every inch of yourself. It's a pity the school doesn't have a fencing team," my mother said wistfully.

And I imagined it: the world's first never-defeated fencer, his identity unknown because he was never seen without a mask.

There was a network of underground tunnels that connected most of the schools on the Mount. They were necessary partly because the Brothers who taught at St. Bon's and St. Pat's lived in the Brothers' Quarters attached to Brother Rice, a tower of modest height. There was no room for Brothers' Quarters on the grounds of the other six schools, and the walk from Brother Rice to them could be a daunting one if done outdoors given that, as Pops said, most of the school year was winter, a cold, windy, snowy winter that made it all but impossible on many days for a Brother encumbered with textbooks, exercise books and exams to make his way up the slippery slope of the Curve of Bonaventure.

The tunnels were essential for the older nuns and Brothers, and for McHugh, who, as the Director of all the Brothers and the supervisor of all the schools, had to make his way several times a day from Brother Rice to the top of the Mount. The Main Tunnel connected Brother Rice to Holy Heart, St. Pat's and St. Bon's, while narrower tunnels branched off to Belvedere, Mercy and Presentation. I had no idea what the tunnels were like, but the way the other boys darkly referred to "the tunnels" made me think of scenes from old movies I had seen on TV, tunnels lit by flickering torches, rat-teeming passages that would have unnerved even such a beast as Lon Chaney always seemed to play. Most of the boys who had been inside the tunnels had only been there to be led from St. Bon's and St. Pat's to Brother Rice to be punished by McHugh—led by older, junior high students who were known among the boys as the MPs, the Military Police, hall monitors who wore white arm bands. "Honour bands," as the teachers called them. It was rumoured that some MPs were undercover, their identities known to no one but McHugh. Rats, finks, squealers could be anywhere, so you had to be careful what you said and did even when there were no white arm bands to be seen.

McHugh's hair was said to have been white since he was in his early twenties. He combed it to the right in a wave that ended in a crescent that hid half his forehead. He was in his mid-forties now, of average height, neither muscular nor fat, but large, soft-looking, with a small double chin that quivered when he spoke. It was easy to spot him from a distance, especially outdoors when it was windy, for his hair went up in a flickering mass of what might have been white flame. He had a smooth, pink complexion; he looked as if he never shaved because he never had to. His neck and hands and wrists were of the same hairless, pink complexion, almost faded versions of my own. These features, combined with his bright blue eyes and his habit of almost always smiling, gave him the jocular, plump look of an easygoing, all-understanding bishop who, you might imagine, was given to merrily making the sign of the cross over everyone and everything. But he had a deep-timbred, flaw-less, far-projecting voice that alone of all his features seemed to match his reputation. He could, at conversational volume, silence a school hallway at lunchtime, his voice clear and unmistakably his. McHugh visited St. Bon's and St. Pat's at lunchtime via the tunnels when the halls were full of boys, among whom he strolled, hands in the pockets of his slacks, shouting out the last names of skylarking boys in a tone that made it clear they would get no second warning. It was said that he not only knew the first and last names of every boy on the Mount but also knew their aca-demic standing and their attendance and detention records. He had an infallible eye for family resemblance and was forever telling boys they would never measure up to their older brothers who had graduated high school under him.

McHugh would stop and look down at me as he had done in the chem lab and the boys would look expectantly at him. McHugh, chewing his gum, would smile as if he was savouring some devas-tating witticism which, but for the Archbishop's edict, he would say aloud and send the boys into derisive fits of unprecedented hilarity. But the smile would abruptly vanish, be replaced by a look of ironic amusement, as if it had occurred to him that, protected or not by the Archbishop, I was not worth toying with.

The boys at St. Bon's tried to goad me into misbehaving—into skip-ping class when I felt like it, talking back to the Brothers, smoking on the school grounds, starting fights in the hallways. "Tell Brother Hogan to go fuck himself, Percy. Come on. Detention is the worst you'll get, if you even get that. Come *on. Do* it. He can't send you to McHugh. McHugh can't lay a finger on you. No one can."

They seemed fascinated by the question of just how much I could get away with, just how far my amnesty might extend. I was intrigued by the question as well. Could I do *anything* and get away with it? Could I steal candy, bubble gum, cigarettes from Collins's store and give them to boys as bribes in return for friendship? *Had* Uncle Paddy conferred upon me absolute clemency for offences committed anywhere on earth?

"You got it made, Percy," the St. Bon's boys said, shaking their heads at my refusal to take advantage of having it made. "Come on, Percy, *you* won't get into trouble. If Uncle Paddy told everyone to leave *me* alone, I'd kick *you* in the balls."

But my mother warned me that the "hands off Percy Joyce" edict could be revoked at any time if someone like McHugh convinced the Archbishop that I was abusing it, and then where would I be? Surrounded by Brothers and boys I had made enemies of when they were forbidden to lay a finger on me. She said that Uncle Paddy, being so old, might pass away and be replaced by someone less interested in my health. Uncle Paddy might be made a cardinal and appointed to the Vatican, where he was unlikely to spend much of his time pondering the fate of Percy Joyce. "Don't push your luck," my mother said. "I can just imagine the field day McHugh would have with you if Uncle Paddy ever changed his mind." She told me to behave as if the Archbishop had never heard of me.

"The boys of St. Bon's seem to think, Medina, that sin won't register on Percy's soul. When the time comes, he'll simply bypass death and Purgatory and ascend directly into Heaven like Christ and the Blessed Virgin. Remember," she said to me, "you can't complain to Uncle Paddy if *I* smack your arse." Medina smiled and winked at me and Pops said he was sure I would never warrant a smacked arse.

"They're right," my mother said. "I wouldn't smack you. I would *never* hit you."

I knew it was true. She would never hit me. Neither at school nor at home would I be punished, at least not in that way. I vowed that I would never take advantage of her love and concern for me. I believed it at the time. But I might as well have made that vow with my fingers crossed behind my back.

HERE COMES PERCY JOYCE

M Y hands hung heavy from my forearms, drooping
when I raised them as if my wrists were made not of
bone but of cartilage, swaying slightly like those of a
marionette or someone hypnotized. When I couldn't avoid raising
my hand in class, I supported the elbow of my raised arm with my
free hand, self-conscious of that bearpaw-like appendage hovering above the other, smaller, proportionate hands. I was thankful
my hands were hairless or else God knows what I would have been
likened to. My feet, at least, were always covered in public, but my
skinny legs struggled to shuffle them along so that I scuffed somewhat with every step, especially in winter, when my balance on the
ice and snow was less sure than that of other children. Whatever
the season, the approach or retreat of Percy Joyce was as audible,
as unmistakable as the voice of Gus McHugh. "Here comes Percy
Joyce," I heard boys shout from inside the classroom as I made my
way to it down the hallway.

In grade three, when I was eight, I started "blabbing," as Pops put it, about my local gigantism at school. I said, not in a boasting but in a confiding, merely informative sort of way, that my *thing* was affected by local gigantism. I started rumours that spread to the grown-ups on the Mount, and those who believed the rumours jumped to the further, and not entirely inaccurate, conclusion that I was hyper-sexed, precociously horny, pathologically infatuated with sex, possessed of a sexual appetite as out of all proportion as my *thing*. To me, gigantism was mostly just a joke, one more thing that I lied about and was teased about, but the rumour was given more credence than others I'd tried to start. Those who believed, feared, worried, fretted about it to any degree assumed that my oversized *thing* was as discoloured and misshapen as my face, my lips, my hands and feet, an unpredictably dangerous, sinister *thing*, as liable to go off or to have some perverse, irresistible appeal to girls as all ugly things in God's creation seemed to have.

In bed at night, I examined my normal, unobjectionable, average but hyperbolized *thing*. I wagged it back and forth as if to prove to myself that no harm would come my way or to anyone else from so innocuous a penis.

I asked my mother: Could things not locally gigantic now become so as I grew older? No, the doctors had told her that my hands and feet would continue to overgrow but their degree of disproportion to the rest of me would not change, and they would stop growing when the rest of me did. The stains would not spread but would enlarge as I enlarged. No new stains would develop. *Nothing else* would spontaneously sprout at some abnormal rate as I grew older. That the source of this information was the doctor who had told her I would vegetate until my early teens then perish peacefully didn't reassure me. I reminded her that she had told me years ago that the doctors had told her of certain complications that might "manifest" as I grew older, but she said they would have done so by now if they were ever going to.

I already knew that to have—or even be rumoured to have—a *big* one was better in the other boys' eyes than having a small one. But I guessed it wouldn't do to have an absurdly big one, one the size of your forearm, a long, limp limb that in full arousal would be of no appeal to anyone but the kind of people who paid money to look at circus freaks. Nevertheless, I said it was too big for a blow job and too big for any girl to have any kind of sex with, which meant it might be impossible for me to do it or ever reproduce—but I wasn't sure. Most of the time, I said, when it wasn't hard, it was just average, so I couldn't prove I was telling the truth by showing it to anyone. And I would tell Uncle Paddy if they forced me to show them or ganged up on me and stripped off my slacks and underwear the way they did with some boys just for the fun of it. I said it was no shame to be descended from a man who had swum ashore from a sinking ship of the Spanish Armada and been taken in by an Irish woman who had never had a proper screw until she did it with my Spanish ancestor who survived the sinking of his Armada by the British who sunk it by sheer fluke as anyone who knew the real story would be glad to tell you.

Every day after I got home from school my mother sent me to Collins's store at the top of the hill, well off Bonaventure, to buy her two packs of cigarettes. She couldn't spare the near hour it would take to get the cigarettes herself and she never had enough money to buy a carton or more at a time once a week. She declined when Pops offered to give her the money and walk with her to Collins's store on Saturdays to get the cigarettes. "And besides," she said, "the more I have in the house, the more I smoke." She said she figured she would probably go through four packs a day if she could afford it. But she didn't want me to carry her ciga-rette money about all day at school, where I might lose it or be relieved of it by some boys who, even knowing what their punishment would be, would be unable to resist, so she'd have me walk home, where she'd give me the money and send me back up the hill to the store.

She gave me a dollar bill. I bought two packages of Rothmans at forty-five cents a package and kept the remaining dime. Children weren't allowed to buy cigarettes, but my mother would phone ahead to let Mrs. Collins know I was coming. In my blue blazer that bore on one chest pocket the yellow crest of St. Bon's, I had to walk back up the hill past Brother Rice, past our rival school St. Pat's, take a left off Bonaventure just before St. Bon's, walk another half-dozen blocks, buy the cigarettes and ten cents' worth of something for myself, and return home.

I set out every day after school for my mother's cigarettes, regarding with dread the maroon-blue-green-blazer-lined sidewalk of Bonaventure, the black-tunic-and-white-blouse-lined sidewalk of the street across from Holy Heart.

For a while, with the dollar bill balled up in a fist that I kept in my pocket, I walked among the students of the Mount, protected by the ever-newly-toughened terms of my immunity, but never entirely convinced that I was safe. I walked above the fray all because of Uncle Paddy. It was like walking among a swarm of muzzled dogs who, though restrained from biting me or even barking, looked at me in a way that made it all too clear what they would do if one day they couldn't help themselves.

Pops kept assuring my mother that no boy who knew what was good for him would lay a hand on me, but it was the boys who *didn't* know what was good for them who worried me. What if some soon-to-drop-out bully with nothing to lose, with no intention of ever going back to Brother Rice, decided to take out his frustrations on me?

Students, boys especially, tried to find ways of circumventing Uncle Paddy's edict. They stopped using my name in remarks, which therefore seemed they might be directed at anyone. They made pacts not to tattle on each other. They shouted from so far back in the pack, their hands cupping their mouths, that no one was sure who had shouted. "Let's get him and hold him down and put a clothespin on his dick."

Pops told me: "Don't think you have less to fear from the girls, Percy. If Brother McHugh hadn't spoken to Sister Celestine, her crowd would set upon you and leave your bones to bleach in the parking lot of Holy Heart."

I walked twice daily—up the hill, down the hill—through a gauntlet of threats that didn't sound as empty as my mother thought they were. Despite Pops' generosity, a dime was more than my mother could afford, more than the daily allowance of even the better-off boys. I'd usually buy candy or chocolate bars with my dimes, things that could be easily hidden and that I could delay eating until I got home. But sometimes I couldn't resist a lemon square or raisin square, or some kind of ice cream treat. Or even a small, warm-from-the-oven blueberry pie. I'd leave Collins's store devouring the pie before it got cold or the ice cream before it melted, watched by hordes of boys and girls, covetously by some but outright hungrily by others, especially the youngest ones, a pack of Rothmans in each of my jacket pockets as I licked an ice cream cone, or ate a square sandwich-fashion, or played hot potato with a blueberry pie as juice the colour of my face and hands spilled down my front.

One day, an older boy decided that, Archbishop or no Archbishop, he would have his say in front of witnesses.

"There's better pie at home, Percy," a chubby, flushed boy named Coffin said. He smacked and licked his lips until they glistened. "Believe me. I've tasted it lots of times." The Coffin Brothers. There were four of them, as well as a network of parents, aunts and uncles whose names were forever appearing in the paper on the occasion of their arrest or conviction for some crime—the

Coffin Clan. No family name was more often spoken in the courts of St. John's.

"Bullshitter," another named Galway said. Galway was in the habit of scorning all claims of sexual conquest, perhaps because his acne-riddled face disgusted girls almost as much as my stained one did. "You've never had your face in Penny Joyce's juicy pie. I had my *fingers* in it last night. Here, Percy, have a whiff. You can still smell your mother's pie on my fingers."

He put two of his fingers under my nose. There was laughter and the girls from Heart sang: "Can you smell your mother's pie, Percy boy, Percy boy, can you smell your mother's pie, charming Percy? He can smell his mother's pie just as well as you or I, but he's a young boy who cannot eat his mother." I wondered why I'd never heard them sing that rhyme before—they couldn't have just made it up.

I knew what they meant by pie. "Shut up," I said, and threw away what was left of mine.

"You should never turn up your nose at a good piece of pie," Coffin said. "I bet you Pops MacDougal never does."

The girls from Heart chanted: "Pops and Pen up in a tree / f-u-c-k-i-n-g / first comes money / then comes Pops / then comes Pen until Pops flops."

"My mother hates Pops," I cried.

"Not what I heard," Coffin said. "Besides, Percy, look at it this way, if they do have a kid, it might not have a face like yours. I'm sure your mother would like to have *one* normal-looking kid even if she has to do it with Pops to get it."

I ran down the hill as a chorus of scorn erupted behind me, my big shoes loudly flapping on the sidewalk as I fought to keep from slipping, my hands working uselessly as if they dangled from my wrists by bits of string. I said nothing to my mother that day or the next about what had happened. I had the feeling, absurd as it seemed, that what Coffin had said was true. Some of it anyway.

I felt sick at the idea that she had done something with one or both of the boys, even as I told myself that their boasts were absurd. But even worse—because more plausible—was what Coffin had said about her and Pops.

BETTER TO BE A PROSTITUTE
THAN DESTITUTE

Pops had to go away later in the week for three days for a teachers' conference. I couldn't remember him ever having spent a night away from the house.

I took the opportunity to confront my mother before Medina arrived. She was setting the kitchen table for their card game, laying out the cribbage board and some potato chips and two beer glasses. I sat at the table when she did.

"Why don't you get rid of Pops?"

"He pays more than any other boarder would."

"Why?"

"He likes to live here. It's close to where he works."

"He makes enough money to have his own house."

"I doubt he makes that much."

"He likes you."

"Yeah, he does. He likes me. He likes you too."

"No he doesn't. He doesn't like anyone but you. And no one

likes him, not *even* you. But you do it with him anyway."

"What?" She grabbed me by the wrist. "Did Pops say something to you?" she shouted so loudly the lamp overhead made a pinging sound.

It *was* true. I knew she wouldn't have reacted that way if it wasn't. I knew she would have thrown her head back, opened her mouth and laughed until I could see her back teeth. She let go of my wrist and began to check the deck of cards, her face scarlet.

"Pops didn't say anything."

"Then where did you get *that* idea? At school, no doubt."

"You *do* it with him," I all but screamed. "Everybody knows. I bet McHugh knows." I began to cry.

"Off to bed before Medina gets here. Off to bed. *Now.*"

"You do it with him because he pays you money," I said, sobbing. "You do it for money."

She stood up and leaned her hands on the table, her head just inches from mine. I smelled her perfumed hair and looked down her blouse, sneaking a peak at the first inch of her cleavage.

"Yes, that's right. I *do* it with him because he *pays* me money."

"That's what whores like Sister Mary Aggie do."

"No. It's not. But I'll always remember this day as the one you called me a whore."

"I'm not sorry," I said, wiping my eyes with the heels of my hands. "Pops is not my father."

"Having a mark on your face—"

"Stain. The right word is *stain*. And it's all over my fucking face, not *on* it."

"Well listen here, Mr. Purple Pimpernel. It's no picnic curling up with Pops, let me tell you."

"Then don't *do* it."

"*I do it for you.* If I didn't, we'd be living in some one-room dump."

"With the Dark Martians on Dark Marsh Road."

"That's right."

"In a house like Medina's."

"No, in a *room* like Medina's. That's all she has, as you well know, a room."

"She doesn't seem to mind. And there's no such thing as a Dark Martian. There's no such place as Dark Marsh Road. You're full of shit."

"If not for Pops and Uncle Paddy, you'd be spending every day beating off the savages on Barter's Hill. And maybe then you wouldn't be such a selfish little *cunt*."

Even as the vehemence of her words hit me, I couldn't help feeling a faint titillation—my mother had said *cunt* to me. She looked as if she wished she hadn't.

"Pops pays more of the mortgage than I do. He pays for the upkeep of this place, for *your* upkeep. If not for Pops, we wouldn't have a pot to piss in."

"*You* wouldn't have your Rothmans."

"So now you're begrudging me my *smokes*? Most people would be human chimneys if they were in my shoes, if they had to put up with—" She paused, bit her lip, shook her head. "What else do I have, Percy? *You* tell *me*."

"I don't *know*."

"You're goddamned right you don't." She started poking me in the chest to emphasize each word. "You—don't—know—*anything*."

By this time I was outright *really* bawling, feeling certain I was right but knowing I would lose no matter what I said. She was doing it with Pops. Even if she never did it again, she'd done it with him. She had crossed the Rubicon of doing it with VP MacD and now there was no going back.

"Pops—" I started, but she cut me off.

"Don't blame Pops. It's not as if he ever makes the first move. And it's only now and then. Just often enough."

"For *what*?"

"I've had enough of you humiliating me. You wouldn't even be able to survive in this neighbourhood or the best one on planet Earth if not for me and Pops and Uncle Paddy and McHugh. You hate us all, but you'd be *crucified* if not for us."

"That's not true."

"All right then. I'll tell Pops to hit the road. I'll tell Uncle Paddy we don't want his protection anymore. I'll tell McHugh to treat you like he treats the other boys. Who do you think will care about what happens to you then? Do you *hear* me?"

"*Yes.*"

"Good. Now." She grabbed me by the shoulders. "You're not going to say a word about this to anyone. Not Medina. Not Pops, especially. He has himself convinced that it's not about the money. And not to anybody else. It could get Pops fired."

"Everybody knows already."

"Everybody *suspects*. There's a big difference."

I stopped crying and glared at her.

"Don't look at me like that," she said. But this time her voice quavered. "A few times. Now and then. Jesus. Better I be a prostitute than we all be destitute." It sounded like something she had rehearsed. She lit up a cigarette.

"You're not a prostitute," I said.

"The word you used was *whore*."

"You're not a whore."

"You have no idea, squirt. Go to bed. *Now.*"

"It's only four-thirty."

"It's a small price to pay for calling me a whore."

"A few times." "Now and then." I wondered how many, how often Pops got more from her for his money than room and board. How strange that what people made jokes about but didn't really believe had turned out to be true. She did it with Pops for money. But not like the women called whores who did it with the fishermen from

Spain and Portugal, waving to their ships from the waterfront and shouting "Mario." The White Fleet. A joke I had lately heard at school. But still, she did it for money. With Pops. Pops sneaking into her room after I had gone to bed. Or maybe she snuck into his—the room with the poster of the Periodic Table on the wall, stuck to it with Scotch tape so old it had gone brown and curled up so that the poster had looked for years as if it was soon to fall. The room whose window faced Brother Rice. Pops on top of her as he stared out the window above the bed.

What if Pops made my mother pregnant? *Pregnant.* I had never said the word out loud and had only rarely heard it said. To me the word called up an incongruously swollen belly attached to a normal-sized woman. Unconcealable. Undisguisable. More conspicuously there than anything on earth. I thought of my mother's belly, my *mother*, her body spoiled, looking like that because of Pops. My mother would have a part-Pops baby. A child of Pops would be my half-brother or half-sister. Unless Pops and my mother got married, he'd get fired. Unless they lied and said the baby wasn't his, Pops would be my father. Maybe Pops was too old to make her pregnant. I pictured all of us walking with the baby carriage along the sidewalk, people crowding round to see if the baby's face and hands and feet looked like mine. If they did, everyone would know that my FSS was my mother's fault, not Jim Joyce's. *I* would know.

I was not to tell Medina. So Medina didn't know.

I waited an hour after I heard Medina come into the house, then went out to the kitchen where they were playing cards.

"Jesus, Perse," Medina said. "Your eyes look like two pissholes in the snow. Been crying?"

My mother smiled when Medina winked at her. That wink—Medina *knew*. Medina had always known.

I looked at my mother, whose face gave evidence that she'd been crying too. I was about to object that she had lied to me, but she spoke first. "Yes, Percy, Medina knows. She's more on your side than on mine. That's because she's not a whore like me."

"I'm not really on your side, Perse," Medina said. "Mothers have done worse to keep their boys in jelly beans."

"I changed my mind and said she wasn't a whore."

"I think you only pardoned me for being one."

Medina sniffed. "Your mother thinks she leads him on, but I think Pops-a-Doodle-do is blackmailing *her*. He's not quite the dork we all like to think he is."

"I hate him," I said. I turned to my mother. "I'll bring back the dime every day."

"A dime a day won't keep Pops away," Medina said.

"I hate Pops."

"Hamlet to my Gertrude."

"Penny," Medina sniffed. "You're the only one here who knows what that means."

"Pardon my education."

Medina sniffed again.

"Did Jim Joyce go away because of Pops?" I asked.

Medina laughed and smacked the table with her hand so hard the big green ashtray jumped. "That's a good one."

"The two of them never met," my mother said. "This is my fault. Talk about an Oedipus complex."

Medina waved her hand. "I already told you, Pen, you're hanging out with the wrong crowd for that kind of material."

"Well then, I'll have to find a new crowd, won't I?"

"Like Pops? I bet Pops understands your every word. Is that how you two talk? After, I mean. I can see you lying side by side, Pops puffing on his pipe, you blowing smoke at the ceiling. I guess you don't talk a lot about Jim Joyce—"

"That's enough, Medina. Off to bed, Percy," my mother said.

"I'll be good," Medina said. "Really, I will."

"*Bed* for you, Perse.

"He could make you have a baby," I shouted.

"No one can *make* me have a baby."

"He's right, though," Medina said. "No matter how careful you are, you *could* get pregnant."

"I won't have a baby."

"Is Pops too old?" I asked.

"I doubt it. Men are never too old."

"They *think* they're never too old," Medina said.

"I really didn't set out to use him. The very first time—well, I just asked him afterward for a top-up to meet the mortgage payment. I said I was looking for a loan, nothing else, but he insisted. He gave me the money. I thought that would be it—but it wasn't. Neither of us wanted it to be. New habits are easy to acquire. It's the kind of thing that would never work if you set out with a plan."

"Pops MacDougal." Medina shook her head in apparent disbelief.

"Don't *you* start. He doesn't just give me a little extra every month. We couldn't afford nearly as nice a place without Pops. I'm not sure we could afford *any* place. Pops carries all three of us. Some of the money I give you comes from him."

"I never *ask* for money." Medina sounded hurt.

"Well, I'm sorry, sweetheart, but it's true. He has full-time, better-paying work than you and me combined. We work part-time and we never know from week to week how many hours we'll get. I'm not proud of what I'm doing, but I'm not ashamed of it either. It's a fair arrangement as far as I'm concerned. I'm not just talking about 'visiting hours.' You may not have noticed, but Pops is head over heels for me. By boarding here and paying so much money, he gets to be around me almost all the time. That's mostly what he's paying for, the company of someone he loves."

"But you don't love him," Medina said. It sounded almost like a question.

"I like him. And I don't *tell* him that I love him. He knows exactly how things stand and he's happy with it."

"What will happen if he goes somewhere else to live?" I said.

"I don't think he ever will."

"When do you do it with Pops?" I asked.

My mother rolled her eyes and stabbed out her cigarette in the ashtray. "Never you mind, Perse. Never mind when or where. I told you, not often. Just often enough. Which is too often, believe me. But that's all I'm telling you."

Medina suddenly pushed back her chair and went over to the kitchen sink, her back to us, head hung down, shoulders shaking with what I thought was silent laughter. She turned and stood there with one arm across her belly, supporting the other arm. I saw that tears streamed down her cheeks.

"What's wrong, Medina?" I couldn't help feeling I had made her cry.

"Nothing, Perse." She was staring through her tears at my mother. "Pops," she said with as much disgust as if he was standing right in front of her. "Of all the people you have to—to take in off the street."

"He bought the beer that's in your glass," my mother said.

"Fuck off," Medina snapped. I'd never heard her say that to my mother. I looked at my mother in astonishment. Her lips were pressed tightly together as if she was suppressing the urge to reply in kind to Medina.

"It's only a few times," I offered. Medina burst out in bitter laughter.

"Perse," my mother said, "this is not the kind of conversation you should be having with your mother and your aunt."

"A few times. Really? Really, Perse? *That's* what you think Pops settles for?" Medina cried. "Tell him how often 'a few' is, Pen." She glared at my mother, who glared back without flinching.

"Enough to mollify him. And don't you dare ask me what that means! Perse, this whore hunt is *over*."

Medina put her hand over her mouth, but this time she *really* laughed. Imitating the deep-timbre monotone Pops had once used on the occasion of giving my mother a sweater for Christmas, she said, "What do you think of it, Paynelope? I wrapped it myself. I can bring it back if it's not your size."

My mother astonished me by letting loose a conspiratorial guffaw.

"I can bring it back if you don't like the colour," Medina continued, her voice becoming softer. "I can bring it back if it doesn't suit your taste. I must say, Paynelope, you have the ripest-looking pair of tits I've ever seen."

My mother threw back her head and laughed until her back teeth showed. I looked back and forth between them, wondering if the argument they were getting over was the first real one they'd ever had and if they'd think of me as the cause of it.

"Does he wear his safety glasses, Pen? Where does he put his pipe? Or should I say pipette. I'll bet he says 'Paynelope' a lot. I must say, Paynelope, your vagana has never looked more becoming."

"There's that look again," my mother said, tapping my forehead with her finger. "Do *not* look at me like that, Percy. Do not judge me, little sanctimony man. I told you, the whore hunt is over."

I turned and ran to my room. I climbed into the upper bunk. I felt sorry for Pops and I wasn't sure why—perhaps it was because Medina had laughed the way she had, at my mother but mostly at Pops. *That's what you think Pops settles for?* I should have felt sorry for her, for her *having* to do such things. But I also—and this is what surprised me—felt envious of Pops, for whom she undid the belt of her bathrobe, as I now realized I'd long hoped she might somehow do by accident, or even on purpose, in front of *me*. My Black Mick mother letting Pops touch what Medina had called her ripe-looking tits, letting him slide his hands the long length of her legs and revel in the smoothness of her thighs. I looked at the Mass cards of Saint Drogo. I was only nine but I knew she'd done it with him because that was all that stood between me and a place like Barter's Hill, a belly grumbling with hunger, the finger-breaking "strops" of Gus McHugh, persecution at the hands of the rabble of the Seven Schools. But I knew that to do it with me was proscribed, forbidden, unthinkable. It had to be. Boys didn't do it with their moms, not even boys like me with moms like mine. I knew I should have been disgusted by the idea—by the idea of her doing it with *anyone*. But I wasn't, and I wondered why. I wasn't at the very bottom of the list of those even hypothetically eligible for a piece of Penny pie—I wasn't even on the list. I cared that I wasn't. I hated it that I wasn't. It seemed that my brain was as warped and stained as my body. Perhaps my FSS proceeded from, was the physical manifestation of, a festering, miscoloured, mis-shapen brain. Perhaps I was becoming Percy the First after all, the terminally ill, mute freak of freaks the doctors had mistaken me for.

I was glad Pops would be away for a while, knowing I would have been even less able than usual to suppress a blush or sit still or look at him, or answer anything he said to me without my voice breaking, or even without crying, which would have been impossible to explain though I would try to and thereby further arouse his suspicions.

Days later, I scrutinized Pops, convinced there must be something about him that I'd missed. *It's not as if he ever makes the first move.* I couldn't imagine her making that *first* first move, let alone imagine Pops' reaction to it. She had known he would be agreeable if she made the first move. She would have had to cajole him through his surprise and nervousness and whatever moral qualms he had or felt obliged to pretend he had. It took more nerve, however, more gumption than I'd thought he had to *let* himself be led to bed by his luscious landlady—and to keep it secret from me for so long. I looked at Pops, sitting in the sunroom in his lab coat in his window-facing chair. I supposed it had been no great feat for my mother to hide their arrangement from me, given how comically repelled by him she and Medina seemed to be. But still—maybe there was more to him than I'd realized, Pops with his scrubbing-brush moustache, his ubiquitous, ever-stained lab coat and his safety goggles that dangled from his neck, making him look like the official inspector of something, one who stuck stubbornly to an odd way of pronouncing certain words. Maybe Pops was not the sum of such parts but had a secret life, carried secretly within him lest it be mocked into non-existence the hope of being loved by my mother, the one woman—it might well be—whom he'd ever done *it* with. I wondered, with a measure of dread, if this secret hope might not be as doomed as my mother made it seem, if she would one day tire of the secrecy and marry Pops. Perhaps, when she decided to rent a room to a boarder, she already had in mind some such arrangement as the one she had with Pops. Perhaps her far-sightedness had had to do with me, because she expected to have me on her hands forever—not that she would have thought of it that way—saw that I lacked the fortitude to prosper in spite of it. My mind was a swarm of conjecture and confusion. Anything, everything, nothing seemed possible now.

THE NIGHT OF THE VAT RAT

SOME noise had woken me. But it must have abruptly stopped since I heard nothing. I listened, thinking that, though the door and windows were closed and though a cement block that no rat could burrow through lay on the heating duct, there might be a Vat Rat in the room. Then I heard the sound again. It was definitely coming from outside the room, from the basement maybe.

We lived around the corner from a beer brewery, a smoking, steaming factory that, when the wind was easterly, sent our way the overwhelming, sickeningly sweet smell of barley malt. And the brewery—and therefore the neighbourhood—had what my mother called a "permanently temporary" problem, a perpetual "outbreak" of rats. She was quoting the brewery, which had been saying since it opened that it would "soon have a handle on the outbreak." My mother predicted they would sooner have a handle on the outbreak of children in China.

The brewery had announced in an ad they took out each spring in the paper that the especially wet spring had softened and eroded the ground around the brewery, exposing pipes and valves, so more rats than usual were making their way in and out of the brewery, hops-and-barley-bloated rats, demented from chronic alcohol consumption, craving more and more of what one day might cause their very stomachs to explode. They were said to have made their way into some houses, gnawed through the very walls, through the paste and glue of Gyproc, while residents of the Mount stood guard around their children's beds with axes and shovels upraised, or lay awake in *their* beds all night, listening for the grimly patient, never-pausing Vat Rats drunkenly incising through the walls.

"They like the beer." Pops shrugged, as if he had in a few words explained something that confounded everyone else in the neighbourhood. My mother said that Pops believed if there was a logical explanation for something, its noteworthiness, dangerousness, even its very existence, was undone.

The attics, basements, crawlspaces of the Mount were set with the largest rat traps that could be found, bought or made. I took as gospel the rumours of rats so fast they stole cheese straight from the traps, rats so smart they knew how to trigger the traps without getting caught. There was a story of a rat so big and strong that it had scuttled backward into a hole in a wall while dragging a large trap that was clamped around its neck. Boys said the rats were bringing back the Black Plague. They pretended my face was evidence of this.

I threw off the blankets, climbed down the ladder of the bunk bed and put my ear to the door. I heard what sounded like a gasp followed by a series of whimpers. I wondered if Pops or my mother was sick. Then it occurred to me that they might be doing *it*. My mother had said it was "no picnic" doing it with Pops.

I eased the door open and heard the same sounds, louder, unmistakably now of two people. They sounded as if they both had bellyaches and were commiserating with each other and suffering and having fun, all somehow at the same time. I went out into the hall and saw that the door of my mother's room was slightly open, a thin slant of light lying across the floor of the hall. I hurried to the door, no longer taking care to be quiet. My hand was an inch from the doorknob when I saw them.

They were lying side by side in my mother's bed, on top of the blankets, naked and making funny noises. I saw my mother's wide bare back and backside, one leg lifted to accommodate Medina's hand, which was buried in her to the nether knuckles as my mother's looked to be in her. I supposed they were kissing, though it looked more as if they were biting each other's lips. Medina, who was facing me, had arched her back, smiling, her teeth parted, her head tilted, corkscrewing into the pillow that was pressed against the wall. She arched more and more until it looked like her back would break, and her breathing, *their* breathing turned into a series of rasps, as if they were soon to perish in each other's arms.

I turned, desperate to tiptoe away, but my elbow hit the door. Brushed it maybe. I wasn't sure I'd made a noise until the sounds inside the bedroom suddenly stopped. I ran back to my room, but in my panic I crossed the hall and wound up in the kitchen, racing through it to the basement door. I could hear nothing now but the thumping of my heart, the pulse of it pounding in my head. I opened the door, turned on the light and hurried down the basement stairs. I swung round at the bottom, one hand on the newel post, and made straight for the sump pump hole, my concocted-in-an-instant plan being to claim that I had heard a Vat Rat in the basement, had come down to investigate, only to see the rat escape into the sump pump hole. I all but posed at the hole, pointing down at the water, where I saw what for a second made me think I was still asleep and dreaming: there *was* a Vat Rat. It had tried to climb in through the sump pump drainpipe and had become wedged in the pipe so that half of it protruded from the pipe into the hole and half of it was still inside the pipe. The half that was sticking out consisted of the head and forefeet and upper torso.

The rat was unmistakably dead, its mouth open so that its teeth were bared, its eyes two narrow slits, its face a rictus that conveyed all the fury and frustration of its final confoundment.

It was not difficult, what with this sight following so closely the one in the bed, to let loose and start bellowing for my mother. "Mom, Mom, Mom!" I was on the verge of shouting for Medina too when I caught myself and called out for Pops instead.

I heard my mother running down the stairs. "Percy, Percy, what's wrong?"

Still pointing down into the hole, I said, "Look, it tried to get in and it got stuck."

"What?"

She joined me beside the sump pump hole. She wore a bathrobe. Her face was flushed and sweat shone on her forehead.

"Merciful God. It must be the size of a cat. Poor creature."

"It's not a poor creature, it's a rat!" I said angrily.

We turned when we heard Pops coming down the stairs.

"Was that you shouting, Percy?" he said. "Or was it Iago trying to wake up all of Venice?"

"Look, Pops," my mother said.

He joined us beside the hole. "Well, there's one that's had its last meal of barley malt." I threw my arms around my mother and pressed my head sideways against her stomach. I smelled Medina's scent and caught the scent of something else I couldn't name. My mother ran the fingers of one hand through my hair.

"You said it tried to get away?" she asked. I nodded into her bathrobe.

"It may have tried about three days ago," Pops said. "That's about how long it's been dead."

"I was in bed and I heard a noise in the basement."

"Well, you didn't hear a peep from this fellow," Pops said. "Smells like last year's cabbage. Don't think he starved or died of thirst. Suffocated probably."

"Maybe I heard another rat."

My mother put her hands on my shoulders and held me at arm's length. I was sweating. I felt my hair matting to my forehead. "Are you all right, Perse?" I looked in her eyes. I wondered what she saw, if she saw that I had seen her and Medina. She turned me around. "Upstairs to bed. I'll be up soon to see how you are."

"That's okay," I said. "I'm pretty sleepy now."

"Are you sure?" She sounded relieved. I nodded.

"I'll see if I can get this beast out of there," Pops said.

"Do you need any help?" my mother asked.

"No," Pops said. "You know what they say about too many rat removers."

"What do they say?" I asked.

My mother rolled her eyes. "They *say*: 'Too many rat removers exponentially complicate the effects of rodent entrapment and consequent morbidity.' You get perfect grades and you've never heard of *that* expression? *I* could rattle it off by the time I was five. Off to bed now."

Climbing the stairs, I also noticed the smell of beer, from my clothes, my hair. She'd been drinking.

I had heard from boys at school about "lizzies," about women reputed to be lizzies, two middle-aged women in particular about whom the parents of the neighbourhood exchanged coy smiles, furtive winks, describing the women as "friends," two spinsters who lived together for companionship, who were tolerated because of their matronly appearance and absolute discretion, because they kept to themselves and didn't *look* the way you would imagine women like that would look, or as if they were capable, even in perfect privacy, of doing such things as were known to be favoured by "lizzies." I doubted that such tolerance would be extended to my mother and Medina, a mother carrying on with the sister of her ever-absent fiancé under the same roof as her child, just feet away, in fact, from where her young son slept, especially if it came out that they were so flagrant that the boy had caught them in the act, the Primal Scene à la Lesbos.

I scrambled up the ladder, lay on my upper bunk on top of the blankets.

The urge to sleep usually trumped everything. I had often nodded off with tears still streaming down my face, only to wake in the morning as fretful as I had been the night before, expecting my mother to convince me that she could somehow restore everything to normal. But nothing could rid my mind of the funny sounds I had heard her making with Medina, or the sight of Medina looking as if she were trying to grind like a corkscrew through the headboard. I had nothing on which to base a guess as to how, if at all, these sounds differed from the sounds a man and a woman lying side by side or otherwise disposed in bed might make.

My mother and Medina. Lizzies. That word from school was all I had. Lizzies. Was it just the once? The first time? Could they have been so unlucky that, while doing it for the first time, they'd been caught? Perhaps it would be the one and only time. Especially if they *knew* they'd been caught, and by whom.

I assumed Medina was no longer in my mother's room, that she'd cleared out, fled the house as quietly as possible when the rest of us were in the basement. She was probably home by now.

My heart pounded. My dick was stiffer than it had ever been. I tried to understand what exactly had been going on, what my mother and Medina had been doing to each other. I thought of Medina, her mouth wide open, eyes shut as if she were relishing the taste of her favourite food. I thought of my mother's wide bare back. Then I wished it was she who'd been facing the door, her tits in full view, the nipples whose shape I had so many times seen outlined through her bra and blouse at last revealed. I found myself rubbing the back of my dick with my thumb, wondering how my mother had made Medina feel what she must have felt, judging by her face and the sounds she made and the way she undulated on the bed, which was so much more than I ever had while precociously self-experimenting. I imagined my hand was my mother's hand, my thumb her thumb. I felt something inside me shudder, and shudder again, and then, swollen past all times before, I spurted onto my hand, my fingers and my belly, my first *real* time, it seemed, the first estimable come of my life, for I'd never so much as woken this wet even from a dream.

The rest of the night I couldn't sleep for wonder of their bodies in the bed. I knew that, from now on, I would see Medina when I saw my mother, smell her mix of musk and sweat on my mother's clothes and in her hair, the blend of their lipstick and my mother's perfume.

I was terrified too: I was certain that if people found out, I would be taken away from my mother. I knew of two boys who'd been taken from their parents who'd done nothing worse than drink too much. I wiped tears from my eyes with the heels of my hands. I wondered if they had heard me, even seen me, at the door. They might have heard *someone* and now be wondering if it was me or Pops.

Word would quickly spread through the school and the neighbourhood about the Vat Rat that had almost made its way into our house, the frightful ingenuity of its assault upon the Joyces, its vicious determination and grisly battle to the death with our drainage pipe. Pops would tell the other teachers. My mother and Medina would tell the neighbours. And every time I overheard the neighbours talking, I would think of the wicked, illicit, inscrutable scene I had witnessed just before discovering the Vat Rat in the sump pump hole.

At breakfast the next morning, I kept my eye on my mother, and I was far from subtle about it, though I'd warned myself not to stare at her or even Pops.

"What are *you* looking at?" my mother said.

"You," I said.

"I can see that. I meant *why* are you looking at me? Jesus, Perse, must you always be so goddamned literal?"

I shrugged.

At first she seemed unfazed, more concerned about me than otherwise. "Perse, you look like you didn't sleep a wink."

"I couldn't stop thinking about the Vat Rat," I said.

"The Vat Rat's gone. Pops heroically disposed of it."

"Another one might try to get in the same way."

"It would have to be a slightly smaller or an even more determined one," Pops said. "I had to use a screwdriver on last night's beast. Came out in pieces—"

"That'll do, Pops."

"I feel sorry for the Vat Rat," I said.

"You didn't look sorry last night," Pops laughed. "You wouldn't feel sorry for one if it climbed up the ladder of your bed and bit off your—"

"Pops, will you for Christ's sake shut up?"

"Sorry, Paynelope."

"It's not *Pay*nelope, it's *Pen*elop*ee*."

Pops, face and neck flushed, got up from the table and left the kitchen, mumbling something about getting his lab coat and doubting that she had ironed it for him as she was always promising she would but never did.

My mother looked at me. "There won't be any more Vat Rats." It didn't sound like reassurance so much as a warning to avoid any further mention of them. But I couldn't help trying to get a rise out of her, to provoke her into blurting out something about last night.

"We can't block up the sump pump pipe"—I darted a glance at her— "the basement will flood."

My mother glared at me and I glared back. "What's wrong with you this morning?" she snapped.

I wondered if it might after all have been the Vat Rat that had so upset her. If she and Medina had seen or heard me at the bedroom door, she would have been careful not to lose her temper with Pops. I realised she didn't know.

In my room, I tried to mimic what I'd seen, looking at myself in the mirror, chewing and moving my head from side to side. Why did they prefer *that*? Why did they like it at all—Medina who had never had a boyfriend and my mother who no longer had a fiancé? I got hard at the very sight of a bare-legged girl from Mercy Convent. I'd all but go off at the sight of scores of them on Bonaventure trying to control their tunics in a gale of wind. My father's sister and my mother. I felt certain it would never have happened if my father hadn't run away and left us. But it also seemed like a betrayal of him in spite of what he'd done to us. And more Medina's fault than my mother's, who had once been engaged and had a child. I told myself Medina would do anything when she was drunk. There might be nothing more to it than that—something women did when they were drunk, and didn't even remember afterward.

But when I looked at my startled, wonderstruck face in the mirror, I knew that if either of them was more to blame, it was my mother, on whose every word and deed Medina hung, as if on an older sister's.

I supposed they didn't have to worry much about being discovered by Pops. His bedroom was farther from my mother's than mine was. And Pops drank six or more beers every night before he went to bed and always kept the door of his room closed after lights out. I kept my door closed as well, for there were nights when my mother and Medina noisily played cards in the kitchen until well after midnight. My mother usually left the door of her room partway open so that she'd hear me if I called out to her or needed to be consoled about a dream. She wouldn't have left the door open on purpose when Medina was in there. In fact, she would likely have locked it; I knew her door could be locked from the inside simply by turning and pushing the knob.

How reckless they had been. Then I thought that if they didn't know they'd been discovered maybe they would soon be back in my mother's bed again. I wasn't sure what I'd do if I heard my mother and Medina go to my mother's room. If they did close and lock the door, I likely wouldn't hear anything unless I eavesdropped just outside the room or worked up the nerve to actually put my ear against the door and risk making it rattle in its frame the way all the doors did on windy nights. Or risk being discovered in the hallway should my mother get up to go to the bathroom or to get a glass of water.

Every night for a week afterward, I listened at the door of my room to see if I could hear the noises again. Some nights Medina would be at our house, but she would always go home before I went to bed. I would hear her leave the house, accompanied to the back porch by my mother, who loudly bade her good night and closed the door. Too loudly. A goodbye that Pops and I were meant to hear, because I didn't know then that it had long been Medina's habit to come back later, sneak up the steps into the house and afterward sneak out again, well before Pops got up at seven.

PART II

ST. JOHN'S DAY, JUNE 24

O N my tenth birthday, my mother insisted we go out walking as we had on my fourth. She and Medina and I went out in the warm rain. Her dark skin showed through her matted white blouses as if they were made of tissue paper. She looked, Medina said, as if she were wearing nothing but a bra above the waist. "So what? Women at the beach show more than me. I'd prove it if we had a way of getting to the beach."

In the early spring, the telephone wires had spun in the wind like long black skipping ropes, glistening with freezing rain, whirring, droning overhead as if, any second, they might snap and, spewing sparks, drop down on whatever, whomever, lay beneath them. Traffic lights and crosswalk signs hovered horizontal to the ground like bedsheets on a clothesline. If you didn't "get" the wind, you didn't "get" St. John's, for its dying down was rare and far more remarkable than its seaborne assault that seemed to come at once from all points of the compass. It funnelled undeterred through the rows of houses whose windows buckled like sheet metal but somehow didn't break. It shook even the largest of parked cars and trucks, bent aerial rods into lethal, lashing tails. I was so skinny it would have blown me over. My mother holding one of my hands, Medina the other, they let the wind lift me clear off the ground, tried to run against it, which made me rise up that much higher, flying for a few seconds, like a gull against the gale.

There had been stains of road salt like chalk outlines on the pavement, shapes as amorphous as the one on my face. A brush cut of sod on top of a five-hundred-foot-high head of rock, that's what the south side hills looked like. Rivers of melted snow ran down every hill, in torrents in the gutters, in wave after gentle wave down the middle of the streets; gathered in mud-coloured, slush-bobbing pools that were too wide to jump so we had no choice but to ford them as fast as we could in the vain hope of being insulated from the icy water by our socks.

My mother often remarked at how the weather controlled my mood. I tried not to revel in the melancholy failure of October, or give in to the urge to brood on the imminence of winter. It was not the seasons but the coming of them that I couldn't stand, the drive of all things in the world to transform themselves, to slough off the old, to promise the smell, look, feel and sound of change. Yet my feet and hands and face persisted as absolutely as I was told my unseen soul did. I hated, therefore, all reminders of time passing—watches, clocks, calendars and radios, the sun and moon and stars, sunset and sunrise.

As we made our way through the city on my birthday, we passed huge bronze statues of the cartoon characters of history, including the bold-looking, sword-wielding visionary John Cabot who was credited with "discovering" the site of St. John's Harbour on June 24, 1497, but had in fact come nowhere near it, having landed on the coast of Maine five years after Columbus "discovered" America.

My mother said that Uncle Paddy was a bit like John Cabot:

"A big fish in a small pond, a small fish in a big pond, a minnow in history, a tide-tossed piece of plankton in the ocean of the world, a dust mote on its last lap of the galaxy." But in St. John's kitchens, she said, walls that bore his image were as numerous as blades of grass.

"Pardon my hyperbole."

"It's pardoned," Medina said. "Whatever it is."

I surveyed the city that for one day each year was mine.

I didn't want to forever give off the Vat Rat–like smell of a festering grievance by nursing the belief that in a rightful world I would be on top.

My mother had quoted to me from a book the night before: "When the soul of a man is born in this country, nets are flung at it to hold it back from flight. You speak to me of nationality, language and religion. I shall try to fly past those nets." It was a quotation from a collection of quotations and she hadn't named the author.

I shall try to fly past those nets. I shall try to fly, he might as well have said, whoever he was. I could not simply "fly past" the desecration of my face and hands and feet.

Nationality. Language. Religion. Add to that what you are born with and every experience of your life. "Nature and nurture," my mother said. How could you fly past those? I asked her. I doubted it was possible. I knew of no one who had done it, not even her. What chance would I have?

But how wonderful it would be if it was possible, my mother said, possible to salute no flag, sing no anthem, adopt no motto, pledge allegiance to no country and no cause, swear no oath, adopt no ideology, silence no voice, suppress no utterance, support no church, subscribe to no religion, abject one's self to none of the legion of imaginary gods.

Young Mother, My Maker. Hold me now and ever in your arms.

THE BLESSING OF 44

CHRISTMAS cards kept coming from the Archbishop, each containing what my mother called her "annual rebuke" from His Grace, a subtle reminder that she had still not had me baptized and was still not taking the sacraments or attending Mass on Sunday. Six such years, six such Christmas cards.

My mother continued to help me frame my replies, making sure I did not inadvertently commit myself or both of us to complying with some adjuration of His Grace, at least one of which was included in each Christmas greeting. The Archbishop always sent the official basilica Christmas card; it bore a photograph of the Basilica on the front and one of the Archbishop on the back. I imagined an official card of my own, 44 Bonaventure on the front, me on the back, my beet-face smiling out at His Grace year after year. My mother always chose a non-religious card with what she called a "pagan" greeting for our reply, something noncommittal about the "Season" or the "Holidays."

Merry Christmas, Your Grace, and thank you for your Christmas card. My mother sends her holiday greetings to you as well and we both hope for your continued good health and prosperity. All the best to you from Percy and Penelope Joyce.

My mother deflected His Grace's invitations year after year.

Should you and your mother attend Sunday Mass, please sit up front where I can see you. It has been years since our one and only meeting. Perhaps, in spite of my busy schedule and your mother's, and the time you must devote to your studies, we will all three be able to meet in private again sometime. I will tell you about my younger days when I planned to be a musician and was quite an accomplished player of the clarinet! If God wills it, my dear friend Percy, it will happen. Yours in Christ, P.J. Scanlon, CJM, Archbishop of St. John's.

My mother's reply, signed by me:

Merry Christmas, Your Grace. Thank you for continuing to be of so much help to me. I promise that my mother and I will sit in the front row if we go to Sunday Mass at the Basilica. I was too young when we met to remember it now but my mother remembers it well. She says that it was very kind of you to make the time to see us and that we will meet again if we are meant to. I hope you get everything you ask for from Santa Claus, maybe a new clarinet ha, ha. Yours truly, Percy Joyce.

As of Vatican II, in October 1962, final-year seminarians no longer served as deacons, that office having since been filled by laymen, so a delivery service had been hired to drop off and pick up my mother's "work."

"Too bad, Pen," Medina had said then, "no more young men to torture with temptation."

That had been a few years ago and it seemed as if Christmas cards were all that would come our way from Uncle Paddy from now on, until the Archbishop told Brother McHugh to ask Pops if our house had ever been blessed. If it hadn't been blessed, McHugh said to Pops, the Archbishop wanted to know if my mother would like it to be blessed, not by him, as his hectic schedule would not allow it, but by one of the basilica priests, preferably Father Bill Slattery, who often said Mass on Sunday at the Brother Rice chapel.

"Having the house blessed doesn't commit us to anything else, does it?" my mother asked nervously. Pops was assured by McHugh that it would begin and end with Father Bill coming to the house, accompanied by an altar boy, and going unobtrusively from room to room, blessing each one with holy water. We would not be required to take part in the blessing in any way, only to witness it, which, if my mother agreed to it, would take place on the next Saturday afternoon.

"I'd hate to turn down Uncle Paddy and risk offending him," my mother replied. Medina announced she would not be on hand for the blessing.

Father Bill, a young, short, chubby priest whose voice was very high-pitched, came to the house with an altar boy. Father Bill did not wear any vestments and he dressed in black—but the altar boy wore his full uniform, a scarlet soutane and a white surplice trimmed with lace, and, Brother Rice being just across the road, a pair of black and red tartan slippers. He carried a kind of metal pail that Father Bill said was called an aspersorium. It was half filled with holy water into which Father Bill dipped a baton with a perforated head: the aspergillum, he called it.

We gathered in the hallway. "You may kneel if you wish, but it's not required," Father Bill instructed us, smiling as if to assure us there was no need to be afraid. Afraid of what, I wondered. Pops knelt and bowed his head. I followed the example of my mother who remained standing, head bowed, one hand gripping the other in front of her.

Father Bill and the boy went only as far as the doorway of each room and the top of the basement stairs, the two of them reciting a prayer as Father Bill, his arm upraised, sprinkled holy water everywhere with an emphatic, practised snap of the wrist, a technique that might have been Vatican prescribed, he did it with such authority. The water went a long way. It spattered across the bed in which my mother and Medina had been entwined the night I touched the door. Drops landed on my bunk beneath the pictures of Saint Drogo, on the blankets beneath which, fuelled by the memory of my mother and my aunt, I had worked my way to a foaming frenzy every night for months.

In each room, Father Bill recited: "Visit this house, we beg Thee, Lord, and banish from it the deadly power of the Evil One. May the holy angels dwell here to keep us in peace and may Thy blessings be always upon us, through our Lord Jesus Christ." Pops intoned "Amen" each time Father Bill and the boy finished the prayer. It was all over in just a few minutes. As they were leaving, Pops gave Father Bill ten dollars, the "remuneration" that McHugh had told him was expected and that Father Bill, without acknowledgement, slipped swiftly into his jacket pocket.

Medina came by to hear my mother describe what had happened. My mother told her she thought that Father Bill should have given us a piece of paper certifying that the house was blessed and setting out the terms of the warranty, such as how long the blessing was guaranteed to keep the Evil One away. All evening long, Medina called Pops the Evil One and Pops said he was surprised she hadn't turned into a puff of smoke the second she set foot inside the house. He teased her that she had waited until the blessing was over to come visit because although it might be true that she was not religious she was certainly superstitious and probably believed in ghosts and was afraid of priests. Medina retorted that he was a hypocrite for kneeling as if *he* was religious.

"I knelt to keep you in cigarettes," Pops fired back.

At St. Bon's, I told the other boys that the Archbishop himself had come to 44 to bless the house. None of them had witnessed, or even heard of, the blessing of a house; my mother told me later that it was not likely most houses on the Mount had been blessed, or perhaps they had been blessed too long ago for the boys who lived in them to remember it. I told them that the Archbishop had been assisted by two priests and four altar boys and that he had sprinkled so much holy water that, by the time he left, almost every inch of 44 was drenched. I told them that my mother had asked the Archbishop to bless the house because we had always known that it was haunted: the lights, the TV, the radio and the stove sometimes came on by themselves in the middle of the afternoon. My mother set the table for breakfast each night before she went to bed and sometimes got up in the morning to find that all the dishes had been put back in the cupboards and the knives and forks and spoons were back in the drawers, which were left open. I told them that the Archbishop usually just sent a priest to bless a house but he knew that our house was "too far gone" for just a priest. He said he wasn't even sure that *he* could do the job, but he did.

I had the most rapt audience ever for my lies. Other boys tried to get attention with stories of how their own houses were haunted, but my story had too much detail. The focus always returned to me.

Still, there were skeptics. Had we *seen* any ghosts? No. Then how did the Archbishop know they were gone? I said things had happened, which the Archbishop said were signs that the ghosts were leaving: the curtains on an open window blew out instead of in, as if someone was climbing out the window . . . we heard footsteps in an empty room . . . and the fire in the chimney suddenly went out. . . .

Complaints were made to Brother McHugh by parents whose boys had come home worried that their houses were haunted.

Word quickly got round St. Bon's that the Archbishop had never been at 44 but had merely sent Father Bill there for a routine, uneventful blessing. And just as they had resented the Joyce boy for being favoured with a Sermon on the Mount, some people in the neighbourhood wondered why the Archbishop himself had asked that our house be blessed, especially as we didn't even go to church and I had yet to be baptized—and many of *their* houses had yet to be blessed. Father Bill was soon collecting house-blessing fees at the rate of two or three per weekend. Boys at school repeated to me things they'd overheard their parents saying: The Joyces are practically Protestants, so why is the Archbishop paying special attention to them? You shouldn't even be *allowed* to have your house blessed if you don't believe in God. Someone should tell the Archbishop that the Joyces are taking advantage of him. How much trouble does the Joyce boy have to cause before he gets what he deserves?

But I stuck to my story. I remembered every word of Father Bill's prayer but amended it to suit my audience, retaining only "Banish from this house the deadly power of the Evil One," which I followed with: "Don't let the Devil get away with anything. Please punish him severely forever and ever. He's not afraid of anyone but Thee because Thou always was and knoweth where he lives. Kick him out of this house, O Lord. Make him think twice about coming back, and try to keep him from setting up shop in the other houses on the Mount. Don't let him touch the dishes or turn on the stove. Make him leave the lights alone. We beg Thee, Lord, and Thy Holy Angels, don't let him change the channel on the TV or the radio and keep him away from Percy, who is not baptized, forever and ever. Amen."

I said that blessing a house was like baptizing it, so at least the house I lived in was baptized. I told the boys it meant that if I died in the house, my soul would go to Heaven, but if I died outdoors, I would go to Hell. I wasn't sure what would happen if I died in the driveway or the yard—maybe I would go to Limbo or Purgatory. I said these things to boys from whom I had gleaned what little knowledge of Catholicism I had acquired by eavesdropping on their conversations or asking them outright what the "rules" of Catholicism were, and then freely embellishing. I said I wasn't baptized because a child couldn't get baptized until his parents were married to each other, so I might be damned for all eternity because my father ran away before the wedding. As no one was even sure he was alive, I might already be a hopeless case. I said my mother and I had often been for drives in the Archbishop's limousine. He often had us over to his house to watch TV. We drank Pepsi with ice cubes made from holy water. I said he and my mother talked on the phone a lot, sometimes about me, sometimes about other people in the neighbourhood, but I was not allowed to say whom. They talked for hours sometimes because the Archbishop was always looking for advice from my mother about what to do with the troublemaking families on the Mount. I said that I talked to him too, but only for a little while. He'd told me he'd have a dog if it wasn't against the rules. And maybe a swimming pool. For an archbishop, there was a rule against almost everything. He said his job was pretty good, better than when he was just a priest. His name was P.J. Scanlon and P.J. were my initials, so we sometimes called each other P.J., but we weren't allowed to do it when other people were around.

"The Archbishop doesn't live in a *house*, he lives in the Basilica," one boy scornfully said. I knew he was wrong, but I merely shrugged as if for him to persist in his ignorance was fine with me. I made only claims that, however absurd, could not be absolutely proved or disproved. I got the goat of many, especially when they saw that the others were unsure if I was lying, or how much I was lying. Then I showed them my basilica Christmas cards personalized by the Archbishop: this silenced even the most derisive skeptic for a while.

PERCY AND FRANCINE

POPS came home from Brother Rice with a note he said was from Brother McHugh. It was printed, not cursively written, and was unsigned: "I don't care how you do it, Miss Joyce, but shut up that son of yours before someone else does."

My mother waved the note in Pops' face. "This is a threat," she said. "He's threatening Percy."

"You can't prove McHugh wrote that note."

"You said he gave it to you."

"Yes. But I'll never say it to anyone else."

My mother said I didn't lie to other children to cheat them out of anything or to convince them to misbehave, and at this point almost no one believed my lies or even *wondered* if they might be true. Other children were so entertained by my lies, she pointed out, that they asked me questions in the hope I would answer with lies. But Pops said McHugh had told him that His Grace believed it demeaned and even blasphemed the Church to invent or modify its doctrine, no matter how transparently untrue and intended to entertain and draw attention to myself my statements were. His Grace felt that I was abusing his patronage, doing things I knew I could get away with only because he was my long-time advocate and protector.

I knew why I felt compelled to make things up, but that made the compulsion no easier to resist. I wanted to be known as the Joyce boy for reasons *other* than my face, my hands and my feet. I wanted to pre-empt teasing, head off my tormentors with the promise of information that was of the sort that grown-ups kept from children; I wanted other children to think that somehow I was privy to things that were kept from them; I wanted to have some power over others to make up for the power that even the least of them had over me. But most of all, it was fun to be impressively, precociously authoritative, whether others found me completely convincing or saw through me for the mythomaniac I was.

It was the year I turned twelve and I was still hoping my life would change. Tick. Tock.

So for the first time on my way up to St. Bon's I fell in beside any girl my age whom I saw walking alone. I knew it was pointless to approach two or more girls, because one of them would never take the risk of seeming amused or charmed by me in front of the others. As it was, a good number of lone girls ran away or started screaming when I approached them. One older girl from Holy Heart didn't. She had long blond hair and a perfect complexion— her name was Abigail. "I'm Percy Joyce," I said.

"Really?" she said. "I thought you were Paul Newman."

"A lot of people make that mistake," I said. "You wouldn't believe how many people ask me for my autograph. I started saying no years ago. I had to draw the line somewhere. Seriously, though, I pity Paul Newman, all those women chasing after him. He doesn't have my coping skills, so it really gets him down."

"I suppose you're pen pals. You're so full of shit."

"What's your name? It's Abigail, right?"

"Do you always ask the name of someone who tells you you're full of shit?"

"No one's ever told me I was full of shit before."

"Look, I hear you're pretty smart, so get this into your head. I don't want to be your girlfriend, or your friend who just happens to be a girl, or your pal, or the girl who tolerates your company or pities you and keeps you around as some kind of errand boy. So point your fucked-up grade six face at someone else, keep your fucked-up hands away from me, and make sure your fucked-up feet never wind up on this side of the street again. Got it?"

"Okay. But you'll be sorry. I can be really nice once you get to blow me." It was something I had heard an older boy say to a girl who seemed to find it funny.

"I said, FUCK OFF."

Word of this encounter got back to McHugh.

"'I can be really nice once you get to blow me'?" my mother said. "You really said that? Jesus, Percy."

"I would have laughed," Medina said, winking at me.

"She certainly didn't have to be so mean," my mother allowed. "And it's not as if her choice of words was any better than yours."

But at that age I thought words had become my weapons, my friends. I aped not just other boys, but my mother. I told different kinds of lies to grown-ups, ones they were meant to know right away were lies but that were also meant to mock the incredulity or shock they showed at the first sight of me. I said to a Mrs. Henley whom I caught staring at me one day in Collins's store: "The woods used to be full of creatures like me, but they put a bounty on us, so most of us are gone. I'm the only one so far to survive in captivity. I still get shot at, but not as much as I used to. I have the knack of knowing when to duck. I don't mind it when you stare at me. My own mother makes fun of me. She says I have a face that looks like the eagle-ravaged liver of Prometheus."

"Don't you complain about how God made you. He knew what He was doing. He had a purpose."

"What was it?"

"No one knows but God. You're part of the Grand Plan He has for all of us."

"The same plan you're part of?"

"Yes. We all play different parts in the same plan. But we'll all be equal when we're in Heaven."

"So, when they roll the credits of history, I'll be way down near the bottom. Across from 'Freak of Nature Number 1197,' it will say 'Percy Joyce.' But in Heaven everyone will get top billing. Everyone's name will fit on one giant marquee."

"That's just self-pity talking. And blasphemy. There are worse-off people in the world than you, Percy Joyce."

"It's my fault. I guess bobbing for apples in boiling oil wasn't such a good idea. It's strange that an all-knowing, all-powerful God couldn't think of a way of getting you into Heaven that didn't involve giving me a purple face."

"Don't you blame that face of yours on me, Percy Joyce!"

That evening, Pops came back with a plan for my future. "His Grace doesn't think this is about lying, not really, although McHugh disagrees with him. His Grace says this is about Percy not fitting in." Pops looked at me. "He's not saying it's your fault, Percy. He just says that, so far, we've only helped you *in*directly and he thinks it's time for a more direct approach. He has offered to write or talk or whatever to some mother on the Mount whose son or daughter is your age or close to it. His Grace says he could ask her to ask her child to set an example for the other students by not making fun of you but instead spending time with you now and then."

"Does Percy really need Uncle Paddy to find him a friend?" my mother asked.

"It's just to get him started. He won't be appointing friends of the month for Percy or anything like that."

"What do you think, Perse?"

I affected a neutral, almost indifferent shrug, as if I were resigned to never being more than a joke among the children of the Mount. What I thought was that it would be a great idea, but only if my conscripted friend turned out to be a girl.

"Wouldn't it make sense for this first friend to be a boy?" my mother said. Pops looked at the floor. "Out with it, Pops," my mother demanded. Pops admitted that His Grace had had no luck in finding a boy who was both acceptable for and agreeable to the task. I suspected agreeability was the bigger problem. The implication that he was somehow *compatible* with Percy Joyce would make any boy the laughingstock of the Mount, whereas an especially self-assured girl might be able to face down whatever mockery came her way for spending time with me. I was euphoric.

Brother McHugh told Pops that His Grace had contacted Patricia—Pat—Dunne, one of whose older sons was a priest who was hoping to be installed close to home at the Basilica. Mrs. Dunne came from a family of long-standing Church service and devotion. Her daughter, Francine, was two years older than me, a grade ten student at Holy Heart. Mrs. Dunne had spoken to Francine about the Archbishop's suggestion and Francine had agreed to conspicuously "befriend" me. We were to meet the next day at the corner of Howley and Bonaventure, directly across from Holy Heart. Despite this being her first year at Holy Heart, Francine, who had been class president at Mercy, was on the student council and serving as treasurer, and was active in many school clubs and associations. She was said to be looked up to by the girls of Mercy and Presentation and was a member of the Holy Heart/Brother Rice coed choir, an approachable but sensible girl who wasn't swayed by the opinions and pastimes of her peers.

Through her younger brother, who attended St. Bon's, she had come to meet many of the boys. McHugh said she had "readily agreed" when her mother passed on to her the Archbishop's request. Sister Celestine, the principal of Holy Heart, had said she also agreed with His Grace's estimation that Francine would help me to fit in with the right sort of students and send a signal to the rest that I was no longer interested in "running with the pack of savages to whom I was merely something they could toy with when they were bored."

"Francine has not agreed to be your girlfriend or anything like that, understand?" my mother said. I nodded. "And you are not to say a word to her about Pops and me, understand?"

"*Yes!*"

After school the next day, I walked from St. Bon's to the corner of Howley and Bonaventure. I had never heard of Francine Dunne and couldn't remember ever having seen the girl who was waiting for me on the corner. There were many girls from Holy Heart milling about, all dressed in the Heart uniform, but none of them was more obviously, more intently *waiting* than the girl who stood motionless, looking at the ground. She had long orange hair and a pale, many-freckled face and she clasped her books against her chest as if she was afraid they might be stolen from her. I didn't think she saw me approach her, but she spoke before I did.

"Mom says you're supposed to walk home with me." She was sullen-faced, shaking her head as she spoke as if she were repeating to a friend some instruction that even coming from her mother seemed ridiculous.

"Hello," I said, "I'm Percy Joyce." She didn't reply. "And you're Francine Dunne," I declared before she could follow Abigail's example and say she had mistaken me for Paul Newman. "It's nice to meet you." She looked about as though, unable to see me, she couldn't account for the voice she could hear. I felt panicked. I didn't know what to say next. I began my "give me myth or give me death" routine. I asked Francine if she had ever met the Archbishop. When she didn't answer, I said my mother had known him since before he became a priest, back when he was one of the best clarinet players in the country. I said he played a lot of other instruments and my mother had taken music lessons from him when she was six. I said that back then he had a show-business name, Chester Walker, so a lot of people didn't know how he started out. I said he still played the clarinet but only when he was by himself, at night in his room in the Basilica. Sometimes, I said, if you walked past the Basilica after dark, you could hear the clarinet music coming through the highest windows. It wasn't a sin for archbishops to play musical instruments, I said, but the Vatican discouraged it because it gave people the idea that archbishops would rather be musicians and have their own orchestras and admire men like Benny Goodman more than God. "I'm sure your mother knows the Archbishop pretty well," I said. "I don't think he would have called her if he didn't know her."

The driver of a car going by blew his horn and waved at us. Francine sighed and began to walk, fast. I asked her if she'd ever been strapped. She gripped her books tighter. I said I had never been strapped and never would be unless the Archbishop was replaced. I thought of my mother's and Medina's tits. I wondered if Francine's tits were bigger than they seemed because they were squashed flat by her books. I told myself that, had she not been holding the books, I would have tried to hold her hand, but I knew I didn't dare. I knew she'd pull it away before I even had time to see what it felt like. Her hands were not full of scrapes and cat scratches and chafed and chapped like those of other girls. They were pale, delicate-looking, small hands with thin, slender fingers.

"Nice boyfriend, Francine," a small girl shouted. "But I think his pants should be on the upper half."

Francine's shoulders rose and fell with a sigh of exasperation.

"Shut up," I shouted.

"Don't *start* anything," Francine said under her breath, her lips as tightly closed as any ventriloquist's.

"Leave them alone, Gloria," another older girl shouted. In the silence that followed, I realized that Francine's mission was common knowledge, that the girls of Heart had been charged by someone, probably Sister Celestine, to let Francine do the bidding of His Grace without interference. I noticed, on the periphery of the clutch of girls from Heart, boys from St. Bon's watching in silence, boys who at the sight of a girl tolerating my near presence, a girl, in fact, *talking* to me would normally have sent up a series of whoops and howls that would have brought the other students of the Mount running from all directions. Clearly, word of Francine's mission had gone out among all the schools, word that, at the behest of His Grace, who would not look kindly on any form of defiance of his wishes, Francine and Percy Joyce would either be left alone or be joined by others who, guided by Francine's example, would take a sincere interest in getting to know me.

"I'm going home," Francine muttered. "You're supposed to walk home with me." Her face was blotched red and white with embarrassment, as was her throat, an archipelago of what might have been the remnants of a stain like mine. Her pale blue eyes blurred with tears. I saw her fighting against the strain of the sort of mass scrutiny I had long ago become accustomed to. I fell in beside her as she began to walk down Howley Avenue. We were not followed. It was October, sunny but chilly, and fallen leaves clattered past us on the street when the wind came up.

"Do you want to go to Collins's store?" I said. "I have enough for two Popsicles." She said nothing. And neither of us said a word more as she led me in and out among a maze of streets until she stopped in front of a large, white, green-trimmed house on Barnes Road, the front door of which came open to reveal a woman wearing a full-length sunflowered smock. She raised her hand, smiled and shouted, "Hello, Percy, you must be Percy." Her eyes went wide and darted from me to Francine. Soon her face was as flushed as her daughter's.

"Hello, Mrs. Dunne," I said. "Yes, I'm Percy." Without a word, Francine hurried up the walkway and, upon reaching the steps, broke into a run, making it necessary for her mother to step aside to let her through.

"All right, then, Percy," Mrs. Dunne said. "See you tomorrow."

I told my mother of my first meeting with Francine, the wordless walk to her house, the uncharacteristic silence and reticent tolerance of the other students.

"It's a good start," my mother said. "Francine and her mother thought it would be better if the two of you got acquainted on your own instead of in a schoolyard surrounded by a lot of other boys and girls." Her source for this information was Pops, who had heard it from McHugh. She told me not to worry—a little awkwardness was normal on the occasion of a first meeting, especially an arranged one.

"Everyone knows what's going on," I said, sighing.

"That doesn't mean it won't work." She said His Grace had asked McHugh to spread the word among the homeroom teachers of the Mount. The boys of my homeroom had been told during religion class, which I had spent, as usual, in the library. I told my mother I didn't think Francine would ever speak to me except to warn me against doing anything that would draw attention to us.

"Well, give her a chance," my mother said. "And don't forget, it's not just up to her to speak to you, you have to speak to her."

"It was your first date ever, Percy," Pops said. "The hard part's over. You're on your way."

"It wasn't a *date*," my mother said. "We're all supposed to be very clear about that." I knew I wasn't the stuff that girls' dreams were made of, not even Francine's; I was two years younger than her and uglier than sin. As for her, she was from that group of girls whose sullen normalcy and plainness seemed self-generated, as if they somehow suppressed whatever allure they might have had out of sheer antipathy to the notion or purpose of attractiveness. And yet I found her enormously attractive. Beautiful.

"So you'll meet her at the same place at the same time tomorrow?" my mother asked. I nodded.

Looking as I did, and attending an all-boys school, I had had almost no contact with girls. Except for that brief encounter with Abigail and now Francine, I had never spoken to one except when mythmaking or in reply to teasing. I had never stood near one except when, for her, it was unavoidable, and only then for seconds.

Now here, on Day Two of our détente, was Francine, voluntarily allowing me to occupy her personal space, throwing a few words my way without the intention of being overheard and gaining a laugh at my expense. While it was true that she could not bring herself to look me in the eye, or even to look at any part of me, it did seem she was doing more than merely tolerating me. I was able to smell her hair, even if it smelled of nothing but shampoo. I was able to smell *her*, her scent that, like my mother's and Medina's, was so nice it defied description. I was able to really *see* her face, her young girl's ineffably feminine complexion, those pale blue eyes of hers, the meeting of her red hair and her forehead, the pout of her small, narrow mouth, the shallow groove beneath her nose that rose to the midpoint of her upper lip, the perfect little furrows in her lips, the swell of her breasts beneath her books, her wind-flattened skirt, the hollow at its middle and the outline of her legs, her lower legs and the freckles that began just above her high-pulled socks, her creased, faintly smudged brass-buckle shoes. Francine.

Francine and I met again at Howley and Bonaventure, watched by many students who pretended not to be watching and said nothing to us.

"Mom says I'm supposed to talk to you today." Francine looked again as if she was on the verge of tears, wincing with the effort of the task she'd been assigned. She stared wistfully off into the distance with the expression of someone determined not to reveal how badly her feelings had been hurt. "Mom says it doesn't take long enough to walk home to have a proper conversation. So we should just sit down somewhere and talk. There's a bench by the bus stop on Military Road."

Without another word, she set off down Bonaventure toward St. Bon's, her books clasped to her chest, her head down. I ran and caught up with her.

She stopped abruptly, turned toward me, her face suggesting that an outburst of anger was imminent—but she bit her lower lip, faced forward and resumed her determined march. Again I had to run to catch up with her, my large feet loudly slapping on the side-walk. Mortified, hobbled, I reached out and grabbed her right arm to make her turn around. As she turned, all but one of her books spilled onto the sidewalk.

"You made me drop my *books*," she said.

"I'm sorry," I protested. "I always leave my books in school. I was just going to ask you to slow down." As she crouched, with one leg bent more than the other, to pick up her books, I saw, for a second, her bare legs entire, and the pale blue, eye-colour-matching V of her underwear. On one of her inner thighs there was a light sprinkle of freckles. I dared not remove my large hands from my pockets to help her. She gathered the books together, wiping dust from their covers.

"The *corners* are bent," she said as she stood up. "They're *spoiled*."

"I'm sorry. I just wanted you to stop walking so fast. I can't keep up. My stupid feet don't work very well."

"Don't you touch me again," she said, and began to walk at her previous pace.

"Can I still walk home with you?" I called. She said nothing, but I ran and caught up with her.

"Do you have any hobbies?" she said, seeming to wipe away a tear.

"What?" I said, my tone that of someone refuting an accusation.

"Hobbies. *Hobbies*. Mom said you might have some hobbies."

I had to say *something* to dispel the excruciating awkwardness. "I'll tell you when we get to the bench," I said. We walked in silence past St. Bon's, where a few boys and girls were hanging about, posted like sentinels but affecting a lack of interest in us. The bench was almost directly in front of the Basilica, just past the bus stop. An elderly man and two elderly women were sitting on it. The man's legs were crossed, his arm over the back of the bench in a way that made it clear he and the two women knew each other and weren't waiting for the bus.

"There's nowhere to sit," Francine said. It might have been a panicked complaint about the utter lack of shelter from lethal objects that were falling from the sky, or a protest against her mother who was supposed to have somehow reserved the bench for us. A tear rolled down her cheek, so I told her I'd been collecting stamps since I was seven. I tried not to think of how lonely and bored you would have to be to collect stamps. I felt as if the Archbishop was watching us from one of the upper windows of the Basilica.

So I said I had hundreds of stamps, some of which my mother had given me, some I had sent away for, some I had seen advertised in comic books. I had a Newfoundland stamp that was over a hundred years old and though it was worth a lot of money, I would never sell it. I told Francine that if not for the invention of the envelope by a girl of about her age back in the time of Rome, there'd be no such things as stamps or letters or the post office. I told her that a man in Russia had collected about six hundred kinds of envelopes and that was the most so far. I said I also collected coins and that coins were invented because they didn't blow away or get worn out the way paper money did. I said I had a lot of Newfoundland coins, mostly Catholic ones. I told her that I was painstakingly constructing a model ship inside a bottle, the SS *Terra Nova*, the tiny pieces of which I had spent a month painting with toothpicks. I said as much about hobbies as I knew or could make up on short notice.

Francine looked as though she was greatly distressed by the detailed account I had just given her of the burning to the ground of her ancestral home.

"I'm going now," she said.

I walked with Francine to her house, where her mother was waiting at the front door again. She hurried up the walkway and the steps as before, shoulders swaying, and all but knocked her mother over as she went inside. Mrs. Dunne waved and said, "Hello, Percy." She looked every bit as fretful and anxious as the day before. I waved back and said hello and then hurried away. But I couldn't help but fib to my mother and Pops that Francine and I had talked about the books we were reading in school. My mother asked if Francine had introduced me to any of her friends. I said no. "Too bad," my mother said. "You two could use some reinforcements. Someone chattier than her and less inclined than you to be a bullshit artist."

"She started *crying*," I said. "I only talked about hobbies because her mother told her to ask me if I had any."

"Crying?" my mother said. "Jesus. Her mother must have been afraid to say no to the Archbishop. Mrs. Dunne should have more sense, but you're not making it any easier for Francine. Maybe I should call it off. Do you think I should?"

"Give it a bit more time," Pops said from the sunroom. "Some girls are just shy."

My mother raised her eyebrows at me. "Well, what do you think?"

What I thought was that for Francine and me to break "it" off now after meeting only twice would confirm, reinforce, the already impenetrable view of me on the Mount as a comical freak who would never fit in even with the lifelong help of Uncle Paddy. So I nodded yes.

"Why don't you meet somewhere different this time?" my mother said. "Maybe the problem is that the two of you are too much on display. I'll try to think of something better, okay?"

"Okay."

My mother's idea, which she had Pops relay to McHugh, who relayed it to Mrs. Dunne, was that Francine and I go to Marty's restaurant on Water Street for ice cream floats.

The next day after school, we walked in silence to Marty's. I held the door open for her, but she stayed put until I went in first. Lisa, the waitress who served my mother, Medina and me on Sundays was sitting by the cash register behind the counter, smoking a cigarette and chewing gum.

"Well, hello, Percy Joyce," she said, smiling.

"Hello, Lisa," I said.

"Who's this, now?" she said, beaming at Francine in a way that convinced me my mother had called her to tell her we were coming. "Is this your girlfriend?"

I turned to look at Francine, only to find that she had already taken a seat in one of the booths along the wall.

"That's Francine," I said. "She goes to Holy Heart."

"Aha, an older woman."

I was relieved to see that the entire restaurant was empty. I joined Francine in the booth and sat facing the front window, which was hidden from me by the other side of the booth and by Francine. Marty's—green booths, wainscotted walls hung with cheap paintings of storm-tossed ships, smiling net-hauling fishermen clad in sou'westers, cheerful-looking Newfoundland dogs with their tongues lolling. But to me the place was the mecca of fine dining. It smelled of deep-frying chips, hot gravy sprinkled with cold brown vinegar, hot fudge brownies buried under Dream Whip and ice cream and chocolate syrup.

Francine sat facing the back of the restaurant. Lisa, who was dressed all in green, put cutlery, two paper place mats and two menus in front of us.

"I just want a plate of chips, please," Francine said, staring at the place mat on which there was a drawing of a smiling man dressed as a chef, his arms folded, *Marty* written in green above his head.

"Mom gave me enough for two floats each," I said, but Francine went on staring at the place mat.

"I'll have a vanilla float with Sprite," I told Lisa, who was one of the few people who didn't look away or at my school tie when I looked at her.

Lisa, taking our menus, smiled and winked at me, cracking her gum again—she cracked her gum to punctuate everything she said and did. When she was gone, I said, "You can have more than just chips, you know."

"Mom said just chips," Francine said.

"I like ice cream floats," I said.

Francine stared away from me at the line of empty booths across the aisle, but we were more privately together in the booth than we had ever been before, closer, sitting down in each other's company for the first time. I looked at her hands. I imagined those lovely fingers doing to Medina whatever my mother's had to make her squirm the way she had and get so out of breath. I imagined them taking the place of my oversized hands and playing with my dick the way I played with it myself. I put both hands in my pockets and covered my hard-on with my left, pressing it against my lower belly. I stared at the freckled skin between the lapels of her Heart blouse, the hollow of her throat, the V of her chest, the tunic that prevented me, I imagined, from seeing the outline of her bra. Beneath the table, our knees and shoes were little more than a foot apart.

"You could have gravy on your chips," I said. She flared her nostrils but said nothing.

"Have you ever been to Marty's before?" I said.

Barely perceptibly, she shook her head.

"We come here almost every Sunday," I said. "We have Sunday sundaes."

I glanced under the table as she bent to pull up her socks. Her knees parted slightly. Her tits pressed against the edge of the table. They were bigger than they had seemed, though not nearly as big as my mother's or even Medina's.

Give me myth or give me death. I said that Marty owned the restaurant but he didn't work there because he owned so many things in town that weren't even named after him that he didn't have to work anywhere. "He never dresses like the man on the menu," I said. I said his real name was Martin Barton but he called himself Marty because he didn't like having two names that rhymed. They didn't really rhyme, I said, because he was French from France and in French *Barton* was pronounced "Bartawn," but people in Newfoundland pronounced it like *Martin*, so he didn't have any choice.

Lisa brought Francine's chips and my float to the table. A vanilla float—I'd had many of them at Marty's—was made with two scoops of vanilla ice cream and came with a side bottle of Sprite; you added as much Sprite as you liked when you liked. The ice cream came in a metal hourglass-shaped goblet that was lined with a cone of paper. The top scoop of ice cream was stabbed with a long narrow spoon and a cardboard straw.

"There you go," Lisa said. "Francine can share her chips with you and here's a straw, Francine, so you can have a taste of Percy's float." She winked at me again and cracked her gum before she went away.

I poured most of the Sprite into the goblet and watched the scoops of ice cream rise up to the top. I sucked on the straw and my mouth filled with creamy Sprite so cold I gasped and lost my breath. I heard Lisa laugh.

"Excuse me," I said. "Do you want some, Francine?" I'd never called her by name before. She gave no sign of having heard me.

There were ketchup, malt vinegar, salt and pepper on the table, but Francine put nothing on her chips. "They look good," I said.

She picked up a chip with her fingers, bit it in half and dropped the other half on her plate. Her small mouth barely moved as she chewed. She pushed away her plate of chips.

"I have to go home," she said as though to someone sitting beside her.

"I'll finish this float really fast then," I said.

I looked at the goblet; the paper cone inside it was about half full. I picked up the goblet with one hand and with the other removed the paper cone, holding it by the rim. "I'm going to drink like a king," I said, and began to pour the creamy Sprite from the paper cone into the goblet.

In all my visits to Marty's I had never noticed that there was nothing at the bottom of a goblet but a hole that the paper cone fit into. The float flowed straight out of the goblet and streamed onto my lap, instantly soaking through my slacks and underwear and onto my hard-on and my balls. Some of the cream spattered onto the table and from there onto the front of Francine's tunic. There was even some on her face and in her hair.

I gasped from the shock of the cold and from embarrassment, unable to say a word.

"WHAT DID YOU DO?" Francine cried. "YOU GOT CREAM ALL OVER ME." She bolted from the booth, dodging Lisa, who was headed for our table. I tried to run past Lisa in pursuit of Francine, but she grabbed me by the collar of my blazer.

"You're not going out there looking like *that*," she said. I looked outside. Francine was halfway up the hill to Duckworth Street, not running but, because of the steep slope, striding as fast as she could, legs splayed as wide as a cross-country skier's, arms pumping.

Lisa stared at my crotch, so I stared too. "I didn't know there was no bottom in it," I said.

No colour registers moisture more clearly than grey. I looked as if I had both come in and pissed my pants. There was a mess of still-white creamy foam over and around my zipper.

Now I was glad Lisa had stopped me. The slope on the far side of Duckworth was even steeper. I would have had to do what Francine was doing now, run and walk, run and walk, through neighbour-hoods I didn't know, my hands and feet flopping all over the place. I would have been jeered at by boys and girls, and by who knows who else, people who though I'd never met them and didn't know their names knew *my* name because they knew *of* me, of my stupid platypus face, and hands and feet as oversized as those of any walrus.

"I'm going to phone your mother and tell her to come down here with some other clothes for you, all right?" Lisa said. I nodded. "You wait in the men's bathroom. Go into one of the stalls and lock the door. Don't take anything off until your mother gets here, all right?" I nodded again and fought back the urge to cry.

I did as she said. I stood in a locked stall in the men's room at Marty's, my thighs sticking together, Sprite and ice cream crusting on my slacks, inside and out, on my underwear, inside my under-wear on pubic hair that, at the best of times, looked like the cheapest, most inexpert and wispy of toupées. I hoped that no one else would come into the bathroom while I was there. I thought again of the bottomless goblet, pictured myself pouring the float into it and announcing with such gleeful aplomb that I planned to drink like a king.

Francine's mother phoned mine and suggested that we all keep the "accident in the restaurant" to ourselves. She and Francine would tell no one, not even McHugh, and she said she hoped Pops would not say a word about it to him or anyone else. My mother assured her that no one at 44 would say a word to anyone, and added that Lisa the waitress had already told her that she would keep it a secret. My mother seemed as relieved as I was and made Pops swear he would not breathe a word to McHugh.

"You'll be *very* sorry if you break that promise, Pops," she said. "*Very* sorry. Understand?" Pops nodded and blushed as if there were *many* mortifying secrets about him that no one knew but him and my mother.

Mrs. Dunne said she thought we should make up some excuse that McHugh could relay to the Archbishop about why Francine and I would have no further meetings.

"An excuse that we can all use when we have to," my mother said. "Mrs. Dunne says she's worried about Francine and hopes that her daughter won't be rewarded for her kindness with ingratitude."

"Her kindness?" Medina said. "You'd think the girl was a martyr. I'd be worried about Francine if I was Mrs. Dunne. She met up with Percy three times and barely said two dozen words."

"It seems her mother had no better sense than to force her into it," my mother said. "Try to imagine a girl less suited to lead by example than Francine. On the other hand, I went along with the whole thing in the first place."

It was decided that our excuse should be that Francine, being involved in so many extracurricular school activities and spending so much time at her schoolwork in order to maintain her high grades in a new school, simply didn't have the time and energy to add to her responsibilities. Given how weary and distressed Francine had appeared since she began to "look out for me," Mrs. Dunne said, the excuse would be believed.

I stuck to the agreed-upon excuse for my "breakup" with Francine. At first it was not openly challenged at St. Bon's, but girls from Holy Heart accused me on the way home of having "tried something" with her. They said they had heard from their parents what "really happened."

Then the boys started in. "Heard you got some from Francine," the boys from Brother Rice shouted. "Percy frenched Francine," they chanted, and the girls answered with a chorus of disgust and sounds of mock retching. "His tongue can't be any worse than his face," a boy yelled, further inciting the girls, who shouted back that they doubted poor Percy-frenched Francine would agree with them. Gloria announced: "One of Francine's brothers wants to be a priest at the Basilica, but Percy told Francine that, unless she put out, the Dunne family would never get anywhere because he'd make sure they wound up in Uncle Paddy's bad books." This, or some version of it, became the story: I had tried to blackmail Francine by threatening to get her and her mother into trouble with the Archbishop

Seeming to lend credence to the accusations was the fact that, day after day, Francine did not show up for school. Girls began saying that she had suffered some sort of breakdown because of something I had done when she wouldn't let me kiss her and "do things" to her. After Francine's fourth consecutive day of absence from school, my mother phoned Mrs. Dunne, who told her that Francine had a bad cold but would soon be back to school. But a week and a half went by with no sign of Francine.

Then word went round that, on the last day she spent with me, Francine had been spotted, red-faced and streaming tears, running up Garrison Hill, sometimes falling in her panic to get home after some sort of "trouble" involving me at Marty's. Francine had run from the restaurant and I had been prevented from leaving it until my mother came to get me.

"I'm going to phone that woman again," my mother declared, but Pops warned her against making accusations she couldn't prove. He said he had heard from Brother McHugh that the Archbishop was "distressed" about all the stories that were going around about me.

"He probably *heard* about them from McHugh," my mother said.

She phoned Mrs. Dunne and had a conversation with her that left her seething. Mrs. Dunne had told her that Francine was in "a very fragile state," that she was under the care of a doctor who said it might be weeks or even months before she was back to normal. In a lisping imitation of Mrs. Dunne, my mother said, "Now I'm not saying that Percy *did* anything. But Francine doesn't like to talk about what really happened in the restaurant. She never had any problems before she made friends with Percy, that's all I'm saying."

My mother, arms folded over her white blouse, stormed around the house in her high heels. "Stupid, selfish woman. Blaming Percy for *her* mistake. If that daughter of hers is that delicate, she should never have put her forward in the first place. She uses her shrinking violet of a daughter to make points with the Archbishop and then she blames Percy when fragile Francine falls apart."

Pops came home the next day after school to announce that McHugh had relayed to him the Archbishop's suggestion that I might benefit from a few sessions with the clerical counsellor at the Basilica.

"Fragile Francine might benefit," my mother fumed, "but it would take more than a few sessions. Frail Francine. Yet-to-be-finger-fucked Francine. Faint Francine. *Feverish* Francine. Francine the Fanciful. Too-tight-to-fart Francine. Francine the Frosty."

But the names didn't help me and the rumours grew.

Francine was confined to bed, completely done in by the five or six hours she had spent with me, profoundly exhausted from the strain of gamely sticking to a task that all her friends had been telling her was hopeless. Francine had endured, in stoic silence, for as long as she could, my filthy language, the filthy suggestions I made to her, the filthy names I called her when she did not co-operate. Francine was bed-bound because of the toll I had taken on her, because of what she could not bring herself to talk about—the darkly hinted-at event at Marty's.

"Jesus, Percy, what did you do to the poor girl?" the boys asked.

"I didn't do anything."

"What did you make her do to you? Did you talk her into a blow job or something? Did you force her into one?"

"Yes," my mother said when I told her what was being said at school. "A blow job. That must have been it." Francine had been prostrate for weeks because the Joyce boy had fooled her into blowing him. My mother said it was a classic case of fellatio exhaustion, from which some young women had been known never to recover.

Francine was in a state. Everything reminded her of Percy. Someone saying "Howley and Bonaventure" set her off. She had no appetite. She couldn't sleep. She'd had, still had, only a sketchy knowledge of the facts of life. She knew half of this and half of that and none of *that* at all. As for a boy's thing, no one had ever told her that anything but pee came out of it. "God only knows how things work on Planet Dunne," my mother said.

Three weeks to the day after she had fled from Marty's, Francine returned to school. When school let out at St. Bon's, I walked homeward, down Bonaventure, past Holy Heart, and saw Francine out front in the parking lot, surrounded by other girls from Heart, many of them older than her, some looking protective, seemingly shielding her even as they plied her with questions. I saw instantly that membership in this circle of Francine's was much prized and that, though the circle would shrink with time, Francine had gained a degree of popularity that she would never lose and that, contrary to what we had been led to believe, she had never had at Mercy. She *looked* as if she had had a breakdown. She was even paler than before, sunken-eyed, had lost weight. On average, it had taken Francine three days to recover from each hour she had spent with me. She looked genuinely convalescent. She probably was, having been so sickly and high-strung to begin with, but she was clearly enjoying herself now, her books pressed as always against her tunic, her long hair brushed back and bunned by what looked like two criss-crossed pencils, but she was chatting, *chatting*, as animatedly as I'd hoped she would with me.

One of the girls on the fringe of the circle looked my way. "There he is," she said. "It's Percy Joyce." For an instant I thought that, en masse, Francine-led, they would come running after me. "Leave Francine alone," one of the older Heart girls shouted, as if she had caught me doing whatever she imagined I had already done with Francine. "Filthy pervert," another girl shouted. I glanced at Francine, who glared at me as if she was reliving all that I had done to her. "Stop looking at her, Freak Face," a tall, skinny girl yelled, then stooped to the parking lot pavement, picked up a piece of asphalt and flung it my way. It landed far short of me, but many of the other girls followed her example and picked up and threw anything they could find. Francine watched them for a while, then gingerly put down her books, picked up a stone and threw it, at which the Heart girls applauded and cheered.

I ran home down the hill.

"What are they saying you *did*?" my mother said. "Someone must have said something to them."

My mother phoned Mrs. Dunne, who wouldn't let her speak to Francine, who, she said, had "already suffered enough."

"Yes," my mother said, "because you are too stupid to know she takes after you, that she too is a febrile, simpering *twit*."

Versions of "what happened at Marty's" and elsewhere were many and various and fast-evolving. I had peed myself. I had dumped an ice cream float into my lap to disguise the fact that I had peed myself. I had squirmed under the table and shoved my ugly face between her thighs. I had smeared ice cream or "something" on her legs. Francine had run home from Marty's with specks of "something" in her hair and on her tunic. I had put "something" in my float, which I tricked her into drinking from. I was endlessly inventive in my vileness. Lisa had locked me in the bathroom and phoned the police, but my mother and Medina, mysteriously alerted that I needed help, had got there before them and forcibly removed me.

"How did Francine even know you were *in* the bathroom?" my mother said. She phoned Lisa, who told her that one of the kitchen staff had seen her hustle me into the bathroom and later told her he suspected I had done something more to upset Francine than spill a float onto my lap. Lisa, who had seen the aftermath of my accident, assured him that she believed me, but the man had since been spreading stories that Lisa guessed had made their way to Holy Heart, where they were further embellished.

My mother said she wondered if Francine, being Francine, was at this point even sure of what happened.

The boys on the Mount began to address me as "Joyce." "What did you do to Francine, Joyce?" they asked, a hint of admiration in their voices. "Come on, Joyce, tell us what you did." The suggestion seemed to be that whatever I had done had proceeded inevitably from my "nature," which could be read from, and was inscrutably bound up with, my appearance. The essential Percy Joyce, for so long foreshadowed by and proceeding from the same dark place as his birthmark and extremities, had finally surfaced and the first hapless victim of that surfacing was Francine Dunne, the most vulnerable target one could imagine for an imposition of any kind, offered up to me by her mother and mine, by her mother who, for naïveté, credulity, lack of assertiveness and dread of authority figures, may have been Francine's only rival.

Through it all, I watched the girls of Heart and Mercy and Presentation from afar, their school books pressed against the bosoms of their dark blue tunics, all wearing pleated skirts, their bare, pink-with-cold legs showing between their school socks and their skirts, the girls, in a gale of wind, trying to control both their skirts and their hair. The latter blew every which way as they turned their heads about, trying to keep it out of their eyes and their mouths, to which wet strands of it clung.

But the principal of Mercy called Brother McHugh, who told Pops I had got into the habit of "creeping" around Mercy Convent

School, "peeping" at them from behind parked cars, the impossibility of my ever finding a girlfriend driving me to acts of depravity that had all of Mercy terrified. Given that, among the girls of Mercy, my mother said, the nickname for the entire student body of St. Bon's was "the St. Bon's Hard-ons," it wouldn't have mattered if any of this was true—but it wasn't. She looked at me. "It *isn't* true, is it, Percy?"

"*No*," I said. "Not all of it. All I ever do with girls is look at them."

The older girls from Heart tried to convince the younger ones that if they kissed me they would catch what I had and wake up the morning after to find that their faces looked like mine. They dared the girls who said they didn't believe it to kiss me and find out, and those girls said they would rather kiss a nun's bare arse than Percy Joyce's lips.

"You're supposed to have your dick circumcised, Percy, not your face." And so I was called Dick Facy.

"I dare you to stick your tongue in his mouth," a tall, heavy-set blond girl said, and the others grimaced and groaned with revulsion. She whispered to the others and they squealed. "Dick Facy," the girl said, "show us your dick and we'll give you a quarter."

"For a quarter," I said, surprising myself and her, "I'll only show you a quarter of my dick." The girls squealed again, their hands over their faces.

That's how close I came to doing something that would have marked me as a fool forever, a boy presumed by parents to be at least half demented, incapable of resisting lewdly exposing himself, so that he'd have to be watched and their children warned from associating with him or ever going near him.

THE SECOND SERMON
ON THE MOUNT

BROTHER McHugh, yet again using Pops as his go-between, suggested that my mother have a "very serious talk" with me. McHugh said he had been fielding calls for days from parents demanding that I be kept away from their daughters even if I had to be expelled.

"He has no intention of expelling Percy," Pops said. "He just wants you both to know how upset the other parents are."

"*They're* upset?"

Brother McHugh said she shouldn't expect the Archbishop to preach a sermon in defence of Percy every time I misbehaved. My mother yelled that I'd done *nothing*, that I hadn't *misbehaved*. She wanted to phone McHugh, but Pops said he was in the Brothers' Quarters and couldn't be reached.

"Girls banding together for safety," my mother growled one afternoon, pacing the kitchen in her pumps, throwing up her arms, setting her tits into a mesmerizing wobble. "Daughters all over the

Mount in flight from Percy Joyce. I can see it now. Parents keeping watch at every window. The sun is soon to set. Penny Joyce can barely hold back Percy, whom she nightly lets loose upon the Mount. Not even boys are safe when Percy is aprowl. Who knows whose milkshake may this time be despoiled? Who knows from what hedge Percy's hands may be outthrust, what girl's legs he may slide his hands up even as she stands talking to her friends?"

When my mother announced she was going to deliver her own Sermon on the Mount, Medina said, "For Christ's sake, Pen, don't do anything stupid. Don't bring us all down because of Francine Dunne." Pops was not there. He was at the East End Club, drinking beer. My mother went to her room for about an hour and came out holding several handwritten pages. Long after dark she went out onto the back step. Medina and I, standing in the open doorway behind her, watched and listened as she raised her voice to a declamatory shout, Medina shaking her head in anxious disbelief.

The Second Sermon on the Mount Regarding Percy Joyce

Unlike other boys, who want nothing from girls until marriage but refreshing conversation, Percy Joyce is aroused by girls and even women, married, unmarried, engaged, the never-kissed, the cock-abhorring girls of Holy Heart. He is aroused by girls he hasn't even met, by pictures of girls whose names he doesn't even know—it doesn't matter to him.

Such a boy as Percy Joyce disrupts the natural order, the time-tested rituals of unhurried courtship of which the one true, proper end is conjugal procreation. He roams the Mount, a grade-school satyr, oaths and obscenities flying from him like sparks from a pinwheel, a runty, rutting beast of lust, a pipsqueak libertine.

Percy Joyce will tell you sex is not a sin, that based on what he has done with himself, he thinks it might be fun to do it with you. You know it is a mortal sin to do it before you're married and that it is a venial sin to do it *when* you're married. You know that a married woman must confess to a priest if she does it with her husband. And that it is also a sin if she doesn't do it with her husband. This, as you know, only *seems* to be a contradiction. It is actually a mystery that no one but an ordained celibate can understand. But Percy Joyce will tell you that you might as well ask a brick wall about sex as ask a priest.

People of the Mount, beware. Percy Joyce goes out at night with binoculars around his neck, so keep your curtains closed. He climbs trees as well as any monkey, so keep your windows closed. If you say you believe in original sin, he may offer to sell you an unpaved stretch of road in Labrador. If you see him, report him immediately to the authorities. Do not try to deal with him yourself. The Purple are known to turn in an instant on even the most cautious and well-meaning person. If you must approach the Purple, do so with extreme caution.

Percy Joyce cannot keep it in his pants: there is only one such boy on the Mount. But there are many good, honest, pale-faced boys who keep theirs in their pants until they get engaged. They might, when they kiss a girl, slip her some tongue, but that is as far as they will go. No harm can come to your daughters from an inch or two of tongue. Repeat: *No harm.* Unless that tongue belongs to Percy Joyce.

Percy Joyce will try to get into a girl's pants. That is a known fact, therefore your daughters must always be careful about their pants. Pants can be removed so quickly. Just like that. And you'll be telling Percy Joyce to do right by your daughter. That certain woman you've been avoiding for years will be your in-law. It is not enough that your daughters believe, however fervently, in premarital purity. They must have sense enough to keep their pants on. But such common sense is not as widespread among your daughters as you may think, and Percy Joyce can talk even the most intelligent offspring of people such as you into anything. Do not blame yourselves. You are as God made you. God did not make Percy Joyce. The Devil did.

Do not let your daughter sit in a booth at Marty's restaurant, not even by herself. There is no telling what her hidden, unseen hands will do. She may play with her you-know-what against her will. It is a well-known fact that girls do not play with themselves on purpose. Nor, except for Percy Joyce, do boys. Your children do it by accident or in their sleep. They do not like it. They are not like Percy Joyce. Percy Joyce will bed your daughter for the fun of it. Look at your daughter. What kind of boy would want to share a bed with her? Percy Joyce would. So tell your daughters they must never share a booth with Percy Joyce.

Daughters of the Mount, if you do somehow find yourself in a booth with Percy Joyce, do not say that all you want is chips. It sets him off. Percy Joyce is always *up* to *something*. He will offer to buy you a float or invite you to share his. Be especially careful if he suggests you put gravy on your chips. As for floats, all he ever does with them is pour them down his pants. It gives him some kind of thrill that we who leave our pants alone will never understand.

Daughters of the Mount, like a wolf, he will try to isolate you from the fold as he did with Francine Dunne. I think we can all agree that the last thing we want is another Francine Dunne. Vicious rumours and false accusations are like kryptonite to Percy Joyce. *Make up* as many as you can. Spread them among your friends. We can only deal with Percy Joyce if we all pull together!

Only a handful of our neighbours were able to make out even bits and pieces of my mother's "Second Sermon on the Mount Regarding Percy Joyce." But word of it got around and people were soon pointing at my mother as the root cause for whatever I had done to Francine Dunne. Boys asked what my mother had shouted from the back steps of our house. They said that some of the Brothers whose windows in the Quarters at Brother Rice had been open had heard what she said but wouldn't repeat it because it was filth and blasphemy. I denied that my mother had said a single bad word, breaking my promise to her that I would ignore all questions about the sermon.

Boys repeated questions they had heard at home: What kind of woman goes out on her steps late at night to give a speech about *anything*? What kind of woman writes a speech and reads it out-doors in the middle of the night, waking up her neighbours? What was she hoping to prove by talking about her own son like that? Hadn't she and her son caused enough trouble for Francine Dunne?

The overheard, intelligible fragments of the speech were fuel for the flames of rumours about Penny Joyce. Men were seen coming and going from her house at all hours. She and "that Medina woman" couldn't get enough of them. They charged the men money for what they did with them. And all of it went on right under the nose of Percy Joyce, so no wonder he had turned out as he had. Why was Brother McHugh allowing a Brother Rice teacher to live in such a house? When was the Archbishop going to wise up and realize that he ought to be using his influence to expel the Joyces from the neighbourhood, not to protect Percy Joyce, whom there was no point being nice to.

Brother McHugh sent word to my mother through Pops that, what with the Francine Dunne matter and her middle-of-the-night obscenity-riddled sermon, the Archbishop was *very* upset and wanted us both to know that he alone could not clear a path through life for me, that my mother and I had to do our part, and unless we did, he would have no choice but to let us fend for our-selves, as we were causing him and therefore the Church, his dio-cese and congregation much anxiety, distress and embarrassment.

"You were right," my mother said to Medina. "It was a stupid thing to do." My mother wrote and mailed to the Archbishop "A Note of Apology" in which she said she had lost her temper because of the lies that were being circulated about me and Francine. The

Archbishop replied to her, indirectly, through McHugh, that he accepted her apology but was "pondering what further measures might be taken to help you and Little Percy."

I started giving a truthful account of what had happened at Marty's, gave it umpteen times at school, but no one believed me. My "drink like a king" story was taken to be typical Percy Joyce BS. As Francine and her mother only hinted darkly at their side of the story, I had only the vaguest notion of what I was expected to refute. I wasn't sure what to do, so I did what I always did in times of uncertainty.

Give me myth or give me death. I said Francine had missed three weeks of school because of the measles, which I didn't catch from her because one of the few good things about my face was that it was better at warding off germs than normal faces were. I said that at Marty's Francine and I had ordered a float each, and when the first float came we each thought it was ours and grabbed it at the same time and I wound up spilling it in my lap, which she blamed herself for and that was why she ran home crying. I said that a bully had come to our booth, picked up my float and threatened to dump it on Francine's head unless I left her alone with him, but I said he should dump it on my head instead, which he did just as I told Francine to run, which she did. But now she felt ashamed because she hadn't stuck up for me as I did for her though my mother had told her disappointment was a part of life and the sooner she learned that the better. My mother was going to tell the Archbishop that Francine should not be disciplined or transferred to another school after all.

I had long thought it was unfair that *my* mother was the best-looking woman on the Mount. Everyone else's mother *looked* like a mother: their backsides and bellies had gone slack though they were not yet thirty-five, their faces tired as if they cried most of the time when they were not in public, as if they knew they couldn't keep up but had no choice but to go on trying and hoping for an ever-elusive easeful moment, a fret-free interval of restoration from which they would emerge looking as they had when they were first engaged.

I had no idea why my mother didn't look like them. Medina said my mother looked so nice because she was spared the bother of a husband and had but one child, who, for all the reasons he gave her to fret, was easier to manage than five or six "normal" children. For whatever reason, my mother had her own exemption, as if the Archbishop had decreed, in opposition to God, that to offset her troubles she should keep her looks longer than usual.

"The mass of boys lead lives of quiet masturbation." My mother, amending Thoreau. When my mother wore blouses that barely buttoned over her bra, I could sometimes see her belly and her bra—a bit of what Medina had seen, and something, I assumed, of what Pops saw and touched from time to time. I couldn't help *trying* to see them. "Percy, stop staring at your mother's tits," Medina growled at me one day. "It's just," I said, "that her blouse doesn't fit right." Medina tipped back her head, waiting to laugh until she locked eyes with my mother, who also laughed.

"Six hundred budding young women on top of the Mount," my mother said. "And six hundred boys with growing concerns. And yours, Percy, seem to be growing much faster than most."

The irony that a woman who looked like my mother had birthed a child who looked like me was not lost on anyone, especially in the wake of Francine and the Second Sermon. I saw people glare at my mother as if her looks had come at the expense of mine, because of some negligence of hers, some moment when, unmindful of me, she was gazing at her own reflection. I think some people saw my looks as a balance or corrective to hers, a demonstration that, in the grand scheme of things, God did not play favourites, even if Uncle Paddy did. We again, as when I was a preschooler, became known on the Mount as Beauty and the Beast; my mother, in the ruthless symmetry of fairy tales and myths, had been brought down to earth by the child she bore, by the husband who left her.

Still, long before I had seen her and Medina writhing on her bed, locked fiercely in their horizontal dance, I had started sneaking peeks up my mother's skirt and down her blouse. At the little furrow of her cleavage that was visible, the back splits in the hems of her skirts. I had watched her putting on lipstick then rubbing her lips together to smooth it all over. When she changed into a housecoat or bathrobe late in the evening, I had hoped her loosely knotted belts would come undone and wondered if I could deftly help them do so without getting caught.

Now I was caught up in a stupefying lust that nothing I had known before came close to; the Mercy, Heart or Presentation girls had not, all together, summoned up such lechery as my mother, in part because she was so constantly nearby and seemingly *available*. I found myself regarding Pops and Medina with jealousy: I was the only one in the house who didn't get to fuck my mother.

I imagined Penny Joyce dressed like a girl from Holy Heart, lying bored and lonely in her uniform on her bed two doors away, smiling as I crept into the room, arching her back as I pushed her tunic up around her waist, her feet flat on the bed as she accommodated me by splaying her sleek Black Mick legs, lifting her bum just a bit to allow me to pull down her pants. . . . Perhaps I wanted, not to have what I didn't have, but to be what I wasn't and could never be, and which my mother was by nothing more than an accident of birth. If I couldn't *be*, then maybe I could be *with* that, joined to it, a moving, breathing, panting part of it, even if only once, if only for a matter of minutes or seconds. In my world, in my circumscribed universe, she was the utmost of what I was denied.

A PITY FUCK FOR PERCY JOYCE

"You might get a pity fuck, if you're really lucky, Percy," a boy from Brother Rice called Moyles said to me one day when, as a shortcut up the hill, I took the rutted path the smokers of Brother Rice took when they left school each afternoon. His maroon blazer, his white shirt, his grey slacks stretched to near bursting. Stately, plump, mischief-making Moyles. He had fashioned a career for himself, planting information and calamitous suggestions in the minds of the boys and girls from the junior schools.

Moyles. The idea that at first seemed so absurd came from him. He was one of those schoolboys who really did know about the adult world, who seemed never to have been a boy like other boys—a know-it-all who, as unlikely as it seemed, knew it all. He had a sly, appraising grin that made me squirm with even more than my usual self-consciousness. "Yeah, pity fuck, if you're really lucky, Percy. Or, when you can afford it, you can get a whore. It'll cost you a lot more than it would cost someone with a normal face, so you better start saving up. Some normal women like to do it with freaks, so you might get lucky there too. Maybe. But no girl will ever *like* you—some girls might feel sorry for you, but not *that* sorry. A whore—well, you'd have to do it from behind so she couldn't see your face. It's called doggy style when you do it from behind. You might go your whole life and never get laid. You might still be a virgin when you die. You should ask your mother for a pity fuck, Percy. That's your best bet. She might say yes. Maybe not now, but when you're a bit older. I'd take a pity fuck from Penny Joyce."

"She's my mother."

"Tell her it's her fault your hands and feet are so weird. It probably is. Fifty-fifty chance, and she can't prove it's not her fault."

I shook my head and smirked to show him I knew what he was up to. But I thought of the words "you might go your whole life and never get laid. You might still be a virgin when you die." It scared me to think about it. And I thought about it a lot.

"Jesus," my mother said. "What's a pity fuck?" We were alone in the living room, my mother trying to read a book, me pretending to watch TV.

"It's when someone does it with you because they feel sorry for you because you haven't got anyone to do it with and never will. Moyles said my only hope of getting laid was if you gave me a pity fuck."

"God Almighty," my mother said. "Is there anything those boys don't think of? Not only is incest against the law, Perse, it's *good* that it's against the law."

"I wouldn't mind a pity fuck from someone else, a girl from Mercy or Presentation maybe."

"Whoa there. After the job that Francine Dunne has done on your reputation, you should stay as far away from girls as you can for a while. For God's sake, do *not* ask one of them for a pity fuck. You might wind up in reform school. And pity, by the way, is not a form of contraception. The girl could still get pregnant."

I nodded. "If I had ten minutes to live and had never been laid, would you give me a pity fuck?"

"I'm your mother, Percy."

"Well, who else would take that much pity on me? Would Medina?"

"No, she wouldn't."

"There's a girl at Mercy who gives blow jobs for money."

"Pity fucks and Mercy blow jobs," my mother said. "What next?"

"She blows a lot of boys. But Moyles said she'd only blow me for five hundred dollars. But he said that in a pitch-dark room I could suck her tits for fifty bucks. I wish we were rich."

"What's this girl's name?"

"I saw her once, but I don't know her name. She's fat and short. I wouldn't really want to do it with her. Moyles said I come from a long line of sheep shaggers. He said sheep were my best bet."

"I think you encourage these boys."

"I don't. What about a pity kiss? We could start with that. I mean a real kiss. Not one on the cheek, but a long one on the lips. I've never had a real kiss and I'm already twelve years old."

"*No.* You are *only* twelve years old. No pity *anythings.* You don't need pity and you know it. From now on you'll be lucky if you get a hug. Why are you talking as if you have a week to live? You haven't decided to hurt yourself or something, have you?"

"No. Forget about the pity kiss. I don't want anything. I changed my mind."

"Good. Because you're not *getting* anything from me, now or twenty-five years from now."

"You'll be an old hag in twenty-five years," I said. "I wouldn't want a pity fuck from an old hag."

I was instantly sorry that I'd said it.

"First a whore and now a hag," my mother said. "I'm coming up in the world."

I protested that I was sorry. And then I reminded her that, in the Beauty and the Beast fairy tale, the Beast becomes a handsome priest when Beauty kisses him.

"The Beast gets Beauty. But I suppose that's only in fairy tales."

"It's not only in fairy tales," my mother said. "But mothers don't sleep with their sons in fairy tales. They do it by accident in Greek tragedies." She told me the story of Oedipus, who unwittingly married and slept with his mother, Jocasta. When they found out what they'd done, Jocasta hanged herself and Oedipus stabbed his eyes out with a pair of golden needles.

"Not exactly a happy ending. Not that it would matter if there was a happy ending—it still wouldn't change my mind."

"I bet I'll never have sex with a girl. Or a woman."

"Most boys your age, or even close to your age, have never had sex."

"I'm not talking about now, I'm talking about *ever*. Other boys will have sex *some*day, but I'll never have it."

"You *will*, Percy."

"Moyles said not to worry, someday I'd meet a nice blind girl and we'd settle down, me, her, her guide dog and her cane."

"Prick."

"Will you promise that if no one else will, you will, you know . . . I mean a long time from now."

"No. The answer is still no. And besides, your notion of a long time is about three weeks. Pity is not the best you can hope for, sweetheart. When the girls who are teasing you now are more mature, they'll see that there are more important things than looks."

I might have believed it if anyone else had said it, but it sounded phony coming from someone who had the kind of looks she did.

"Will you promise I'll get married?"

"Sweetheart, I can't tell the future. I couldn't *promise* you a girlfriend even if you looked like a movie star. I can't make a promise like that to *anyone*."

"You can promise me I'll die, but you can't promise me a girlfriend or a wife."

"What has dying got to do with it? When did I ever promise that you'd die?"

"You don't have to. I know I will. You won't promise because you're afraid you'll break your promise."

"No. That's not it."

"Then promise."

"I don't know why you're doing this, Percy. It's not just the boys at school, is it? A promise is not a guarantee, you know. Not always."

"Well, maybe someday you could *help* me get a girlfriend. You could promise me you'll *try*. Not like you did with Francine Dunne."

"Percy, I don't know what to say. How would I go about trying? When or where would I start?"

"You figured out how to get Pops to pay the rent—"

"That's enough. *Stop*. All right, I'll do everything I can, when the time comes, but I'll have to think about it first. This is something that sooner or later you'll have to do for yourself, just like everybody else."

"I know. But I'm talking about *now*—"

"You said you weren't talking about now."

"Never mind, never mind, never *mind*," I yelled. I stomped to the door of my room. Before I went inside, I looked back at her. Her book was closed on her lap, her head leaned back against the sofa, her eyes closed, her cheeks puffed out. She exhaled audibly and shook her head ever so slightly.

A few days later, my mother, wearing her bathrobe, came into my room after I'd gone to bed. She stood by my upper bunk, her hands behind her back.

"I assume you've never seen a naked woman. A real one or a picture of one?"

I shook my head. My heart pounded. I thought she was about to undo the belt and let the robe fall to the floor.

"I'll bring you home a picture of one. You can keep it. Give her a name and promise her you'll never be inspired by anyone but her."

"A *picture* of one? Can't you just undo your robe and let me look? Just for a minute. I won't move. When I was a baby, I must have seen you stark naked all the time, but now I'm too *old*?"

"Jesus Christ. Yes, you're too old. You're my son. Stop trying to seduce me."

She wouldn't say where she found the glossy, colour, full-page picture she brought home. She left it on my pillow with a note paper-clipped to it: "Hold her tight and treat her right. Call her Tina. T-I-N-A—Stands for Tits 'n' Ass. Call her anything you like. Just don't call her Francine. She wasn't easy to get, so make her last."

I taped her to the wall beside my pillow in the upper bunk. The woman in the picture did indeed bare all—hence my decision not to call her Tina. Arms over her head, legs splayed, lying slightly on one side to show her bum, she had the kind of face that my mother said later was known as "bland blond," but it seemed anything but bland to me. Her vagina looked like something that had been revealed by expert surgery, pink layers and folds surrounded by more hair than I had ever imagined down there. I told my mother that I'd call her Vivian after a girl from the Mercy Convent I had long lusted after and longed for from afar. But I thought of her as Francine, Francine sublimated into this bland and naked, blond, grown woman.

I couldn't imagine that, where boys were concerned, girls might be generous, receptive, that there was a kind of game going on between boys and girls that wasn't all that easy to play and that, unless both sides did their part, would fail. I assumed that girls held on to everything they had—words, lips, sex—and that it was the boys' job to take those things away. I suppose that I was a little in love with Francine in spite of everything. I thought of how her legs looked, pink with cold, when, in the mornings, right in front of Heart, she pulled her slacks down from her tunic. I imagined us getting secretly engaged, then having to break it off because her parents disapproved of me. I imagined no great anguish, no heart-rending goodbyes, only silent suffering. I imagined saving her from gangs of boys like Moyles. I hurled myself in front of a car to knock her out of the way. And I imagined meetings, the two of us, sensitive loners, meeting, walking after dark behind St. Bon's, unaware of one another and then somehow colliding and falling together into snowdrifts, kissing, holding hands, each discovering that, after all, there was someone just like us. So there was *that* Francine.

But there were the two other Francines too, the real one who scorned me and the one on the wall. I never could quite reconcile the three of them. They were like the Holy Trinity of Francine, joined but separate, individual but seamlessly linked, co-equal and co-eternal. At first, I much preferred to look at "Francine's" face whenever I was, as my mother put it, "answering the call." But I moved on from there.

When Pops or Medina asked where I was, my mother said, "He's in his room, answering the call of Vivian." Sometimes, if I worked up the nerve, I would tell them later that I hadn't been answering the call of Vivian but had been reading a book. But mostly I skulked, shame-faced, about the house, feeling like what I supposed I was half the time, a kind of lust-driven robot programmed to jerk off in "secret."

"What if he tells someone at school that his own mother is supplying him with pornographic pictures?" Pops said.

"He won't. And no one would believe him anyway. They'd think that it was just another one of his stories."

"I think they would believe him. They think you're capable of anything. Now he'll be no better than all the other rabble on the Mount. A *teacher*, I call myself. For the past twenty years all I've done is oversee a non-stop pecker convention. The lives of these boys outside of school is one long, continuous *cunt* hunt. I'm sorry. I shouldn't have said—that word."

My mother reminded him that a pecker that fell into the wrong hands could do a lot of damage. Better I be so drained by the time I left the house that I wouldn't notice if the girls stampeded topless down the hill.

"He doesn't work on batteries," Pops said. He said I was plugged into a grid like the one that lit Manhattan. "He'll never run down," Pops said. "Mark my words. He'll just improve with practice."

We shopped for boots and shoes in the men's department of a store called Parker and Monroe where the clerks pretended not to notice that my feet were as purple as my face and larger than those of many of their grown-up customers. They—all men— blushed at the sight of me as we came into the store, blushed deeper still at the sight of my mother, their eyes darting back and forth between the two of us as they tried to shoehorn my feet into a pair of shoes that I would soon outgrow.

Once, when we left the store, my mother said, "Maybe you only think your face bothers other people. Maybe they see that it bothers you and that's why it bothers them."

"Everyone cares what everyone looks like," I said. "I care what you look like. I'm glad you're pretty. But don't tell me you're glad my feet are so big. Some people say I'm nice, like being nice makes up for all that. They pretend. But who are they pretending for? Not me. I bug people. They'd fix me if they could because I bug them, not because I bug me."

"Do you think that's entirely true?"

"You would if you were in my shoes."

"Boo hoo. Poor Percy."

"Nice try, Aphrodite."

I admit that it might be that my inner self has been altered by my outer one. It *might* be, as my mother suggested, that a life of looking as I did made me think and act the way I did. But there's no way of knowing if that's true.

Would I have fallen in love with my mother if I was normal-looking? Here's a better question: Would I have fallen in love with my mother if *she* was normal-looking? Maybe she was as much a product of her looks as I was of mine. We were both exceptional.

This might be just the kind of thinking that led to me looking as I do. It might be that the generations of people who regarded incest as I do are the reason that I regard incest as I do. It might be nothing more than too small a gene pool that—who knows how long ago—led to my inner/outer aberrations.

You may know by now that there's nowhere else for this to go but to the question of free will. Is there, was there, in the sum of me, even the smallest of undetermined fractions? I think . . . that it's too soon to say.

The seasons went round and returned as predictably as Halley's comet. Summer. Tick. Fall. Tock. Winter. Tick. Spring. Tock. But for me, they didn't seem to change. It was as if my mood altered so instantly with the weather that every season seemed to be the norm, the persisting, year-round season, the others lost to memory. It seemed, on hot days, that there was no season but summer, on cold and snowy ones that there was none but winter. It seemed the drowsy, dozing days of fall would never end and that spring was a herald of nothing but more damp days of spring. Time, which had previously seemed to race, now stood still, leaving me hopelessly at odds with everything.

THE PERCY JOYCE COMPLEX

ON a Friday night in late May, a month before I turned thirteen, my mother said she was going to rent a car and take us up Signal Hill for a picnic the next day.

"I assume I'm not invited?" Pops said.

"It's a family occasion," my mother replied.

She mixed bottles of orange Freshie, made bologna and butter and mustard sandwiches, wrapped some brownies and other cookies in waxed paper, and put it all in a cardboard box.

"You'll freeze to death up on that hill," Pops said. "They've made a National Park out of a place where criminals were hanged and there was a smallpox epidemic. I bet you'll have to eat inside the car. A typical Newfoundland indoor picnic."

"If we have to, we will," my mother said.

"Maybe you can build a fire. I can build a safe one for you. They may even have firepits—"

"No thanks, Pops."

She walked to the rental outlet the next day and came back in a car called a Rambler Ambassador that Pops said was the size and shape of a hearse. The car was light pastel blue with brown panelling on the sides, a roof rack, and large fin-shaped fenders on the back. She parked the car on the Brother Rice side of the road, directly across from the Block. Pops went out in his lab coat and walked around the car like an expert.

"Never mind a hearse, it's the size of a boat," he announced. "It should be christened with a bottle of champagne."

"I packed a bottle of red wine," my mother told Medina when she arrived.

"The problem with cars is the upkeep," Pops continued. "Repairs, gas, tires, insurance. On and on. It's not worth the bother. Better to leave the upkeep to someone else and take a bus."

"Buses don't go up Signal Hill."

"An excellent reason to go somewhere else for a picnic," Pops said. "Or you could take a taxi."

"Have you ever taken a taxi, Pops?" my mother asked.

"No," Pops said, "but if I ever have to, I will."

"And what phone would you use from Signal Hill to call a cab to take you home?"

"Just a suggestion. I thought the three of you might be able to walk downhill. I assume Medina's been invited."

"Yes, she has. She's family, remember? You can sulk till we get back."

"It was the only car they had left," my mother said to me, as we sat, uncertain, in the car a few moments later. "It's a goddamn stick shift."

I was in the front with her. I had only been in a car a few times in my life. Medina had never been in one and had told my mother she'd rather walk, even up Signal Hill, so she was going to meet us there. My mother said it was years since she'd driven a car. The Rambler roared but didn't move, then seemed to go dead but *did* move, lurched a few feet, stopped, lurched again, slowly jumping up Bonaventure.

"The hills are the hardest part," my mother said, looking at the dashboard as if at the console of an airplane. "As soon as I remember how to use the clutch, I'll be okay. I learned on Jim Joyce's bread van, but I don't think it's the same."

She seemed to get the knack of it on the hill between Brother Rice and Holy Heart. I had to grab on to the ashtray to keep from tipping over each time we turned.

I waved at pedestrians, who waved back when they were close enough to see who I was.

"You shouldn't wave at strangers," my mother said.

"Why?" I waved again, happily. Someone shouted my name. "Everyone knows me."

"Everyone thinks they do," my mother said. "And don't roll down the window—May 25 and it's still too cold."

My mother looked tiny, almost childlike, making the wheel seem comically oversized. I wasn't sure if she could see over it or was looking through it at the windshield.

"Cars behind us are blowing their horns."

"Too bad. The goddamned clutch is supposed to make some kind of shape, the shape of a letter of the alphabet I think, but I can't remember which one."

We drove haltingly up Bonaventure, past St. Bon's and St. Pat's, the two schools opposing each other in a kind of eternal stand-off that made me fancy one of them was Protestant. We went past the Basilica on our left, its vast parking lot empty but for a looming statue of the Blessed Virgin. My mother said she thought the steep slope of Garrison Hill was best avoided, so I didn't get to see if Sister Mary Aggie was back in her room, the luridly flashing Sacred Heart once again hanging in the window. Instead, we went left onto Military Road, followed it past what my mother said was the Colonial Building—it was fronted by a colonnade of concrete pillars—to Cavendish Square, where I got my first look at the Newfoundland Hotel, an old but elegant-looking brown brick structure in which, my mother said, some of the guests were permanent. We turned left onto the east end of Duckworth Street and, leaving the city proper, started up Signal Hill, where my mother once again had problems with the clutch, jerking it from side to side, forward and back, as if she were trying to wrench it free of the car altogether. The rear of the car bounced and there was a gunshot-like blast of exhaust, after which the car at last began to climb until it reached the edge of a billowing wall of fog that instantly blocked out the sun.

"Perse, I'm afraid this picnic won't be any picnic," my mother said.

Medina was standing against a rock by the side of the road, bundled up in winter clothes though my mother and I were dressed for the fall-like spring in heavy sweaters. It was especially windy on top of Signal Hill where the cliff overlooked the open sea on less foggy days—but even halfway up I felt the wind gust against the car. Medina was smoking a cigarette, puffing on it without removing it from her mouth, both hands in the pockets of her parka, the hood of which was partway down, as was the zipper. My mother waved to her and Medina smiled briefly, waved back, then looked away from us, away from the road. She looked as if she was trying to make it seem perfectly normal for a woman to be alone, with no car in sight, smoking a cigarette while leaning against a rock in thick fog halfway up Signal Hill, as if it was well-known as a place where people went on foot to reflect. One of her feet was raised, the sole of her boot against the rock, as if she were posing for a photograph.

My mother parked the car on the edge of the road and told me to roll down my window. "Get in," she shouted, but Medina shook her head.

"There's some shelter from the wind over there." Medina pointed back to a rise of rock.

"Wait," my mother called, but Medina was already walking away from us.

We spread a blanket on the ground and had to weigh it down with rocks at the corners to keep it from blowing away. The three of us knelt on the blanket because the ground was cold and damp. We sat back on our heels. Medina looked around.

"Nice place for a murder," she said.

We couldn't see the road, presumably couldn't be seen from the road. The fog was so thick it felt more like mist. Dew gathered in our hair and trickled down our faces like beads of sweat. I smelled the ocean and heard it rumble in and out through the caves of shale that I knew lay beneath us, channels that went deep inside the hill, which sounded hollow. We were able to see only about fifteen feet in any direction. It felt as though we were three actors on a stage, hemmed in by fake fog, about to speak our lines, unable to make out anything but each other, the set and the few props we'd been provided with.

We ate in silence and then my mother said, "We brought you here to tell you something, Percy."

"Something bad?"

"No. Something important, though."

Medina stood and, lighting a cigarette, resumed her one-legged pose against the lichen-covered wall of rock.

My mother took my hand in hers.

"I love Medina," she said.

"So do I," I said.

"I mean I'm *in* love with her," my mother said. I looked at Medina, who wiped a tear from one eye with the back of her hand. Her face was red, but not just from the cold. She looked away from us at the same spot as before.

"I know, I saw you in your bed," I said.

My mother dropped my hand. "What?"

"The night I found the Vat Rat stuck in the sump pump hole."

"Merciful God," Medina said. She turned sideways to face the road.

"What did you see?" my mother said, her face and neck now as red as Medina's.

"You and Medina in your bed. You were both on top of the blankets and making funny noises, especially Medina. The door was open a bit. I didn't push it open. I didn't even touch it." My eyes filled with tears that didn't quite spill out. "I never told anyone," I said, "I promise." My mother took me in her arms and kissed me on the head.

"Medina's crying," I said. I'd noticed her shoulders shaking.

"I know she's crying," my mother said. "And we thought we were the ones with the secret." She let me go and tried to smile. "We figured you'd guess what was up sooner or later. Or discover us by accident just the way you did. We know when Pops is down for the count—he never gets up again once he goes to bed. But you—no offence, Perse, but you're kind of unpredictable. So we thought it would be better if we told you and explained to you why you must never say a word to anyone, ever, about us, rather than leave it to chance. No offence again, and no pun intended, but you've got very loose lips. And besides, I think it's right that you should know. I don't like keeping secrets from you."

She said that, when she was pregnant, she told Jim Joyce about her love for Medina because she knew what he would do and she wanted him to do it. She wanted him to disappear. She wanted him gone. She knew he would never tell another soul because he'd be too ashamed to tell and too worried that no one would believe him but instead would think he was just spreading lies about a woman he didn't want to marry even though she was pregnant, or who wanted nothing more to do with him because he cheated on her or beat her up. What had he done, people would wonder, to make her reject him?

"I wanted a baby," my mother said. "I didn't want *him*. I wanted a baby very much. Don't look so surprised. Just because I prefer women to men doesn't mean I don't want to be a mother. And lucky for you, or else you wouldn't exist."

She had used him, used Jim Joyce. She knew that, she said, and wasn't proud of it. She might even have destroyed him, she didn't know. She was so young and so very much in love with someone else. A woman. Medina. She hadn't known what else to do. She hoped that, wherever he was, he had put the past behind him.

"You didn't have to get engaged to him," I objected. "You didn't have to tell him you like girls."

She said that if she hadn't done both, he wouldn't have run away. She partly got engaged to him, him in particular, so that she'd have a safe reason to spend time with Medina, her almost sister-in-law, if he didn't leave St. John's. She didn't want him having anything to do with the three of us, her, me and Medina. He'd have known I was his son—he wasn't the smartest person in the world, but he could count and he knew, or at least was as certain as any man could be, that she'd been with no one else. But she couldn't have him interfering in our lives. Imagine, she said, looking beseechingly at me, how things would be now for Medina if Jim Joyce were still around: she'd have to spend time with him or conspicuously go out of her way to avoid him.

So my mother did one thing more than ask him to marry her and then tell him she liked girls: she told him which girl she liked. She and Medina planned it together, told him together. It was very hard for both of them—nowhere near as hard as it was for Jim Joyce probably, but hard. And terrifying—he was the only person they'd ever told, and they couldn't help imagining what was in store for them if Jim Joyce acted out of character and did his best to convince others that they were what they told him they were, two women in love, one of them his sister, one his fiancée. They'd wind up in the Mental for longer than Sister Mary Aggie had ever been confined, perhaps for ever, or they'd be arrested and sent to some special prison on the Mainland where women like them were sent to be "cured" by means that were not very pleasant—and I would have had no one to care for me but Jim Joyce, from whom I would almost certainly have been taken because of my "specialness" and put in some home unless he beat the authorities to it and, before fleeing the province, left me on the doorstep of people whose job it was to be the custodians of ill-fated children.

"But you tricked him. That's why he went away. You *made* him go away. You made him feel so bad he went away. But you've always *blamed* him for going away."

"I've just been keeping up a false front. People expect me to be bitter and to blame him for leaving me, pregnant and engaged. So I do."

"I bet he still feels bad."

"Maybe."

"He might have told on you."

"Yes. No. I don't know. No one would have believed him. He knocked me up, after all. He wasn't in love with me and he wasn't close with Medina. His own *sister* doesn't miss him. I doubt that he misses her."

"Maybe he misses me."

"If he misses anyone, he misses you."

"He wouldn't if he ever met me. If he ever saw me."

I started crying, not bothering to hide or wipe away the tears that streamed down my cheeks. "I bet he isn't very happy now. I bet he hates you and Medina. And he'd hate me too."

"People have moved on from far worse."

"You don't feel sorry for what you did, do you?" I clambered to my ungainly feet and turned my back to her.

She said she did feel sorry but she'd lose no sleep if she had to do it again. If you couldn't control certain circumstances, you had to find a way to deal with them. If people knew about Medina and her, we'd have no friends, no allies, and I'd certainly have no one looking out for me, let alone someone on a par with Uncle Paddy. Everyone would be against us. She wanted a child and knew of only one way of having one that she and Medina could bear to live with. And even so, she was taking a big risk with the lives of all four of us, five if you included Pops.

I turned in time to see Medina, eyes red and swollen, walking back to the blanket, a fresh cigarette between her fingers. Medina knelt and sat on her heels beside my mother. I wiped my own eyes but stayed put. I asked my mother if she liked doing it with Pops and she asked me if I thought *I* would like to do it with Pops. I asked Medina if she would do it with a man if she had to and she said that a man would only do it with *her* if he had to. She said that, where men were concerned, she was still a virgin.

"Girls who do it with girls are lizzies," I shouted at them. I'd known for years, but it felt, now that they were confiding in me, as if I had just discovered that my mother and my aunt were lizzies. "Lizzies are crazy. The Mental is full of Crazy Lizzies."

"I'm sure they could find room for two more. Officially, the powers that be may have just decided lizzies aren't criminals anymore but it's not the long arm of the law we have to worry about, it's the long arm of Uncle Paddy—at a word from him, we could *all* be locked up in one place or another. Anyway, people would find a way to get us into the Mental—things don't just change overnight because of some law that almost everyone in this city and this country disapproves of. So please, please keep this to yourself," my mother said. "We decided we could trust you. You're almost thirteen. We thought you should know the truth. We love you."

"I won't tell on you. Who'd believe a fucking retard like Percy Joyce?"

"*Perse*," my mother cried. Medina stood up and started toward me, arms outstretched. I backed up and she stopped.

"Maybe I'll just run off like your *brother* did," I taunted her. "You made your own *brother* run away. You were jealous of your own *brother*. You still are." I turned my back on them, stumbling to the nearest rock and sat down, staring away into the fog as if I wanted to be left there, wanted my mother and Medina to go home and forget they'd ever heard of me.

"Get used to it, Perse," my mother said, gently raising her voice. "I like girls. Men just don't float my boat. No offence. They don't float my boat, or turn my crank, and they're not my cup of tea."

Now, bawling from sheer spite, I cried at her that I bet that, if she'd liked boys, if Jim Joyce had floated her boat, I might have been a normal baby, because women who didn't like men had babies who were all fucked up.

She said she knew of other girl-loving women whose babies were not fucked up, not that she thought of me as being fucked up.

"I had boyfriends, Perse. Before Jim Joyce. They did it *to* me, but they didn't do it *for* me, that's all. I thought that would change when I got older. I'm not sorry it didn't. And I'm not going to apologize to you for being what you call a Crazy Lizzie. I lost a whole fleet of boats before I found out what was sinking them."

"That's a pretty picture," Medina muttered.

. I began to feel foolish staring off into the fog. I went back to the blanket and sat down. "Some night," I said, my voice barely above a whisper, "Pops is going to catch you. You *think* he won't, but he will."

"We're careful. I phone Medina after Pops has gone to bed. Then Medina comes over. Late. About once a week. Sometimes she's at our house, she goes home, I call her, she comes back, and later she goes home again."

"The things we do for love," Medina said. "Not to mention the things we do for the mortgage."

"The mortgage is why I do it," my mother said. "And just once a month. I always go to his room. He's never been in my bed. We don't kiss on the lips."

"Every night that you don't call, I think about it." Medina smiled at her. "And I sit by the phone every night, even when you've told me you won't be calling, just in case you do. I fall asleep by it. And when you do call, I have to go down the garbage lane and sneak in by the back, and later sneak back home again. All you have to do is use the phone."

"It's not ideal for either one of us," my mother said.

"What would Pops do if he caught you?" I said.

"Jesus." Medina put her head in her hands and shook it back and forth.

"Pops is Pops, thank God. Just remember that if we're caught by *anyone*, they'll take you away from me. For good. So keep your mouth shut, Perse. No tall tales at school. I don't want to hear that you suddenly claimed to be well versed in the ways of Crazy Lizzies. We'll all be fine, we'll all stay together, as long as we keep this a secret. A solemn secret. I wasn't sure about telling you because nothing is more important than this. Perse, you have to be as careful as Medina and me. Understand?"

I nodded.

Medina resumed her station against the rock, one foot flat against it as she smoked a cigarette of which little remained but the glowing filter. I watched her throw it aside emphatically as if thereby to rid herself of all the thoughts that were running through her mind. She turned back to us.

"The two of you would be just fine if not for me," Medina said. "A mother and her son. If I stay, it will always be the way it is. Lies and secrets and sneaking around, wondering when we'll be caught, how much time we still have left. It would be better for you two with me out of the picture. Maybe Percy's right. What if Pops *had* heard me making funny noises? What if he had looked into the room? I remember how upset you said Percy was that night. I didn't see him, I was too busy clearing out of the house like a thief who'd been caught in the act. Percy could just as easily have gone to Pops' room instead of to the basement."

Medina came over to me, stood me up and took me in her arms, resting her cheek on my head. "Completely out of the picture is where I need to be," she said. "But what would be the point of me if not for you and Perse, Pen? I don't even have the nerve to ride in a car. You'd get by no matter what. Not me."

My mother quickly stood, pried me apart from Medina, took her face between her hands and firmly kissed her on the lips. She just as quickly moved away and glanced back at the road.

"You see?" Medina said. "You never know who might be watching, even up here."

"Don't ever speak again about completely removing yourself," my mother said. "It would destroy me. And Perse. We've had our talk with Perse, so let's go home."

The fog cleared for an instant, and we stood silently, looking down to the harbour far below. My mother and I picked up the remains of the picnic and packed them in the cardboard box.

"Why do you love me, Pen?" Medina demanded.

"Oh Jesus, Medina, don't start up with that again. Why do you love me?"

"I think maybe I'm the only lizzie you've ever met. I think maybe if you met one who could read and write and was smart and looked even half as good as you, you'd say so long to Medina."

"You know that's not true. It's a hurtful thing to say."

Medina angrily tossed aside her cigarette. "You don't know what it's like. Who would want to steal *me* away from *you*? Who would want to steal me away from anyone?"

"Beggars can't be choosers? That's what you're saying. I didn't settle for you. Jesus, Medina."

"Well, I'm sorry. I'm just saying it's not easy—"

"—having what you think you don't deserve and what everybody else not only wants but thinks is available?"

"See? You put me into words better than I do. But why do you need me?"

"I need you because you're you, period. I love you. I love what I see when I look at you. I don't have to count the ways. I don't have to put it into words."

Medina turned back to look at her. My mother smiled at her. "I'll start down the hill after you're gone," Medina said.

My mother took my hand and we walked to the car. She put the cardboard box in the back seat again, and after a great deal of effort she managed to turn the Rambler around, spinning the steering wheel as fast as she could.

As we began down the hill, with our headlights cutting a thin path through the fog, I knelt backward in my seat to watch Medina. She was posed exactly as she had been when we arrived, leaning against the rock. But she was watching us this time. I waved to her and she waved back. I turned to see my mother wave to her in the rear-view mirror, then blow her a kiss. I turned again and saw Medina blow back her kiss, then put her cigarette in her mouth, both hands in her parka, the sole of one foot lifted against the rock. She receded into the distance, faded into the fog as the car took us back down into the sunlight of St. John's. "She should have come with us," I said.

"She'll be all right. She's used to walking by herself. God knows what we've done to your mind, Percy," she said as she struggled with the clutch. She tried to explain the Oedipus and Electra complexes to me. "For you, it must be like having a head-on collision of complexes." I had witnessed, she said, a version of what Freud called "the primal scene." Not my mother and father, but my mother and my father's sister, having sex. So she modified the Freudian complexes to fit my circumstances and hers: I subconsciously wanted to murder my father for abandoning me, my father's sister for sleeping with my mother, Pops for sleeping with my mother, my mother for sleeping with everyone, my father included, every male on the Mount for wanting to sleep with my mother, every female on the Mount for pretending not to want to sleep with her. According to the new Percy Joyce complex, she said, a boy's early childhood instills in him a desire to kill everyone he ever meets. "But I suppose it only works that way if the boy's mother is Penny Joyce. Christ, I'm such a slut." Smiling wryly, she added, "But feel free to contradict me. I contradicted you when you said I was a whore and a hag."

"Once a month with Pops?" I said. "The same day every month?"

"Yes," she said, "Pops' time of the month. I go to his room. For a little while. Late. But don't even bother asking me which day. And promise me you'll never listen at his door."

"I never listened at your door," I said. "You left the door open."

"Promise," she said.

"I promise. You and Medina—I bet it's more than once a week."

"That's none of your business. If you try to catch us, you'll wind up staying awake all night every night. We're very discreet."

"I already caught you once."

"Jesus, 44 is not your average Bonaventure house, is it, Perse?"

"No."

"I doubt it would qualify as an average house anywhere in the world. So, are you all right? Never mind the complexes—that was just for fun."

"I'm all right." I said it with as much conviction as I could muster, which was a great deal more than I felt. I had long known that Crazy Lizzies could wind up in the Mental, but the furtive manner of my mother and Medina's admission, the fog they had conjured up, it almost seemed to me for the occasion, had made that fate seem real at last. I could lose them both. They could lose each other. Where would I end up? What would be my version of the Mental, what sort of institution would a boy as disfigured as I was, a boy whose mother and aunt had humiliated Uncle Paddy, end up in?

There followed nights when they put on the record player after Pops had gone to bed. Taking off their shoes, they slow-danced to Patsy Cline, Jim Reeves and Kitty Wells. "I'm crazy for lovin' you," Patsy Cline sang as my mother and Medina made their way around the living room floor, Medina leaning her head on my mother's shoulder, my mother smiling at me as I watched, sometimes beckoning to me to join them, which I did, the three of us in a huddle, my arms around their waists, my face pressed sideways against my mother's breast. "Your mother's a good dancer," Medina said dreamily, her eyes closed as Patsy sang about walking after midnight, in the moonlight. I knew why, on such nights, I was allowed to stay up so late, knew that it was in case Pops, for whatever unlikely reason, emerged from his room. If he did, there I'd be, making the sight of my mother and Medina, and sometimes me, dancing seem fun, harmless, innocent, two tipsy women dancing with each other and a boy for lack of a man to dance with. They turned off the lights, but they left the TV on, the volume turned down low but the screen conspicuously flickering, visible to anyone who might be watching from the street, walking or driving past 44. Medina would slide her hands up and down my mother's back, sometimes lower, and I'd watch my mother hastily grab them away and whisper something urgent in her ear, after which Medina's hands climbed back to where they'd been, one on my mother's shoulder, one in her shoulder-high hand; my mother always led, one hand on Medina's hip.

It's strange to think of your mother in bed with anyone, especially when you know your father hasn't been to bed with her—or even seen her—in years. But it's especially strange when you know that, just rooms away from yours, she sleeps with a man once a month and with a woman once a week—with the man for money, though the man in question convinces himself it might one day be for love, and with the woman for love that puts them in jeopardy of losing everything they have. How, being in love with a woman, could my mother stand to do it with a man? How could the man who knew the price that he was paying not sense or guess what *her* price was? It is also strange when you are a boy who has never really touched a girl except by accident, to know that on any given

night such things might be going on behind the closed door of
your mother's room.

"Mom, will you sleep in the bottom bunk tonight?" I asked my
mother. She shot me a dubious look as if to say she had guessed my
ulterior motive. "You in your bunk, me in mine, that's all."

"I might snore. And I'll definitely smoke a cigarette whenever I
wake up. And I wake up a lot."

"So do I."

"Okay. But just for tonight. And I'm not staying if you start in
about pity fucks again. I'm not going to wake up to find you in bed
with me, am I?" I told her no and sighed as if I couldn't believe she
thought I was still obsessed with *that*. By having her sleep in my
room, I could at least make sure that, on certain nights, she didn't
go to bed with Pops or Medina.

When she came into my room that first night, she was wearing
her bathrobe over her pyjamas as she sometimes did on cool nights
after she had had a bath. My mother's wool-woven bathrobe was a
modest heirloom of her mother's. It was jet black, an almost perfect match with her hair, as were her eyes the perfect complement
of her dark complexion. If not for the pyjamas, I would have seen
the parts of her not hidden when she wore nothing but the robe—
her long, thin neck, the first knob of her breastbone, her wrists,
her beautiful brown feet which she so rarely displayed around the
house. She undid the belt of the robe, shrugged off the robe with
a single flex of her shoulders. The pyjamas were light blue and
covered every inch of her from the neck down.

She climbed into the lower bunk, the bedsprings squeaking.
"Jesus, Perse, I can't stretch out full length."

"Lie on your side," I said. My bunk shook every time she moved.
Until she lit up for the first time, I could smell her perfume. It
mixed with the smoke already in her pyjamas and her hair.

"Some people were made for sleep," she murmured. "And some people were made for keeping one eye open all the time."

"One eye?"

"It's just an expression. It means you're never less than half awake, never more than half asleep. Just in case."

"Of what?"

"Sabre-tooth tigers. Other night owls who might steal your food. Or worse."

"Evolution."

"That's right. The survival of the lightest sleepers."

"What kind of fuck is Pops?"

"*Perse.*"

"I just mean what is it called. It's not a pity fuck."

"Desperation."

"A desperation fuck?"

"Remuneration. Maybe. Jesus, I don't know."

"If you did it with me—"

"My only child, my only son, is trying to seduce me. It would be a felony fuck! I told you, don't start."

"If no one knew, what would it be called?"

"A deep, dark secret. Very deep and very dark."

I leaned out over my bunk to see if I could make her out. She lit up another cigarette. I briefly saw her face flash in the dark. She briefly saw mine.

"What if you knew my face was your fault?"

"That's it," she said. "You're on your own." I heard the bunk loudly squeak again as she climbed out. "Your face is not my fault." She sounded as if she was crying as she stormed out of the room. She slammed the door behind her.

For nights on end, I listened at the door of my bedroom, trying to hear other doors opening and closing. Pops' door, my mother's door. The back door and then my mother's. My mother tiptoeing to Pops' room then back to hers. My mother and Medina tiptoeing from the back porch to my mother's room. I was certain my mother would have an excuse ready if Pops opened his door and saw them in the hallway. But no excuse would do if he saw them as I had. I told my mother that I could stay up and keep lookout for Pops the nights that Medina came by for a second visit, but she said, "Nice try," and added that the when-and-what of her and Medina and her and Pops was none of my business. "That's all I need, knowing that you're in the living room, one door away, ears open for every sound, waiting for Medina to come out and go home. Can you imagine how embarrassed she'd be if she had to pass by you each time? Or how embarrassed I'd be? You stay put in your room and don't leave it except to use the bathroom." Some nights I heard my mother dial what I had no doubt was Medina's number and later heard the door open for her. But I knew that I wouldn't have heard it if I hadn't been trying to, or if I was drunk like Pops. Once or twice, I thought I heard my mother go to Pops' room, but I wasn't sure. Always too sleepy to listen for the end of the visits, I'd fall asleep.

Ours *was* a strange household, as my mother had said on Signal Hill. My mother spent some nights with her male boarder, wishing she wasn't in his bed, some nights with her sister-in-law, most nights alone but, I felt certain, wishing that she wasn't. She knew everything. I knew almost everything. Pops thought I knew nothing. I knew some things Pops didn't know. Medina may have thought I knew something about Pops' "turn" with my mother that I didn't know. Some of the things that went on behind Pops' door, the things my mother did with Pops, I didn't want to witness, but I dearly wanted to witness whatever she and Medina did, partly because I was mostly ignorant of what women did and nothing my imagination came up with seemed commensurate with even the little I'd seen and heard, and partly because I wanted to see my mother's face as contorted with pleasure as Medina's had been, my mother helpless, abject, all guards down, reliant on someone else's hand to give her some inscrutable release.

It seemed that the "I know something you don't know" games made up the subtext of every evening. And after lights out, it was even stranger. I didn't know who was in which room, or if Medina was even in the house. The only whereabouts I was certain of were my own, but I knew that, under whatever circumstances they spent the night, my mother and Medina wondered what I was up to.

From now on, my mother said, there were things we could talk about only in our house and only when Pops was either absent from it or drunk and asleep behind the closed door of his room. In the latter case we spoke in a kind of code, for we were never, could never be, in spite of what my mother said, *absolutely* certain that Pops wouldn't rouse himself from his beer-induced sleep to rejoin us in the living room. Even when he wasn't in the house, we used only a less rigid version of the same code, for a kind of discretion was necessary lest we fall into the habit of speaking openly of anything and thereby be the least bit more inclined to drop our guard when others were around. My mother said we must agree not to exchange knowing looks or to laugh as though at inside jokes or adopt facial expressions that might be the first of a series of steps that led to self-betrayal. Our house was the Trojan Horse, she said. We—except for Pops—were the Greeks, living secretly among the enemy, staying silent until—well, in our case, until the end of never. "Remember, sweetheart," my mother said, "you can't even hint to other people. You can't talk about us out loud to yourself because you might be overheard."

"I don't talk to myself," I replied defensively.

"Then you must be the only person in this world that you don't talk to. Anyway, don't start. When you and I and Medina go to some place like Marty's restaurant, act as if everyone you know, Pops included, can hear our every word."

So 44, in the rare absences of Pops, was the one place my mother and Medina could speak even close to openly, and now they included me. In the living room, behind the locked door of my mother's room or mine, we could at least relax the code if Pops had gone to bed. The house at 44 Bonaventure was our sanctuary. It was almost as if we spoke a language there that elsewhere was forbidden, illicit, a language not wholly understood by others but known to be the language of deviance, the keeping of shameful secrets, the breaking of universally accepted codes of conduct, the commission of crimes and sins against all who were not one of us.

"It's like being a member of the resistance in an occupied country," my mother said. "We can't trust anyone we haven't always trusted. We never know—and neither do they—who might be one of *them*." We were the not-them who "they" feared would somehow subvert who they were and spread through their ranks the ever-possible contagion of insurrection. They might catch what we had.

"If I had friends, *real* friends, would I be allowed to tell them?"

"*No.*"

"If I had a best friend?"

"No."

"A girlfriend?"

"No."

"If I got engaged—"

"You wouldn't be engaged very long if you told your fiancée about your mother and your aunt. The way things stand now, or are ever likely to stand, you have to keep this secret from everyone."

"If I was married—"

"You couldn't tell your wife and children. Listen, Perse, the problem is that you can't know how a person will react to the truth until you tell them the truth."

"Then it's just as well I'm so ugly no one will ever marry me."

"It's not just as well because you're not ugly."

"Don't talk about my 'specialness' like that guidance counsellor did."

Medina, walking in at that moment, laughed.

"You're different," she said.

"From everyone!"

"Well, you wouldn't want to be the same as everyone else, would you?"

"All people are different." My mother pulled me to her, hugging me. "But some are more different than others, that's all. Medina and I are different from most other people."

"Would you trade places with me if you could?"

"You have no reason to want to change places with anyone."

I felt like saying, but didn't, that I wished I could trade places with Medina so it could be me who was in bed with Penny Joyce, and Medina who had to make do with nothing but the picture of a woman on the wall and two pictures of the voyeuristic Patron Saint of Unattractive People flanking a pointless prayer for my salvation.

ST. JOHN'S DAY, JUNE 24

I F I come across, sometimes or always, as a one-trick pony—
lust, lust and again lust—if I seem insensitive to the needs and
feelings of others, I can only say that it's not as if I thought
everyone's lot in life was better than mine and that therefore other
people needed no support or sympathy from me. But I didn't
think that "we" were all in the same boat, either, just because "we"
had mortality and other awful inevitabilities in common. I was
my boat's sole occupant most of the time, surrounded by heavily
manned ships whose guns were ever aimed at the SS *Percy*. That
kind of attention keeps you busy and vigilant.

I saw such things as disappointment, heartache and loneliness
all around me. I also saw that no one wanted to seem so desperate as to need consolation from Percy Joyce, as to have no one but
Percy Joyce to lend them a sympathetic ear. You may be thinking: "I
bet there were some people, special, strong-minded, self-possessed,
who would have liked to be his friend, who admired his intelligence,

his sense of humour, his perseverance, his imagination, his courage; boys and girls, perhaps, who made overtures of friendship, who openly approached him, only to be rebuffed by a boy too full of self-pity, too self-absorbed, too lust-preoccupied to accept an outheld hand." Well, I believe such people exist in great numbers in books and movies for the simple reason that they don't exist anywhere else.

I encountered no one who looked as though they were trying to put themselves in my freakishly oversized shoes, no one who looked as if they had lain awake grappling with their bedsheets as they tortured over the question of what being me must be like or how best to solve the conundrum of mercy and compassion that was daily posed to them by the sight of me. No, what others felt at the sight of me was relief—and I don't blame them. Relief that, no matter how bad things got for them, they would never be as bad as they were for me. That, I've no doubt they were told by priests and parents, was my purpose in God's plan, to be a chastening reminder to them that things could have been worse. Of course, not all of them were right—witness the girl who left Holy Heart after a diagnosis of incurable leukemia. I've no doubt that, in adulthood, many of them realized they'd been wrong. Car accident injuries, the deaths of children and spouses, alcoholism, debt, mental illness—all these and many more were on offer in the same world as the one lived in by Percy Joyce.

But what beggar was ever gladdened at being stepped over by a nattily attired millionaire? Has word that the net worth of a billionaire has doubled ever set off a celebration in a flophouse? In this, if in nothing else, I was like you. I didn't want to be *that* guy. I hated being *that* guy for other people who thanked God they hadn't drawn a straw as short as mine. Would I have thought this way if I was normal-looking? Whom have you ever met who didn't think they were somehow insufficient?

For the first time, I went for a birthday walk after dinner by myself. School was newly out, which emboldened children to tease me.

"Percy's mitts match Penny's tits / His hands are like two frying pans."
I would walk quickly past my tormentors, seeming lost in thought.

My face, at thirteen, looked as if it had been hacked from the
red granite of Signal Hill, like the rust-encrusted hulls of ships
moored bows to sterns in the harbour, like the blood sausage in the
butcher shop. It looked like the red brick of the Anglican cathedral in the rain. It looked like everyone's face does when coming
in from the bitter cold, like the pyramids of five-point apples in
the supermarket, like fillets of salmon laid out for inspection on
crushed ice, like the lobsters that clinked their claws against their
tanks while curious, pitiless people pressed their faces to the glass.

Earlier in the year, one of the Brothers had brought to my attention a quotation from Samuel Johnson, no doubt thinking I should
have been finding solace in books, poetry, novels: "The only end of
writing is to enable readers better to enjoy life or better to endure
it." I had no doubt which camp he thought I belonged to, but I
didn't think my life was such that I had to settle for enduring it.
I liked books, but didn't see them as alternatives to life or as rem-
edies for the terms of my existence. I didn't believe the inspiring
stories my mother had read to me when I was younger. I doubted
that even Mary Shelley would have given me the time of day any
more than she would have given it to Dr. Frankenstein's creation
had she encountered him for real while palling around with my
namesake. Or that Beauty gave a flying fuck about the Beast. A
woman as beautiful as Esmerelda wouldn't have imperilled her life
by publicly giving the hunchbacked Quasimodo a drink of water
as he lay chained astride a millstone in the searing sun of Paris. I
knew that big-conked Cyrano would not have gotten close enough
to Roxanne to make himself heard to her, let alone perish in her
arms as she told him she loved him.

I walked far afield from 44 Bonaventure. Downtown, the row
houses reminded me of trains whose every double-decker car was
painted differently; the people, arms folded, who gazed out of

the open windows might have been the passengers except it was me who moved past them and they who stayed in place. They waved, nodded their heads, winked in acknowledgement not so much of me as of the collegial feeling of evening, the dying down of the wind, the abatement of traffic and skylarking children, the slow-rolling fog that, when the air cooled after sunset, came in through the Narrows from the sea. The evening-out of all things, all people, as time moved once more into night as inexorably for others as for me, a reassuring reminder to me of an ultimate commonality that was otherwise all too easy to ignore. I remembered the winter look of the city, the frozen froth on the rock face of the Brow, green because it was pickled by the sea salt in the air. The torrents of blowing snow in the gaps between the trees on the ridges of the hills before a storm. I watched the dark lop on Quidi Vidi Lake, each wave's "skin" faintly wrinkled by the wind. Seagulls screeching and diving and gliding on the gale, hovering above the waves, staying in one spot like low-flying, soon-to-crash kites just for the fun of it, just because they knew they were being watched by the landbound likes of me. At such moments I felt I had as much right to be there—and to be as I was—as everything else. The birds took me to be no more or less of an intrusion than they would any human.

I encountered the *Telegram* boys, delivery boys who, late each afternoon, fanned out across the city, referred to as "boys" though every one of them was a grown man and some of them looked as if they were in their sixties. Shabbily dressed at best, they lugged around their beige canvas bags that barely legibly read *The Telegram*, the straps slung tightly like the sashes of uniforms across their chests, their hands blackened and their faces smudged by the fresh, still-warm newsprint. They earned one cent per delivery; all wore the same fierce-faced, cold-besieged expression of those who, though they worked outdoors, had never grown accustomed to the weather. These boy-men cocked their heads and grinned ironically at me as if our lots in life were much the same, and had been apportioned to us by that same not-to-be-trusted-respected-or-defied "crowd," the nebulous never-seen few who ran the world. There was something wrong, physically or mentally, with almost all of them—they walked with a limp, were toothless, illiterate, had a speech impediment, were missing a hand, had the IQ of a child half my age, were runty, squat or in some minor way mal-formed—as if they had been culled from the freaks and misfits of the city. There was an army of them, whose ranks, if not for my family, I might have had no choice but to join. Yet there were times when I wished I could have joined them.

Once, sitting at a sidewalk picnic table, I was startled by my reflec-tion in a store window. It was not my stain that startled me so much as my slobbering lower lip. I looked as if I had caught myself in the act of nodding off, my head leaned sideways on one large hand like some animal pondering a sight it had never seen before. I quickly removed and hid my hand, straightened up, and looked away so there was nothing in my line of sight but the normal-seeming world.

Did I have greater and more oddly focused carnal appetites than other boys my age? Perhaps. Perhaps not. I did wonder what hold-ing hands with a girl, what kissing one would be like, how it would be if there were no impediments between us but simple shyness, awkwardness, nervousness born of nothing more than inexperi-ence. I could, I did, imagine not just physical normalcy but nor-malcy of personality and character, but I could not, by doing so, simply become a normal boy who was incidentally—who just hap-pened by the by—to be misshapen, for I could not be other than what growing up that way had made me. It made no sense to me to wonder how I would have turned out if I had not been so differ-ent. I could not will my heart into bleeding like a saint's for other people. Merely to survive tasked me to the limits of my soul.

I was, to the people of my city, as my city was to the rest of the world—except that, for the most part, my city was oblivious to the rest of the world, not out of ignorance but out of simple disdain. Had the people of St. John's known how they were regarded by outsiders, they wouldn't have cared much. But I didn't have the luxury of disdaining all opinions of me but my own. I was not a city of seventy thousand people, not a community of individuals who could bolster each other's self-esteem by regarding, or pretending to regard, St. John's as either the only or the only worthwhile place on earth. Medina had done it, but only by the grace of another's love for her, the fierce, unqualified, unassailable love of a fellow soul. I wasn't, yet, loved like that, and I had reason to doubt I ever would be. But what if you are so singular, so alone, as to be your own "audience"? You can't get more regional than that. Yeats, the Irish poet my mother sometimes declaimed aloud when typing Uncle Paddy's letters, said that to maintain faith in yourself in the face of corrupt but universal opposition, to believe yourself to be the sole keeper of the truth, was "of all things known . . . most difficult." And so it seemed to me.

THE SLAP HEARD
ROUND THE MOUNT

THIRTEEN. I wondered if the year would be lucky or unlucky for me. My eighth September of school. A boy I'd never seen before but who looked as if he might be one of the Coffin family came out of the gauntlet on the Curve of Bonaventure, left the anonymity of the other students and stood in front of me, blocking my way. He was coming up the hill, but he was taller, so we looked each other in the eye. He wore a maroon Brother Rice blazer. His eyes were as hate filled as if he bore me some lifelong grudge.

"Your mother is a slut," he said. "She does it with the Brothers in the Brothers' Quarters. All she has to do is go across the street to Brother Rice. A hundred Brothers, a hundred bucks. A-Fuck-a-Buck Penelope, that's what the Brothers call her. She even does it with McHugh."

I mashed my still-warm lemon pie into his face, then ran as close to full out as my flipper feet would allow—though, as I discovered near the Block, no one was chasing me. On the hill, the gauntlet had dispersed. I never saw the boy again.

One day about a week later, just seconds after I left Collins' store with my mother's Rothmans in the pockets of my jacket and an ice cream sandwich partially unwrapped in one hand, a man wearing a khaki shirt and black overalls fell into step with me. I looked up at him and smiled back when he smiled. He was young but had a stubble of a beard and black hair that was slicked back from his forehead. A cigarette was tucked between his ear and his head.

"You're Percy Joyce," he said. He was red-faced, as if he was angry or had been drinking. I nodded.

"I'm Buddy Coffin. Stevie Coffin's brother. Did you know McHugh gave him fifty straps because of you? Broke two of his fingers. Hit him in the face. He said Stevie hit him first. Stevie came home bleeding all over the place and said he was expelled."

"What do you mean, 'because of me'?" I said.

Buddy knocked the ice cream sandwich from my hand. "You told on him. You said he called you names and you went bawling to McHugh."

"No I didn't. I don't even know Stevie Coffin."

Suddenly, boys and girls wearing the colours of all the schools on the Mount seemed to appear from out of nowhere, surrounding us, following us, saying nothing. I tried to run, but Buddy grabbed me by the collar of my blazer, turned me around to face him and punched me in the nose. I fell back onto the ground, put my hand to my face. When I took it away, my fingers were smeared with blood. I heard boys shouting his name and mine. Some exhorted him to hit me again, others to leave me alone. A loud cheer went up. I found I was on my feet, holding with both hands to a pack of Rothmans that Buddy was trying to take from me. The package ripped. I had the lower half, shreds of tobacco and broken cigarettes. I was on the ground again, felt a kick in my stomach, I wanted to retch but couldn't breathe. "Little fucker," someone said.

The boys and girls shouted and screamed. Buddy's face was very close to mine. "Now you knows what will happen if you tells on anyone again," he said. Then: "Now go the fuck home. All of ye, go the fuck home."

Two girls, one on each side, held me up, helped me walk down Bonaventure. I tried to say "thanks" but my mouth was so full of blood and so sore I couldn't make a sound. They sat me on the Block and ran away. My mother and Pops came out. The next thing I knew, I was in a chair in the front room, my head tipped back, my mother holding over my nose a towel filled with ice cubes. My head stopped buzzing. I was still holding the half pack of Rothmans, the shredded cigarettes. I patted my jacket pockets. They were empty. My St. Bon's crest hung by a few threads from the pocket of my blazer. My slacks were torn at the knees and smeared with mud.

"If he doesn't say something soon, he's going to the hospital," my mother said.

"No," I protested. "I don't want to go to hospital." I put my hand on my stomach where Buddy had kicked me and felt a bruise that had swollen to the size of an apple. I wasn't sure what else he'd done. It felt as if it was mainly my stomach and my nose. And my left upper arm, though I had no idea why it hurt so much.

"I'm all right," I said.

"His nose is not broken," I heard Pops say. "I've seen plenty of broken noses, Paynelope."

"Shut up," she said, and took the towel of ice away and put her arms around my neck. She began to cry. I breathed out and blood bubbled from my nose.

I heard voices in the kitchen when I woke up on my bunk. The room was not quite dark. The door was partially open. I raised a hand to my face, which had a soft bandage on it, placed there by the doctor who had come and gone. It didn't hurt. My stomach didn't either, but I felt dizzy. Later, I woke again and heard voices in the kitchen. I went down and through the half-open door saw my mother standing over Pops, who was sitting at the kitchen table, somewhere he rarely sat. Medina was watching, leaning back against the sink.

"So do you know why McHugh beat up the younger Coffin brother?" my mother was demanding.

"I heard the boy made some filthy remarks about you. *Especially* filthy ones."

"Every boy on Bonaventure makes remarks about me."

"Not like these."

"Who would have repeated them to *you*? McHugh?"

"It wasn't McHugh."

"It must have been *some* grown-up. No student would have—they'd be too embarrassed. And too afraid they'd wind up like Percy. Some grown-up must have told you. Who was it, Pops? Whoever it was probably told McHugh—"

"It doesn't matter who it was."

"It does to me. If McHugh had never heard about what the boy said, he'd never have strapped him and this would never have happened to Percy. I'll call around the neighbourhood—"

"Don't," Pops said.

"Then tell me who told you."

"No one told me. I overheard the boy talking to Percy, I'm the one who told McHugh. If you knew what that boy said—"

"I don't give a damn about what some *boy* says about me." She furiously tapped the side of her head with her forefinger. "You are so stupid, Pops! Stupid."

"He's so banged up you can hardly see his stains." Medina sounded equally mad. "You should teach Buddy Coffin a lesson, Pops."

"In what?" my mother said. "Chemistry?"

"I really think you should stick up for Percy, Pops," Medina went on relentlessly. "You owe it to him. You should put the fear of

God into Buddy Coffin, and his father too. I can show you where they live."

"Revenge is for cowards," Pops said.

"Yes," my mother laughed. "The Coffins would be in big trouble if not for your moral opposition to revenge."

"Jim Joyce would have paid the Coffins a visit," Medina said.

Pops rose from his chair and, beer bottle in hand, turned to face her. "He might have if he hadn't run away. But I guess we'll never know, will we?"

"Jim Joyce would have kicked the shit out of you using nothing but a loaf of bread," Medina said. "If they'd made *How Green Was My Valley* about Pops, they would have called it *How Yellow Was My Belly*."

"Big Bad Jim," Pops mimicked her, "driving his big bad bread truck. So brave he ran out on his fiancée while she was pregnant. He never left a mark on anyone but Percy."

"One more word, Pops," my mother fumed, "and you'll be looking for another place to live."

"I'm sorry, Paynelope," Pops said, "but Big Bad Jim's sister brings out the worst in me."

"Fuck off," Medina said.

"*Stop it*," my mother yelled. "Pops, everyone, and I mean everyone, knew what would happen to Percy if Buddy Coffin thought he'd laid a finger on his little brother. Half the Coffin boys have criminal records. The half that doesn't isn't old enough."

"Stevie Coffin told Percy you do it with the Brothers. I wasn't very far away. I guess the students didn't see me. Percy shoved a lemon pie in the boy's face. He was going to chase Percy down the hill, but I intervened. And then I went back down to Brother Rice and told Brother McHugh what happened. That Coffin boy said such awful things, Paynelope."

"So you turned him in and Percy got blamed for it."

"I suppose."

"*You* will get my cigarettes for me from now on, Pops. You will pay for them and you will give Percy a dime a day."

"Yes, yes, all right."

Pops went out—not to Collins' store—to buy my mother's cigarettes. I was curled up on the sofa under a blanket when he came back, his hands shoved in the pockets of his lab coat. He put the Rothmans down beside her typewriter—put them down with an emphatic thump but never said a word. Next he presented my dime to her like a child bringing back the change as directed, except that he put his index finger on it as he pushed it closer to her. He made his way to the fridge for a beer then to the sunroom, where the empty bottles from the night before still stood around his chair. "No one cleans up in this house anymore," he said.

"Clean up after yourself," my mother answered. "If you bring your empties back, you won't have to pay as much for my cigarettes."

I didn't go back to school for a while. It turned out that I did have a broken nose, which, though it was wrenched back into place by the doctor, blackened both my eyes. I looked like a red-faced, black mask–wearing bandit, the world's first red raccoon. The doctor wrapped my torso with tight bandages because my ribs were bruised. They hurt when I coughed or laughed, and at night, in bed, they woke me every time I moved. The doctor said my arm was sprained, probably from a half nelson, but I didn't need a sling. I had assorted other scrapes and bruises, and my entire school uniform—blazer, slacks, shirt and tie—looked, as my mother put it, as if I had been "dragged behind a horse."

She badgered Pops into buying me a new uniform from St. Bon's. One night, as I lay in my bunk, I heard her say, "I bet McHugh knew what Buddy Coffin would do if his little brother was so severely punished. Buddy Coffin was one of McHugh's students years ago."

"Wouldn't it be nice if Percy beat up McHugh? But there's not much of Jim Joyce in him," I heard Medina tell my mother.

"A hundred in everything. Jim Joyce couldn't *count* to a hundred. All his grades together didn't add up to a hundred. He beat up his teacher just to get expelled."

I felt wounded when my mother laughed and whispered things I couldn't hear. I conjured up an image of Jim Joyce by twisting what my mother and Medina had said about him. A boy who wouldn't let the prospect of an encounter with McHugh stop him from stealing cigarettes from a boy like me. A boy who could beat up McHugh. A boy who wouldn't let another boy walk past him enjoying some treat he couldn't afford. I could conceive of no match for the man such a boy had become. Wherever Jim Joyce was, he walked about like me, unscathed, but for different reasons. So what if he had done nothing better than drive a bread truck? He was probably doing something better now. There must have been something for which he was uniquely qualified by his nature to achieve, something he resisted until one day he left my mother as abruptly as he left Brother Rice.

My mother called the police about the possibility of pressing charges against Buddy Coffin. "The prosecutor said he wouldn't advise involving a boy like Percy in something as *public* as court proceedings."

"I don't want to go to court," I said.

"It doesn't matter anyway," my mother said. "There isn't a single person who's willing to say in court that Buddy Coffin laid a finger on you." She brooded more on my beating than I did.

Eight days after my encounter with Buddy Coffin, when the bruises around my eyes had faded to the shade of iodine, I went back to school, accompanied, in spite of my protests that I wanted to go alone, by my mother and Medina, one on either side of me, though I refused to hold their hands. Pops volunteered to join us, but my mother said he would only make the trouble he had caused me even worse.

As usual, the button just above my mother's tits, the highest one she ever fastened, looked as though it would pop at any second and her tits would tumble out. Her blouse was tightly tucked inside her skirt, the white cloth pulled flat against her back. Her skirt, navy blue, with small zippers on each side of her waist, made of her bum a perfect peach. She had on the heels she wore while typing and a pair of nylons, down the outer thigh of which ran a thin white seam. On my other side walked Medina, dressed in her lime-green hospital overalls and her flat-soled grey shoes.

The boys and girls of Bonaventure lined the street, which made me feel like the sole attraction in a miniature parade. There were a few shouted remarks from deep in the pack. "Nice bodyguards, Percy. One nice one, anyway. Nice new face too." There were wolf whistles and shouts of "Penelope." I couldn't help but identify with the boys who merely groaned, as if to themselves, "Jesus, will you look at that piece of ass."

Just outside the gates of St. Bon's, my mother looked around at all the boys and girls until they fell silent. My mother, her fists clenched at her sides, rose slightly on the balls of her feet. "LISTEN TO ME," she shouted, "every last one of you little snotbags. What Brother McHugh does to you is not Percy's fault. Percy Joyce is not a tattletale. It wasn't because of Percy that Brother McHugh beat up Stevie Coffin. Tell your older brothers and sisters, tell your fathers and your mothers. It is not open season on Percy Joyce. Buddy Coffin will get what's coming to him. The next person who harms a hair on my son's head will end up with a broken nose."

"Who's going to break *my* nose? You and her?" one of the older boys from Brother Rice laughed. "Who's gonna take on Buddy Coffin? You?" He pointed to Medina.

My mother pointed back at him. "Would you like me to demonstrate? If I have to make an example of someone, it might as well be you." The boy grinned. My mother walked straight up to him and slapped him in the face so hard he almost fell over backward.

"Jesus," one of the boys whispered. "Did you see that?"

"You can't just go around hitting people," one of the older Heart girls declared, but she did not step forward. My mother pointed at the boy she'd struck. "Ask him what I can or cannot do. I live at 44 Bonaventure Avenue. I'm not hiding out like Buddy Coffin."

The boy moved off, his hand to his face, into the mass of tunics and blazers that parted for him, no one saying a word.

"Let's hope *he* doesn't have an older brother with nothing to lose," Medina said.

"In you go, Percy, into school," my mother said as she walked back toward me and Medina, her face as scarlet as if she was the one who had been slapped. "Now!"

I ran across the field in front of St. Bon's, unsure if I was being pursued or if any of the Brothers had witnessed what had happened on the street. "Slut," I heard some girl say. The word was taken up in a half-hearted staccato, ringing out like the word "here" during the taking of attendance in my homeroom. "You're a slut and Percy's a bastard," some boy shouted. I wondered what they meant, *really* meant, by "slut"—perhaps not, or not just, that she had been knocked up. Perhaps there were rumours spread by some growing minority who suspected the truth, who were able to *see* the truth, piece it together from what was commonly known and the way my mother and my aunt couldn't help but look at one another or stand side by side, a little too close, their shoulders sometimes touching, lingering just that tiny bit that didn't seem quite right. Perhaps they were giving themselves away by furtive eye contact, the briefest exchanges of conspiring smiles. Was anyone on the Mount watching them *that* closely, as closely as, for other reasons, I did? On the school steps, I looked back.

All I could see were students, students who sounded as if they were exhorting two combatants to tear each other limb from limb. But then the first bells rang out more or less at once from all of the Seven Schools, and the boys and girls resolved into streams of like-coloured uniforms and went their separate ways. I couldn't see my mother or Medina.

I hurried inside and sat by myself in my homeroom until the other boys poured in, whooping and laughing. "Your mother knocked O'Keefe into last week," the boy who sat behind me said. "Penny Joyce could take on all the Coffins at once," another ambiguously said. I stared at my desk, still unable to credit what I had seen my mother do.

THE TUNNEL AND THE
SUITE OF GUS McHUGH

My homeroom teacher, Brother Hogan, said that Brother McHugh wanted to have a word with me. I was escorted by a monitor to Brother Hogan's little office, where Brother McHugh, still wearing his overcoat and gloves, was sitting side on to a desk as if to impress upon anyone who saw him that he had long ago outgrown such meagre accommodations.

"Percy Joyce," McHugh said, turning about in his chair to face me.

"Yes, Brother." I sat in the chair opposite his. Both chairs were like the armless wooden ones we used for assembly in the gym.

"You seem fine," he said. "No major damage?"

"No, Brother."

He said he bet he was the first person I'd ever met who regarded me with neither mockery nor pity. "I've respected you," he said. "Everyone deserves respect. But I'm told that your mother has been making threats against my students. Making threats is against the law. And it will only make things worse for you. If something else happens to you, it will be because she provoked it. There is only so much that I can do to protect you. I keep telling the Archbishop that. His Grace is most distressed about what happened to you, but even more distressed about what your mother did today. It took him a while to convince the parents of the student she struck not to have her charged for assaulting their son. Tell your mother that God helps those who help themselves, not those who strike boys and make threats. Violence solves nothing. Those to whom evil is done do evil in return. It is one thing for *me* to discipline a student, another altogether for *her* to take matters into her own hands. And still another to say in public that I beat up a student."

He went on to say that I needed to be disabused of the notion that I was exceptional, a notion so many people in my life had indulged that I took it for granted everyone would do so, now and in the future, here and elsewhere. Did I think he had fallen in line with all the others and was catering to my "sulking sense of griev-ance against all people and all things"? Those who set themselves above others would be brought down—not as Buddy Coffin had brought me down, but more profoundly. "I know you have no idea what it is like to be laid so low, to have not a single thing in the world to rely on but yourself, to feel as if even God no longer cares about your fate. You revel in your so-called loneliness. I can't stand boys who use their allotment at birth as a crutch, a way of begging sympathy from others. Such a person might as well go cap in hand through the streets." He leaned across the desk and put his face close to mine. "You've seen how dangerous it can be to assume that someone is always looking out for you. My life's purpose is to lead the Christian Brothers of the Mount, not to play guardian angel to some prideful misfit. I was asked by His Grace himself to keep you out of trouble. But you're a far cry from being one of my primary concerns. You are a nuisance, nothing more. And you and your mother have done nothing to make my task the least bit easier. Tell her I said so. Tell her the two of you have to do your part as well. Now don't go back to class. I told your teacher you'd be going straight home. It's best you leave before the other boys. There's no telling how worked up they are because of what your mother did and said this morning."

The end-of-class bell rang. As if that was his cue, McHugh stood, came round to my side of the desk and grabbed me by the upper left arm, which still hurt from whatever Buddy Coffin had done to it. "*Ow*," I shouted.

"You know what? I've changed my mind. I have an idea."

"What do you mean?" I managed in a quavering voice. I knew he hadn't changed his mind, that he'd all along been planning whatever he was about to do and only told me I was free to go to give me an unwarranted sense of relief that, when he broke it, would terrify me that much more.

"Get up," he ordered. So scared I thought my legs would give way, I managed to stand. He all but dragged me out into the hall-way, which was thronged with boys rummaging through their lock-ers and heading to their next class. At first, the boys nearest us fell silent, they were so surprised to see me in the clutch of McHugh, who was so vigorously chewing his gum it might have been me he was gnashing between his teeth. Then the boys erupted in scorn and derision: "Looks like the little Joyce boy broke up with His Grace." "It's tunnel time, Percy, time for the long march to Brother Rice." "Percy, Percy, what *did* you do? Mom and Pops can't help you now."

"*Shut up*," McHugh roared, shoving boys out of the way with his free arm, sending one of them flying headfirst into an open locker door.

"I can take him for you, Brother McHugh," one of the hall monitors said, but McHugh ignored him.

"*Make way*," McHugh shouted. "Make way unless you want to come with us."

The blue blazer–wearing boys of St. Bon's made way as best they could, though McHugh all but trampled some of them, while others did their best to incite him further by sticking out their feet to trip me.

"Don't make me drag you," McHugh warned.

We reached the two steps that led down to the iron tunnel door. McHugh, who must have had the key in his hand all along, shoved it in the lock, leaning down from the top step and pulling the door open.

"So long, Percy," a boy behind us called out. "Not everyone comes back. Ask Stevie Coffin."

"In you go." McHugh flung me inside.

For a second I thought he planned to close the door but stay on the St. Bon's side of it, leaving me locked in the tunnel by myself. But he stepped inside, relocked the door behind us and put the key in the pocket of his black slacks. To our left was another door, on which there was a sign that said: "To Holy Heart High School. Please lock the door behind you."

"Follow me," he muttered, setting off down the tunnel at such a clip I stumbled to keep up. Water pipes painted white ran through the tunnel at the juncture of the ceiling and the walls. The air was chilly, the tunnel dimly lit by flickering fluorescent lamps spaced far apart on the ceiling; the walls, floors and ceilings were made of concrete and had that oily basement smell that I remembered from the night I found the Vat Rat in the sump pump hole. They were stained with what looked like sweat marks, water seeping slowly in through cracks too small to see. In places, water dripped in greater volume from the ceiling and collected in small puddles on the floor. On the walls were hung framed, glass-encased photographs and portraits of the Christian Brothers, the first of whom came from Ireland to Newfoundland in 1875.

"Are you going to strap me?" I called, but I kept losing ground on him and he didn't turn around. I couldn't help but picture my oversized hands as they would look when McHugh was done stropping them, my oversized fingers bloodied and broken, gory stumps such as Pops had once described. "You're not allowed to strap me. The Archbishop said!"

"That's right." McHugh's voice echoed between the tunnel walls. "Maybe he'll send you a Get Well Soon card. But I'm in charge of all the schools on the Mount. That means I'm in charge of you."

"No!" My voice sounded thin, even to me. "My mother and the Archbishop are in charge of me."

"Maybe. But he said he wants someone to do *something* about you. He says you and your mother are out of control. You can't control yourself, and she can't control herself or you. Spouting filth on her back steps late at night. Uttering threats. Slapping a mere boy in the face."

I wanted to turn and run back to the tunnel door, though I knew I couldn't open it and McHugh would likely enjoy dragging me back again toward the Brother Rice end while I struggled to escape. Unexpectedly, at that moment, a young Presentation nun, her shoes echoing as loudly as ours in the empty tunnel, appeared around a turn in the distance, her arms pressing books to her habit. "Sister," McHugh said, sounding quite matter-of-fact. "Brother McHugh," the nun answered. They passed each other without another word. As the nun drew closer to me, she slowed almost to a stop. I knew she recognized me and was surprised to see me in the tunnel, following McHugh to Brother Rice. "Sister?" I implored, hoping she might make some sort of objection to McHugh on my behalf. "Keep following Brother McHugh," she said, and sped up, rounding the turn out of sight.

Ahead of me, McHugh stopped and leaned his back against the wall of the tunnel. As I caught up with him, he reached into the pocket of his slacks and withdrew a stick of spearmint gum that he slowly unwrapped, then rolled the paper and tinfoil into a tight ball that he slipped into the chest pocket of my blazer. He put the gum in his mouth and chewed it with his front teeth. He patted the wall to indicate that I should lean against it as he was doing. Soon we were standing side by side, our backs against the cold concrete of the tunnel wall, like two people who, having met while going in opposite directions, had stopped to talk. He turned toward me, leaning his shoulder against the wall and putting his hands in the pockets of his slacks. I looked up at him and he smiled with his mouth closed, still working the gum with his front teeth, his white hair a touch dishevelled, his clerical collar askew. I waited for him to speak, but he said nothing, only regarded me for so long that I couldn't hold his stare and looked at the floor.

"It doesn't show any signs of clearing up, does it, that face of yours? Not from Buddy Coffin, I mean, but from the mess you came into the world with. We're all so tired of it. Everyone must make allowances for Percy Joyce. Because of his face, because his father ran away and left his mother holding something like a baby. Because of the Archbishop. What would you do if His Grace wasn't in your corner? He has himself convinced that you were born on June 24 for some divine purpose, that your face and hands and feet are therefore signs of that divine purpose. I know several people who were born on June 24 and each of them is far more likely than you to accomplish something of note in the name of God.

"His Grace sees a fatherless only child whose face looks like a leper's, whose mother lives in the past, hoping her lost love will come back for her and who, until he does, will go on blaming God and never set foot inside a church.

"But you know what I see, Little Percy Joyce? I see a spoiled, coddled mommy's boy whose mommy is glad Daddy is gone and doesn't lose a second of sleep wondering why God has been so mean to her. I don't know what your mother gives a damn about besides her Little Percy.

"I know she's not the miserable, discarded woman His Grace thinks she is. Would she be married if not for you, Percy? Is it the prospect of having you as a stepson that keeps men away? His

Grace believes that, partly, your mother is reluctant to remarry because she's afraid that a man who's not your blood father would mistreat you. Perhaps he would. I'm sick and tired of you and I don't even have to live with you.

"Somehow it doesn't all add up, though. My vice-principal tells me that, for a woman with a problem child, Penny Joyce is pretty cheerful." McHugh moved his head closer to mine. Blood pounded in my temples. I was terrified of what he'd say next and had no idea what my response should be. It occurred to me that he might be working up to telling me that he knew about my mother and Medina, that, contrary to their belief, Pops knew about them and had told him.

"Listen to me. Are you listening?"

I nodded. He moved away from the wall.

"I know how to hurt boys in ways that leave nothing but little red marks that can easily be explained away. It's called 'snapping.' It's not like getting strapped. Some boys think it's worse. You're about to get snapped." I thought he had misspoken. "Yes, snapped," he said. "Not strapped or stropped. That comes later. Snapped comes first. Do you know what it is?" I shook my head. "Every schoolboy except one as coddled and as spoiled as you knows what it is."

His hand darting out so fast I couldn't dodge it, he snapped my left eye, launching his index finger from his thumb. I stared at the floor through a blur of tears, feeling as though there were a million grains of sand behind my eyelid.

Still I thought this was some sort of prelude to strapping. I was certain I would be strapped, stropped, certain he would make minced meat of my hands and explain it to the Archbishop in some way that exonerated him, that would convince the Archbishop that I was a lost cause who had made many look like fools. I foresaw the end of Uncle Paddy's patronage and protection, the start of open season on Percy Joyce.

But the "snapping" continued. He "snapped" each of my ear-lobes. It felt as if he were holding a match to them. I covered them with my hands. He snapped me in the diaphragm with such force I couldn't breathe. I had to fight to keep from throwing up. He flicked the head of my dick with his finger as precisely as if its location were traced on the outside of my slacks. A sickening ache shot all the way to my stomach. I almost puked. I grabbed my crotch with both hands and would have doubled over had he not prevented it by cupping my chin in his hand. With his other hand he pulled my hands apart.

He snapped my left nut. Even as I was doubling over with pain, it occurred to me that he had been using that index finger of his on boys for years, so casually adept he was at hitting just the right spot. He snapped my septum and my eyes and nose watered freely, my nose stinging so I thought it must be bleeding.

"That's what I can do by barely lifting a finger," he said. "Think about that. Remember it. You'd best keep this little dust-up to yourself. His Grace would never believe you if you told him what I did. And he'd know that I'd never make up those things you said about me."

I squinted, pressed the heels of my hands against my eyes, which felt as if they would otherwise have popped straight out of my head. "Say one word and I'll start all over again," he said. "Understand?"

Hands still pressed to my eyes, I nodded my head. He pulled my hands away from my face. I saw him through a reddish blur of tears. He gave me a plaid handkerchief. "Clean yourself up," he said. "You look even worse than usual." I wiped my eyes, my running nose, my face. "Fold the handkerchief and tuck it neatly in my jacket pocket, all the way in where no one can see it." I did as he told me.

"Now follow me. There's something at the school that you should see."

"Are you going to strap me?"

"Follow me."

At the end of the tunnel, there was an iron door that read: "Brother Rice High School. Please lock the door behind you."

He put the key into the lock. "Who said anything about strapping? Though I must say, you're quite the little crybaby, aren't you? The other boys take their punishment like men. But you will always be your mommy's little boy. 'Little Percy' she'll be calling you when you're thirty-five and she's still wondering if your diaper might be of better use if she put it on your head."

I felt myself turning crimson with shame from head to toe. He opened the door. Directly in front of us was a set of steps that led up to what I assumed was the bottom floor of Brother Rice. On our right, a closed door read: "Quarters of the Christian Brothers of the Mount: Absolutely No Admittance." McHugh opened the door and eased me through, his manner now relaxed, his expression one of faint amusement.

We were in a narrow, barely lit vestibule of some kind, facing an elevator door above which a panel was numbered from one to eight. McHugh pressed the button and the door opened abruptly. "After you," McHugh said with a mock flourish of his hand. He followed me into the elevator, which was lined with imitation wood panelling. "Press eight," he said. I pressed the button and the elevator slowly rose, shuddering slightly each time we passed a floor. When the eight above the door lit up and the door slid open, I saw what looked like the corridor of a cheap hotel; on the floor was a light blue carpet that set off to garish advantage the lemon-coloured walls.

"Follow me," he said again as he slowly turned left and sauntered down the corridor with his hands in the pockets of his slacks, whistling with his gum still in his mouth.

There were no doors, it seemed, but at last we reached one. There was nothing written on it, not even a number. With a key much smaller than the tunnel door keys, he opened the door to what he said was his "suite." "I have the whole eighth floor to myself, so to speak." He sounded boastful. "There's nothing else up here but storage space."

The suite was more expensively decorated and furnished than our house—two leather sofas, a gleaming cherry wood dining-room table, overhead a grapnel-like chandelier. There was a framed copy of da Vinci's *Last Supper* on the wall above the couch, stretching from one armrest to the other. On the wall opposite, there was a silver-framed certificate of some kind, a citation of service perhaps, that bore what I recognized as the official stamp of the Vatican. Although I saw but one room of it, I could tell the suite was small, smaller than his office, where, for reasons I had never considered but now understood, he spent so much of his time. The suite was too cramped, even for a single person.

The floor was made of hardwood that gleamed as if it had just been polished. I detected the smell of some sort of detergent; it seemed the place had been cleaned just before my "visit." I pictured one of the Presentation nuns on her hands and knees, doggedly scrubbing the floor with both hands beside a pail of grey soapy water. There were many small crucifixes on the walls or on wooden stands on the two coffee tables—silver, bronze, marble, wooden crucifixes—as though a collector of them, a hobbyist who sought them out, lived here. But there were no depictions of the Sacred Heart or the Blessed Virgin Mary.

"The living room," he said. "Now you've seen more of where I live than most people have." The only other door to the room was shut. I assumed it led to his bedroom.

On the far wall was a large south-facing window. "Take a look," he said.

I went to the window and noticed first the distant view—St. John's, the part of it to the east of downtown, the brightly coloured houses of the Battery, Signal Hill topped by Cabot Tower, the grey Atlantic whose whitecaps were lopping through the Narrows, causing the hull of a small outbound ship to rise and fall as though it was deadlocked with the current. I looked down at a sharper angle and saw, first, Bonaventure Avenue and, second, our house, the red and green facade of 44, the leaf-strewn veranda, the massive Block out front. I could see straight into the kitchen, which was unoccupied, and almost straight into the living room, where I saw my mother typing at the Helm, a cigarette in her mouth. McHugh stood beside me, the sleeve of his jacket touching mine, the two of us sharing the view in a manner so seemingly congenial it was as if the "snapping" had never happened—though every part of me that he had snapped still ached or burned.

"That's Mom," I said, pointing. She was wearing a pink blouse and her hair was pinned up behind.

"Yes," McHugh said. "That is your mother. There she is, beavering away to buy men's gloves and boots for those paddles you call hands and feet. I sometimes, when I happen to look out, see her at that table, or in the kitchen. The view at night is especially good. I've seen Medina Joyce, I've seen our Vice-Principal MacDougal in his chair, with his back to all of you as if he's been punished and put in the corner. And, of course, I've seen you."

"I didn't know where you lived," I said. "I mean, which floor you lived on or which side of the Quarters."

"I've lived here since before you were born. Then I used to watch the deacons come and go with their duffle bags. Your mother wore a bathrobe, a black bathrobe, when she worked back then, and when she met those young men at the door. But now she dresses like someone who deals with the public even though it's always the same old man who comes by to fetch things from her. Why is that? It seems like it should have been the other way around, don't you think? Proper businesswear for those poor young deacons and a bathrobe for a man too old to give a damn about a woman like your mother."

I said nothing for fear of setting him off.

"Whenever you look out your kitchen window at night and you look up and see that the lights on the top floor are on, you'll know I'm home, still up, still wide awake. I stay up late. I don't sleep very well, sometimes. My job is always foremost in my mind. It's possible that, some night when you look up here, you'll see me standing at the window. If you do, wave to me. I'll wave back. Just like two close friends."

"Why did you make all the boys think you were going to strap me?"

"The boys jumped to their own conclusions. I never said a word about strapping you, did I?"

"No, but—"

"Not even in the tunnel, when there was just the two of us, did I say I would strap you, let alone do it, did I?"

"No, but you snapped me."

"I have no idea what you mean. I was angry with you. The other boys saw that. His Grace hasn't forbidden me from getting angry with you. But I didn't do anything to you. Can you prove that I did? You already look—well—you look like your old self again."

"You hurt me."

"I had to drag you to get you out of harm's reach. The things those boys were saying, the way they were ganging up on you—I had to get you out of there as fast as I could. I'm sorry I hurt your arm, but I couldn't help it. I wouldn't repeat those lies of yours to your mother if I were you. She'll lose her temper again. His Grace has only so much patience."

I knew he was right. My mother would almost certainly provoke some sort of showdown with McHugh that would imperil Uncle Paddy's patronage of me.

"Why did you bring me up here?"

"I've seen where you live. I wanted you to see where I live."

"Why?"

"It makes us even."

"But you've never been *inside* our house."

"Yes, I have. Once, when you and your mother went out, Vice-Principal MacDougal invited me over and showed me around. It's a very nice house. More spacious than my suite, but not as well appointed. Tell your mother that."

"I will. But she'll be mad with Pops."

"He'll tell her that I called him and told him I was coming over and asked to be let in."

"Is that true?"

"It might be. I can't remember. But no harm's done either way, right?"

"I suppose."

"You let McHugh in here and didn't tell me?"

"He showed up at the door when everyone was out. He knocked. What was I supposed to do? Send him away? He's my boss."

"Jesus," my mother said over and over as she pulled the curtains on the Bonaventure-facing windows.

"Pulling the curtains shut in the afternoon will make him think we have something to hide," Pops said, with a furtive glance at me.

"It will make him think *I* have something to hide," my mother retorted. "Pops, I don't give a damn about what McHugh thinks. But I can't believe that he said what he said, that I don't seem the least bit bothered that Jim Joyce ran off, that I don't seem the least bit bothered about anything."

"Then why close the curtains?"

"Because I don't like being spied upon. I don't like the idea that Big Brother McHugh is always watching. The eye in the sky that sees everything. Did you know his window was so high up and overlooked Bonaventure?"

"I had no idea. I've never been up there. He never mentioned it."

"Jesus. Scaring the shit out of Percy. Hurting his arm. I'm sorry I hit that O'Keefe boy. I shouldn't have. But I was face to face, for the first time, with what Percy has to go through every day. Why did McHugh take Percy up there? What point does he think he's made?"

"I don't know."

"Why does he want us all to know he's got his eye on us? You tell him everything that goes on here anyway."

"I never volunteer anything. I just answer his questions."

"I'm sure you do."

"You should have let me go to St. Bon's by myself," I said. "Boys like O'Keefe never *do* anything to me. All they ever do is call me names. I'm used to it."

"You shouldn't have had to get used to it. And what was I supposed to do, with you coming home beat up like that?"

"All *you* ever do is make things worse because you lose your temper. Like you did with that stupid sermon. Like you did with Francine Dunne's mother."

"That's because I just don't know what the *fuck* it is I'm supposed to do with you." She began to cry and laid her head on her arms, which were folded on the kitchen table.

"Paynelope—" Pops said. He moved a step toward her, but I rushed to her, put my arm around her neck and laid my head sideways on hers.

"I didn't mean what I said," I cried, and it was true. But I also noticed how nice it was to bury my face in the soft scent of her hair and to feel her shoulders and her back, as they rose and fell, warm beneath my arm.

I stayed up after Pops went to bed and sat at the kitchen table while my mother told Medina that McHugh wanted Uncle Paddy to think I was beyond help, that we both were a pair of conniving, unbalanced cranks, nuisances whom he should divest himself of before we started making real trouble for him.

"Something's up, Pen. Something more than that. I'm scared to death about what McHugh said to Percy. The part about things not adding up. I can't imagine McHugh saying that. I can imagine him thinking it but not saying it, especially to Percy. I wonder if he ever saw the two of us."

My mother said that all they'd ever done outside her bedroom they had done at night, with the lights down low or even off, and even then they'd only done little more than sit beside each other and almost always remembered to close the drapes and curtains. I wondered how many times McHugh had seen her with no clothes on when she was alone by day in the house, walking from her bedroom to the bathroom or vice versa, her hair up in a towel as she waited for the tub to fill with water. I envied McHugh his peeping perch from which, through even the most basic of telescopes, he could see my mother as close up as if he were watching her through the window from our side of the street.

Medina rubbed her stomach and winced as if she might be sick. My mother put her hand on her arm. "He was just fishing," my mother said. "Hoping Percy would let something slip. All the suspicions in the world are useless unless they're backed up by proof."

"That might be true in court, Pen, but it's not true on the Mount."

"He suspects what he wants to be true, which is that I give it away to any man who asks. If I knew when McHugh was watching, I'd let some stranger in and do him on the kitchen floor. That would erase any suspicions good old McHugh might have."

"Oh yes," Medina said. "You know the old saying: When in doubt, fuck the milkman in the kitchen."

THE CHAPEL

THAT January, after coming back from Mass one Sunday, Pops announced that McHugh had told him that, unless my mother and I started going to Mass, Pops would have to find another place to live. If he refused to do that, he would have to find himself another job. Pops told my mother that McHugh had said he had never liked the fact that his vice-principal boarded in a house whose landlady was a lapsed Catholic who didn't go to church and who hadn't had her son baptized in *any* Christian faith. Now, given all the "trouble and upset" she and I had caused, the Archbishop shared his belief that what he called my mother's "indifference" to religion might be transformed into true faith by regular attendance at Mass, and ultimately by the resumption of the sacraments.

"No," my mother said. "Out of the question. Tell McHugh to tell Uncle Paddy I said no. I said no to his henchmen priests years ago and I'm saying no now."

The following Sunday morning, as Pops dressed for Mass, the rest of us sat around the breakfast table. Every so often Pops poked his head out of his room and urged my mother to change her mind.

"If only for the boy's sake, Paynelope," he said.

"It was *because* of what McHugh did to the Coffin boy that Percy was beaten senseless. And you want us to go to Mass at his chapel?"

"What am I supposed to tell McHugh when I show up for Mass alone?"

"Tell him whatever you want," my mother said.

"Why haven't *you* told him something? You've had all week to speak your mind. He's just across the road. You can reach him by phone any time you want."

"Tell him that Percy and I are sick," my mother said. "Tell him Medina's looking after Percy because I'm too sick."

"McHugh doesn't give a damn about Medina."

"The feeling is mutual, believe me." Medina turned her back on him.

"And what about next week?" Pops asked my mother. "What do I tell him then?"

"All right, all right, we'll go to Mass next week," she said. "But *this* week I'm making a point."

"What point?"

"I don't know, Pops. Just go to Mass."

We sat at the table, mostly in silence, until Pops came back about an hour later.

"No harm's been done," Pops said. "McHugh told me to tell you and Percy that he hopes you'll feel better soon and that he'll see you at Mass next week."

"How did he look when you told him we were sick?" my mother asked.

"Like he always looks, Paynelope. He smiled. He knows you're just trying to save face." Pops said the Archbishop merely wanted my mother and me to *attend* Mass. She didn't have to take the sacraments yet and I didn't have to be baptized. The Archbishop said he believed that merely attending Mass would have a salutary effect on me, who he feared might otherwise lose my way for good.

The next Sunday, all four of us went to Mass.

Medina had breakfast with us before Mass, telling Pops that since, like her, he was going to Communion "just for show," he didn't need to fast, but Pops said that, as always, he would wait until after Mass to eat.

"He's probably afraid," my mother said, "that McHugh will smell bacon on his breath."

My mother and Medina wore nylon bandanas, my mother complaining that she hadn't worn one since she was last in church and wondering why women had to cover their heads. She'd known women who forgot or lost their head coverings to lay napkins or even paper tissues on their heads. If the Church had its way, women would wear their hats to bed even if they wore nothing else.

"Modesty insists," Pops said, adding that he didn't know why men had to go bareheaded in church but he didn't really care since he never wore a hat even in the coldest months of winter.

"We look about thirty years older with these things on, Medina," my mother complained, looking at herself in the hallway mirror. "Heaven forbid that any man should be distracted by an immodest head of hair while he's trying to concentrate on the death by crucifixion of someone who, two thousand years ago, got Himself into trouble on purpose by telling everyone He met that He was God." Medina laughed.

"I'm not even sure I know how or when to genuflect," my mother mused.

"You do it when you cross in front of the tabernacle," Medina said, "and when you first arrive at your pew and when you last leave it. And you'll remember how, don't worry, although that skirt might be a bit too tight for genuflecting."

My mother smoothed her skirt down the front and on her hips as though trying to stretch it. "I'll just do a little dip. I think that's all I ever did."

"Should I show Perse how to genuflect?" Medina asked,

"No. I don't want him blessing himself and genuflecting just to be polite."

Only the Brothers, and the lay teachers of Brother Rice and other Christian Brothers schools on the Mount who wished to, attended Sunday Mass at the chapel. There were not many lay teachers on the Mount and only a small percentage of those went with their spouses and their children to the chapel instead of to the Basilica or one of the lesser churches, so the congregation in the chapel consisted almost exclusively of Brothers clad in black from head to toe but for the white collars at their throats. It was as if they wore not the colour of their religious order but that of their religion itself, the colour of mourning and bereavement, as if they belonged to a local, exclusively male ascetic cult whose leader, ostensibly the presiding priest, was in fact Brother McHugh, who joined them in grieving for the death of Christ and the lives they had renounced.

My mother said the chapel looked like a coven of warlocks. It *was* strange-looking, the near-homogeneous blackness of the chapel. It was even true that, as Medina observed, most of the Brothers had dark hair, as well as heavy five o'clock shadow complexions, as if the cult was so ascetic that even razor blades were in short supply, the Brothers taking turns with them until they were too blunt to shave the fuzz from a peach. "A band of hirsute brutes," my mother called them, noting that even the youngest had hairy wrists and hands. They made for a strange sight from behind, that line of kneeling, black-clad Brothers, in the pews and at the altar rail, the soles of their shoes showing as they otherwise never did, the only part of what they wore that was less than spotlessly clean. "They must have their names sewn into their uniforms," Medina said. "Do they always wear nothing but black?" My mother said that, among themselves, they dressed more or less normally. "That's good," Medina said. "I hate to think of them all wandering about at bedtime in black pyjamas."

Instead of the priest, it was Brother McHugh who at the door bade everyone welcome and goodbye, calling them by name: "Brother Riggs, Brother Hogan, Brother Cull, Mr. and Mrs. Macnamara."

Pops began to introduce us to "Director McHugh," but Brother McHugh ignored him. "Miss Joyce," he said, taking my mother's hand in both of his, patting the back of hers as he looked her in the eye so intensely that she turned away. I had never known my mother unable to meet someone's gaze.

"Nice to meet you, Brother McHugh," she said.

"What a momentous occasion," McHugh said. "Percy a guest in God's house for the first time in his life, you returning to it after so long an absence. It's been, what, thirteen years? Something of a sabbatical. Why don't we call it that?"

"Sabbaticals are every seventh year," my mother said. "But call it what you like, this is where my rehabilitation stops. I'm here as a spectator, not a guest. The same is true of Percy. By the way, no confession or Communion for me."

"Well. We'll take things one at a time." He turned to Medina. "*Miss* Joyce," he said, slightly stressing "Miss" as if to differentiate Medina from my mother for memory's sake, but also, it seemed, to emphasize that her singleness was different from my mother's, hers being no one's fault but her own.

"Percy Joyce," he said, "the last male of the Joyce clan." He was so clearly invoking my missing father that my mother couldn't help herself.

"The last but for one," she said, pursing her lips in a half smile. "You're pretending to forget my prodigal fiancé, a.k.a. Jim Joyce. Call me naive, but I still set a place for him at dinner."

Brother McHugh smiled at me in that wise, all-understanding way I had seen other Brothers smile at children, as if to say that he lived already in the Heaven that the rest of us were only hoping for and therefore knew how laughably insignificant our earthly tribulations would seem to us from there. My earthly tribulations. But there was something else about that smile that didn't so much betray his insincerity as invite you to apprehend it and so also to see that the near perfection of his mask was the measure of what lay behind it, the measure of the power of the man you were dealing with. It was this, I think, this glimpse that one was meant to get of the real "Director," that made people look away.

"The Joyce family is welcome in my chapel, witnesses to the sacraments of the Mass. Perhaps someday you will be more than mere witnesses."

He squeezed my shoulder, turning upon me an unblinking gaze. He seemed to think he had not impressed himself upon someone sufficiently to address them until they had looked away. "Don't think you're fooling me, because you're not," those eyes seemed to say at first, but it was more personal than that, something like, "Don't think you're forgiven for having betrayed my generosity just because you've come to Mass. Don't think you can't be snapped again."

McHugh's look made me feel guilty, made me feel not only that I had done something wrong but that I had wronged *him*, made him lose face in front of others in a way so blatant it must one day be addressed. "The Brothers at St. Bon's have told me a great deal about you, Percy." He smiled at me as if we had just met for the first time. "They say you have a gift for learning but have difficulty making friends, blending in."

"They want him to be gifted *and* blend in?" my mother said. "I don't think that's possible."

"A gifted person should not exalt himself above others," Brother McHugh replied. "After all, his gift comes not from himself but from God."

"Well, Percy is really not much of an exalter. I hardly ever catch him exalting anymore."

"There's no need to speak like that to Brother McHugh, Paynelope."

"Don't worry, Vice-Principal MacDougal, I've faced bigger challenges than Miss Joyce before."

My mother put her hand on my back. "Come on, Percy." She turned one last time to McHugh. "Don't you think that a God who gets the credit should also get the blame?" I knew she was speaking of my face, but I didn't mind.

As we found and slid into a pew, I watched Brother McHugh. His demeanour was one of exaggerated piety and gentleness. He moved about very slowly, his hands joined palm to palm in front of himself, nodding slightly, deferentially, whenever he caught someone's eye. His chapel voice was low but sonorous, intelligible from a distance, a voice that somehow matched the early morning sunshine that obliquely slanted through the stained glass windows and the hushed sounds of congregants who, somehow both bored and expectant, made their way to their usual numbered stations in the pews.

Brother McHugh's demeanour may have been deferential, but the other Brothers deferred to him as he walked about, making way for him, groups of them parting to let him pass slowly among them. He was not the tallest or largest of the Brothers or the most fit and solid-looking of them; that prize went to a square-shouldered and square-jawed Brother with thick, black-framed glasses that magnified his eyes. He had the most prominent and volatile Adam's apple I had ever seen. I half expected it to pop out of his mouth. McHugh looked effeminate by comparison, forever brushing back his white hair with one hand, shaking his head slightly from side to side as if to rid his face of some imaginary fly, a little wattle of fat quivering beneath his chin. A small wooden crucifix hung from a black belt around his waist, but he was otherwise unadorned.

About half of the schools on the Mount didn't front onto Bonaventure, so many of the Brothers and lay teachers who attended chapel Mass had never seen me before. They recognized me instantly, of course, by what I heard one of them, in a whisper, call my funny-coloured face and oversized, sagging lip. "That's the boy with the funny-coloured face," a man said, as if the woman beside him couldn't see as much with her own eyes. Why, said the expressions of the lay teachers, some of whose own children went to Brother Rice or St. Bon's, should the only Limbo-bound/freak/ father-deserted student on the Mount, an oddball triple threat, also be the only boy who didn't have to prove himself in any way, didn't have to get by on his toughness or his wits or his good looks or his athletic prowess, the only boy who got an Uncle Paddy– conferred free pass through the prolonged boot camp known as "school" and the proving ground for Heaven known as "life"?

Before Mass began, I watched people going into and emerging from the confessional. They looked, stepping out, as if they'd been hiding in the wall. There were a few other children, including some lower school girls, dressed as though for their own birthday parties in frilly dresses and white tights and gleaming black, silver-buckled shoes.

"What's going to confession like?" I said.

"It's not for claustrophobics," my mother whispered. "Especially not for claustrophobic priests."

"What do you do?"

"You pretend to tell the priest your sins. Most people recite a list of made-up minor ones. The priest forgives you for doing things he knows you never did. When you come out, you go up to the altar rail and pretend to say your penance—the prayers he instructed you to say, the number of times he instructed you to say them."

"Is that what you did?"

"Always."

Father Bill Slattery, the priest who had blessed our house, said Mass when he was finished hearing confessions. I was surprised to see him step out of the wall space as if he too had been hiding in there.

Brother McHugh sat alone at the aisle end of the left front pew. Each time Father Bill made us sit or kneel, Brother McHugh turned around slightly and smiled, seemingly instructing us to do as he was about to do, not so much superfluously translating for us the priest's command as making it seem to come from him, as if we needed extra instruction because, in spite of Vatican II, Father Bill still said Mass with his back to the congregation and his gaze on the tabernacle. I imagined McHugh standing at his window in the darkness late at night, looking out at the world that he was set apart from, could no longer consort with as he once had and so many other men he had known still did. His suite, his office, this little chapel, the tunnels, the Basilica, the stations of his life, a tiny, nameless constellation in the night sky of the world.

I had never been inside a church before. I paid close attention to everything—Father Bill in his gleaming, heavy-looking vestments, the many glittering, ornate vessels, the crystal cruets of water and wine, the Biblical scenes depicted in the stations of the cross that lined the walls and the ones in the intervening stained glass windows, the incense-puffing thurible that hung from chains that clinked like pocket change, the set of four angelus bells that one of the altar boys rang, making them sound like the advance of a colony of lepers. Father Bill said the Mass in Latin, again in spite of Vatican II, and might as well have given the sermon in the same language for all the attention it was paid. I ignored every word of it in favour of looking about at people who I thought were spellbound until I saw that most of them were fighting to keep from nodding off to the singsong sound of Father Bill's high-pitched voice, a voice that would not have been taken seriously if it had emanated from an executioner. I had seen crucifixes before, at school, in McHugh's suite, but none as graphically coloured and detailed as the one behind the tabernacle, which my mother said was a kind of "oven" where the Communion wafers, the Holy Hosts, were kept.

The most appealing thing I saw was the statue of the Blessed Virgin Mary recessed in the wall on the outer right-hand corner of the altar, the counterpart to one of Christ on the left-hand side whose weirdly glowing Sacred Heart was like the one I'd seen years ago in Sister Mary Aggie's window. Mary, alone of all the people in any way depicted in the chapel, looked serene in spite of the gasping serpent she was crushing with her foot. "A virgin with her foot on the head of a snake," my mother whispered. "I wonder what that's meant to symbolize, Perse."

On the way out, Pops dipped his hand into a holy water font just inside the door and blessed himself.

"So what did you think, Perse?" my mother said. What I thought was that, so far, it was fun to have done once and might be fun again a year from now, the way it was fun to go to the circus on its annual stop in St. John's. But all I did was shrug as if to say I didn't see what the fuss was about.

"He didn't understand any of it," Pops said.

"I should have taught him Latin."

"You should not have spoken to McHugh like that," Pops whispered. "He's done a lot for Percy."

"And for you. He lets you board in a heretic's house as long as the heretic goes to Mass. Good thing for you that I agreed to go."

"You mean good thing for you," Pops said. "An abandoned woman with a child could find herself in worse circumstances than yours."

At Pops' after-Mass breakfast, my mother all but dropped a plate of food on the table in front of him.

"Big plans for tonight, Miss Joyce?" Pops said. "Two or three men lined up as usual? Maybe if you learned to cook, you could find a man." He grinned.

"Don't be too smug, Pops. A man never knows what might be in his food."

Pops smiled at me. "I'm just pulling your mother's leg," he said. "My leg isn't yours to pull," she retorted.

From then on, once a week, my mother was Pops' "captive date," as she put it. "He thinks I'll relapse by long-term exposure to Catholicism," my mother said. Or else, she said, McHugh had directed Pops to try to wear her down. "McHugh's missionary," she called him, saying that Pops' comportment, his "humbly holy look," in Mass almost had her fooled. My mother said you only had to look at the world to see that no one was running it. Pops said that his disbelief in God was based on science. He said that my mother and Medina couldn't be bothered to give the question of God enough thought to find out if they believed in Him.

Medina kept going to Mass with us, forgoing her usual church on Patrick Street, spoiling what my mother called Pops and McHugh's "fantasy pageant." My mother and I would watch as Medina and Pops made their way to the altar and joined the others kneeling at the rail for Communion, often having no choice but to kneel side by side, looking almost like a married couple. Because of the angle to the altar at which we sat, I was able to see some people sticking out their tongues. Everyone's tongue was a different size and shape, but all of them were wet and all of them quivered as though they were terrified of something. I saw Pops, hands folded on the rail, eyes closed, mouth open, his purple tongue hanging out as if he were presenting it for examination by a specialist. Medina barely extended hers and didn't close her eyes. It looked as if the entire congregation had come out to have their tongues inspected by the priest, as if he could tell by their tongues what they'd been up to since last Sunday.

Pops and Medina would come back from the altar and kneel in our pew, Pops with his head bowed and eyes closed, his mouth closed but barely moving as he chewed the Host—the very picture of fervent piety and unassailable faith. Medina would kneel briefly, then sit down.

"Pops, you're *such* a hypocrite," my mother would say later, each time laughing until she had to bend over and put her hands on her knees.

"I'm merely doing what I must," Pops said. "At a word from that priest, I could lose my job."

"One more look at that tongue of yours," Medina said, "and I could lose my breakfast."

I've no doubt that to people who didn't know us, Medina was the odd one out, appended to a complete family like the maiden aunt she was. No doubt they mistook Pops for my mother's husband and my father unless they noticed that he wore no wedding ring. My mother always wore her engagement ring in public as she did at home, sometimes rubbed it in the chapel when she talked about Jim Joyce. We always sat in the same order in the pew. From left to right: Pops, Medina, me, my mother.

"I feel sorry for the priest," my mother said, "but it's hard to join in with someone when they're standing back on to you and singing like that in a language that no one else can understand."

"One can disbelieve in something and not stoop to mocking it, Paynelope."

I asked Pops what the Holy Host tasted like.

"Like paper and glue," Pops said. "Like taking a bite of an envelope that someone else just licked."

The altar boys didn't look embarrassed in spite of what they wore. They had plaid slippers like the ones I had at home, but the priest had shiny black boots like the ones sailors wore. Pops said the boys' frilly, ruffled white blouses were called surplices and the red dresses they wore underneath were called soutanes. He sighed.

"Your mother's right. It's all a lot of flim-flam. Hocus-pocus, smoke and mirrors. Don't ask me any more about it."

I recognized the Brother Rice boys—they were some of the grade elevens who during the week stopped traffic on Bonaventure, sauntering across the street in their maroon blazers and grey slacks as if they owned the very pavement they were walking on.

"You should see the way McHugh looks at you," Medina said to my mother. "He must have picked it up from Perse."

Nowhere did I sit so close to my mother for as long as I did at Mass. The pews of the small chapel were snugly full each Sunday, bodies pressed to bodies, strangers, mere acquaintances at best, pressed shoulder to shoulder, hip to hip, thigh to thigh, everyone squeezing their knees tightly together to make room. My mother on one side of me, Medina on the other, the two of them separated by nothing more than me, the three of us, where we touched, faintly damp with sweat, my mother's and Medina's scents mixed with mine, and even, to some degree, with that of Pops, away from whom—and therefore into me—Medina leaned as much as she could, which gave me an excuse to lean even more into my mother than I had to. When we knelt or sat, or rose to stand, my mother's right breast was often squashed against my shoulder, firm, barely yielding. When we sat, her skirt hiked up above her knees so far that when she crossed her legs, she overexposed one leg instead of merely baring the lower halves of both. I was glad I didn't have to leave the pew, glad that neither she nor I went up to the altar for Communion, for what I had could be hidden by nothing less than the Catholic Book of Worship, in spite of which, I felt certain, my mother saw the bulge in my school slacks and knew the reason for it—not that I minded that she saw it or that she knew she inspired it.

ST. JOHN'S DAY, JUNE 24

JUNE 24. My fourteenth birthday. I hitched a ride to the top of Signal Hill in the back of a pickup truck, in the cab of which rode a man, his wife and their little girl, who kept alternately scowling and smiling at me from the small back window, pulling her mouth into shapes in an effort to look like me. As we passed the site of the picnic my mother, Medina and I had had there, I thought of what we had said and had not spoken of so openly since. That day we had been hemmed in by fog and rock, but this day was cool, clear and windy.

There were many other people on the hill, most of them gazing out to sea on this rare day of perfect visibility, shielding their eyes from the sun with one hand to get a better look and holding their coats together at the throat with the other, their hair and scarves blown back horizontal by the wind. Some children and even a few grown-ups whom I had never set eyes on before said, "Hi Percy," and I nodded to them.

Even people who live by it are spellbound by the sea, gape at it in the morning as if it wasn't there the night before. What a curiously urbanized people we were, I thought, gazing in wonder at the sea as if word of it had been spreading since the sun came up, rumours of a great tract of water by which we would henceforth be separated from the main. We stared as, in 1905, our ancestors had stared at the towering iceberg uncannily shaped like the Virgin Mary that had floated by on this very day, the feast day of the Baptist. Late in the season for an iceberg and therefore all the more miraculous. The Ice Queen of Heaven. The Virgin Berg. Our Lady of the Frigid Fjords.

Like me, these people knew nothing of boats, of ocean navigation, of fishing except the kind you could do while standing knee-deep in a pond. They saw the weather as nothing more than an unrelenting nuisance. They didn't understand the inextricable connectedness of wind and water. In many ways, we were almost as urban as the people of Lower Manhattan. Islanders living right on the edge of the Atlantic Ocean—without at least an hour's notice they could not have said from which direction the wind was blowing or what the implications of that information would have been for the weather forecast.

Yeats had heard the "sea-wind scream upon the tower." My mother had several times read to me his "prayer" for his daughter: that she not be granted beauty overmuch . . . lest she consider beauty a sufficient end . . . and never find a friend. What was my mother trying to tell me—that it might be for the best that I was "not granted beauty overmuch"? Self-infatuation, the curse of beauty. Not quite the same as that of ugliness. Or that no one knew better than she did what to live with "beauty overmuch" was like? I imagined her waking up one morning to find her face stained, her hands and feet both stained and doubled in size. How much solace would she have found in the poetry of Yeats? A Prayer for Penelope. A Prayer for My Son.

But I wouldn't have minded the company of a girl who, from having been granted beauty overmuch, was so shallow as to want nothing from others but adulation—it would be fine with me. Throw me your bone and I'll throw you mine. Does that seem crude and pathetic? Very well, then, I was crude and pathetic, and in that way, if in few others, typical of teenage boys. I'm trying to distinguish between lust and love lust. I have lusted, unrequited, after hundreds, but I have love-lusted after no one but my mother. Would this have been the case but for my FSS? Who knows?

There are many things that, barring apocalypse, will always be taboo: murder, rape, molestation, tyranny and torture. And so on. Of taboos, mine is not the first, much less the last. It is anomalous, not typical, even as taboos go. There's no point in asking if it's right or wrong. It happens by the confluence of circumstances, every one of which is unlikely, and that very confluence beggars belief. Just remember, I'm the one who said my mother was a prostitute for sleeping with the man who kept a roof above my head. I am not some sexual iconoclast. My case is just a tad more hopeless than that of the few among us who have truly been in love. My story is not an alibi, not a euphemistic closing argument in defence of breaking what many people call the worst taboo.

Standing on Signal Hill, I found I could look down at the ruins of the old smallpox sanatorium, beyond which the lone and level sea stretched far away. It was easy to imagine that there was no far shore, that all of us had come to the top of the hill as though to the edge of a never-ending universe of water, the origin of all four winds, the realm of Aeolus. Guglielmo Marconi, second only to Ben Franklin among the famed flyers of kites, gave Signal Hill its name when he flew his kite, antenna attached, from the top of the hill, and claimed to hear, in Morse code, the letter *S* sent by wireless telegraph from Clifden, Ireland—supposedly the first transatlantic telegraph transmission. Marconi's claim was contested by

Thomas Edison, who called him a hoaxster, but Marconi stuck to his story. His credibility was somewhat weakened years later when he became one of Italy's most decorated pre-war Fascists, honoured by Benito Mussolini agreeing to be the best man at his wedding.

Far down below, I could glimpse the Purity Factory, makers and purveyors for decades of what my mother called "cram," cheap confections that I loved as much as other children did. In what looked like liquor bottles came alcohol-free, distilled syrup so sweet you had to mix it with four parts water; children added ice cubes to it and strolled about sipping, like grown-ups, from tumblers of what looked like Scotch. There were Purity raisin squares that were more like raisin sandwiches, raisins layered between two goo-soaked slabs of pastry. Red jelly balls—balls of cake with centres of generic jam. Jam-jams and lemon creams. Sweet bread, also called excursion bread, which looked like loaves of hard tack but was not as hard and split into slate-like pieces when you pierced them with a knife. Peppermint knobs that looked like white, pink-striped bumblebees. Candy kisses—peanut butter, rum and butter, butterscotch, coconut, banana. I loved them all.

A silent, blank-faced young man clad in a white T-shirt and blue jeans walked about among us, holding a sign that read:

MOVE ON, MOVE ON
NEWFOUNDLAND IS DEAD AND GONE
CONFEDERATION PUT HER IN THE GRAVE

No one paid him much attention. Nationality. "You speak to me of nationality . . . and religion." A net harder for some to fly by than for others. I too could summon up no interest in the cause that he was mourning. Born after confederation with Canada, I had never been what most of these people thought of as a "real

Newfoundlander." But even for the old Newfoundlanders there had been no pledge of allegiance, no exam such as immigrants have to pass these days, no oath to swear. Canadian citizenship required nothing of them. It was conferred upon them while they slept on March 31, 1949. They went to bed Newfoundlanders and woke up Canadians. It must have been like being baptized without giving your consent. Now they sat in mute bewilderment in front of television sets that brought them news from a foreign country. It would have made little difference to most of them if they were told they were citizens of Patagonia. They couldn't opt out, couldn't be conscientious objectors. Not unless they left, exiled themselves and lived their lives in unacknowledged protest of defeat.

Most, but not all, parts of "the bay" were outports situated on the coast. To townies, the bay was a nebulous elsewhere in which they didn't have much interest. "The bay" had always been, would always be, another country. The unconsolidated "bay," settlements, strung out like Christmas lights on the perimeter of Newfoundland and so widely scattered that each one knew little more of its nearest neighbours than the names of the fabled places they lived in, places never seen by most that existed as much in rumour as in fact, as real to those who lived elsewhere as London was to me. The real bay was the one you could not get to from St. John's except by boat—hypothetical boat, for demand for such a thing was non-existent.

I looked down at the place from which The Attempt was often made. St. John's was the starting point, or finishing point, for world record–seeking crossers of the Atlantic. There was a monument somewhere down there to Alcock and Brown, who had taken off from Lester's Field in their Vickers Vimy bomber and crash-landed safely in a bog in Clifden, Ireland, becoming the first aviators to survive a non-stop transatlantic aircraft flight. There was no monument to the man from Minnesota who tried to water-ski from St. John's to Clifden, only to die of hypothermia less than a mile from the Narrows when the boat that was towing him broke down. An endless variety of unlikely mariners made The Attempt in unlikely vessels. A man in a one-man submarine was given a rousing send-off to what proved to be the bottom of the ocean, for no trace of him or his craft was ever found. The Attempt was unsuccessfully made by hot-air balloonists, most of whom were kept from freezing to death by their hydrogen-heating flame propellant, which immolated one man in mid-air. He fell, flaming, Icarus-like, into the ocean, thankfully out of range of spectators, his unmanned balloon travelling for seventy miles before ditching on the deck of a cruise ship bound for Greenland. Rowboats, canoes, kayaks, leg-powered bicycle kites, near-weightless gliders and a host of mini dirigibles all failed in The Attempt.

The City of Percy Joyce.

The City of Percy.

I am Percy Joyce, lord of all that I survey. I felt like shouting it out loud. How quickly word would spread that I'd been seen and heard asserting my identity. Anyone who knew me would have been more amused than surprised to hear me claiming suzerainty over all I gazed upon. Percy Joyce, King of Kings. Look, ye Mighty, on my works and despair. Still, I thought, better not to swell the legend in case my compos mentis was ever called into question, as, under certain circumstances, it might one day be.

This is my city, awarded to me by my mother, Penelope, as a birthday present. This is my day and my city, mine and John the Baptist's.

This is my city, as is whatever can be seen from any part of it: the harbour, buffered from the sea by the south-side hill known as the Brow; the city on the north side of the hill with its almost fully blooming, house-camouflaging trees; the Basilica atop the Mount in the centre of the ridge; the towering Confederation Building to the east, topping yet another hill, affrontingly, undeniably there for every citizen of anti-Canada St. John's to see.

Omphalos. It is the Greek word for navel, belly button. The centre of the universe, the site of the Delphic Oracle that spoke in fateful riddles. My omphalos was surrounded by a stain, my belly button like the bull's eye of a target.

THE BLESSING OF THE FLEET

AFTER the first day of school in the winter of grade nine, I went down to the parking lot at Holy Heart, just down Bonaventure from St. Bon's, where the yellow buses for various parts of the near-bay—essentially any place that was not St. John's but within driving distance of it—lined up in vertical and horizontal rows, the smoke from their idling exhaust pipes rising straight up in the air on the coldest days.

Having given up hope of ever achieving credibility among the townies, I was desperately seeking out new territory and possible friends. For the new boys and girls who came to Holy Heart and Brother Rice by bus because there were no high schools where they lived, I was still something of a novelty—just the sort of exotic one would expect to find in a place so big that it must have one of everything. Many of the bay crowd had been raised to think of St. John's as a place that was laughably full of itself. They made it clear they were only going to school in St. John's because they had to, and planned to have no more to do with the city or their new schools or the townies than they had to.

To them, I was the measure of how short St. John's fell of being the great place the townies liked to think it was—a place of boys with purple faces, swollen, misshapen lips, hands and feet too big for the arms and legs they were attached to. If that was what a cursory glance turned up when they arrived, the place was not worth investigation.

But for me, they were a sub-faction who kept to themselves and didn't know my full history and with whom I might therefore be able to make a "fresh start" of the sort I had thought I might make when I began school.

I wandered in and out among the buses, conspicuous because of my face and because of being an incongruous townie whose blazer identified him as being from St. Bon's, which even the bay crowd knew was not a high school.

"What do *you* want, Jam-Jaws?" a boy in a Rice blazer asked me, rolling down a window of one of the buses.

"My mother works in Holy Heart," I said.

"His mother is a nun," the boy said to the others. "You're what she got for getting knocked up."

Boys and girls crowded his side of the bus, looking out the windows at me.

"Some ugly mug on you?" a girl said, making it sound like a question. I nodded as if she had not insulted me but had merely said what no one knew better than I did was a truth I no longer cared about.

"Yeah," I said, nodding and looking about as if my face had long since ceased to be uppermost in the minds of anyone who knew me. "Where does this bus go? How come it doesn't say on the buses where they go?"

"Portugal Cove," the girl said, adding, "What's your name?"

A girl who didn't know my name. I hoped there were many.

"Percy Joyce," I said.

"Is your mother a teacher?"

"No."

"Then what does she do at Holy Heart?"

"Oh. She's the secretary in the principal's office."

"There are two secretaries in Sister Celestine's office, and they're both older than my grandmother," the girl said.

"I meant my mother used to work here. I used to come up here and wait for her to get out of school."

"So what are you here for now? What are you standing out there in the cold between the buses for? Looking for a girlfriend, I suppose. Good luck!"

Some of the boys and girls got off the bus and crowded around me. I said I had a girlfriend but she went to Holy Cross, an all-boys school on Patrick Street. She was the only girl who went there, the only girl in the history of Newfoundland who'd ever gone to an all-boys school. Her father taught there, he made her go there so that he could keep his eye on her, her name was Tina. I saw it in one girl's eyes, the hesitation, the uncertainty, for me a near moment of being, in the best sense, exceptional. It soon vanished, as it always did. "You're full of shit," she said, but at least she was laughing as she got back on the bus and drew her window closed. I saw her huddle with some other girls and point at me through the window.

The next day, I walked among the maze of buses, happy, even under such circumstances, to be the centre of attention. Though the drivers ordered them not to, the children got off the buses, surrounding me, grinning, their hands in their coat pockets. I told them about Sister Mary Aggie and the Mass cards of Saint Drogo, the Patron Saint of Unattractive People, all of which they took to be more lies, but I didn't care. "Tell us another one, Percy," they shouted. I told them my father was a missionary doctor in Africa and that on one of his rare visits home he had passed on to me a fever that he had contracted from a Nigerian tribe. "My father has a face like mine," I said.

Word of what I was telling the bus children somehow got back to my mother. "You should try to find friends you don't have to impress by lying to them, Perse," she said.

"Or," Pops said, "he could comb the woods in search of ostrich eggs."

I could tell by the look on my mother's face that she knew Pops was right. But I was, for a while, something the bay boys and girls looked forward to, a highlight of their day. By that time, the townies had long since dispersed to their homes, or their after-school hangouts, places where they could smoke without being seen from any of the Seven Schools. The buses parked in exactly the same formation every afternoon, each bus in exactly the same place—the Goulds, Petty Harbour, Kelligrews, Portugal Cove, Torbay, Kilbride—and when they departed for all those places that I'd never set eyes on, the traffic on Bonaventure stopped by a traffic cop at 3:45 every afternoon to make way for the caravan of buses, I'd be left there in the empty parking lot, waving to the children in the rear of the bus to Kelligrews, which always pulled out last.

When the traffic cop told me to stand clear of the buses, I posted myself just up Bonaventure from Holy Heart, where I redundantly guided the buses on their way, waving my hands and arms exactly as the policeman did, ignoring him when he told me to go home.

"Have you been to Torbay, Percy?" a red-haired boy named Sully asked me through the open rear window of the Torbay bus one afternoon.

"No."

"You should come with us."

"How will I get home?"

"You can come back with us tomorrow morning."

"But what about tonight?"

"We'll all sleep on the bus tonight. We'll leave the engine on so it won't be too cold, but you might have to snuggle up with a girl if she needs someone to keep her warm. It'll be like camping out. We do it all the time. Cyril, he's the driver. He doesn't mind, just ask him."

I knew it was a ruse, but merely because I liked the sound of camping out with the Torbay boys and snuggling up with a warmth-seeking girl, I went to the open bus door and asked Cyril, a short, white-T-shirt-wearing man with rheumy eyes who reeked of rum, if he would take me to Torbay and let me spend the night in his bus with the other children.

Cyril turned round and roared, "Stop telling him lies or you'll all be walking to Torbay." He turned to me. "Go on now. You should have better sense."

But the next day, when Cyril was stretching his legs and having a smoke, the same boy, Sully, opened his window and said that I should get on the bus while Cyril wasn't looking and they would smuggle me to Torbay.

"You have to ask your mother, I suppose," he said.

I shook my head.

"Then get on the bus before Cyril turns around."

As I scrambled on board and ran down the middle aisle to where the boy was sitting, mine the only blue blazer amidst rows of maroons and dark blue tunics, the whole bus fell silent. I sat beside Sully, who told me to crouch down behind the seat in front of him. Just as I was doing so, I heard a girl up front say, "Cyril, Percy Joyce is on the bus."

"See ya, Percy," Sully said, laughing, as I stood up and ran back to the front of the bus, where Cyril grabbed me by the collar and addressed the back of my head as he held me in front of the open door: "Don't you ever sneak on board this bus again, you ugly little frigger," he said. He let me go and I tumbled out.

"Cyril the Squirrel," I yelled up at him.

"What?"

"Cyril the Squirrel!"

I ran down the bus steps, out of the parking lot and onto Bonaventure before I slowed to a walk.

Every day after school, I made my way from St. Bon's to the parking lot of Holy Heart, a mere few hundred feet, and spoke to Sully. I told him I had Mass cards that I'd had to send away to the Vatican for, and I recounted the story of Saint Drogo, the Patron Saint of Unattractive People, as Sister Mary Aggie had told it to me. I said he was made a saint because he hid himself away for life lest his ugliness not only terrify people but test their belief in a God who could create such a Hellish-looking beast. Sully asked if he could see the cards and I told him I would bring them from home and show them to him the next day. The next day, and the one after that, I told him I'd forgotten the cards. I was certain that whatever I passed in through that bus window I would never see again. He said he bet I was lying about the Saint Drogo cards. "I have three of them," I said, "but they're pasted to my wall. They might tear if I try to take them off."

"I bet you haven't even got one," he said. "I bet you a dollar."

In an effort to divert him, I told him I also had on the wall of my bedroom a "dirty" picture of a woman showing everything. He said he bet I was lying. I shook my head. I didn't mind losing "Francine." I was, as my mother said, no less "priapically preoc- cupied," but I had grown bored with Francine from having used her for inspiration so many times. I would have liked to replace her with a picture of my mother, just as naked and as wantonly disposed. I asked her to get Medina to take that kind of picture of her so she could give it to me. A pity picture, a compromise—a picture she would never see me use, never be embarrassed by, for I wouldn't tape it on the wall beside the Mass cards of Saint Drogo but would keep it hidden somewhere in my room.

"And where would I get *that* picture developed?" she said. "Not that I'd give it to you anyway."

That night, I heard her say to Medina: "I think I've lost all sense of just how far from normal he's become."

I untaped Francine's picture from the wall above my bed, folded it in half once so as not to spoil it with too many creases, and snuck it out of the house inside my school shirt. At St. Bon's, I spent the entire school day with Francine partly tucked inside my pants and partly hidden by my shirt, taking care to avoid contact with anyone who might audibly crumple the paper and discover I was hiding something. I had to restrict my own movements lest I cause the paper to crackle and give away my secret.

After school I went down to the Holy Heart parking lot, slipped Francine out between two buttons on my shirt and handed it in through the back window of the Torbay bus to Sully. Sully, his arms out the window, unfolded the picture.

"Her name is Vivian," I said. "You can keep her if you want to, but I won the bet, so you owe me a dollar."

"Holy fuck," Sully said under his breath as other boys tried to grab the picture from his hands. "You can see *more* than everything in this picture, Percy. Where did you get it?"

"From a *Playboy* magazine," I said. "Pops has a subscription."

Sully shook his head. "I've seen *Playboy* magazines," he said. "They don't look like this."

Francine is sullied now, I thought. Sullied by Sully.

"My mother gave it to me," I said, knowing that he would be much less convinced by the truth than by a lie.

"Yeah, right," he said. "Thanks a lot, Percy." He raised his window as he was set upon by other boys and even some girls. I heard shrieks and squeals from inside the bus and shouts from Cyril the Squirrel. I really didn't mind that it was the last I would see of Vivian and smiled up at Sully, who winked at me.

Among the bus children, knowledge of female anatomy exponentially increased for a few days until Sully was caught with

Vivian, strapped by McHugh and suspended for a week. I was apprised of this by one of the boys on the Torbay bus.

"Sully told McHugh he got the picture from you. McHugh called your mother. This might be a good time for you to run away."

I knew McHugh wouldn't strap me, but another "snapping" seemed all too likely. I wasn't sure what he had told my mother or exactly what Sully had told him, but I put off going home for as long as I could, wandering down every street that intersected with the Curve of Bonaventure. It was after five when I turned up at 44. My mother was still at the Helm, squinting at the page she was typing through a pall of cigarette smoke.

"Well, if it isn't the pornographer of Bonaventure Avenue," she said.

"*You're* the pornographer of Bonaventure Avenue," I said peevishly. "You gave me the picture."

"And I told you never to take it from the house or to school or to mention it to anyone."

"Yeah, well, I'm sorry," I said, "but how was I supposed to know that Sully would show Vivian to everyone? I thought he would just keep her for himself like I did. Sully said he would give me a dollar, but he didn't."

"McHugh said your friend Sully told him that, according to you, I gave you the picture."

"Sully didn't believe me."

"McHugh believed Sully. Or at least he did after I confessed. I thought admitting to giving you the picture might make you seem less delinquent."

"This is all so tawdry and disgusting," Pops said from the sunroom. "I told you that you shouldn't have provided Percy with pornography."

"You may have been right, Pops. McHugh asked me why I would incite my son on to acts of lewd behaviour."

"A good question," Pops said.

My mother said she told McHugh she thought it was better that I get a piece of paper into trouble than some orphan girl from Belvedere. He said that such pictures only incited boys to seek out the real thing. He said that pornography was known to lead to rape, which in my case would be even more likely because, with girls finding me repulsive, I might someday be driven to take by force what other men got through marriage.

"You have no idea how much harm you and Percy may have done," Pops said. "You especially. You act recklessly, Paynelope. You speak too provocatively."

"Taking a reasonable tone with unreasonable people can be very wearisome. It's the heretics against the lunatics. And I'm aware that, historically, the lunatics are way out in front."

Sully showed me the scabs and red welts on his hands. "You should have seen them a week ago," he said. "They got infected and swelled up like tomatoes."

"Did it hurt?"

"Did it *hurt?*" Sully laughed. "Never been strapped?"

I shook my head. I was glad he didn't know why I'd never been strapped.

Word of Vivian was soon rampant on the Mount, Percy's paper girlfriend, given to him by his mother, his paper girlfriend whom he had jilted for a dollar he would never get, like father like son, but at least Jim Joyce had made off with the family car in spite of being such a fool as to dump a woman like my mother. The boys of Brother Rice called out to my mother as they were leaving school: "Come out, Miss Cunny Penny. James Bond is here to see you."

The boys chanted: "Come out, come out, Penelope, And spread your Black Mick legs for me."

The grown-ups in the houses across from the school—the Conways and the Macnamaras—parents with whom my mother had not exchanged more than a word or two in years, chased the boys away, shouting at them to shut their filthy mouths, then glared at me as I watched them from the front window, as if I was somehow responsible, after which they closed their curtains.

When we next left the house, the corpulent Mrs. Conway came out and accosted my mother. "What kind of woman would give that kind of picture to a child?"

"The kind who didn't want him knocking up some tart from Holy Heart."

"You've corrupted those boys."

"Yes, I remember well what angels they used to be. For instance, here's a little ditty that I remember from my pre-pornographer days, composed and beautifully delivered by your son Danny:

"How much is that Mommy in the window,
The one who's a great piece of tail?
How much is that Mommy in the window?
I do hope that Mommy's for sale."

"Apparently," Pops said, repeating the words of McHugh, who had found out from the monitors what I was up to, "he told them a few days ago that his father was an African missionary and that they adopted him as their leader or witch doctor or something."

"Ah. Like Lord Jim," my mother said. "I think I read that book to Perse. Lord Jim. A white man named Jim, running away from his past, winds up as the leader of a tribe in Africa. The tribe calls him Lord Jim. He becomes almost like a god to them. He sacrifices himself in the end, gives up his life."

Give me myth or give me death. It was painfully fun to incite so many people to such antic jubilation no matter by what means or at what cost to me. I elaborated, amended my story about Jim Joyce going to Africa. "The tribe calls my father Lord Jim," I told Sully. "He's almost like a god to them." It wasn't long before word of my latest grandiose story spread through the bus crowd, by whom it was endlessly altered. "Cannibals in Africa think Percy's father is Jesus Christ."

"In Africa, they think Percy's father is God the Father, so Percy calls himself the Son of God. He says his second name is Jesus. Percy Jesus Joyce."

"Percy says he's Jesus Christ."

"Are you the son of God, Percy?"

I had about a year of Sunday masses under my belt. I was well prepared. I grinned and nodded.

"So this is the Second Coming of Christ?" Again I grinned and nodded.

Then why hadn't I descended in clouds of glory from the sky? I retreated a step and said I was His brother. They insisted Christ had no brothers and sisters. I said He did but that most of them stayed home in Heaven to keep God the Father company because Jesus and the Holy Ghost were on the road a lot. They insisted again—no brothers or sisters—so I again told them I was Christ.

I said God the Father was my father and the Holy Ghost was His brother, making him my uncle.

That means your mother is the Blessed Virgin Mary.

Right.

What do God the Father and the Holy Ghost look like?

I shrugged.

You don't know what they look like?

Yes, I do.

Come on, Percy, you're one-third of the Holy Trinity, so you should know what the other two-thirds look like.

I shrugged.

How come you can't heal your own face?

I don't want to.

You like it the way it is?

I nodded.

Hear that? Percy likes his face the way it is.

You're supposed to have long hair and a beard, Percy. You're supposed to wear nothing but a bed sheet and a pair of sandals, even in the winter. Do your feet get cold?

No. Because they're so big.

You have to be crucified when you grow up.

I know.

Are you afraid?

No.

Hear that? Percy's not afraid of being crucified.

Good. We need a cross, a hammer, three nails, two thieves and a crown of thorns.

It seemed to me that this was less harmful than telling lies that people were unlikely to believe. These were blatant, outright lies that no one but a fool would tell. It was fine with me if my new role was the fool, for it was better than having no role at all.

"It's a sin to talk like that," a short brunette named Daphne said. "It's a sin for you and it's a sin for him. Leave him alone. Tell him to go home. Tell him to go away. I'm telling your teachers."

"You should bless us," the children chanted before she could utter another syllable. "You should bless us, Percy." So I did, with the thumb and the index and middle fingers of one hand, I blessed a bus as it began to pull away, blessed it as I had seen Father Bill bless the tabernacle.

"Cure me, cure me, Percy," the boys and girls on another bus said. "Heal me, heal me." I kept making the sign of the cross.

Day after day, I took my act to other buses with more or less the same result. I bought a roll of lemon drops and gave Communion to anyone on the Torbay bus who, while Cyril was having a cigarette or sipping from a bottle of what he said was Coke, closed their eyes and stuck out their tongue.

"The Body of Christ," I said, as I had so often heard Father Bill say on Sunday mornings in the chapel of the school across the street. I married pairs of boys and girls who sat together. I walked down the aisle, saying over and over, "I now pronounce you man and wife."

The children on all the outport buses got to know me and came to expect me and look forward to my appearance in the parking lot each afternoon. I felt euphoric. I sat all day in class, mentally rehearsing my performances. In the library I excitedly made notes like a priest preparing a sermon.

Nancy has a great big wart that she wants you to heal. I healed it.

There's a crowd of lepers on the Petty Harbour bus, Percy. Go heal them. I healed them.

"McHugh says Percy has ordained himself," Pops said. "He said he pretends to say the Mass on the Torbay bus every afternoon. McHugh says there's nothing he can do because the buses are off limits to him and all the other teachers on the Mount. The bus drivers are supposed to keep order but all they do is drive the buses and ignore the children, whom Percy has goaded into calling him all kinds of things: Percy of the Parking Lot, Saint Percival the Merciful."

"Percy, why can't you stop telling lies?" my mother said.

I shrugged. "They're not really lies. They're just jokes."

"You're making a joke of *yourself*," she said. "Making up stupid lies to impress children who aren't half as smart as you."

Still, I couldn't stay away from the buses. I told the children I'd written a letter to the Pope, Pope Paul VI, and included with it a picture of myself, which had prompted the Pope to write me back to tell me that my stained face was part of God's plan and that one day the purpose of it would be revealed to me. I said he joked that I should take heart from the very fact that someone with a nose the size of his had been so successful. I said we were now writing each other about once a month and plans were being put in place for me to visit him one day and for him to be the first Pope to visit Newfoundland, where, if he had time, he would have dinner with the Joyces.

"Percy is pen pals with the Pope," Sully announced loudly. "What do you and the Pope say in your letters?" I said it was mostly small talk because the Pope's English wasn't very good. I said my name in Italian was Percifico and his was Paolo, though I never called him that.

McHugh called my mother again and complained I was an even more compulsive liar than I had shown myself to be by my mistreatment of Francine. Now, however, I was lying almost exclusively about things related to the Catholic Church, which would not be countenanced.

My mother and McHugh had a conversation by phone that my mother recounted like this:

"His Grace still wonders if Percy might not benefit from professional help."

"No. You know, His Grace seems to do more than his share of wondering, especially in front of you. Or is it really you who does the wondering? Is it part of your job to wonder for His Grace?"

"I can assure you that when I say I am quoting His Grace, I am quoting His Grace."

"Quoting what he says in reaction to what you say, which, for all he knows, may not be entirely true."

"You're accusing *me* of lying?"

"It's quite a life you've made for yourself, isn't it, Brother McHugh? You never have to worry about getting the old pink slip some Friday afternoon. You've never in your life had to support yourself and you never will. Let alone support yourself and a child.

You've never been faced with having to do something about as pleasant as swallowing thumbtacks to keep your child from going hungry. I'd like to see you in the winter on a picket line, shouting 'scabs' at replacement priests and nuns and Brothers and singing, 'We don't mind a bit of snow, But Uncle Paddy's got to go,' while you tried to keep warm around a barrel of burning picket signs."

"You think I have it easy."

"I think that, if not for confession, the only thing between you and damnation would be a coma that lasted from cradle to grave."

"You believe in confession?"

"There was a time when a woman would have been burnt at the stake for having a baby with a face like Percy's, and the baby would have had its brains dashed out on the ground. And the Church would have presided over the proceedings. Did you enjoy the Classics Illustrated version of the Spanish Inquisition as much as I did when you were growing up? Maybe you're just suffering from a bad case of historical nostalgia, Brother Those-Must-Have-Been-the-Days McHugh."

Pops said, "McHugh says it's the same in all the schools, all the grades. Anarchy. They're all repeating Percy stories, Percy lies, Percy Joyce tall tales, all making fun of the Bible and Catholicism."

I stood in the parking lot, in front of the fleet of buses, extended my arms and shouted, "Gentlemen, start your buses." I was over-joyed that the drivers, even Cyril, now played along for a while, starting their buses at more or less the same time, grinning at me, cocking their heads in amusement at each other. I knew that I was playing the very sort of role my mother feared I would end up play-ing. But I felt that I wasn't *really* playing it, just pretending to, doing a kind of send-up of it: the poor disfigured boy who had found a place for himself in the hearts of at least some of the students on the Mount, cheerful in spite of an allotment at birth that would have embittered most, the irrepressible, inspiring Percy Joyce, who believed that there was goodness at the core of every heart.

"Bless the bus, Percy, bless the bus," the children chanted. "Bless the brakes, bless the steering wheel, bless the tires. Perform a miracle. Make Cyril sober." One moment I was Christ, the next I was a priest, the next I was the Pope, the next I was Saint John the Baptist.

The Torbay children cheered, laughed, shouted. "Bless the other buses, Percy, bless the other buses." I went from bus to bus as the children on each of the buses took up and modified the chant. "Bless us, bless the bus, bless us, bless the bus."

I found a discarded tin can, filled it with ditchwater and, dipping a stick into the water, blessed the buses as I remembered Father Bill doing when he blessed our house. I made my way among the buses, blessing each of them, shaking water from the stick with a snap of my wrist, gaped at and for this sometimes rebuked by the drivers, in spite of whom I carried on. "Dear God," I said, "banish the Evil One from the tires of this bus, and from the brakes and from the steering wheel as well. Dear Lord, don't let this bus break down before it gets to Kelligrews. Banish the Evil One from the driver of this bus and from the boys of Brother Rice and the girls of Holy Heart, and save them from the agonies of Hell."

"Bless us, bless the bus." I became so caught up in their chanting exhortations I hardly knew what I was doing. I did and said whatever came to mind.

One of the boys shouted, "Go out on the street and bless the fleet, go out on the street and bless the fleet."

Soon everyone was chanting it.

When there was a pause in the traffic, I went out to the icy middle of Bonaventure to the spot where the traffic cop stood each afternoon. He had yet to arrive, so I faced the parking lot, the fleet of buses, the red facade of Holy Heart behind them, raised my sceptre-like stick, benedictory fashion, and began repeatedly to bless the fleet, flinging drops of water from the stick, which set the children on the buses and those still standing in the parking lot to cheering. Several drivers who were standing about in front of the buses, smoking, yelled at me. I dimly heard, "Get off the street before you're killed by a car."

"I baptize you all," I shouted. "I baptize you all. In the name of the Father, and of the Son, and of the Holy Ghost."

Behind me I heard a woman shout from what sounded like the distance of the sidewalk, "You stop doing that, that's a sin for you, Percy Joyce."

I put aside the can and stick, clasped my hands, fell to my knees, then bent over and kissed the ground as if thereby to confer sacredness upon it as I had seen the Pope do on TV when arriving by plane in a foreign country. I wound up with a lump of road salt in my mouth and spat it out, and continued to spit to rid myself of the acrid taste. The motorists seemed to think I was spitting out of contempt for the Pope whom I had just imitated; they honked their horns and shouted in protest. I stood.

"Hey, get off the road," a man said, stepping partway out of his gleaming green car, one foot inside, one on the street. Jubilant at the sound of the cheering, chanting children, I blessed him and gave him silent absolution, then genuflected in the middle of Bonaventure as if Holy Heart were a giant tabernacle. Suddenly I felt as much as saw that some boys had joined me in the space between the cars. I turned around. They knelt behind me on the pavement like some grade school congregation, blessing themselves, clasping their hands and bowing their heads. I had moved them to imitate me, to choose *me*, Percy Joyce.

"You little bastards," the man said, but he stood behind the open door of his green car as if thereby to shield himself from us or to make possible a quick escape. "*Stop it*," he yelled. He wore a fur hat and a long black overcoat. He was as red-faced as if he had spent his entire life protesting the very kind of blasphemy that he was witnessing. Behind me, the boys stood and snowballs sailed past me as they threw them at him and at the cars, the snowballs spattering across windshields, hoods and hood ornaments, grilles and blinking headlights.

As I stood on the double white line in the middle of the street—the traffic on either side of me stalled, my newly acquired followers behind me, chanting my name—I looked up at the sky and held out my arms as if to embrace the end-of-time Rapture brought on by me, by my blasphemies and exhortations. From the corner of my eye I glimpsed one of the bus drivers start to run toward me. I managed to lower my arms before he slammed into me with the fervour and force of a man determined to head off the very conflagration I was trying to invoke. Slipping and skidding on the icy street, I got up, made for the far sidewalk, and started sprinting and sliding down Bonaventure on my clown's feet to the renewed cheers of the children on the buses, some of whom blew the bus horns and noisily opened and closed the doors. I looked behind to see if anyone was chasing me and saw that the driver had slipped on the sidewalk and fallen down, arms out in front of him as he lay with his face pressed to the pavement. He slowly rose and limped back up the hill. Gasping for breath, I walked slowly down Bonaventure, wondering how long it would be before a phone call was made from Holy Heart to Brother Rice, and another from Brother Rice to 44. The faster the better, it seemed to me, for I couldn't wait for everyone to learn of the mass subversion I had engineered, winning over to my side dozens, perhaps hundreds of children of whose lives I had made myself the focal point, the centre of attention, the object, it might even be, of their friendship and their loyalty.

I had not even made it from the porch to the front room when my mother came out and threw her arms around me.

"Percy, what have you been *doing*?" she said. "My God, you're drenched in sweat, you're as hot as an oven." She felt my forehead, then put her face close to mine and looked straight into my eyes as if to spy out there the answer to her question. Out of breath but still exhilarated, I pushed past her into the house, where Pops was pacing about the front room.

"I've been getting calls from both Brother McHugh and Father Bill from the Basilica," he shouted at me. "You strayed onto public property. You caused a traffic jam on Bonaventure. No one seems to know what you thought you were up to. Word of what you did is all over the Mount!"

"You'll be all over the Mount if you raise your voice to him again," my mother said. "Perse, Perse, they said you were standing in the middle of the street with all the traffic around you. You could've been hit by a car standing there in the street like that."

"They always stop the traffic around that time to let the buses out." I was still out of breath. "You should have seen me, Mom, you should have seen me. You should have seen all the other kids. They were cheering like I scored the winning goal."

"Father Bill—" Pops began, but my mother interrupted, "I'll handle this, Pops." She turned to me. "What really happened?"

"The boys and girls on the Torbay bus dared me to cure them, so I did."

"What do you mean 'cure them'—cure them of what?"

"Not *really* cure them. I just did this." I made the benedictory sign of the cross. "Then the ones on the other buses dared me, so I cured them too, one bus at a time. And then they dared me to go out onto the street and cure all the buses at the same time. Like blessing the sealing fleet, a boy said. So I did it. Lots of times. As many times as I could before one of the bus drivers came running after me and tackled me. But he didn't hurt me."

"That's it?"

"Yes, but you should have seen me, Mom. Everyone was shouting out my name and all the girls were watching me and—"

"I've never seen McHugh worked up like this. People have

complained to the Basilica, to His Grace, to the principal of Holy Heart. People are saying Percy's out of his mind," Pops said.

"That's *enough*, Pops. But Perse, you *could* have been hurt, hit by a car."

"That's not the *point*," Pops shouted. "The two of you shouldn't be pissing off McHugh no matter how unlikeable you think he is. I wouldn't care about upsetting him or His Grace or Father Bill if I didn't have to care, but I *do*. And so do you and Percy."

My mother waved her hand dismissively. "It was just a joke. A joke that got a bit out of hand. When I was in school, I wouldn't part with a candy unless someone let me put it on their tongue. Percy is only fourteen years old."

Pops was pacing back and forth, his hands shoved into the pockets of his lab coat. "It wasn't just a joke. It got everyone worked up and made them laugh. They were laughing *at* you, don't you understand, Percy? Will you never understand? They were making fun of you. The joke was on you."

"No it wasn't," I said bitterly. "The joke was on Uncle Paddy and McHugh."

I stormed off to my room, lay in the upper bunk and hit Saint Drogo in the face, over and over, pounding the wall with my fist. Stupid, ugly, fucking saint. They didn't make him a saint until long after he was dead. What good did that do him?

The next day, as I walked up the Curve of Bonaventure toward St. Bon's, boys genuflected in front of me and blessed themselves. Others asked if I would let them touch the hem of my blazer. Girls trailed after me, saying, "Bless me, Percy, for I have sinned." Making a megaphone of his hands, a grade eleven boy from Brother Rice announced that Percy Joyce would be hearing confessions in the bathroom of a bus from three to five that afternoon. I would walk on water at three, turn water into wine at three-fifteen, calm the ocean at three-thirty, be crucified at four o'clock and rise from the dead at four-fifteen. I clasped my fists and shook them in triumph above my head. Triumph, mock triumph—what was the difference when the only alternative was to be ignored?

A fury-faced middle-aged woman with jet-black dyed hair and eyebrows came out of one of the largest houses on Bonaventure, still in her slippers. She grabbed me by the arm and said, "You see what you've done, you sinful, selfish little brute. You've got them all at it now. A lot of good boys and girls all saying God knows what. And you had us fooled. We thought you were a good boy. A smack across that face of yours is what you need! A good smack across the face from your mother like the one she gave to someone else's boy. Maybe she needs one too. Your face and those hands and feet are your excuse for everything, you saucy little crackie. You bless one more bus, kiss one more piece of pavement, make fun of the Holy Father one more time, and I'll send you home to Penny Joyce without a tooth left in your head. It might be an improvement."

I slapped her in the face hard, as hard as I could. I left the white marks of my oversized fingers on her cold red face. Her eyes went wide and she put one hand up to her cheek as if to gauge how much damage I had done. "You *hit* me," she said, staring at me with astonishment. I expected her to hit me back. I wouldn't have ducked, I wouldn't have run. I knew that I had crossed a line that children never cross. I wanted to be punished for it right away because I knew that, the longer my punishment was deferred, the worse it would be. But she turned slowly around and began to cry. "I'm sorry," I said. "I shouldn't— I'm sorry." She quickly made her way back to her house and went inside.

"McHugh said you hit Mrs. Madden," my mother said. "You hit her so hard you made her cry."

"You hit that boy from Brother Rice! Mrs. Madden said that if she knocked out all my teeth, it might improve my face. And she said that what *you* need is a good slap in the face like the one you gave O'Keefe."

"In that case, you should have hit her harder than you did." She took me in her arms and began to hug me, but in spite of the scent of perfume on her neck, I pulled away, pushed her aside, my hands on her hips.

In my room, I lay down on the upper bunk. I wished I hadn't given "Francine" to Sully, from whom she had been confiscated by McHugh, who, I fancied, now had her on *his* wall above *his* lonely bed. All I had now was a square on the wall that was less faded than the wall around it, the place that Francine had occupied for years.

Pops said that McHugh wanted to pay us a visit, to come to the house and talk things over with everyone present.

"Everyone?" my mother said. "You can tell McHugh what I told you: *You* are not one of us. *He* is not one of us. Us is, we are, Percy and me and Medina, so even if I was inclined to let McHugh inside the house, I'd send you away until after he was gone. I might even send you to your room. Second, McHugh will never set foot inside this house again. It's bad enough that he did it once without my permission. It's bad enough that he can *see* this house from where he lives or whatever he calls what he does after school. It's bad enough knowing that he is always just across the street without having him over to *counsel* us about our lives, to advise me in front of Percy, and Percy in front of me. Pops, here is something that will never happen: I will never serve McHugh a cup of tea, never ask him, 'Milk or sugar?' I will never put out a tray of biscuits for him, sit on the edge of my seat and wait for him to speak while my hands are folded primly in my lap. I will never watch him cross the street as he makes his way to 44, never open the door and stand back to welcome him inside. McHugh, in his all-black uniform and his clerical collar, will never see the inside of this house again unless he breaks the goddamn door down."

"He said he would be here at seven-thirty," Pops said.

My mother took Pops by the elbow and guided him toward the front door. "Go over there now," she said. "Don't phone him. Go over there. I don't care what you tell him, but if you have to, tell him I will call the police if he turns up on my doorstep. Or tell him that he and I can have a nice inconspicuous chat on the sidewalk in front of Brother Rice. I'll keep grabbing his hand and I'm fairly certain he'll keep pulling it away. I don't think it will set the neighbours to talking at all, do you?"

More than anything, she said, McHugh wanted to be *seen* crossing the street to our house. In fact, he would probably go back and forth half a dozen times just to make sure he was seen, make sure that it spread through the neighbourhood that Director McHugh was at last taking unprecedented measures to deal with the Joyces.

From the front window, I watched Pops, who had donned his lab coat, cross the street, all but running.

"Get away from the window, Perse," my mother said. "Let's not give McHugh reason to think he has us worried."

I reluctantly moved away from the window. A few minutes later, Pops returned, holding in his hand a sheet of paper that bore the official stamp of the Basilica.

"It's for Percy." Pops held it out to me. "It's from the Archbishop."

"I'll read it," my mother said. She did so in silence and then out loud:

My dear Percy:

I hope this note finds you in good health. It has been a joy for me to keep in touch with you all these years, to track your progress through school and to do whatever little bit I can to help you. As of late, however, I have been receiving reports about you that have caused me great concern. I have come to fear for your spiritual well-being. I once preached a sermon on your behalf and I have exempted you from corporal punishment throughout your years in school. I still believe that I was right to do so. But, my dear Percy, I feel that some gesture of atonement from you would be appropriate, some acknowledgement of, and contrition for, your recent misbehaviours. As to what this gesture should be, I leave it to your mother, in consultation with Brother McHugh, to decide, though I have, as you will hear, made some suggestions. Please understand that my affection for you has not lessened. I pray for you daily, as I trust you do for me.

Yours in Christ,

P.J. Scanlon, Archbishop of St. John's.

Pops handed her another piece of paper, this one unadorned with a stamp or letterhead of any kind. She read it out loud.

Dear Miss Joyce:

My superiors and I think that, in light of recent events, it would be wise for you, Percy and me to meet at my office at Brother Rice as soon as possible. I hope that you and Percy can come at five-thirty tomorrow—Vice-Principal MacDougal tells me that you believe your house to be too untidy at that time of day for you to receive me as a visitor. I appreciate your concern, though I have no doubt that it is unfounded and that you are an exemplary housekeeper. But if you feel you'd be more comfortable in my office, that too is acceptable. I must insist that my vice-principal be present at our meeting, as he is always present at meetings regarding matters of importance, not only to this school but to others on the Mount. I would not oppose the presence at the meeting of your sister-in-law, the other Miss Joyce, if you would like to have her there. If five-thirty is not convenient, please

indicate a suitable time. I will do my utmost to accommodate what
I am sure is your busy schedule.

    Yours in Christ,

    Director G.M. McHugh

My mother thrust the second letter back at Pops. "Tell him
that Percy and I will meet him in his office at five-thirty. You will
meet us there—don't come home before the meeting, and after the
meeting don't leave the school until half an hour after we do. Do
whatever you like with that letter, but get it out of this house."

She asked Medina if she would go with us to the meeting, for
moral support. "Jesus." Medina sighed. "All right."

"I don't understand why everyone is so upset."

"McHugh says that just to hear someone claiming he can perform miracles or to see him pretending to perform them makes
some people doubt that miracles ever happened," Pops said.

"I've never witnessed a miracle." She blew smoke in Pops' direction. "It's easy to claim that someone walked on water two thousand years ago. It's not as if you can dare them to try it again."

"The stain doesn't help," Medina said. "Some people are superstitious about that stain. They pretend to feel sorry for Percy, and I
guess they do, but deep down . . . I don't know . . . they don't want
to get too close to someone God might have it in for."

When I got home from school the next day, my mother told me not
to change out of my St. Bon's uniform. She told me to sit and watch
television until it was time for our meeting with McHugh. I watched
her at the Helm from the living room. She stopped typing for long
periods of time, nervously smoking one cigarette after another. She
was wearing her newest blouse, a plain but tight-fitting dark blue
one, and a tight black skirt and black pumps. She looked relieved
when, still wearing her green hospital uniform, Medina arrived.

"Didn't have time to change," Medina said. "I guess it's time to face the music." She sounded even more nervous than my mother looked.

"I guess so," my mother said. She looked at me and faintly smiled. "I thought girls would be his biggest problem. I guess I can't be blamed for not preparing for the day my son would claim that he was God."

In McHugh's office, the walls were festooned with diplomas, certificates of merit, awards, depictions of the Sacred Heart and the Blessed Virgin, small but ornate and finely detailed crucifixes like the ones in his suite.

I was surprised to see Sister Celestine, the long-reigning principal of Holy Heart, Sister C as she was called, sitting beside McHugh behind his desk, the two of them in high-backed leather chairs. Medina, my mother and I sat opposite them on wooden chairs, and Pops sat at the window, half on the sill, half on the radiator, awkwardly posed. He wore his lab coat, the strap of his safety goggles dangling from one pocket. I noted—and it seemed strange—that the only person there not wearing a uniform of some kind was my mother.

Sister C sat rigidly upright, her hourglass-shaped headdress rising high above her head. McHugh said Sister C was there because the "foment" I had caused had taken place on the grounds, the parking lot, of her school, and involved many of her students. Sister C wore black glasses, from behind the thick lenses of which she stared coldly at me. She spoke slowly, deliberately, giving an air of impenetrable composure. I wondered if, years ago, Mary Aggie had been imitating Sister C when she spoke as if she was unfazed even by the fact of her mortality and imminent entrance into Purgatory.

"I remember you." Sister C turned to Medina, who was so startled she all but jumped from her chair. "You were in my grade three class. I remember all my students, everything they said and did and didn't do. Yes."

Instead of answering as I was sure she would, Medina blushed and examined one of her hands as if she had never noticed the shape of it before.

"I remember you too." Sister C faced my mother. "The smart one. Smart but lazy. Full of backtalk even after you were strapped. So long ago."

"I remember you too, Sister," my mother said. "Less fondly, I'm sorry to say, than you remember me."

"Still the same," Sister C said, sighing as if she had known when my mother was a child that she would never change. She closed her eyes as she spoke, as if reciting from memory. "Both of you. Yes. But God has seen to it that you got what you deserve." She looked at me as if to say, "You're what they deserved."

"I'm glad to see they've modernized the Mercy habit," my mother said.

"Are you aware I am now Mother Superior at the Mercy Convent?"

"No, but that explains the air of superiority. Mother Superior. That's quite an accomplishment for a woman who has never had a child. Are you aware that I am now Mother Hysteria at 44 Bonaventure Avenue? Give my regards to Mothers Inferior, Mediocre and Deplorable."

"The one beside you isn't saying much," Sister C said, again closing her eyes, faintly smiling. "She learned what was what long ago. We wouldn't be hearing a peep from you either if you'd been dealt with in the same way that I dealt with her. Oh no, not a peep."

"But here I am, a Peeping Mom."

I watched in surprise as Medina raised a hand to wipe a tear from her eye, but her hand shook so badly she let it drop into her lap.

"What's wrong, Medina?" I asked. My voice broke, I was so nervous.

"Medina's fine," my mother said. "It's a classic case of protégé and tormentor meeting up after years apart."

"Be careful, Penelope. It's never too late for comeuppance." Sister C smiled.

"Or to somehow lose your living daylights. A woman your age could easily misplace them."

"Miss Joyce," McHugh said, "perhaps someday you'll put your clever words to better use."

"That tongue of hers," Sister Celestine said, her tone gentle, "will never be of better use until someone removes it from her head and feeds it to a dog."

McHugh turned to me suddenly, as if he felt the conversation was derailing and he needed to regain control, and asked if I understood why we were meeting. Before I could answer, Sister C leaned forward. "An air of disrespect, irreverence, even near insurrection is sweeping the Mount. The students are flouting all that they've been taught, at home, at school, in church. They are making jokes about the teachings of the Church. Percy Joyce, do you think your troubles are more important than those of others? Do you think you've been overburdened, singled out for persecution? It would be a mistake for you to assume that, because of His Grace, you can do what you like and get away with it. You are as God created you. One day you will stand alone before God, without an alibi, without excuses, without someone like your mother to plead your case. All alone, yes." She nodded, smiled, as if picturing the moment of my reckoning.

"Well said," my mother exclaimed. "It really is a shame that someone so given to nurturing has no children of her own."

McHugh, persevering, asked me again if I understood why we were meeting. I nodded, but he said, "Tell us why, Percy."

"I made up some stories. Just for a joke."

"What stories?"

"Just for a joke?" Sister C interrupted incredulously. I nodded. She turned and faced McHugh. "His backside would be the colour of his face if he were one of mine." She said it matter-of-factly, as if for her to lose her temper was simply not possible.

"But he is not one of yours," my mother said. "Nor is he one of Brother McHugh's. He is one of mine. He is my only one. My only child. By your own free choices and to the great detriment of the human gene pool, neither of you has a child."

"Such insolence." Sister C coldly faced McHugh, her voice when she spoke still eerily serene. "Why are you permitting this? I can see now why this wicked boy acts up the way he does."

McHugh addressed my mother. "None of the students on the Mount will ever forget what he's done. When he blessed the buses, they cheered him on as if he was an athlete. Sister Celestine tells me she has never seen students in such a frenzy. When they witness the flouting of the one thing that, as we tell them daily, will sustain them through their lives, the Truth as it was shown to us by the One True God, their impulse—their common but unnatural impulse—is to rebel, run wild. They saw that the least among them blasphemed but was not struck down, not punished in any way. The heavens did not open in protest. So? The contagion of Satan, whose greatest sin was Pride, spread through them like a plague. Satan knows he is foredoomed and will lose the war, yet he has his little victories. The frenzy of which Sister Celestine spoke is something I have seen before, children running en masse to their destruction like the Swine of Gadarene. It is something that must be put down or disorder will prevail."

"You have found your voice at last, Brother McHugh," Sister Celestine said, eyes closed. "You have found your voice at last, praise be to Our Heavenly Father." She looked at my mother and faintly smiled.

"I believe none of this would have happened if Percy had had a proper religious upbringing and family guidance," McHugh said. "If he had been baptized and raised as a Catholic. If he were taking the sacraments, going to confession and Communion, none of this would have happened."

"That's right," my mother said. "Baptism would have washed the stain right off his face."

Sister C turned her thick lenses on my mother. "That's how the Devil talks, Penelope. In mockery of God Himself. Ironic riddles. Irony is the trademark of the Devil." She slowly crossed herself.

"Not to mention the foundation of most of the world's great literature," my mother said. "Hence the famous expression: Shakespeare's hands are the Devil's workshop."

McHugh smiled as though at a failed attempt at wit.

"You don't seem content, Brother McHugh," my mother said. "Being a Christian Brother must be like being a male nurse. Answering to priests who are less than half your age—acne-ridden boys who can forgive your sins and give you whatever penance they wish. Most Catholic parents pray they'll have a boy, but if they have one, they don't go on to pray: 'Dear Lord, please endow my son with wisdom and guide him through his studies so that he may honour You and us by growing up to be a Christian Brother. May he one day teach grade eleven, live all his life in a single room and be a good sport about it.' No, it's a priest they pray for. To parents who wanted a priest, a Christian Brother would be a kind of consolation prize. A consolation priest. Honourable mention in the clerical sweepstakes.

"And what about you, Sister? The Brides of Christ are the charladies of the Church. Who are the celebrated women of the Church? A handful of horribly martyred saints, most of them virgins up to the day that they were raped. And the Blessed Virgin Mary."

"Mocking the Blessed Virgin," Sister Celestine said as placidly as if she were identifying a species of bird. She pointed at me. "No wonder you look like something that slithered out of Hell itself. You need to have the demon beaten out of you. Yes. All the meetings in the world won't make any difference to the likes of him and these two."

"Brother McHugh mentioned Pride," my mother said. "Whenever I think of Pride, I think of the getup priests say Mass in, preening like gold-laméd peacocks."

"God's generosity is *infinite*." Sister Celestine bowed her coif. "But his patience is not."

"That makes him imperfect."

"No wonder that boy has the mark of the Beast," Sister Celestine said, regarding me as if Satan himself could not disturb her equanimity.

Medina suddenly stood up. "Leave my nephew alone," she hissed, "or so help me God, I will break that beak you call a nose." She shook her fist at the nun, and I saw her face was smeared with tears. "You used to strap me all the time. But do you remember the day you told me to stay behind in the classroom for doing something wrong? Because I do. I don't even remember what it was, but you locked the door of the classroom and you beat me black and blue with a yardstick. I was eight years old. Eight. You hit me like you were chopping down a tree and you kept hitting me after I fell down. If I hadn't covered my face with my arms, you would have knocked my teeth down my throat. I don't know how you didn't break my arms. And all the while you screamed like I was a fire you were trying to put out." My mother put her hand on Medina's arm, but Medina shook it off. "A grown woman of God does that to a helpless little girl? That's why I dropped out. I was afraid to go back. I told my mother I would run away if she sent me back to school. But I'm not a helpless little girl anymore, Sister C. You get out of here now or so help me God, I'll jump across this desk and stuff your sacred rosary down your throat and use your teeth to make a new one. Go. Now. Get the fuck out, you sadistic cunt."

Sister C looked blank-faced at McHugh, who looked away. She slowly rose. Boots faintly scuffing, she eased past the desk. "Little

Medina," she said softly. "You'll be nothing but the little girl you once were when you stand before the Lord on Judgment Day and wish you'd heeded me. But it will be too late." She coasted past me out of McHugh's office, her headdress held high. Except for the sound of her shoes, she seemed to glide out, easing the door closed behind her. We listened to the measured, unhurried receding of her footsteps.

Medina sat down. "Bitch," she whispered, her hands shaking even as they lay there in her lap.

"Sister Celestine is . . . very devout," McHugh said. "And now, no doubt—in spite of how she seems—very upset. She is not accustomed to the sort of words you used."

"Quite right," my mother said. "A lifetime of celibacy has such a mellowing effect on people. Even if she'd been dressed like me, no one who witnessed that display of inner peace would doubt she was anything but a nun. And certainly Percy looks unfazed, as I would expect any wicked beast with an indwelling demon to be."

"Thank Christ she's gone," Medina said, exhaling as if she'd been waiting to breathe since she walked into the room and saw Sister C beside McHugh.

"You are mocking a clerical order of the Church and you are mocking me, a servant of God, a teacher and a servant of the poor," McHugh said, but he didn't sound upset and he wasn't looking at Medina but at my mother. "You're trying to provoke me, Miss Joyce. It won't work. Driving Sister Celestine away is one thing, but driving me away is something else. Percy's aunt would be well advised not to misjudge *me*." He paused and smiled gently at us all. "Let's get back to the matter at hand. His Grace requires some sort of gesture of contrition from Percy. He says that such a gesture is absolutely necessary if you wish to maintain your present . . . arrangement."

"If Pops goes on boarding with us, Pops loses his job. Or Pops moves out and keeps his job. Either way, I lose the room and board he pays me for, is that it?"

"I don't believe that's all he pays you for, unless he's been mis-leading me. I'd tell you to find another tenant, but I'm aware of just how much you . . . rely on my vice-principal. And how much he relies on you. His Grace is aware of these things as well."

I glanced at Pops, who was twisting the strap of his safety gog-gles round his finger, his face as pale as I had ever seen it. I looked at my mother, who was trying in vain to seem unperturbed.

"Do you"—she managed—"have an actual recommendation of some sort to make?"

"I do," McHugh said. "I would like Percy to apologize."

My mother shrugged and looked at me. "Say you're sorry," she said.

"I'm sorry," I said. I realized I was fighting back the urge to cry.

McHugh laughed. He said I couldn't discharge my debt by apol-ogizing only to him. I must apologize to everyone. Every student in every school. Every nun and priest, every Brother and teacher and staff member in each of the Seven Schools. I must apologize in person to His Grace.

"And how is he supposed to do all that?" my mother said.

"Not in print," McHugh said. "A printed apology that appeared in, say, the *Monitor* would end up blowing around the neighbour-hood, plastered to telephone poles, the door of your house, Miss Joyce, even those of your neighbours. Percy, because of his delicate nature, his usual passivity, would probably come home with copies of such an apology taped to the back of his blazer or stuck in his hair."

"What, then?" my mother said.

"Via the public address systems, Percy would read an apology written by me, with counsel from His Grace, to the students, cler-ics, teachers and staff of every school."

"No," my mother said. "I'll do it. Put the words in *my* mouth, not his. Everyone thinks I'm more to blame than him anyway. Perhaps I am. I'll read the apology. I'll testify before the Committee on Un-Basilican Activities. I'll name names."

McHugh smiled and shook his head. "Percy must apologize.

His Grace was very insistent about that. I need your decision as soon as possible. We can't have this situation getting worse."

"Or blowing over and being forgotten."

"An apology is not nearly as severe a punishment as any other student would receive. This is how we'll proceed. We'll record Percy reading the apology and play it over the public address system in the schools. He could read it into a tape recorder, right here in this office, in front of no one but his mother and me."

"Can you not see the absurdity of this? You want to treat my son like some sort of prisoner of war who, unless he wants to be shot, has to say over the radio that the cause he was fighting for is evil and therefore doomed to fail."

"It's your exaggerations that are absurd. Students at Brother Rice and other schools on the Mount have apologized to the entire student body in their own words in person during assembly in the gym. The point of having someone apologize in front of his peers is to teach them the value of contrition and humility. What I'm proposing would be much easier for Percy."

"Percy doesn't even belong to the Church he supposedly sinned against."

"He enjoys, and therefore has abused, the protection of the Church."

My mother sighed. "What do you think, Percy? You read into a tape recorder and get it over with?"

I shook my head.

"That wouldn't quite be getting it over with," McHugh said. "Percy would have to sit among his classmates as the tape was played. Just once. Just his own classmates. Not all of St. Bon's School or all of the other schools."

"You're *negotiating*," my mother said. "You're negotiating the terms of my son's surrender."

"There is another option. Percy need not apologize. You and he could agree that he be baptized and make his first confession and take his First Communion. That would more than make up for what he's done. When it comes to religion, conversion is the most profound and sincere form of apology."

"He's not going to become a Catholic just to satisfy your notion of revenge, are you, Percy?"

I shook my head again.

"We'll think about the apology," my mother said.

"Get back to me very soon, Miss Joyce," McHugh said.

Pops remained behind with McHugh as the three of us left his office and the school and crossed Bonaventure to 44.

"Pops," my mother said when he got home—he had just opened the door and was still standing in the doorway of the porch—"why did you tell McHugh about our arrangement?"

We were sitting around the kitchen table. From across the room, Pops looked sheepishly at her, at me and then at Medina.

"They *know*, Pops," my mother said, rolling her eyes. "They've known for some time."

"Why did you tell *them*?" Pops said, gesturing at Medina and me.

"I didn't. They figured it out for themselves. Just like everyone else on the Mount seems to have done."

"Well, so did McHugh," Pops said. "He guessed it. Or he heard the rumours in the neighbourhood. Everyone guesses, assumes. Or something, I don't know. He caught me by surprise."

"Did he really?" my mother asked. "Are you sure that, deep down, you weren't just dying to tell him, to brag to him that you were banging Penny Joyce no matter what the consequences of such a boast might be?"

Pops shook his head. "No, no, it was nothing like that."

My mother tongued her front teeth, her lips pursed. "You might have told us Sister C would be there."

"I didn't know about Sister C. Look, Paynelope, what am I

supposed to do? On the one hand he's my boss. On the other—"

"There is no other hand, Pops. Not another word."

Pops crossed the floor to his room and slammed the door.

I begged my mother again and again to go back and ask McHugh to let me "write" a letter of apology for the *Monitor* rather than read one into a microphone, even once.

"I'm with Percy," Medina declared. "Even if I could read, I'd be so nervous I'd choke up or something."

I was suddenly terrified of the idea of "choking up," even of crying while hundreds of students listened to me sob and struggle to find my voice. And what if I couldn't make it through the apology? I suspected that McHugh would make me try another day, and another, over and over until I managed it. I pictured students in classrooms all over the Mount listening to my disembodied voice the way they did to the principal's, my voice louder than ever before, its every tremor magnified. I pictured the kids cracking up at the sound of Little Percy Joyce's voice making a public announcement, Percy Joyce's eerily magnified voice emanating from the metal box above the classroom door. And who knew what McHugh would write for me—what an exercise in self-humiliation the apology itself might be? Who knew what he would make me admit to? Perhaps things that I had neither said nor done. I thought that an apology in the *Monitor* was far preferable, especially given that almost no one read the *Monitor* anyway.

But my mother said McHugh was right, that every student in the neighbourhood would be going round with a copy of my apology in their pocket, that copies of it would be blowing around the neighbourhood for months, years, there, always there, on the ground, everywhere I looked. She sent Pops back to McHugh, telling him to return with a copy of the apology. Pops came back with a single sheet of paper. It bore the title, centred over the text,

"The Apology of Percy Joyce." My mother said it seemed that McHugh and His Grace meant it to be as famous and influential a recantation as Galileo's. She read it, shook her head, rolled her eyes and sighed, "I suppose it could be worse."

So as not to disrupt classes on the Mount, my apology would be played over the PA systems of the seven Mount schools more or less simultaneously just before school let out, after which Brother Hogan would escort me from my homeroom down the hill to 44.

The next afternoon, Pops returned from Brother Rice with a large reel-to-reel tape recorder in the use of which, he said, the head of the audiovisual department at Brother Rice had instructed him at length. My mother briefly glanced at it, then went on typing. Medina came over just after five and shook her head when she saw the machine resting on the table at the opposite end of the Helm from my mother and her typewriter.

We all stared at it as if we couldn't account for its presence in the house.

"Brother McHugh says that he will read a recorded introduction to Percy's apology," Pops said. "He's recording it tonight at the school."

I thought of Brother McHugh and I simultaneously engaged in the same strange task, he on one side of Bonaventure, me on the other.

"I suppose it's not much comfort to you," my mother said to me, "that, during the Inquisition, people who pissed off the Church would have much preferred your punishment to the one they got."

"Very funny. You wouldn't be making jokes if you had to apologize into a tape recorder."

"What is it with McHugh and punishment anyway?" my mother asked. "He must have been a delightful, pet-torturing tot. I can just see him practising on walnuts with a thumbscrew. Experimenting on himself with the rack he got for Christmas."

"Paynelope."

My mother said all I deserved was a good talking-to from no one else but her—a talking-to which, because of the apology, had been cancelled. She said that, as there was no knowing how long it would take to get the apology right, we should have dinner first.

While we were eating my mother's macaroni and cheese—usually one of my favourites, but I could barely force down a few bites—Medina said she had never witnessed a more "foolish" situation than the one we were in.

"In what sense are you in it?" Pops said. "What about me? If Percy doesn't do this, I either have to move out or lose my job."

"Why would moving out be such a big deal for a ladies' man like you, Pops?" Medina replied, winking at me. My mother shot her a look.

"Well, it's just that I'm used to it here," Pops said, his face and neck blotched red from embarrassment. "I've always found it difficult to adjust to new situations. And this location is very convenient, being so close to Brother Rice."

"Jesus, Pops," my mother said. "We all know why you live here. Even Percy. Why are you still pretending?"

"I really wouldn't want to leave you and Percy in the lurch," Pops said. "What other boarder would pay half as much as I do?"

"Why *do* you pay *soooo* much?" Medina said, her grin lapsing quickly into a frown.

"Has kindness become a crime?" Pops said.

"Oh no," Medina said, "not if you're saving someone from the lurch. There's no worse place to be left than in the lurch. You're a saint for keeping them out of it out of the goodness of your heart. I'd rather be left in St. Anthony, where you were born, than in the lurch."

"Really," Pops said. "How would you get there? It's a long walk."

"It's time for you to make your insincere apology, Perse," my mother said. "You can read it with your fingers crossed behind your back. You can make faces at the tape recorder. Just say the words."

"We wouldn't need Pops if you made more money," I said. "You're really smart and you're a dropout. I'll still be smart if I drop out."

"It's not about how smart you are. It's about a piece of paper that certifies how smart you are, even if you're not. People are very impressed by documents that bear the official seal of someone or something. They will believe a lie if someone certifies it as the truth. In fact, the lie becomes the truth. The village idiot is certified as the village sage, and a sage is born. When so certified, right becomes wrong and good becomes evil. It's too late for me to get a certifying piece of paper, but it's not too late for you. All you have to do is read what's on *that* piece of paper. We know that none of it is true. I bet a lot of other people do as well. I'll help you with it. All you have to do is speak close to the machine, okay?"

I nodded.

"We'll do the dishes later," my mother told Medina. "I don't know how long this will take and I don't want to keep Percy up too late."

We sat at the Helm, me opposite my mother's typewriter, my mother on my left, Pops on my right, Medina sitting beside my mother, arms folded, lips pressed tightly together as if she were staging some kind of silent protest. Pops put the printed apology on the table in front of me.

"While Percy's reading, no one else should make a sound," he said. He told me not to touch the piece of paper.

He pressed the record and play buttons on the tape recorder and nodded at me. My mother put her hand on my shoulder. I was startled when the reels began to move and the tape from one wound around the other with a faint whirring noise. Until then, I suppose, I believed that I wouldn't have to go through with it, that McHugh would relent or my mother would think of an alternative that he would agree to.

Everyone looked solemnly at the tape recorder when it started making noise. It was as though they had coaxed me into going through with some medical test and only now, as they were face to face with the device that would perform the test, did they realize what they had talked me into. And there, to complete the picture, was Pops, looking every bit the doctor in his lab coat, his stethoscope-like goggles poking from one pocket. I felt as though I would now be somehow attached to the machine, hooked up to it, and it would perform its task exactly as it had many times before, and that Pops, to whom it was all routine, would have no more regard for me than the tape recorder did. As if he was reading my mind, he said to my mother, "I'm going to record his voice, not extract his bone marrow." But he might as well have said "vital signs" instead of "voice," as if the machine's purpose was to help them find out what was wrong with me, to coerce apologies from misbehaving children. My apology. I would soon be without my apology. I fancied it was something like the spleen. An apology that Pops would transport in the machine across the street to Brother Rice, where McHugh would regard it like a body part of mine that had been lopped off—a trophy he would keep forever on display in his office, a chastening reminder to all boys that their apologies could be removed.

"Perse looks as white as a ghost," Medina said.

"Are you all right, sweetheart?" My mother put her hand on my forehead. "Damp. You're sweating. You're not feeling sick, are you, sweetheart?"

"Not really," I said.

"Well, don't throw up on McHugh's machine," Pops cautioned. But I couldn't stop the train of thought that had started in my head. Apology. Biology. You must biologize. Boys dissecting formaldehyde-preserved apologies that boys before them had offered up to science.

"Even your face looks pale," my mother said. But I didn't want to think of my face. I tried not to think of anything.

"I may not be a nurse, but I know what someone who's about to be sick looks like," Medina said. "You should get him to the bathroom, Pen."

But I shook my head, convinced that, if I were to stand, I would get sick. I thought of Medina's dislike of cars as I looked at the two spools of tape spinning slowly in opposite directions.

"Can you turn the machine off, Pops?" I said. He jabbed at the stop button with such speed and force he must have thought that every fraction of a second counted. My mother went to the kitchen and brought back a glass of water, which I pretended to sip. I felt a little better now that I was no longer mesmerized by the spinning tapes that had reminded me of the close-up of relentless train wheels I had seen on TV the night before. When I nodded at him, Pops hit record and play.

"To His Grace, the Archbishop of St. John's," I read, my voice so high-pitched from nervousness it came out as barely more than a squeak. Pops hit stop.

"Don't worry," Pops said, "you can do it in bits and pieces. The head of the AV department will clean it up later with McHugh."

Pops hit record and play, I read the phrase again and Pops hit stop again.

"He's never going to sound like a grown man reading the nightly news," my mother said.

"I just want to make sure that his voice is as clear as it can be," Pops said. "I want to make sure it's intelligible. We wouldn't want Percy to have to do it all over again tomorrow night."

"I bet Brother McHugh is finished recording his introduction," I said, looking out through the window and up, across the street to the lights of Brother Rice high above us. I felt that I was reading to the Archbishop while standing right in front of him, reading the words he "wrote," the ones McHugh rewrote for him, and which he would therefore want me to get just right. I tried not to think of the pictures of him in St. Bon's in which, despite the shepherd's staff he held and the pointy, funny-looking mitre on his head, he looked so severe.

"Pretend that you're just reading to the three of us," my mother said.

I next read the opening phrase almost buoyantly, as if I were introducing His Grace the Archbishop of St. John's to an adoring crowd on the day of his triumphant installation. Pops hit stop again.

"You're not directing a movie here, Pops," my mother said. "Percy, don't worry about what it sounds like or even what the words mean. Just read it like you were reading the back of a cereal box. Read it through no matter what you think your voice sounds like. If you're not sure how to say a word, I'll tell you, then you say it and keep going."

"Don't go too fast," Pops said.

"And you keep your hands off the tape recorder," my mother told him. "He's had all the coaching from you he's going to get. He's not trying to boost the spirits of his people after some dreadful setback in the war. He's just a boy who's having words put in his mouth by a man he met once and hopefully will never meet again."

My mother hit record and play and I began to read in what seemed to be a monotone. I got to the phrase "I do hereby humbly apologize" and felt suddenly that I was guilty of far more than anyone, even Brother McHugh, suspected, far more than I was apologizing for, a life of transgression that forever set me apart from the rest of humankind. I burst into tears. My shirt and hair were soaked with sweat. My mother hugged me from behind, her arms around my chest, and kissed my cheek. I was too upset to derive any tittilation from the feel of her breasts crushed against my back. The transgressions that had set me apart and would set me apart forever seemed huge and far greater than what I was being asked to apologize for but didn't feel the least bit apologetic about. So what that I had claimed to be the Son of God and a pen pal of the Pope. So what that I had brought to school a pornographic photograph acquired for me by my mother. *I* hadn't changed the colour of the face of Baby Jesus in the missal in the chapel with a red Magic Marker as some boy, inspired by my claim to be Christ, was said to have done. It wouldn't have bothered *me* if some other boy had claimed to be the nephew of the Holy Ghost or denied that God the Father had a beard, or claimed that his father worked with the lepers of Nigeria.

"Hello, everyone, this is Percy Joyce . . . I am a grade nine student at St. Bonaventure College on Bonaventure Avenue in St. John's. In the vicinity of Holy Heart High School I recently did and said some things that I should not have done and said. Many of you witnessed my inappropriate behaviour. Many of you heard about it from your fellow students . . . I claimed to be a worker of miracles, but I am just an ordinary boy with ordinary problems of my own. I pretended I could cure the sick. I made an even more grandiose claim that I think it would be best not to repeat even by way of apologizing for it . . . I made a mockery of the sacraments, which can be administered only by an ordained priest of God. I mocked our Holy Father. I made certain claims about my mother and father that were false . . . I assaulted Mrs. Madden. I made fun of humble Saint Joseph. Jesus, Mary and Joseph exemplify the proper relations that should exist between husband and wife, and parents and children. We should often ask them to sanctify our families by their example and intercession . . . I should not have pretended that I could confer upon myself the power to preserve others from harm by granting them my blessing. Although I bear the mark of my Creator, that mark has not endowed me with special powers or capacities . . . I mocked the doctrine of the Holy Trinity, which is the central dogma of the Church. In the unity of the Godhead there are three persons, God the Father, God the Son and God the Holy Spirit. They are co-eternal and co-equal but truly distinct from one another. I confess to having done all these things . . . I am heartily sorry for having done them. I have made this apology of my own free will by way of asking forgiveness from anyone who, because of my behaviour, may have been troubled, offended or upset, and in the hope of returning the Seven

Schools of the Mount to the state of studious quietude in which learning and the love of God may flourish. Again, I do hereby humbly apologize and solemnly vow never to repeat the transgressions to which I have confessed."

It seemed to me, as I made the recording, that there was no one else within miles. As if I had lugged the recorder to some remote, silent place on Signal Hill and shamefully apologized, unheard by anyone or anything but my machine, had gone to some long-ago-designated official place of apology where, in solitude, many others, some of them famous, had humbled themselves before technology and God.

"It doesn't sound very contrite," Pops said after hitting stop. "He could at least sound sorry even if he's not."

"He's not going to sob his way through it," my mother said. "That would make him a hypocrite, and hypocrisy the subject of next week's apology. No wailing, no gnashing of teeth. You have enough there that McHugh and his minions can patch together any way they want."

"All right," Pops said. "McHugh is waiting for me in his office. He plans to broadcast the apology tomorrow afternoon if possible."

My mother sighed and shook her head. "Well," she said, "don't keep the Grand Inquisitor waiting."

Pops picked up the tape recorder and, holding it in front of him as if it might otherwise explode, hurried from the house.

"There you go, Perse," my mother said. "That part's done. By this time tomorrow, all this silliness will be behind you."

I was relieved when, about fifteen minutes later, Pops came back without the tape recorder.

"McHugh says that it will need a great deal of work," he said. "He said that he and the AV people might be at it half the night."

"How did he seem when he listened to it?" my mother said.

"Obviously not pleased," Pops said.

"I don't suppose he let you hear his introduction."

"I didn't ask to hear it. He didn't offer. Maybe he hasn't recorded it yet."

Pops told me about the Protestant archbishop Thomas Cranmer who, trying to avoid execution, recanted his Protestantism, then later recanted his recantation when he discovered that the Catholic Church meant to burn him at the stake no matter what he said or did. "You can recant your recantation all you like when you're at home," Pops said, "but don't do it out there. Remember Cranmer."

"Cranmer. Wonderful example, Pops," my mother said. "From now on, let's keep to a minimum the analogies to Percy's life that end with people being burned alive."

"Physician, heal thyself," Pops said.

My mother smiled at that and nodded a subtle touché.

"Well, you should at least talk to him about how to comport himself after his apology," Pops said.

"Come straight home with Brother Hogan," my mother said later when Pops had gone to his room. "Don't say a word to any of those children on the buses, especially that boy Sully from Torbay. Forget about the dollar that he owes you—you'll never see it. If anyone tries to goad you into making the kind of jokes you made before, just ignore them. No more stories, not even about Jim Joyce. If you've given him a new identity, keep it to yourself. I don't want it getting back to me that you're saying now he's the captain of a submarine so top secret it never surfaces or something. God, if people knew what you *could* have told those children, all this would seem pretty pale by comparison."

I lay awake that night thinking of McHugh at work on my apology across the street. Perhaps he was finished and watching 44 from the window of his suite. I wondered what he was thinking at that second, if *he* wondered if I'd been able to get to sleep or had even gone to bed yet, much of the house still being lit. I imagined him on the eighth floor of the Quarters looking down at the now-curtained windows of 44, watching for any sign of movement, any sign that Pops might be in my mother's room or she might be in Pops'. I was sure he wondered what it was like to sleep with Penny Joyce and, in spite of himself, envied Pops. He probably found it as hard to believe as any of the boys that Pops had landed her or that Pops could do justice to a body such as hers.

I fell asleep at some point and woke about three-thirty to the sound of footsteps and muted whispers in the hall. I recognized the footsteps as my mother's. She was heading back to her bedroom. I faintly heard the back screen door being eased open then shut with a click. Medina had been in my mother's room. It was the first time I had ever heard her re-arrival or departure. Now that she was gone, my mother was free to pad less quietly back to bed in her slippers. It seemed strange that she had invited Medina over on a night when she must have known I would sleep lightly, if at all, unless she wanted company on a night when she knew *she* would sleep lightly, if at all. I thought of getting up and going to her room and asking her if she would come to mine and lie in the lower bunk for a while, perhaps until one of us fell asleep or even until morning. But she hadn't slept at all yet. I felt jealous of Medina. I had no idea what it felt like to a woman when she came, and I wondered if it was possible for any boy or man to feel that way. I looked at the faded square of wall above my bed, and at the pictures of Saint Drogo that flanked Sister Mary Aggie's prayer for unattractive people.

I could rationalize my lust for my mother this way: Throughout adolescence and young manhood and beyond, every heterosexual male not only harbours the desire, at some point in his life, to sleep with a truly beautiful, sensual, fuck-loving woman, but *believes* that he will, that it is not yet, not ever, too late, no matter how old he is. It is, of course, a delusion in most cases, but a sustaining one. To abandon all hope, however delusional, is impossible. It seemed to me, at fourteen, that the only truly beautiful woman I would ever have the faintest hope of sleeping with was my mother. It was as simple as that. I was not goaded by any sort of neurosis or incest fetish to pursue her. She wasn't just my best bet, she was my *only* bet.

But I know that it was not for these reasons that I pursued my mother. I pursued her because I was in love with her, body and soul.

THE GREAT UNVEILING

I FELL asleep and was again wakened by a noise. The door of my room opened. My mother came in, wearing her bathrobe. "Shhhh—" she said. "Not a word, not a peep."

She went to the window of my room and opened the curtains, backed away from the window, still staring at it, lit by what might have been a street light or the first full moon in March. She slowly, almost teasingly, undid the belt of her black robe and let the robe hang open, let it part, the two halves of the front flanked by the loose ends of the belt. She wore nothing beneath it. I saw, in the silver light, a wider, lower cleavage than I ever had before, and, lower still, the full length of her legs, the insides of her thighs that I knew would be smoother than mine or any boy's or girl's. I saw finally her feet, slightly akimbo, as if she were posing for some lover photographer whose camera lens was pressed against the window from outside. In a movement that looked long practised, as if she had performed it many times, she drew back her shoulders, causing the robe to shed like skin, slide slowly from her, pause around her upper arms, then fall to the floor around her feet. She looked like a statue whose loving sculptor was unveiling her at last. The Great Unveiling of Penelope. I saw her breasts, her nipples in what might have been a state of full arousal, her breasts at such angles to each other that a series of faint knobs— her sternum—showed in between. Below that, I saw more clearly what I had only seen in shade so far, the small swell of her lower belly, rapidly rising and falling as, I fancied, it must have done the night I found her with Medina, her wide back bared to me. I heard her breathe, saw her breasts and shoulders rise. Just below her left breast, her skin pulsed at a rate that seemed to match the racing of my heart. I saw the out-jutting of her hips, the V of her long legs that ended at the hollow that was darker than her robe. She stood thus for perhaps ten seconds, staring out the window as if mesmerized by some sight that had moved her to show herself at last to her one, her only child, the strangeling whom she must have known wanted even more, who wanted, wanted, wanted everything because he might otherwise have to reconcile himself to nothing, wanted her to hoist herself, climb into my bed and give me what she gave Jim Joyce the night I was conceived, what she gave to Pops for my sake, and something like what she gave, and was given by, Medina. I hoped I would not have to make do with what she had just now bestowed upon me, a gift offered at a cost I might forever be too young to understand. As though departing from a stage as a scene was ending and the curtains and the lights were going down, she swiftly crouched and grabbed her robe and left the room and gently shut the door, leaving the curtains open and my room lit pale and silver by what might still have been a street light or the first full moon in March.

THE APOLOGY OF PERCY JOYCE

I WOKE a third time to the smell of toast. My mother, Medina and Pops were in the kitchen. My mother and Medina were using an empty boiled-egg shell as an ashtray. I looked at my mother, who didn't look like a woman who had performed a striptease for her son the night before; there was no hint of self-consciousness or embarrassment in her eyes. I wondered if this meant she assumed I understood that the Great Unveiling would neither be repeated nor be outdone, that she had done all she was willing to do for me.

"So it looks like this *is* the big day, Perse," my mother said. "McHugh phoned Pops just a few minutes ago."

Pops, in his lab coat, slumped in his chair, looked as though he wished his day hadn't started with a phone call from McHugh.

"None of the other children know," my mother said, "so don't say a word about it to them."

"They'll be surprised," I said gloomily.

"Good. Maybe your apology will be half over before they even know what's up."

"No, it won't."

Pops looked up. "Ready to face the firing squad, Percy?"

"Could you be a little more ominous, Pops?" my mother said. "We don't want to send Percy off to school feeling too carefree, now, do we? Perhaps the offer of a blindfold and a final cigarette would put him more at ease."

"Well, *I'm* here for moral support," Medina said.

"Who can feel apprehensive now that Medina's here?" Pops said.

"Knock it off, you two. Perse, you don't have to do anything today but sit there. You don't even have to listen. Cover your ears. You already know what you said."

"Except for McHugh's introduction," Pops said.

"You're not gifted when it comes to reassurance, are you, Pops?"

"I'm a realist."

"Well, Percy isn't. He's one of those rare early-teens optimists. Unlike you, he doesn't believe that the worst will be over when he's dead."

I left them there and walked up icy Bonaventure, past Brother Rice and Holy Heart to St. Bon's. The day dragged as I knew it would.

At 2:45, the PA box in my homeroom let loose a squawk of static that set the whole class, even me, to laughing.

"Hush up," Brother Hogan commanded. Next there sounded the only voice other than that of the principal of St. Bon's that I had ever heard coming from the PA system.

"Attention faculty, students and staff. This is Director McHugh. Please pardon this interruption of the last class of the day."

I scrutinized Brother Hogan, by whose blank expression I could tell that all the teachers of the Mount had known of this "interruption" in advance.

"You're about to hear a recorded announcement from one of your fellow students. It was recorded, and copies were made of the recording, so that all the faculty, students and staff of the Seven Schools could hear it at once and so that the burden on Percy Joyce could therefore be minimized.

"The announcement as such speaks for itself, but I would like to say a few words before I hand things over to Percy Joyce."

I stared at my desk and felt myself blushing all over, my face and body, I fancied, all the same colour for the first time in my life. The boy behind me nudged my arm and a murmur of surprise started up among the boys, only to be quelled by Brother Hogan, who whacked the blackboard with a yardstick so hard that a cloud of chalk dust formed, rose and fell.

"As most of you know, Percy is an academically outstanding student, an obedient student, respectful of his peers and his teachers. You may also know that he began and continues to live his life in somewhat unusual circumstances. To speak publicly of all of these would be neither appropriate nor necessary.

"You all know Percy, in the sense that he is easily recognizable. But no one is disfigured in the eyes of their Creator, nor should they be in their own eyes or in the eyes of others. God has given us the free will to choose how we deal with things that cannot be controlled or changed. One such thing is Percy's supposed disfigurement, which, for the most part, he has borne with grace and forbearance, in such a manner that it has made him a stronger, more appealing, more exemplary person than he might otherwise have been.

"There are times in life, however, when all of us stray from what we know is the one true path of righteousness that, because of the mercy and sacrifice of God, will lead us to salvation.

"Most of you, perhaps all of you, know just how far Percy has strayed from that path in recent days. There is no better person to speak of this matter than Percy himself. Both he and his mother have repeatedly told me that he wants nothing more than to make amends. I ask that you listen to his remarks with open minds and reward him as God Himself rewards all true confessors—with forgiveness and the everlasting gift of hope."

For a while after McHugh stopped speaking, nothing but low-level static came from the PA box. I could feel the other boys staring at me but didn't dare look up.

"All eyes on the blackboard," Brother Hogan said. "You don't need to look at Percy while you listen to his voice."

Finally, "I" began to speak. That is, the words "Hello, everyone, this is Percy Joyce" boomed from the PA box at a much higher volume than McHugh's voice had. It sounded as if it were coming from one giant loudspeaker located somewhere outdoors on the Mount so that even pedestrians, motorists and people in their houses could hear me. "I am a grade nine student at St. Bonaventure College. . . ." Even had my voice not been so surreally amplified, the version of my apology that was being broadcast sounded nothing like any of the versions we had recorded at home the night before. The person speaking sounded so unlike me that several boys turned round and looked in awe at me, as if they believed they were just now hearing my real voice, the real, commanding, confident, forthright Percy Joyce who spoke as grown men did in public service announcements. I wondered if my voice was thus magnified and flaw-free on all the PA boxes in the school, in all the classrooms at St. Bon's, in all the classrooms in all the Seven Schools of the Mount.

Through the half-open windows at the back of the classroom came what seemed to be a faint echo of my apology until I realized that I was hearing it from the also-open windows of St. Pat's across the street, delayed by about a second.

"I recently said and did some things that I should not have said and done," I bellowed as if daring someone to contradict me. "I claimed to be a worker of miracles," blared the boy with the authority and conviction of someone whose claim to be a miracle worker was beyond dispute and would not be revoked. A couple of boys put their hands over their ears until Brother Hogan mimed that they should remove them.

"I was born on an important day in the calendar of the Church, a day especially important to the faithful of St. John's, whose city is named after the saint who prophesied the birth of Christ, who prepared the way for Him, baptizing believers in His Name.

"My birthday falls on the day this city was discovered almost five hundred years ago by a namesake of the Baptist, John Cabot, a man named to invoke his blessing on the life of exploration he would lead. I should not have blasphemed against my patron, the greatest of all the saints."

Even my inner voice was drowned out by my recorded one, every trace of my self-consciousness was shouted down. I went on staring at my desk but did so wide-eyed, for I was half convinced that, at long last, it was the real me I was hearing. "I made certain claims about my mother and father that were false . . . I made fun of humble Saint Joseph—"

It sounded more as if I had bullied the helpless henpecked husband of the Blessed Virgin Mary, who, together with the Son of God who had been fathered by the Holy Ghost, was forever scorning history's most famous cuckold.

"I mocked the doctrine of the Holy Trinity—" I said as if I understood that doctrine as well as any Church theologian and had therefore mocked it more cleverly than anyone ever had before. It went on like that to my final line. "I confess to having done all these things. I am heartily sorry for having done them," I said as heartily as the whole apology had been delivered. "I do hereby humbly apologize and solemnly vow never to repeat the transgressions to which I have confessed."

I knew the apology was over, but for a few moments no one else did, not even, it seemed, Brother Hogan, who for some reason stared expectantly at me. I wondered if I should have concluded by saying, "Thank you for listening," by signing off in some manner not indicated by Brother McHugh. Then came a smattering of applause that Brother Hogan put a stop to by once more whacking the blackboard with his yardstick. The PA box squawked again.

"Thank you, Percy Joyce," Brother McHugh's recorded voice said at normal volume. I exhaled for what seemed like the first time in minutes. The apology was over. My mother had been right. It seemed—quite miraculously—all behind me now. McHugh, having overseen the editing of the tape itself, was surely satisfied. I looked forward to my walk home down Bonaventure, not even minding that Brother Hogan would escort me, for I would surely not need his protection. I was once again the Boy of the Hour. A sense of triumph replaced the one of dread I had felt since I first set eyes on the tape recorder. I was astonished, exultant, to find myself unscathed by Uncle Paddy and Brother Gus McHugh.

The PA box squawked again. "On a final note," Brother McHugh's voice said. I imagined him in his office at Brother Rice, listening to himself as he was about to add his final note. I thought of Sully in some classroom at Brother Rice with my dollar in his pocket. I thought of Pops in the chem lab, no doubt feeling as relieved as I did, soon to return to 44, as I was.

"I would like to inform you," Brother McHugh said, "of a decision that Percy and his mother made between them just today. I'm sure many of you know that Percy has not yet been baptized in the Catholic faith or any other, although his mother and father were both baptized in the Catholic faith just after they were born. Percy and his mother have decided that Percy will be baptized a Catholic at some point in the near future and as soon as possible thereafter take the sacraments of Confession and Communion. They wish to announce also that Percy will take Jerome as his baptismal name, which is the Christian name of Brother Rice vice-principal MacDougal. I hope that all of you who are listening will congratulate Percy and welcome him at last into the One True Holy Catholic and Apostolic Church."

The sound of several pairs of hands clapping came from the PA box. "God bless you, Percy Joyce," McHugh said. Brother Hogan, smiling warmly at me, put down his yardstick and began to applaud, inciting the boys of my homeroom to do the same.

The classrooms on either side of ours erupted in applause, followed by those on the other side of the hall. Soon the whole school was ablaze with noise, clapping, howling, thumping, stamping, cheering. I heard the same tumult from St. Pat's across the street, from Holy Heart and Brother Rice down the hill, from Our Lady of Mercy Convent School, the Presentation Convent School on Barnes Road, the squeals of the little orphan girls of Belvedere.

The boys of St. Bon's stood up, desks scraping on the floor, and soon I was certain that all the students of the Mount, except for me, were on their feet. I was certain that my mother could at least *hear* Brother Rice celebrating. I wondered what she would think was going on. Such a riotous celebration for the apology I had laboured to record? And what would she do when she heard what McHugh had done? Still, though I foresaw something of the tumult that was imminent, I couldn't help smiling, grinning from ear to ear.

Brother Hogan yelled that class was dismissed. I stood, but before I could move toward him or he toward me, two of the bigger boys in class hoisted me on their shoulders and carried me from the classroom into the hallway, downstairs to the lobby and outside to the parking lot in front of the playing field. They turned right and carried me to Bonaventure as throngs of cheering and laughing boys followed. But I saw, my heart sinking, that it was a mock celebration, that the world had tilted in an instant in favour of my supposed champions, His Grace and the Director, that all things were to be enfolded in their outstretched arms, that my mother and I, and Pops, and Medina, had been duped by powers whose pawns we seemed fated forever to be. Different, variously coloured rivers of students poured from the snow-covered side streets onto Bonaventure, the blue of St. Bon's, the green of

St. Pat's, the dark blue tunics and light blue blouses of Holy Heart, the maroon of Brother Rice. I should have felt, as I had when I pretended to be God Himself, like some champion athlete who had just returned home from victory on the Mainland. But the sounds of it all around me were changing subtly, more laughing than cheering, and I realized that the point of this celebration had become as much to mock the importance of my conversion as to acknowledge it. There I was, displayed aloft at the confluence of the rivers, surrounded by a mob of boys and girls performing a kind of mass parody of adulation, some chanting my name but more simply skylarking, wrestling, throwing hats and even textbooks into the air, the melee blocking Bonaventure, on which some cars were hemmed in by students who looked bent on overturning the vehicles or dragging their occupants out onto the street.

The neighbourhood residents who were at home at that time of day may have spotted me and attributed the uproar and traffic stoppage once again to that disfigured, flounder-faced, trouble-making Joyce boy. The cars blew their horns in protest, but the boys and girls would not give way until, at the Curve of Bonaventure, they began to peel off home onto the side streets on the right or race back up the hill along the sidewalk. The two boys on whose shoulders I had ridden down Bonaventure set me on the sidewalk outside 44. One kicked me in the backside and said, "There you go, Percy, now you're a Catholic." Then the two of them ran back up the hill.

Many other boys and girls still milled about and, now that the mob had dispersed, yelled less complimentary things at me.

"Nice apology, Percy. Getting baptized. Easier than getting strapped, I suppose. I wouldn't mind apologizing instead of getting strapped."

"Don't worry, Percy, we still believe you're one of the Holy Triplets. Three in one. Like a Swiss Army knife."

"Percy Jerome Joyce. Got a nice ring to it!"

"Maybe a ring came with it—did Pops pop the question to Penny, Percy? Why else would you take his name? I bet you and your mother will be taking his last name too. Did Penny pop her buttons? Jesus, I'd love to see that."

"Oh Brother McHugh, I'm sorry I lied, but I'd rather not be crucified."

Still, I couldn't resist the urge to wave just before I went inside, a final acknowledgement it might have been of the worshipful adulation of my peers I had so longed for. When I opened the door, my mother came running to meet me and took me in her arms.

"Well, if it isn't Jerome the Baptist, home at last," my mother said when Pops arrived just after eight. Medina had come over as soon as she could get away from work, and they'd been there for hours, sipping beer at the kitchen table.

"I'm sorry, Paynelope," Pops said, slurring his words, his hands hooked thumbs out in the pockets of his lab coat. "I was afraid to come home, so I went to the East End Club for a beer. No overcoat. Dressed like this. Got a lot of compliments."

"Welcome home, Jerome," Medina said.

"Saint Jerome is one of the Doctors of the Church," Pops said. "There are thirty Doctors of the Church and *none* of them are women. Too bad."

"There are no Nurses of the Church either," my mother said, "but if you don't soon shut up, you may need a doctor *and* a nurse."

He laughed sheepishly, went to the fridge and took out a beer, forgot to open it, then slumped noisily into his armchair in the sunroom.

"Well, that's *it*," my mother said. "That's the last straw. I can't go around telling the truth, telling people that what McHugh said isn't true. At best, people will think I'm even crazier than they thought. I can't get away with calling McHugh a liar. What proof do I have? And with all of the Mount celebrating Percy's conversion, what am I supposed to do? Uncle Paddy either connived with McHugh about this, or he's as pleased as punch to hear I've come round at last to his way of thinking. Either way, there's no turning back from this."

She got up from the table, a glass of beer in one hand, went to the sunroom and spun around Pops' chair. "You knew about it all along, didn't you? Percy getting baptized. Taking your name. McHugh may as well have announced the day of our wedding."

"I'm sorry, Paynelope, but McHugh is a hard man to argue with. No one will think all this has anything to do with *us*."

"For the umpteenth time, there *is* no us," she said quietly, then slowly poured her glass of beer over his head. It must have been warm, for he didn't draw so much as a single extra breath but merely sat there, eyes closed, as the beer ran down all sides of his head, frothing up his face, trickling down beneath the collar of his lab coat and his shirt. He wiped the beer from his eyes and the rest of his face with the sleeves of his lab coat.

"There," my mother said. "There you go, Jerome. Properly baptized." She went back to the table, sat down and lit up a cigarette.

Medina threw back her head and laughed. "That head has a big beer on it."

Pops struggled out of the chair and, removing the lab coat as he walked, slowly zigzagged to his room and closed the door behind him. Medina laughed again. "He's so drunk he barely noticed." Pops soon emerged from his room wearing a different shirt and pair of slacks, his hair matted down with beer.

"No harm done," he muttered.

"The harm is being done at this very moment," my mother said. "The Apology of Percy Joyce. A famous day in the history of the Mount. I don't suppose you and McHugh have set a date for the baptism yet. Don't lie to me again, Pops."

"I've never lied to you, Paynelope. Left out some things, that's all. Sins of omission, that's all. No date set yet. But His Grace has agreed to baptize Percy in the Basilica."

"I don't care if the Pope has agreed to baptize him in the Sistine Chapel. Have you and McHugh made any other plans that I should know about?"

"World domination," Pops said.

"You do understand that you and I will never get married, don't you?"

"Never say never."

"You should say it in this case."

"Why don't you want to marry me? No one else is beating down your door. There is a dearth of suitors in your life."

"My door gets banged on more often than you think, but I keep it locked."

"Sorry. Where do I rank among the many thousands beating down your door?"

"You're all deadlocked in a last-place tie." She looked at me and smiled and faintly shook her head. I wasn't sure if she meant to tell me that she didn't see me as being on a par with sub-par Pops or that I must keep quiet about Medina.

"Do you still carry a torch for Jim Joyce, Paynelope?"

"I do not carry so much as a single unlit match for Jim Joyce."

"He turned you off marriage for life?"

"Something like that."

"Still. You never know. That's what McHugh says. You never know. He tells me don't give up, you never know, she might come round."

"So there it is. That's what he wants."

"I've asked you three times to marry me, Paynelope."

"*Three times?*" I said.

"Yes," my mother said as offhandedly as if she had meant to provoke this disclosure from him.

"McHugh says we'd all be better off with your sort-of sister-in-law out of the picture."

My mother and Medina traded looks. "Why did he say that, Pops?" my mother asked gently.

"I don't know. I give him such glowing accounts of her."

"What do you tell McHugh about Medina?"

He turned to Medina. "I wouldn't pick you if you were the last woman left on earth. You are loathsome."

"I'm so loathsome I could cry."

"Go to bed, Pops," my mother said. "Go on, now. Unless you'd like another beer, so to speak."

"I'll go to bed," Pops said. "Why not? Women and children last."

"That's right. Women and children last."

Pops tried to negotiate the floor, taking one step back for every one forward, until he achieved some momentum and all but ran across the room to his bedroom, the door of which was partly open. He banged into it, went inside and closed it behind him.

"Pops asked you to marry him?" I said to my mother.

"I was worried you might tell the boys at school. But now that you're through your phase of far-fetched fabrication, I trust you completely."

"Pen," Medina said, "I think McHugh knows. About us. I'm almost sure he knows. Jesus Christ."

My mother, her face turning pale and blank, tried to smile. Medina started to cry. Moving her chair close to my mother, she rested her head on her shoulder.

"Oh fuck, Pen, I'm so scared. What will we do? I have no one in the world but you and Perse. Maybe we should take off, get out of here."

"McHugh may be hoping that we'll run. He knows we have no money. He knows that we'd be caught." Medina nodded faintly, then buried her face in the crook of my mother's neck. I thought my mother might flash me a reassuring look, but all she did was stare as if at the approach of something she couldn't quite make out.

PENELOPE'S PROPOSITION

WORD of my apology and upcoming Baptism, Confession and Communion spread beyond the Mount. Over the next few days, every grown-up I encountered congratulated me. As I walked up Bonaventure to St. Bon's, some of them opened their doors to shout greetings to me. "Good morning, Percy." "Well done, Percy." "We're so proud of you, Percy." "We're so happy for you and your mother." "God bless you and your mom, Percy. And God bless Mr. MacDougal." I wouldn't have been surprised to see Mrs. Madden waving to me from her window, holding no grudge for my having slapped her in the face. Motorists honked their horns and waved in earnest, their faces devoid of the usual ironic expressions. At St. Bon's, Brothers whom I knew by little more than name tousled my hair, beamed at me, clapped me on the back, winked at me, called me "the man of the hour." Everyone was as congenial and jocular as if, through the sheer power of prayer, my face had been healed, and everything thought to have proceeded from it and my "non-affiliation" had been undone and would soon be forgotten. Their delusional sincerity made me feel like shouting out the truth. They thought my longed-for day had come at last. I wished beyond expression that it had, hated that my supposed triumph was a sham that I could never reveal with impunity or even with the expectation that a single soul would believe me.

Most of the students of the Mount were not so forthcoming in their offerings of praise or congratulations; for the first time in my life, I knew what it was like to be envied by others. There was a general muting of even the most covert teasing that I had gone through every day. Moyles, who I felt certain had been put up to it by a teacher, invited me to join the Math Club, handing me a small card on which were written the number of the classroom and the times of the weekly meetings of the club—Moyles, from whom the idea of bargaining with my mother for a pity fuck had come. "Percy, you should join the Math Club," was all he said, grinning as he hurried off. I received likewise laconic, terse invitations to join the Chess Club and the band.

We went to chapel that Sunday again and McHugh met us at the door as always.

"You must be very excited about Percy's baptism," he said to my mother. "What?" she said. "Oh, *that*." She badly feigned a laugh. McHugh looked about, no doubt wondering if anyone had overheard what provoked her to laugh in the chapel. He could not reply as he would have liked for fear of also being overheard. He could not even alter his smile, though I could see his jaw muscle moving. He went on smiling, able only with his eyes to tell her what he would have said were he free to speak. "The soon-to-be-baptized Percy Joyce," he said as he turned his gaze on me. "Soon to join the Church after all this time." I nodded and was about to utter a perfunctory, "Yes, Brother," when my mother all but pushed me past him.

As I walked down Bonaventure, a man who looked too young to wear a fedora but was wearing one nonetheless, and who was carrying a large flash camera, came toward me. "Can I take a picture of you, Percy?" he said. I nodded. "Stop right there and smile," he said. "Nice big smile."

He snapped several pictures, said, "Thanks, Percy," and headed past me up the hill. That Sunday, a short article about me that bore no byline appeared in the *Monitor*, along with a photograph of me smiling down at the camera—if those swollen lips of mine could be said to "smile." I looked more as if I were sneering at those who would see the picture. There I was in the pages of the *Monitor*, my disfigurement on full display, my stain clearly outlined though the photograph was black-and-white, my swollen lips making me look as though I had got the worst by far of a fist fight. I suspected that, for many people in St. John's, though for no one on the Mount, this was the first look they had ever had of Percy Joyce, though they had heard of me for years.

ST. BON'S BOY TO BE BAPTIZED, the headline read. The story told of my surprise announcement over the PA systems of the schools on the Mount, making it sound as if *I* had announced my upcoming Baptism, Confession and Communion, and highlighting my former "non-affiliation," the fact that I was fourteen, describing the encouragement I had received from my mother, Penelope Joyce, my decision to take as my baptismal name the first name of "Brother Rice vice-principal Jerome MacDougal, a long-time resident of the Joyce household and a special family friend."

The article made no mention whatsoever of my apology. "Percy is well known throughout the city because of a distinctive congenital condition which has not prevented him from achieving academic excellence or the admiration and friendship of his peers. His Baptism will be performed by His Grace Archbishop P.J.

Scanlon at the Basilica of St. John the Baptist on Saturday, June 24th, at two in the afternoon."

Three months away. On my fifteenth birthday.

"And people think of *Percy* as a liar," my mother said to Pops. "Is there anything else I should know? Have any other dates been set? You haven't booked a church for our wedding, have you, Pops?"

"McHugh thinks that Percy should start preparing for his first confession and Communion right after he's baptized. He has a lot of catching up to do, starting with the catechism."

"Go to the East End Club, Pops," my mother said. "And don't come back for a good long while."

I listened to Medina from the doorway of my bedroom.

"McHugh has Pops convinced that you'll be his someday. I can tell just by looking at Pops. That's what that Jerome business is all about. What else *could* it be about? McHugh's going to insist you marry Pops or else, make an honest man of him and spare Uncle Paddy any more embarrassment and scandal. Uncle Paddy will settle for nothing less, I guarantee you. In which case you *should* marry him. For Percy's sake. Poor Perse. He'll never make it on his own. Never. You *know* that. So there'll never come a time when you don't need Pops. Or let's say that Perse does want to go out there and go to university someday. Who's going to pay for that if Pops is gone? You? Me? He hasn't even started high school. It will be, what, ten years before he finishes university? And then what? Where on earth would he fit in? Maybe nowhere. Probably nowhere. You can't take that risk. In which case, *this* can't go on. You can't marry Pops *and* keep him holed up in the sunroom and his bedroom while you and I go on as usual."

He'll never make it on his own. I felt sick with shame. I wondered if I ought to go out to the kitchen and contradict her. But I couldn't have done it with conviction, for I wasn't sure that she was wrong.

I heard my mother cry. "You're crying because you know I'm right," Medina said.

I went out to the kitchen.

Medina grabbed her jacket from her chair and hurried toward the back door. "Don't follow me outside, Pen," she said. "The last thing you need is to be seen chasing me down the street."

"I'll call you tonight," my mother said, looking worriedly at me as she wiped tears from her eyes. Medina said nothing. She left as quietly, as stealthily as, I imagined, she left the nights she came back for a second visit. She had become an expert with that door.

My mother told Medina first. She called her on the phone and it took some doing to convince her to come to 44. Medina, still in her hospital greens, arrived with eyes red and swollen, a wad of paper tissue clenched in one hand. When my mother told her she was going to marry Pops, Medina began to cry again and was almost out the door before my mother caught her by the arm and led her back inside. They entered the living room, arms linked, Medina with her head on my mother's shoulder, looking as inconsolable as someone being led from church behind a casket.

Jerome. My mother said Medina was right. It was a not very subtle suggestion—more like a command that would soon become an ultimatum—from His Grace, especially with McHugh prodding him about it daily. If she and I, and even Medina, wished to go on being supported by Pops, it had to happen in the one Church-approved way: she and Pops had to be married. His Grace knew that Pops was sleeping with her. It was an open scandal that he could not be seen by his diocese as tacitly tolerating, much less approving of, or as being powerless to end. His Grace had as good as proclaimed their engagement to the people of the Mount by including in the apology that I would take Pops' name. She said that McHugh might suspend, or at least relax, his "witch hunt" if she and Pops mollified him by marrying. It would make it near certain that McHugh would never tell His Grace about his suspicions regarding her and Medina; McHugh would not want to be the messenger who told His Grace that the perfect parable of the Joyces was a sham. She didn't talk explicitly about my chances of "making it out there." But I saw in her eyes when she looked at me that she agreed with Medina that it was at least likely that I would forever need protection and support—and would certainly need it for a long time to come.

"I'm going to steal their thunder," she said. "I'm not going to wait for them to tell me what to do." She would rob them of the "final flourish" of announcing her engagement to Pops without first convening with her. "It won't be much of a victory for us," she said, "but it will be *something*."

She told Medina of all the conditions that Pops would have to agree to first, foremost among which was that they would not have, not try to have, children. Second, that Medina would be as welcome and as frequent a visitor as she had been before, would still be my aunt with whom my mother would remain best friends and confer about all things, especially me, whom Medina loved as if I were her child, the two of them raising me as they saw fit, without consulting Pops. She told her about "visiting hours," about how they would stay the same for her and for Pops. She said she would tell Pops that, having had her own bed to herself for so long, she was not about to share one with him. She would have her room and her bed, and he would have his. Things would be just as they had always been at 44.

When my mother was finished, Medina said, "You're going to marry Pops?" as if that was all she had heard, as if she herself had not seen as inevitable that very course of action the day before.

My mother nodded.

"He's going to ask you to marry him and you're going to say yes?"

Medina kept shaking her head, eyes fixed on the table as though she were entranced. My mother said no, she was going to ask Pops, who, like Jim Joyce, was going to say yes. Medina slumped back in her chair and sighed.

"And when Pops tells McHugh about all these conditions you've attached, even if one of the conditions is that he *not* tell McHugh about the conditions?"

"We'll be married. Everything will seem, look, legitimate to people who, if truth be told, have even more rigid conditions attached to their own marriages. Besides, I think I can convince Pops to keep even more secrets from McHugh than he kept before."

"He won't settle for that."

"I think he will."

"You'll have to take his name," Medina said.

"Yes, but Percy won't. That will also be one of the conditions, that he still be known as Percy Joyce. And as far as I'm concerned, I'll still be Penny Joyce. You and I will still have the same last name."

"Except that everyone will call you Mrs. MacDougal. I can think of myself as Cleopatra, but that won't make me her."

"I don't know what else to do, Medina. If there comes a point when you can't stand it, or I can't, or Pops can't, we'll deal with it then."

"Well, Pen, I will *not* be your maid of honour. I won't go to the wedding. I don't care how it looks, how strange it might look to McHugh. You can tell him it's out of loyalty to Jim Joyce, my brother, your first fiancé and the father of my nephew."

"I will. Look, it will be a very small, bare-minimum wedding. I still have the dress I chose when I got engaged. I'm sure it still fits.

I'll wear that. There'll be no reception, no honeymoon. Pops will pay every cent of what little it costs."

"I don't want to see you in that wedding dress."

"There won't even be a wedding night, I promise."

"We'll see," Medina said. "I bet it won't go like you think it will."

"Pops will be home soon. He might be drunk. If he is, I won't say a word about getting married."

"Then I should go."

"Please, Medina, don't. I'm going to need all the support I can get."

"You want me to witness you asking him to marry you?"

"I'm not going to get down on one knee or anything. And there won't be any visiting hours for Pops tonight. I promise."

"I still have to get baptized, don't I?" I said.

"Yes," my mother said. "Yes, you do."

"I don't know," Medina said. "One way or another, McHugh will sniff this out."

"I didn't go to the East End Club again." Pops closed the front door behind him, sounding as if he had come home with good news that would make us all feel better, as if his patronage of the East End Club were the main bone of contention at 44. "I went to the chem lab," he said, announcing what might have been a bonus to his shunning of the East End Club. In his hands-but-for-thumbs-in-pockets pose, he walked in. I sat at the kitchen table where my mother and Medina were already seated, nervously smoking and nursing glasses of beer that were going flat.

"Here he is," Medina said, "dressed in wedding white."

Pops ignored her and, coming into the kitchen, headed straight for the fridge. Before he could grab the handle of the fridge door, my mother said, "Guess what, Pops." Her face and throat scarlet red, as was her chest down to the first, ever-on-the-verge-of-popping button of her blouse, she said, "We're getting married, you and me."

Pops smiled, opened the fridge door and took out a stubby brown bottle of Dominion Ale that he opened as always on the buckle of his belt.

"Really," Pops said. "What game have you two cooked up for me tonight?"

Medina, looking at no one, said as if to herself, "It's a game called, 'Let's see what Pops will fall for next.'"

Pops nodded and turned to face the sunroom.

"That's it, Pops," Medina taunted, stabbing out a cigarette among the many butts already in the ashtray. "Go to your little playroom like a good little boy."

"Enough, Medina," my mother said.

"There is nothing," Pops observed, "that looks worse than lipstick on the filter of a cigarette."

My mother pushed her chair away from the table and stood up. "I mean it, Pops," she said. "We're getting married."

She removed Jim Joyce's engagement ring and put it on the table. I'd half expected her to hand it to Medina. Pops stared at it.

My mother forced a smile. "So, Pops, where's that engagement ring you keep offering to me?"

"It's in the pocket of my lab coat," Pops said. He patted his left pocket. "Please don't play this joke on me in front of them."

My mother held out her left hand, ring finger extended. Pops glanced at me. He looked so dumbstruck I couldn't help but smile, which seemed to reassure him. He reached into the pocket of his coat and took out a ball of wrapping paper, from which he removed a ring box covered in green velvet. He snapped it open and took out the sapphire ring, holding it between his thumb and forefinger. The hand that held the ring trembled.

"I think you know the rest, Pops," my mother said.

Pops took two steps toward my mother then lowered himself to one knee.

"Will you marry me, Paynelope?" he asked, sounding perplexed, as if he couldn't believe the words had been prompted from him by her.

Medina sniffed with derision. "It doesn't count unless you say her name right."

"I will," my mother said, her own hand and voice trembling as badly as Pops'. Pops managed to slide the ring onto her finger. Medina, sullen-faced, crossed her arms and shook her head at me in scornful disbelief.

"There," my mother all but gasped, "we're engaged."

Pops, her hand still in his, stood up, his blue eyes blurred with tears. Her arms at her sides, my mother quickly leaned forward and pecked Pops on the cheek, then withdrew her hand from his and resumed her seat beside Medina.

"I don't know what to do," Pops confessed. "One normally doesn't get engaged—"

"While wearing a grimy lab coat?" Medina said.

My mother ever so gently brushed Medina's arm with the back of her hand. Pops seemed not to notice.

"It's even more romantic in front of witnesses," my mother said.

"In front of strangers, yes." Pops nodded. "Such as in a restaurant where everyone applauds if the surprised woman says yes."

"Well," Medina said, "I'm so happy for you both it's all I can do to keep breathing, let alone applaud."

"We're going to be married?" Pops asked.

"Yes," my mother said, lighting up a cigarette.

"When?"

"Just before Percy gets baptized," my mother said.

Pops beamed at me as if I too had agreed to marry him.

"I don't understand," he murmured. "Only the other day you were all, all of you, against doing *anything*. You were so upset with me, Paynelope, you poured a beer over my head."

"Drier heads prevailed," Medina said.

Pops had popped the question three times. Three times he must have opened that little velvet box with the engagement ring inside—three times, perhaps abruptly, without preamble—then said, "Paynelope, will you marry me?" looking up at her on bended knee or while lying in his bed beside her. Three times she had refused.

"Today is a new day," my mother exclaimed.

"For me especially," Medina said.

"Not even you can spoil this moment." Pops smiled at her.

"Oh, I think I could if I really tried," Medina said.

"I have so much to say to you, Paynelope," he declared.

"I have far more things to say to you," my mother said. "Have a seat at the table with us. I have a list of—let's call them stipulations."

She told him of all the stipulations he would have to agree to unless he wanted her to be abandoned by yet another fiancé. Pops, drinking bottle after bottle of beer, agreed to everything, but looked all the more puzzled and dismayed. When my mother was through, Medina said, "Oh well, I guess bachelors can't be choosers, Pops."

"We should celebrate or something, don't you think?" Pops said. "If I'd have known, I would have bought champagne."

"We're already celebrating," my mother said. "And I think it's time for Percy to have his first glass of beer to celebrate his upcoming baptism."

"Yes," Pops said. "But we mustn't tell McHugh we let him have some beer. He'll be so pleased when he hears the news, mine and yours and Percy's, Paynelope."

My mother poured me a half glass of beer. I almost gagged on the first mouthful. "Sip it slowly," Pops said, then downed an entire bottle without a pause for breath.

"A short engagement," Pops said. "McHugh will be glad to hear that. His Grace, too. McHugh will be on the phone to him—Aren't you going to congratulate us, Medina?"

"Sure, Pops," Medina said, raising her glass. "Here's to you, Pen, McHugh and Uncle Paddy. And Sir Percival the Merciful, of course. I hope the five of you will be very happy."

"Why must you always be so sour?" he asked.

"It's been a very long day for me, Pops."

"Well, perhaps now *you'll* get married."

"I haven't been preventing her from getting married," my mother said, closely watching his reaction.

"You wouldn't see me so often then, Pops," Medina pointed out. "Wouldn't you miss me?"

"Like a toothache."

My mother looked relieved.

"Paynelope, you've set some draconian stipulations for our marriage. Are they completely non-negotiable?"

"Completely," my mother said.

"Well," Pops admitted, "I've never really wanted children of my own. No offence, Percy. And I've come to think of Medina as a fact of life. But separate rooms? Separate beds? And the visiting privileges seem"—he glanced at me—"well, they seem like visiting privileges. Like you're behind bars. Or I am."

"Don't look a gift wife in the mouth, Pops," Medina said.

"You're getting a bit tipsy, Pops," my mother said. "Why don't you go to bed?"

"I'm not tipsy," Pops corrected her. "I'm good and drunk. It's not every day I get engaged. That ring looks quite becoming on your finger. It's Percy who should go to bed, and Medina should go home. Then we could have a proper celebration, you and me."

"Go to bed, Pops," my mother said, looking uneasily at Medina. My mother stood, took him under the arm, got him to his feet and led him to his bedroom door.

"Tuck me in?" Pops said. "After we're married, I'll carry you across the threshold," he said, flinging out one arm in a triumphant flourish.

"Off to bed, there you go."

"No good night kiss, my darling fiancée?"

My mother kissed him on the cheek, gently pushed him inside and closed the door. She sat at the table again and flashed Medina a mischievous, conspiratorial smile that Medina ignored.

"He'll soon see that nothing has changed," my mother said.

"Nothing will have changed except that he'll be married to you. His dream come true. Till death do you part."

"I'm not looking forward to the first time someone calls me Mrs. Jerome MacDougal. It will be as if both my names have simply disappeared."

"You and me, Perse," Medina said, "we'll be the last of the Joyces until you have children of your own." She looked instantly as if she wished she hadn't said it. I decided not to make her feel worse by estimating the chances of my ever having children.

Medina complained that many of the things that my mother had excluded Pops from for fear of giving people the wrong impression would now be things that people would *expect* Pops to take part in. She could just see it now, the Triple P family, Penny, Pops and Percy, strolling to Marty's for ice cream sodas after Mass on Sunday or to a movie at the Capitol on Henry Street, Pops with his wife and stepson, wholesome pillars of the community whom people would regard as proof that, in the end, things could work out for the best for everyone, even abandoned, pregnant fiancées, disfigured children and lonely bachelors.

"Maybe it's just as well that you and Pops are getting married," she said. "I'll no longer have to think of Pops and I as having the same girlfriend. You'll be his wife. I'll be the woman you're having an affair with. And everyone knows that having an affair is more fun than being married. Especially if the affair never ends."

"It won't," my mother said.

"If you've already made up your mind, Pen, you should tell me now," Medina insisted. "I wouldn't blame you for putting Percy ahead of me, but I'll blame you if you lead me along until I get the point just because you haven't got it in you to send me away or because you want to make it seem that I'm the one who ended it."

She started to cry. My mother let go of me and motioned with her head that I should go to my room.

THE INSTRUCTION OF PENELOPE

A T McHugh's request, my mother, Pops and I went to visit McHugh in Brother Rice one evening after dinner in late May. McHugh told Pops we should come to the chapel instead of to his office. There would be no one else there, he said, because he had told the other Brothers that it would be occupied.

McHugh was sitting in one of the two front pews when we went inside, the one just to the left of the aisle that was in line with the tabernacle. The chapel was so dimly lit, mostly by two banks of votive candles flanking the altar, that I couldn't see more than a few pews past McHugh.

McHugh rose and smiled. He held out his hand to me and squeezed it firmly when I took it.

"God bless you, Percy," he said. "Baptism is the first and greatest of the seven sacraments."

"Thank you, Brother," I said, as if baptism's primacy and greatness were solely my doing.

McHugh next took my mother's hand. "Congratulations, Miss Joyce. I have been praying that you would accept Vice-Principal MacDougal as your husband. He had begun to lose hope. It is wise for a woman not to lightly give up her body, heart and soul to another, but you did have the two of us worried for a while."

He laughed and looked at Pops, who, incongruously attired in his lab coat, smiled as if he was casting back with ironic fondness to the days of disappointment through which nothing but the encouragement of a close friend had sustained him, days whose happy end McHugh alone had been able to foresee.

"I don't feel as though I have given up anything," my mother said. "Nor did I realize until recently that you and my husband-to-be were such close confidants. By the way, it was I who proposed."

"Mr. MacDougal told me," McHugh countered, "that you did not quite do that. You simply informed him that you and he were getting married, at which point *he* proposed, asked for your hand in marriage on bended knee just as he had done three times before. But this time you said yes."

"There doesn't appear to be much that Mr. MacDougal doesn't tell you."

"I have no way of knowing what he doesn't tell me," said McHugh.

My mother sat in the front pew and I sat beside her. Pops remained standing until McHugh motioned for him to join us, at which he sat beside my mother. McHugh clasped his hands behind his back and, looking at the floor, frock slightly swishing, began to pace back and forth in front of us, between us and the altar rail. He spoke in a voice that was gentle, serene, modulated, as if he wished to leave the silence of the empty chapel undisturbed, as if every word he was saying was part of some official clerical instruction to those about to begin or resume their lives in the Church.

"I asked you to come here this evening so that I could speak about a few things that still somewhat trouble me." He smiled and continued pacing as if savouring what he was about to say. "I have news. Father Bill will perform the marriage right here, in the chapel. A week before Percy is baptized. His baptism, as you know, will take place June 24, a Saturday. Percy's birthday. As always on that day, the Feast of Saint John the Baptist will be celebrated, as will the Basilica itself, and the city of St. John's as well. Your baptism, Percy, will be the least of the reasons for the great celebration that will occur that day.

"His Grace will administer all three of the sacraments on the same day to Percy in the Basilica. Father Bill is going to hear *your* confession, Miss Joyce. You will have to go to Confession and Communion before you can be married. The Church, you see, has some stipulations of its own. You will be required to take these sacraments seriously, to make a full and sincere confession before you take Holy Communion. You must confess to what the Church deems to be a sin, not just to what *you* deem to be one. I believe it's been quite some time since you went to Confession, hasn't it?"

"I stopped going just after Percy was born. Don't assume cause and effect."

"By the way, His Grace wishes that Percy's Baptism, Confession and Communion be witnessed by as many students of the Mount as possible. And bishops and priests from all over the island will attend and take part—not for Percy, of course, but as I said, for the usual celebration of the Basilica. For reasons that elude me, Percy has for years been a favourite of His Grace, and his long-delayed induction into the Church is, His Grace believes, an important event for all of us. But His Grace does not want to dilute the momentousness of Percy's big day by combining it with yours. Otherwise, you'd have been married in the Basilica immediately before Percy was baptized."

"Pops—" my mother said, but McHugh interrupted her.

"That is also one of the things I wish to discuss. I'm hoping that, once you are married, you won't go on using the students' nickname for Mr. MacDougal. It seems—disrespectful, frivolous, even demeaning. Mr. MacDougal shares the Christian name of one of the great Doctors of the Church, a name that your son has decided to take as his baptismal name—"

"Pops is Pops," my mother said. "He has been for a very long time. He is not *Jerome*. Not to us."

"You'll think about it?"

"Only when I'm in need of a good giggle."

"Then there is the question of children."

"There is no question. We won't be having any."

"None?"

"I *have* a child."

"You had him outside of wedlock."

"He will soon be inside wedlock. Soon, all three of us will be wedlocked."

"Mr. MacDougal has no children. Nor, he tells me, will he have any say in how Percy is raised."

"What did you do, Pops, give him a written list of my stipulations?"

"Is your concern that another child of yours might be born with a disfigurement like Percy's?"

"It never crossed my mind."

"In the eyes of God, Percy is beautiful."

"As he is in mine."

"I have a gift for you, Miss Joyce." McHugh held out to my mother a small but thick black book. "This is a new copy of Saint Joseph's Daily Missal." He opened it near the beginning. "You see, it says 'This missal belongs to . . .' I've written in your marriage name, Penelope MacDougal." He closed the book and again held it out to my mother, who grabbed it from him as if she meant to throw it aside.

"Thank you," she said. "I've always wanted one of these."

"Saint Joseph is the Patron Saint of the Universal Church."

My mother held the missal in one hand at her side.

"How can you be certain that you won't have another child, Miss Joyce? Need I remind you that any unnatural form of prevention is deemed by the Church to be a sin?"

"I think it's time the three of us went home," my mother said.

McHugh, now pacing faster back and forth in front of the altar rail, said, "Just a couple more points. For Percy's sake, I'll use the euphemism which Mr. MacDougal tells me you used: separate rooms and 'visiting hours.'"

My mother laughed, not mirthfully.

"Is there anyone in your home at the moment?" McHugh said.

"Medina is there," my mother said.

"Is it Medina night again so soon?"

"What do you mean by that?"

"She seems to visit quite a lot. Mr. MacDougal tells me it's hard for him to hold your attention while she's there. Would you mind if Percy went home so that we could speak more freely?"

My mother sighed. "Go home, Perse. Tell Medina we'll be there soon."

As I rose, Brother McHugh stopped pacing and again took my large hand, this time holding on when I tried to pull away. "*I* will be instructing you in religion—"

"Don't tell me, let me guess," my mother said. "His Grace agreed to that while the two of you were relaxing in the steam room."

"—and in your preparation for your baptism and the other sacraments. There is much for you to learn in a short amount of time."

I said, "Yes, Brother," and he released my hand. I walked quickly to the chapel door and hurried across the road to 44, where, by the time I'd given Medina a full account of the meeting, she was unable to keep still. She went to the front window and looked across the street at Brother Rice. "He said that, Perse?" she said. "He said 'Medina night'?"

"Yes," I said.

"He *must* know, Perse, he must. Why else would he say 'Medina night'? I'm here almost *every* night."

My mother and Pops arrived, Pops trailing behind her. My mother, Saint Joseph's Daily Missal in one hand, kicked off her shoes, slamming them against the wall, and tossed her bandana on the floor.

"Paynelope," Pops said.

"Shut up," my mother said. She crossed the front room into the kitchen and smacked the missal on the table so hard that some of Medina's beer spilled and foamed.

"Percy should go to his room," Pops said.

"I decide when Percy should go to his room." My mother sat down at the kitchen table and lit a cigarette. "McHugh objected to all my conditions of marriage, my stipulations as he somehow knew I call them, including the matter of how many times a month Pops should be allowed to *fuck* me."

"*Paynelope*," Pops said. "Percy—"

"Is none of your fucking business and has many times heard and said the word 'fuck' before."

"What happened, Pen?" Medina said.

"I was lectured in a *chapel* against the use of contraception and the obligation of all married couples to contribute to the continuance of the human species."

"I'm going out," Pops informed my mother. "I hope you'll have cooled down by the time I return, which may not be for a while." She said nothing and he slammed the front door behind him.

"More children McHugh said I should have," my mother fumed. She said she asked him if it was a rule of the Church that every woman had to have at least one child who was not a bastard.

"But Pen—'*Medina* night.' Perse told me."

"Pops doesn't know. I can tell. I'm less sure of McHugh. But once Pops and I are married, what could he do? They'd rather burn down the Vatican than annul a marriage. I think we'll be all right if we're careful."

"I don't know," Medina said. "All I know is that, if someone has to go, that someone will be me."

My mother took her hand, kissed her lightly on the lips and tugged on a curl of her hair.

It was possible, McHugh had told my mother, who told Medina the next day, that there would be some radio, television and newspaper coverage of my baptism.

Medina said it sounded as if they were planning a "big do" at the Basilica. She began to refer to it as "the Big Do at the Big B." "Whereas the marriage of Pops and Pen," she said, "won't even make Wedding of the Week."

My mother pointed out that she would be making her first confession in fourteen, almost fifteen years, but I would only have to summarize the past eight years, seven being the age when, according to the Church, the capacity for guilt kicked in. In everyone. No exceptions. There was neither precocity nor backwardness where guilt was concerned. There were no delayed children who didn't give a damn till they were eight. Seven was the age of guilt. You were ushered into it while dressed to the nines, your hair newly cut, ribbons pinned to you, proud parents bawling because they were so happy to witness you become suddenly and keenly aware of your innate malevolence and the evil that you harboured in your soul.

When you turned seven, a lot of things that had never bothered your conscience began to bother it a lot. Thanks to your catechism instruction, you became aware that Satan is forever slyly at work in your mind, tempting you to perform such nefarious acts as withholding jelly beans from your friends or even misleading them about how many jelly beans you have. Formerly able to greedily relish your jelly beans in secret, you are now kept from doing so by consciousness of guilt, despite the many rationalizations for hoarding candy that the Evil One supplies you with. You think of the eons of immolation in Purgatory that your jelly bean dishonesty will get you if you leave it unconfessed. You hold out for as long as you can until, giving in to the Evil One's exhortation that you gobble all your jelly beans at once, you are overwhelmed by guilt and a desire to return to the state of wholesome innocence you once inhabited, and you confess to a priest that your jelly bean assets are greater than you have led others to believe. You are forgiven, assigned penance and told to go and sin no more by a priest who is as certain that you *will* sin again as he is that your enjoyment of jelly beans will never be the same.

And so it goes, my mother said. Satan shouts down or impersonates the voice of God and soon you cannot lift a finger, move a muscle, think a thought or say a word except at the behest of the indwelling, near-omnipotent demon whose existence, until a few days ago, you had somehow overlooked. At least, my mother said, I had had seven more years of lightheartedly breaking the commandments than she'd had, but I would soon be all too aware of how much coveting I did in the course of a day, of the impossibility of drawing an uncovetous breath.

THE PARABLES OF PERCY
AND PENELOPE

"His Grace believes that the other students will learn a lot from the example that you set and that your mother sets."

Brother McHugh had told Brother Hogan to bring me to Hogan's little office, which was hardly more than a closet, though I remembered it as the place from which McHugh had dragged me the day that he snapped me in the tunnel, and I wondered in fright if another snapping might be imminent. But it turned out that he really did just want to speak to me. He sat sideways to the desk as before, legs crossed, affecting disdain for his modest surroundings.

"The Archbishop says your life stories are like parables. Your mother, as a younger woman, suffered great disappointment and betrayal, humiliation—in part because of her own premarital wrongdoing. Her fiancé left her when she was with child. Her child was born with a disfigurement that she foresaw would cause him and her great distress, the scorn of those who, never having truly suffered, would not understand the wounds that their cruelty inflicted. Your mother became bitter and turned away from God and from the Church. For fourteen years. Only by the humility and innocence of the very child who seemed to be at the root of her unhappiness did she come to realize her mistake, a realization that brought her back to God and the Church, by whose grace she was rewarded with the restoration of the very thing that years ago she had lost—a loving husband.

"And you, Percy Joyce, your story, His Grace believes, is equally inspiring. A child is not only born out of wedlock to a mother who, because of trials that were devised to test her faith, has lost her way in the world, has become cynical, hardened and blind to the wonder of Creation, but he is born disfigured. He is encouraged by his mother to see only what is bad in others, but in spite of this, in spite of the persecution that he suffers because of his disfigurement and his shyness and his shame, he grows up to be a gentle, loving and forgiving child. With the help of wise, God-guided men of faith, he comes to see that, for him and his mother, the one and only path to true and full salvation is through the Church. The mark that hides your face is the outward sign of your inner gift, of the working within you of the Holy Spirit.

"These are the two stories that His Grace believes will be told the day you are baptized and the day your mother is married. In each of these stories, a new and more glorious chapter will begin. That is what His Grace believes. It is not what I believe. I am not so easily fooled. I know snake oil when I smell it. Your mother rubs herself all over with it."

At home, my mother fretted about making her first confession in so many years. "'Bless me, Father, for I have sinned. I've had amnesia since breakfast.' Do you think that might work?"

Pops said he didn't think Father Bill or His Grace would let either one of us get away with a perfunctory, itemized confession.

"Confessions aren't *supposed* to sound like inventories," Pops added, heading to the sunroom.

"McHugh has told me to be open, sincere and entire. Or something like that. If I'm all those things with Father Bill, the odds of the wedding going ahead would not be good. The odds of the poor man's life going ahead would not be good."

"Your odds wouldn't be so good either." Medina glanced toward Pops, who had settled in his chair in the sunroom. "What you say in confession is supposed to be a secret between you and the priest. But I've seen priests drag people out of that box and beat the daylights out of them."

My mother decided her best bet was to more or less recite the Archbishop's parable. She would confess that being dumped while pregnant and engaged had made her bitter, her bitterness had caused her to turn her back on the Church, as had her child's disfigurement. She would paint a portrait of a jaded, jilted woman who, for my entire life, had sought solace for the loss of Jim Joyce in the bottom of a beer glass.

She said she expected a lecture on the sinfulness of, and consequent troubles that derived from, premarital sex. She would say that she constantly complained about the unfairness of her lot, her man-deficient existence, her miserable Jim-less, Joyce-less, joyless, empty life. She begrudged other women their husbands, wondered aloud why fate had sought her out but spared them. What had she done to deserve her manlessness? What had those other women done to deserve their lifelong man-mates? She had grown weary of asking God such questions and getting no reply. But she would also tell her confessor that she had emerged from the darkness of despair to discover that living in her house, almost since Jim Joyce had left, was the remedy for her misery—a man who surpassed in manliness the man who had rejected her and her child. And so she was about to begin her man-renewed, revived-by-man life, never more to stray from the Church, never more to be unmanned, never again to live in a husbandless house without a Church-sanctioned husband in the marriage bed beside her.

Or nearby at least.

She would say that now, almost fifteen years later, she was repentant because she knew that it was all part of God's plan for her and her son, which was itself a tiny but inscrutably crucial part of His all-inclusive, universal plan by which all the atrocities of history would not only be redeemed but be seen as necessary. The parents of murdered children would see that, according to the plan, the murder of their children made perfect sense, there being no other way that an all-knowing, all-powerful, all-loving God could think of to bring about the eternal harmony and happiness of others.

I thought of *my* confession. It would be strange enough going into the confessional with an entire church full of students watching me, timing my confession, the whole Basilica so silent on my birthday they would, I fancied, be able to hear my every word or at least gauge the severity and complexity of my sins by the length of time I was holed up in the wall space, by the length of time it took me to finally spill my guts after all these years. It would be stranger still to be watched by all those students as I made my way to the altar rail to say my penance—which they would also time, and for the same reason.

My mother said that in the confessional I should just assume the tone of my famous apology, repeat it word for word, and throw in some other disclosures that my confessor was already familiar with, such as my Vivian period, my Peeping Percy phase, my Francine phase, my bus-blessing, Pope-imitating phase, my ongoing "give me myth or give me death" campaign. "Pile it on," she said. "There's nothing Catholics like more than a reformed sinner—the worse the sinner, the greater the reformation."

McHugh reminded me that Catholicism was not a buffet from which you could pick and choose what you wanted to believe and ignore the rest. It was a prix fixe menu that allowed for no substitutes. This was especially true of the Catholic doctrine that he would teach me. He said I would also have to memorize, in preparation for my confession, not the condensed and simplified version of the Baltimore Catechism that my schoolmates had studied in grade two, but the much longer and complex version that was prescribed for those who made their First Communion as young adults.

"His Grace has allowed me the use of a room in the Basilica of St. John the Baptist. This is a special privilege as there is no more appropriate place for a boy about to be baptized to study the catechism than a basilica named after the first and greatest of all Baptists. It is a privilege for which, one day, you will thank His Grace personally, even if your gratitude is insincere."

One afternoon when Pops was attending a teachers' meeting, I returned home from school and found my mother and Medina kissing on the couch in the living room— kissing, not even with their arms around each other, but also not just pressing their lips together—rather having a slow, deep kiss that they didn't pull out of when I walked into the room. I stayed silent but I had a curious feeling that they had wanted me to "catch" them, that they may have seen me coming down the hill and up the driveway. After about a minute, during which I watched, rapt, from the doorway, noting every movement of their mouths, I disguised my hard-on by sitting down. They pulled apart.

"I was just kissing the bride," Medina said.

My mother said, "Guess what, Perse? Medina's changed her mind. She's going to be my maid of honour after all. I've already phoned McHugh and given him the good news."

"I'm sure he's doing cartwheels," Medina said.

"How come you changed your mind, Medina?" I asked.

Because she'd be jealous, she admitted, not only of Pops but of whoever was my mother's maid of honour, and she wouldn't be able to stand spending the wedding day alone in her room or wandering the streets in some other part of town. "I'm not going to enjoy it, but I think I'd like it even less if I wasn't there."

"I'm so glad," my mother said. "It won't be as hard to pretend when everyone I'm pretending for is there." I was surprised to see tears on her cheeks.

Medina said we shouldn't be surprised if, when Father Bill said, "You may kiss the bride," she got to my mother before Pops did. "I feel sick when I think of Pops lifting that veil and planting one right on your lips."

"Well, it will be the first and last time he ever kisses me on the lips. There has been no real kissing during 'visiting hours' and there never will be. That's always been a stipulation, as you know."

Medina said she would be bawling from the outset and she couldn't guarantee that her tears would seem like tears of joy.

"I might start bawling myself," my mother added.

Pops merely frowned when my mother told him Medina would be her maid of honour. "It's your choice, Paynelope," he said. He announced that the grade eleven history teacher at Brother Rice, a colleague of many years, had agreed to be his best man. "I really hardly know him," Pops said. "McHugh asked him for me. And McHugh said he would do his best to find godparents for Percy."

"If a good confession is humble, sincere and entire, that means there hasn't been one yet," my mother told us.

Nevertheless, she made her fourteen-years-delayed confession to Father Bill in the chapel confessional at Brother Rice. She said she paraphrased for Father Bill the Archbishop's Parable of Penny Joyce, which Father Bill listened to wordlessly and seemed disappointed by, judging by the tone of his voice as he assigned her penance. She described how Father Bill sat sideways to the wire mesh window to the other side of which her face was all but pressed, so that her lips were hardly more than an inch from his ear. She said that confession was like whispering to someone through a screen door in the darkness, asking the man on the other side to make you pure of heart and white of soul, even though you both knew that he couldn't.

"Have you ever been in the Basilica?" I asked her.

She said that she hadn't. She said that most rich Catholics, or those who wanted to be mistaken for rich, went to Mass at the Basilica, for the same reason that they shopped at the most expensive stores: to be seen by their rich fellows, to attend the highest-quality Mass that could be found in Newfoundland, Mass that did your soul more good than Mass at a mere church. At the Basilica, people believed, the sacraments counted for more. Better to confess to a bishop than to some hack priest who would botch the forgiveness of your sins and send you away in worse shape than you were before. Better to be baptized in the Basilica than in some church whose baptisms came without a warranty and might wear off at the worst possible time. Better to be married at the Basilica than at some discount church where grace of inferior quality was doled out like food at a homeless shelter.

THE CATECHIST AND
THE CATACHUMEN

WHEN McHugh heard that I had never been inside the main part of the Basilica, he told me not to go in there before the day of my baptism. The first sight of the Basilica might help put even me in the proper state of awe and wonder to receive the sacraments.

I had to study the answers to four hundred and twenty-one questions, as well as many prayers, hymns and the entire Mass. In the catechism for older students and adults, the official, unabridged Baltimore Catechism, there were fourteen hundred questions and answers, most of them much longer than in the abridged version. McHugh reluctantly decided there was not enough time for me to study the longest version. There were, however, among the four hundred and twenty-one questions in *my* catechism, Fifty Primary Questions that I would have to answer word for word on an exam because, he said, every one of the words was exactly the right word, chosen by the anonymous author of the catechism in 1885. As with the Ten Commandments, no other words, no synonyms or summaries would do, because the slightest departure of nuance or connotation could lead the student of the catechism into sin. There were no grey areas between right and wrong. The Truth was the Truth. The questions and answers in the Baltimore Catechism were channelled through the Infallible Pope by the Holy Spirit. They could not be argued with, qualified, modified or otherwise altered in any way or any context.

I always arrived first, "promptly at 3:45," as McHugh instructed me. He arrived promptly at 3:50. On McHugh's instructions, I entered the Basilica by one of the rear doors that opened onto a large, circular stone vestibule rung round with Roman arches, each arch leading to a windowless door, each door numbered.

Our study room, number six of six, seemed to be a conference room. There was a long, wide, gleaming wooden table with chairs on either side but none at the head or the end. The walls were lined with shelves containing ancient-looking leather-bound books, their titles inscribed in Latin on their spines, books that I fancied contained, volume by volume, the Ultimate Catechism, the Summa Cum Laude of catechisms, millions, perhaps billions of ever-proliferating questions and answers that gave rise to other questions and answers ad infinitum, the whole thing not omitting a single footnote of Church doctrine or the most scrupulously fine of fine distinctions.

There were many holy pictures on the walls above the books. The one above the door by which I entered was a photograph of the Archbishop. Above the door at the opposite end of the room, by which McHugh entered, was a photograph of the Pope. Encircling the room were other photographs or portraits of other popes and Newfoundland archbishops, almost all of them in profile, as if to face the viewer directly would have been profane. Like the doors, the room was windowless, lit solely by lamps, for there were no overhead lights. The room always gave me the impression that, outside, it would have been dark no matter what the time of day or year, so dark, so "late" that I ought to have been home hours ago.

McHugh and I sat at the centre of the table on opposite sides. Every chair had a corresponding large glass ashtray, green notebook and gleaming silver pen. I always half expected the balance of a catechism committee, a delegation of Church sages hand-picked by Uncle Paddy, to pour into the room and occupy the empty chairs.

McHugh quizzed me each afternoon from a catechism that he held in his hands, never leaning it on the table, as if he believed that, even from that distance, I would be able to read the answers.

He always brought with him four versions of the catechism, the smallest a mere paperback chapbook for seven-year-olds, the next biggest a slim hardbound copy of my catechism. And two larger catechisms, the one with fourteen hundred questions and answers, and the fourth, which was an annotated version of it that was exclusively for the use of teachers. He never consulted the other three books, but the four of them sometimes lay side by side on the table like a symbol of the duration of a lifetime, from boyhood to adolescence to young manhood to middle and old age.

McHugh announced that he was the Catechist, the person whose responsibility it was before God to instruct and prepare me for baptism, penance and Communion by the use of the catechism. I was the Catechumen, the person being instructed and prepared. Catechist and Catechumen, we sat face to face each day like devil's advocate and would-be saint, doing battle in the manner prescribed by the Church.

We began each day this way:

"What is the full name of this book?"

"The full name of the book is the Baltimore Catechism."

"What am I?"

"You are the Catechist."

"What are you?"

"I am the Catechumen."

"Let us begin."

And so we began: "We cannot fully understand how the three Divine Persons are one and the same God because this is a mystery. What is a mystery, Percy?"

"A mystery is a truth which we cannot fully understand."

"What gender is the Holy Ghost?"

"He is without gender."

"Then why do you refer to the Holy Ghost as 'he'?"

"I'm sorry, Brother. *The Holy Ghost* is without gender."

"Why are there no images of God the Father in Catholic churches?"

"There are none because He has never shown Himself to us."

"Does the corruption of our nature remain in us after original sin has been forgiven?"

"It does. It remains in us until we enter into Heaven, throughout our lives and our time in Purgatory."

"What should be done with bad and immodest books and newspapers?"

"Bad and immodest books and newspapers should be destroyed."

What are the six reasons for Holy Communion?

What are the five qualities of proper prayer?

What is the difference between the particular judgment and the general judgment?

What are the seven sayings of Jesus on the Cross?

What are the twelve fruits of the Holy Ghost?

Every now and then he lowered the catechism, closed it on the desk and placed his hands on it, one on top of the other. This was a signal that we were taking a break of sorts—that is, that he was now about to ask questions of a different kind, questions mostly having to do with 44 Bonaventure and its occupants, which he asked in the same imperious, challenging tone as the catechism questions. He stood beneath and looked up at the round white clock on the wall as he spoke, as if the clock, whose second hand was the only moving thing in the room, somehow helped him find the right words, words by which to pose me the "extra" questions that would be, like the words of the questions and answers of the catechism, and the words of the Bible, the exact, right words, without the faintest hint of an inappropriate nuance or connotation, infallible questions in search of infallible answers.

After staring at the clock for several minutes, he would move on to a portrait of one of the popes, a photograph of one of the archbishops, and so on. In this manner he would make his way completely around the room, as if he were performing the Stations of the Cross, sometimes seeming to examine the walls themselves in the hope of being instructed by them as to what questions he should put to me.

The first "extra" question he ever asked was, "What are your mother's middle names?" I didn't know. He frowned as if he believed I was lying. He wrote something in his notebook. "Her second name is Anne," he said. "She is named after Saint Anne, the mother of the Blessed Virgin Mary. She herself may not know whom she is named after or why. Her confirmation name is Elizabeth who was the mother of John the Baptist. When I told His Grace her confirmation name, he seemed to take it as further proof that you were born on the feast day of John the Baptist for a purpose. I told him it might merely be a coincidence but he has his mind made up."

Sometimes he walked about the room as he asked his extra questions, the catechism clasped behind his back. He said I was not to follow him with my eyes or turn in my chair but was simply to face straight ahead as if he were still sitting at the table. Over a period of such days, he interspersed seemingly insignificant questions about the middle and third names of Pops, Medina and Jim Joyce. A couple of times I asked him why he was asking extra questions, but he ignored me.

Soon, he began to randomly alternate the two kinds of questions, no longer getting up to walk around but still not lowering the catechism, as if even the answers to the extra questions were

written in the book. One day, "What are the Seven Chief Spiritual
Works of Mercy?" was followed by "Who would you say is your
mother's best friend?" I responded Catechumen fashion to the
second question, repeating the question in my answer. "I would
say that my mother's best friend is Medina Joyce."

"It's disrespectful to the catechism and therefore to the Church
to answer *my* questions like that," McHugh said.

"I'm sorry, Brother."

"And who is Medina Joyce's best friend?"

"My mother, Brother."

"Who would you say was Medina Joyce's second-best friend?"

"I'm not sure."

"Vice-Principal MacDougal?"

"Maybe."

"You and I know that they are far from friends."

"I guess they don't like each other all that much."

"How did your mother meet Medina Joyce?"

"I don't know."

"She met her before she met your father?"

"I think so."

"So your mother met your father through Medina?"

"I think so."

"Your mother and Medina, the two Miss Joyces, remained
friends in spite of what your father, Medina's brother, did?"

"Yes. Medina is nice."

"And yet she seems to have no other friends. Does she?"

"I think she does. At St. Clare's, where she works."

"But when she isn't working, she spends most of her time at your
mother's house. Vice-Principal MacDougal told me so. How many
hours a week would you say she spends at your mother's house?"

"I'm not sure. She doesn't like it where she lives, but that's all she
can afford. She only gets twenty hours of work a week. My mother
gives her money sometimes."

"She gives Medina money that Mr. MacDougal gives *her*?"

"Sometimes. I don't know how much."

"Do you think she could afford a better place to live if she did not spend so much money on alcohol and cigarettes?"

"I don't know."

"Smoking and drinking are unseemly habits for a woman. Mr. MacDougal tells me that your mother drinks and smokes a lot. Is that true?"

"She doesn't drink as much as him, but he doesn't smoke. Except a pipe sometimes."

"So you like Miss Medina Joyce? Your aunt by blood. Your common-law aunt."

"Yes."

"Why does she spend so much time at your mother's house?"

"They like to play cards."

"Cards, yes. Another bad habit. Well, I expect you'll see much less of her after Vice-Principal MacDougal marries your mother. Is that right?"

"I suppose so."

"I will see to it that Vice-Principal MacDougal will not be so foolish as to tolerate the frequent presence in his house of an ignoramus who exploits and despises him."

The part of the catechizing that concerned Medina spanned two days. On the second day, McHugh brought with him to the Basilica, along with the usual four books, a small cardboard box from which he removed a pair of black binoculars. He placed them on the table in front of me.

"Do you know what those are?" he said. I nodded. "I like to look at the city through them from the window of my room. Have you ever looked through a pair of binoculars?"

"No."

"Give it a try."

I picked them up. They were much heavier than they looked,

thick and made of metal. I raised them to my eyes. Everything looked blurred until McHugh adjusted a little wheel on the top. The room came into focus, everything eerily enlarged. I was able to read the writing beneath the portrait of the Pope. McHugh snatched the binoculars away from me and again laid them on the table.

"One night, it must have been a year ago, I couldn't sleep. I got up and looked out the window as I often do. And I happened to see, to faintly make out, someone standing in the little patch of woods behind your house. It was winter. The trees were bare. A cold night. I couldn't make out who it was until I looked through these binoculars. It was your aunt, Miss Joyce. She was simply standing there among the trees, her hands in the pockets of her yellow coat, staring at your house. She stood there for perhaps ten minutes. Then she went inside and the last of the lights in the house went off. I realized that she'd been waiting for something, a signal of some kind perhaps. Why was she out there on such a night? What was she waiting for?"

"I don't know."

"I've since seen her come and go from the house at all hours of the night. Sometimes she waits outside. Sometimes she goes inside the moment she arrives. She always approaches the house from the back, in the dark, like some sort of thief."

"She's not a thief. She has trouble sleeping where she lives. It's noisy. When it's really bad, she comes over to our house and sleeps on the chesterfield."

"But why would she wait outside like that?"

"I'm not sure. Maybe she's making sure that we're all the way asleep so that she doesn't wake us up when she comes in."

"She doesn't call first to tell your mother she's coming, to ask if it's all right?"

"Medina doesn't have her own phone. There's a phone in her boarding house, but it's almost always broken."

"She *does* have her own phone. Mr. MacDougal told me so."

"It *was* broken for a while. She must have got it fixed."

"So she just comes over and walks right in, sometimes after all of you have gone to bed and are sound asleep?"

I nodded.

"She doesn't need a key?"

"Mom never locks the house, not even when everyone goes out."

"It was odd, the sight of her behind your mother's house, staring. I can't see the back door of your house, not even with binoculars, so I don't know if your mother let her in or she let herself in. What do you think?"

"I don't know."

"You think Miss Joyce somehow knows, somehow guesses when it would be best to come inside so as not to wake anyone?"

"Maybe."

"Is she sometimes on the sofa when you wake up in the morning?"

"No. She gets up before me and helps my mother make breakfast."

"You're lying."

"No, I'm not."

"I spoke to Vice-Principal MacDougal about this matter just this afternoon. He never mentioned that Miss Joyce sometimes spends the night at your mother's house. He said he had no idea why Miss Joyce comes and goes the way that I described. He went home and asked your mother about it and came back to my office just before I left to come here. He said she told him Miss Joyce has absolute freedom of the house. She told my vice-principal that he retires early, is a heavy sleeper and always gets up late, so it's no wonder he doesn't know about Miss Joyce's visits. She said Miss Joyce feels lonely where she lives, especially at night, a place where she has no family and where most people are merely passing through and so hardly even talk to one another. So she comes over to your mother's house because it's the closest thing to a real home that she has."

"Oh," I said. "I thought she couldn't sleep because it's too noisy where she lives."

"But now you think your mother's right?"

I nodded.

He stared at me, smiling, chewing his gum at the front of his mouth. "Oh what a tangled web we weave," he said.

When I got home, my mother was at the Helm but not typing. She put her finger to her lips and motioned with her eyes toward Pops' sunroom, where he sat drinking beer. She looked frightened, and seemed on edge, drifting into episodes of self-absorption while we played Scrabble. She seemed especially nervous after Medina arrived. They smoked a pack of cigarettes between them before Pops at last left the sunroom and went to bed. The three of us sat at the kitchen table.

"I didn't have time to warn you," my mother whispered, reaching for my hand. "I knew if I went to the Basilica to get you for some made-up reason that McHugh would be even more suspicious. What did he say and what did you tell him? And keep your voice down." As I recounted my session with McHugh, Medina kept shaking her head and saying "sweet Jesus" under her breath. "It's fine," my mother said when I was finished.

"Fine?" Medina said. "He's been watching me for a year through his *binoculars* and you think everything is fine? Your story and Perse's don't match and you think everything is fine?"

"They almost match. It's plausible that Perse wouldn't have the reason for your visits quite clear in his head." She took me in her arms and hugged me hard. "You did good, Perse. Better than I did, I think." She let me go and turned to Medina. "McHugh doesn't know anything, so he can't *prove* anything. I keep telling you that. Let him have his suspicions. Soon enough it won't matter what he thinks."

"Well, you'll be the one who's safely married within the Church. To McHugh, I'll still just be a Crazy Lizzie."

"He won't dare cause trouble for you once Pops and I are married—he won't want to do anything that might bring to light the truth about Percy Joyce's reformed mother and humiliate Uncle Paddy."

"Jesus, Pen, I hope you're right."

Later, my mother came into my room and folded her arms on my bunk. She said she would take my place at catechism if she could and she hated the thought of my being interrogated by McHugh. She said she wasn't sure to what degree Uncle Paddy shared McHugh's suspicions, and she'd wondered to what degree my catechism was being directed by Uncle Paddy. "It's only a few more days," she said. "We'll be home free once I'm married and you've been baptized. After the Big Do at the Big B, there'll be no turning back for them. Do you think you can hang in there for a few more days?"

"I think so, Mom."

That night, I drifted in and out of sleep, lucidly, continuously dreaming that McHugh was standing atop the long table in the Basilica, strolling its length with his hands in his pockets, his black boots clumping on the wood, while every chair at the table was occupied by a Christian Brother, all of whom were smoking, chewing gum and taking notes.

I woke once to hear voices in the hallway, my mother's and Medina's. Medina urgently: "I wish the three of us could just go away." "Where? How?" my mother said. "I'm just wishing, Pen. I'm not saying we should." I wondered if she was really wishing that I wasn't in the picture. Maybe then the two of them could have run away. But wherever they went, they would have to live much as they did now, in some acceptable, fictional arrangement. Nevertheless, I felt that I was a major complication, a nuisance who crimped what little space they might otherwise have had.

I spent the next day at St. Bon's fretting over the looming catechism with McHugh, knowing that, at the end of it, I would be so tired that, by the time I got to 44, I would want to go straight to bed without having had a bite to eat.

I was now required to sit in on religion class with the other boys. I sat side on in my desk, legs crossed, arms folded across my chest, looking appraisingly at elderly Brother Trask as he recited from his notes a highly condensed and simplified form of Saint Thomas Aquinas's ontological proof of God's existence, having to do with the Prime Unmoved Mover who was God. My mother had read a book about this very proof and had spoken enough about it that I thought I might be able to cause some mischief.

So I raised my hand and said that an all-powerful know-it-all wouldn't need to write or read a book. Maybe God only thought He was all-powerful but found out the hard way that He wasn't. Maybe there used to be someone in charge of everything but now, for some reason, there wasn't. Maybe God had abdicated. How would we know? "The Bible," was always the answer Brother Trask gave. So I asked him why, if the Bible held all the answers, the Church had commissioned Saint Thomas Aquinas to prove the existence of God. Why were we taught that proof? Wasn't faith alone enough? God might not know it all, I said, He might just know a lot, the most. He might know more than everyone else but not everything. Maybe He was just doing the best He could.

"No," Brother Trask said, "God knows infinitely more than the smartest person who ever lived. And His Plan is perfect."

"But there can't be an infinite amount of knowledge if only God is infinite."

"You're showing off. That's called sophistry."

It was a small consolation but I could tell that Brother Trask was intimidated by me, and all the more by my appearance, as if my being disfigured had conferred upon me some of the seven-foot

Aquinas's genius, as if I were his descendant, slowly slobbering my objections to his own pedestrian misreading of the Proof.

"The world might be like a game God gave Himself for Christmas that He doesn't play with anymore. We might be stored away in the basement of the universe with a bunch of other games He got bored with. If you know everything and can do everything, it must be hard to entertain yourself, hard to set goals and think of challenges. It must be impossible."

"Nothing is impossible for God. The Word of God is in the Bible. You're giving offence, Percy."

"But God is perfect. You'd think the last thing on His mind would be critical appraisals."

It was mean of me to speak that way to Brother Trask, but it was hard not to vent a little when I knew that a session with McHugh was imminent, McHugh to whom Brother Trask would report every word I said.

At home, my mother thumbed through my catechism.

"You never hear about Mary being kept up all night because God won't stop bawling no matter what she tries. You never hear about her burping Baby Jesus or changing his diaper. Did Mary suckle God? Do you lactate if the Holy Ghost makes you pregnant? When did Jesus first realize that he was God? Did he start out with a sneaking suspicion that just kept growing on him, or did he not have a clue until Mary broke it to him at a certain age? It would have been like me trying to convince Perse that he was Santa Claus."

She read aloud the catechism entry concerning the sixth commandment, Thou shalt not commit adultery. "It covers a lot more than adultery," she said thoughtfully. "It says that 'even unacted upon, lust summons up the corruption of men, brings everlasting death and damnation on their souls, causes them to risk the laws of Heaven and the pains of Hell, begets in their souls a distaste for holy things, gives them a perverted conscience, a hatred for God and possibly leads to a complete loss of their faith.' Well, I notice when I turn men's heads, so it seems to me that if I summon up the corruption of the nature of men, I should notice that as well. I don't *feel* as if, by wearing short skirts, I bring everlasting death and damnation on the souls of men, do you, Medina? It certainly puts choosing what to wear in a whole new light. From now on I won't say, 'Is this a nice blouse?' I'll say, 'Will this blouse cause men to risk the loss of Heaven and the pains of Hell?' I'll tell shopkeepers I'm looking for clothes that come with a guarantee that they won't do that. If I wear my hair up, will it beget in the soul of the man next door a distaste for holy things, a perverted conscience, a hatred for God, and possibly lead to a complete loss of his faith?" She paused. "I doubt it's healthy for a man to regard his wife as one of the main causes of the downfall of humankind. What a wedding night the bride would have."

Medina got up from the table and threw her cigarette into the sink and turned on the tap. She stood on her toes and peered out through the kitchen curtains at Brother Rice.

"I'm sure McHugh has a crush on you," Medina said. "I can see it in his eyes when he looks at you."

"I am a woman in love with another woman, and I sleep with my male boarder because he pays me to and is better read than most, and I do this because, having been abandoned by my fiancé when I was pregnant, I can't find a more reliable way to support myself, not to mention my son—so pardon me if it takes me more time than it would take the average person to get used to the notion that a neighbouring member of the clergy might be in love with me."

McHugh had me recite the Confiteor: "I confess that I have sinned exceedingly. . . ."

"God knows all things, even our most secret thoughts, words and actions. Do you believe that, Percy Joyce?"

"Yes," I said.

"Do you believe that there is nothing in the world more perfect than man because he is made to the image and likeness of God?"

"Yes."

"Are you lying?"

"No, Brother."

"Why did Jim Joyce go away?"

"I don't know."

"Yes you do."

"I don't."

"Your mother must know."

"She says she doesn't."

"The other Miss Joyce?"

"She says she doesn't know."

"They must miss him."

"They don't talk about him very much."

"You must remind them of him."

"Maybe if I looked like him, I would. But I don't look like anyone. Anyone could be my father. It might not even be Jim Joyce."

"Is your mother unsure of who your father is?"

"I just meant that I don't remind anyone of anyone."

"You're unprecedented, unique, one of a kind."

"I suppose."

"Thousands of people in the world have wine stains on their faces. You're not unique"

"How do you know?"

"I looked it up. Do you think your mother keeps secrets from you?"

"No."

"So you know everything she knows."

"She knows more than me. But that's not the same as secrets. Can I go to the bathroom? I have to pee."

"Not yet. Listen to me. His Grace says he will never give up on either you or your mother. That means I must never give up, even though I know that neither of you is worth a second thought. If you drop out of school, if you drop out of the Church, if Vice-Principal MacDougal no longer lives with you or works at Brother Rice, we will still not give up, because His Grace believes that God has charged him with the mission of saving Penelope and Percy Joyce. That His Grace singled you out as special cases long ago is common knowledge. You are both, for better or worse, very conspicuous. There may be no one left on the Mount but him who believes you're worth the bother. But he thinks he must not be seen as having failed you or, by extension, the rest of the Mount, whom he long ago directed to look out for you as Christ Himself, in words and deeds, directed His disciples to look out for the least among them. His Grace believes that a congregation's faith could be diminished if its Church-appointed leader were made to look like a failure or a fool."

I sat up straight in my chair and stared at the brass buttons on the cuffs of my blazer. The whole room, McHugh included, was reflected in them. I was both thirsty and bursting to pee but didn't dare complain to McHugh whose ever-growing candour I was growing frightened of provoking into an outright accusation against my mother and Medina.

"How many kinds of sin are there?" McHugh demanded.

"The number of kinds of sin is ten. First there is Original Sin, which we are all guilty of because our first parents, Adam and Eve, were guilty of it. A person born of a person with an impure spirit has himself an impure spirit at the instant of his conception. Therefore, all the people who ever were or ever will be born, except the Blessed Virgin Mary, bear on their souls the sins committed by the pair in which all the people of the world have their origin and from whom they are descended and related to by blood—Adam and Eve. Next, there is actual sin, of which there are two kinds— mortal and venial. The seven mortal sins are called the seven capital sins and sometimes the Seven Deadly Sins. The number of lesser, or venial, sins is infinite, but all of them together are less grave than a single mortal sin. Can I please go to the bathroom?"

My mother had other worries besides being discovered: She said she hoped I was holding up well against McHugh's relentless cat-echizing and I would not come home one day a broken, indoctrinated boy, convinced of my utter corruption and terrified that I would die before a priest could pour a cup of water on my head and thereby pardon me for an ancient crime attributed to two people universally known to have never existed—the crime of having sex and thereby creating a child.

"At least women like Medina and me don't *add* to the amount of original sin in the world," my mother said as I sat with them at the table. She pointed out that the history of the world would have been very brief if the first two humans God created had been women, lesbians or not. After their expulsion from Eden, there would have been a very brief, uneventful historical period followed by the quiet extinction of the human race and the non-invention of religion.

"Original sin. You inherit it by being born. You didn't conceive yourself, or give birth to yourself but, because it began with sex, every birth there ever was needs a fall guy, so it's you. We're born with more guilt coursing through our veins than blood. The second sin is your first breath, and so it goes. You detox in confession every month or so, only to come out and get hooked on guilt again."

She pored over a copy of the fourteen-hundred-question cat-echism that she'd borrowed from the library.

"You think you have it tough, Perse, but it could be worse. There are subcategories within subcategories, answers with the ring of divine authority to the most bizarre hypothetical questions: If you suffer amnesia and forget to confess a mortal sin, do you go to Hell? No. But if your memory comes back, you must not only confess the mortal sin but reconfess every sin you've committed since you inadvertently forgot the mortal sin, no matter how long your amnesia lasts, or else you do go to Hell."

She leafed slowly through the pages of the catechism, hardly aware, it seemed, of the cigarette between her fingers.

"How they love numbers—I suppose because they're exact, precise. They seem to forbid debate. What are the six of these, the seven of that? And they're very big on the whole pecking-order thing. I mean, they rank everything and everyone. There are separate hierarchies for the living, the dead, the angels and the saints—but the Holy Mother is the One and Only. The Blessed Virgin Mary. Born of a woman but without the taint of original sin. She was given a get-out-of-guilt-free card, and a get-out-of-life-alive card—she never died, just went straight up into Heaven in the pink of health. There is a pontiff but no nuntiff. Nuns have no upward mobility. Why not have a women's Vatican led by an über-nun elected by her peers on the advice of the Holy Ghost, a Most Holy Nun whose every utterance is true and through whom God speaks like the greatest of ventriloquists? How about some arch nuns, a College of Cardinelles?"

"Just what we need," Medina said, sipping on her beer, "more nuns."

"Listen to this: Saint Thomas Aquinas is a Dr. Angelicus, Saint Anselm a Dr. Magnificus, Saint John of the Cross a Dr. Mysticus. Men must not be as angelic, magnificent or mystical as they used to be. Not a woman to be found among the eternal host of angels, who, though supposed to be genderless, all bear the names of men—Michael, Gabriel, Raphael and that nameless guy who wrestled all night with Jacob. In pictures, they all have lots of muscles and long hair—I swear they look like beatnik bodybuilders."

I was glad to see a smile on Medina's haggard-looking face. My mother smiled back at her and caressed her cheek with the back of her hand. She pursed her lips in a kiss that she blew at me.

"As far as I can tell," she said, pushing aside the catechism, "God Himself is guilty of the Seven Deadly Sins. The Wrath of God: no explanation necessary. Pride: He created millions of angels to praise Him in song for all eternity. Envy: nothing raised His wrath more than the worshipping of other gods. Sloth: everything is effortless for Him. Gluttony: hard to make a case for that against a God who, being all-powerful, requires neither food nor drink. But He didn't have a worry in the world before He made, well, the *world*, so He must be a glutton for punishment. Greed: He created us so He could share Himself with us, an act, we are told, of immense generosity. And if you have boundless self-replenishing wealth, no overhead, no upkeep, no mortgage, no payroll and no dependants, how generous can you be? Lust: the sole taint of Paradise and ever since the driving force of humankind. But He made everything, including everything in Paradise, so He must have come up with lust so that Adam and Eve could come down with it."

Medina and I laughed as my mother continued her avalanche of forbidden fruit. She stared off into space, composing on the fly:

"When it comes to women, the Church pretty much puts all its eggs into one basket: the eggless Blessed Virgin Mary.

"So imagine that the most famous of all virgins was a man. The Blessed Virgin Gary, the only man to have ever made a woman pregnant while maintaining his virginity. The Angel Gabriel appears to Gary and tells him that even though he long ago vowed to give himself to no one but the Church, his wife will soon be made pregnant during a middle-of-the-night visit from the Holy Ghost. Imagine that Gary's story is as widely believed at first as Mary's must have been. His wife, Josephine, gives birth to a baby girl—Jessica. The Holy Trinity would then be God the Father, God the Daughter and God the Holy Ghost. At thirty-three, Jessica Christ, after choosing twelve women as Apostles, will be crucified and ascend into Heaven to redeem the sins of humankind. So now everything is changed. There are no early Church

Fathers, only early Church Mothers. Only women can be popes—and therefore, at any one time, the only infallible person on the planet is a woman known as Mama Pope Trish. Pope Ramona. Pope Donna the Twenty-third. Only women can be priests and forgive men's sins. Or withhold forgiveness from men. Only women get to listen to the confessions of lust-drunk adolescent boys. Men receive penance and Communion exclusively from women, cannot marry without the permission and blessing of a woman. Only men must cover their heads in church, and they must sit and listen while women preach at them in church for the immodest way they dress. A way is invented to determine if a man is a virgin. There is no longer a way to prove that a woman is a virgin. Our Lord of the Immaculate Conception."

"If McHugh is watching from his suite through binoculars," Medina said, "I hope he can't read lips. He might be wondering what we're all laughing at."

"Let him wonder," my mother said. "So let's see, what's left? How about the sacraments:

"Baptism: The Sacrament That Almost No One Remembers. (I don't think you'll ever forget yours, Perse.)

"Confession: The Sacrament of Perfunctory Duplicity and Repentance for Fictitious Misdemeanours.

"Communion: The Sacrament of Looking as Humbly Holy as an Athiest Like Pops. (He calls himself an agnostic but he's an atheist.)

"Confirmation: The Sacrament That No One Understands the Purpose of.

"Holy Orders: The Sacrament That Has Nothing to Do with Women.

"Matrimony: The Sacrament That Precedes Priest-Approved Sex.

"Last Rites: The Sacrament That No One Remembers. Excluding false alarms of course.

"The Seven Deadly Sins should be called the Seven Sinful Hobbies.

"Fourteen hundred catechism questions and only Ten Commandments. Ten is a far better number to conjure with than fourteen hundred. If Moses had come down from Mount Sinai with Fourteen Hundred Catechism Questions, who would have taken him seriously? He would have needed two hundred and eighty stone tablets and who knows how many times he would have had to go up and down that mountain while the Hebrews were losing patience with him at the bottom."

"You better be right about there being no Hell, Pen," Medina said.

"I'll risk it. I'm so tired of this whole Mary-meek-and-mild thing. Mary Queen of Peace. Mary Queen of the World. Mary ever-patient, always in a good mood. She must have had her bad days just like everybody else. Why not name a school the Vicious Virgin Mary? Mary of the Monthly Cramps. Mary Who Could Be a Real Bitch. Mary Fit to Be Tied. Mary Bored Out of Her Mind. Mary Fed Up to Here. Mary Without a Smoke or a Beer in the House. And the orders of nuns should have very different names: the Sisters of Eternal Aggravation, the Sisters of Celestial Assault.

"I suppose Mary had it pretty good—God for a son, and a saint who never went near her for a husband. What would *I* get for being a married virgin? Or you Medina? A good talking to from a priest. It must have been rough on Joseph, though. Keep your hands off the wife and if you know what's good for you, don't look sideways at the youngster. If he happens to tell you he's God, just play along." She went on and on and, when she finished, we applauded.

"Well," she said, "if wishes were horses, women would ride."

I was well primed for a session of give me myth or give me death, my first in a long time. I told the other students—only minutes before joining McHugh in the Basilica that, according to my studies, the catechism stated that, if a mother and her son were stranded on a desert island, they were allowed to do *it* but only after waiting for seven years. In fact, the rule of the Church was that, after seven years, they *had* to do it. I said the mother had to be on top, always, or else it was incest. I said that after Jim Joyce left, my mother had sworn never to have sex again. I said that after she took one look at me, she *swore* she would never have sex again. Then I said my mother had told me that, if I hadn't fucked a woman by the time I was twenty-one, she would let me fuck her. I said she was really looking forward to getting laid after all these years. But because she felt sorry for me, she let me see her tits sometimes, and once she let me touch one of them just so that I wouldn't die not knowing what a naked tit felt like. Because she felt sorry for me, she let me see and touch any part of her I wanted to when we took baths together. But she wouldn't let me do it to her or anything like that. She let me do anything except go all the way.

I didn't notice the reaction of the other students. I couldn't swear I *had* an audience once I was through. My head was a buzzing, swarming tumult of salacious lies. I foresaw a day when I might myth myself to death.

"So now we turn at last to you, Percy Joyce. Do you know what marriage banns are?" McHugh held the catechism as if he meant to throw it at me.

"The priest announces at Mass on three Sundays in a row that a man and a woman of the parish are engaged and says that if anyone knows why these two people should not be married, they should tell the priest in private after Mass." I liked to imagine them going up *during* Mass, whispering in the priest's ear and pointing accusingly at members of the congregation.

"Do you know of any reason why Penelope Joyce and Jerome MacDougal should not be married, Percy Joyce? Remember that it is a mortal sin to withhold such information from the priest or someone able to communicate it to him."

"I don't know of any reason," I said, but, unable to keep my voice from quavering, I swallowed with a gulp.

McHugh laid his catechism face down on the table, then leaned on the table on his outspread hands, which brought his face closer to mine than it had ever been during our catechisms. "You don't sound very sure of yourself. Is there something you would like me to pass on to His Grace? The eternals souls of Penelope and Jerome depend on this as well, as might those of other people if other people are involved. You *must* be certain."

"I am. I'm certain, Brother."

I thought he'd keep after me for hours, but he announced that this was our next-to-last meeting. The last would take place after the wedding and would consist of an exam on the Fifty Primary Questions.

"Between now and then," he said, "I want you to think very hard about the questions I asked you today."

"Only one more, sweetheart?" my mother exclaimed when I got home. "We should celebrate!"

Some celebration. She and Medina drank beer in the kitchen and Pops drank in the sunroom. But they ordered out for pizza. My mother playfully said McHugh suspected Pops of having one or more secret wives in his past, women who were still alive and to whom he was therefore still married, divorce being forbidden to good Catholics such as he was. "Is he right? Is there a Mrs. VP MacD back in St. Anthony, Pops? A brood of kids, perhaps? Or are you even from St. Anthony, or Newfoundland for that matter? What town in what country did you hightail it out of years ago, and what did you run away from? Tell us all! A series of shotgun weddings, probably. Or a gambling debt? A posse of homicide detectives? You're a man of mystery, many mysteries. Maybe you have other girlfriends, even fiancées that I don't know about. Pops the secret rascal. We're not related, are we, Pops? You're not Jim Joyce's first cousin, are you? This would be an awful time to tell me you're the brother I never knew I had."

"Don't be absurd," Pops said, smiling, dismissing her with a wave of his hand but clearly enjoying her tongue-in-cheek flirtation with him. He smiled almost sheepishly, as if it tickled him that my mother would, however jestingly, speculate about his darkly romantic past.

Medina said sulkily that the only mystery about Pops was what the pair who were to blame for his existence could possibly be like and by what manner of mating their species reproduced.

"What did your father do for a living, Pops?" my mother asked. "I might as well get to know you since we're getting married."

Pops told her that his father had been a fisherman and his mother had earned money cleaning other people's houses. But Medina said there was no way that Pops had ever been a child or that there had ever been an entire family of MacDougals.

MacDoug-aliens was the best explanation for Pops, my mother said, suddenly switching sides because of how sullen Medina looked. "MacDoug-aliens from Planet Doug. What are people like on Doug?" My mother tipped back her head in laughter. "They probably all work in labs and wear white coats. A safety-goggle-wearing Pops-like race that lives primarily on beer."

Pops sighed with impatience. "Why do you let her influence you, Paynelope? Why can you not be as nice all the time as you are sometimes?"

"Variety is the nice of life," my mother said. "Besides, it's so much more fun being mean than nice. You'd get bored with me if I was always nice."

"*I* would," Medina said.

"She *is* always nice to you," Pops said.

THE CHEMISTRY LAB

Much later, unable to sleep, I went out to the kitchen for a glass of water. I saw that Pops was still in the sunroom. There were, I guessed, ten empty beer bottles beside his chair, but he was awake and talking as though to his reflection in the window. For the first time, it occurred to me that it could just as easily have been my mother and *him* that I had heard and seen in the bed that night. I was glad it hadn't been.

"What are you doing up this late, Percy?" he said. "Having dreams about the girls of Mercy? Tell Vivian to think of England."

"Thirsty," I said. "Vivian's gone."

"Here," he said, "have some beer." He laughed and drank from the bottle in his hand. I stood beside that old reclining chair of his.

"I've had beer before," I said. "Remember, when you and Mom got engaged—"

He laughed again. "Do you think about little orphan girls from Belvedere playing with your jelly beans?"

"I'm not afraid of girls."

"If it wasn't for me, you'd be coming home from school every day with your pants put on backward by the girls of Holy Heart."

"If it wasn't for Uncle Paddy and McHugh, you mean."

"Yes. You're right. The albatross of 44, the albatross of Penny Joyce, is right."

"Mom doesn't think of me as her albatross," I said. But his words stung. Percy the albatross forever hung about his mother's neck, weighing her down, a dead, leaden *thing* against which she would forever struggle in vain, forever have to lug around until she died.

"Shouldn't have said that, Percy. She loves you."

"Is something wrong, Pops?"

"Is something wrong? Everything is wrong, Percy."

"But you and Mom are getting married soon."

Pops sniffed. "Married," he said. "Don't you think I know what that woman and your mother have been up to all these years? Don't you think I *know*?"

I was so frightened I started to cry.

"Please don't tell anyone, Pops."

"Who is there to tell? Everyone knows."

"No they don't. Please, Pops. If anyone finds out they're lizzies, they'll take me away from Mom."

He slapped me across the face with the back of his hand. I fell, wound up palms flat on the floor, my hands gaining purchase just in time to keep my face from hitting the carpet. I sat partway up, supported by my hands and feet, no longer crying.

"That's not true," he whispered.

"I saw her and Medina," I said, unable to curb the spite his slap and the word "albatross" had stirred up in me. He stood, put his hands under my armpits, lifted me off my feet and all but threw me into his chair.

"What lies are you telling about your mother, Percy?"

Then, because he had hit me and thrown me into the chair, I realized that he'd been talking about something else—how my mother and Medina had been soaking him for money for so long. But I couldn't stop myself now.

"I saw them. Kissing. They had no clothes on and they were making noises. My mother loves Medina, not you. Doing it with you almost makes her puke. She loves to do it with Medina. I saw them in my mother's room, in her bed—"

"That's not true."

"It *is* true."

"What did you see?" He put his hands on the arms of the chair and brought his face to within an inch of mine.

"I saw her and Medina. Doing it. Mom was doing it to Medina with her whole hand."

"Shut your filthy little mouth. What lies are you telling?" But his voice was a whisper now.

"In my mother's bed."

He raised his fist but slowly lowered it. And I saw by his eyes that, until I told him, he'd had no idea.

"I was just kidding, Pops," I said. "They're not lizzies. I was just kidding. Because you hit me. And said I was an albatross."

"You know that's not true," he said, as if he was talking to himself. He was almost crying, his voice husky and weak. "Go to your room, Percy. Close the door, get into bed and go to sleep."

"Are you going to tell anyone?"

"No. I'm not going to tell anyone. Are you? Are you going to tell your mother or Medina what you said to me?"

"If you promise not to tell, I'll promise not to tell."

"I promise, Percy. Believe me. I won't say a word. Not another word. And you won't say a word. No matter what happens. Right? For your mother's sake."

I nodded. I scrambled out of Pops' chair, ran to my room, shut the door, got in bed and ducked my head beneath the blankets. I lay there, my heart pounding, waiting for Pops to wake my mother, waiting for the shouting to begin. I waited for Pops to confront my mother, to walk right into her room so that she'd wake up to see him standing over her. I thought of how scared she'd be, and I hoped he wouldn't hurt her. I wondered if I should phone Medina. And then wondered if, even now, Medina might be in my mother's room, asleep in bed beside her. I wished I'd said nothing to him, felt so stupid for having misunderstood what he was about to say, for presuming to know, and not, as my mother would have done, waiting for him to speak.

I waited and waited, but I heard nothing. I wondered if Pops had become so drunk he had fallen asleep in his chair, but I didn't dare get up to see. I silently consulted with Saint Drogo. I stared at him as he peered out between the bars of his self-made cell. He was a cartoon-like depiction of deformity that, for the second time since I'd acquired the Mass card from Sister Mary Aggie, didn't make me smile. The first time, the sight of him had made me punch the wall. But even this Quasimodo of a man had made his mark and been canonized, immortalized. The Patron Saint of Unattractive People. I thought of going to my mother's room to tell her what had happened, what I had said to Pops, to tell her that, because of me, Pops *knew* and might tell McHugh. But the more I thought about it, the more certain I felt that he would never tell McHugh, never tell anyone, in part because he loved my mother and knew what the consequences would be for her and me, and in part because, like Jim Joyce, he wanted as few people as possible to know of his humiliation. If my mother and Medina knew that he had learned the truth about them and believed he might now or soon or sometime in the future tell McHugh, that would be the end of it, of him and Paynelope, of his life and all our lives at 44. With the truth out, we would have to run, my mother, Medina and I, run to God knows where, live as best we could after starting all over far from Newfoundland, an unlikely threesome of fugitives whom he would never see again.

So I decided that, the best thing would be to say nothing to my mother, to wait and see what Pops would do next. I doubted he would wait long to speak with me again for fear that I *would* go to my mother. As I lay there on the bunk, I expected to hear the sound of my door being eased open, expected that, in whispers, Pops and I would soon be working out the terms of our silence, Pops impressing upon me what I already knew, the importance to all of us of me keeping my mouth shut.

There wasn't a sound, but I felt as if I'd been wakened by one after just a few minutes of sleep. Pops never used the back door, so I went to the front porch, to the vestibule, and looked out through one of the teardrop-shaped windows in the door. Though there was no street light nearby, I was just able to make him out, wearing his lab coat, slowly, slump-shouldered, trudging up the steps of Brother Rice. I wondered if he intended to wake McHugh in the middle of the night. The access tunnel from the school to the Brothers' Quarters would be, as always, locked from the school side of the door. Pops *could* phone McHugh from somewhere in the school. Maybe he hadn't used our phone because he didn't want to risk waking me or my mother. Or maybe he had used it and was now on his way to see McHugh. But then I remembered that McHugh was the only one of the Brothers who had a private phone in the Quarters, and I doubted that Pops even knew the number; McHugh was always in his office when they spoke by phone. So what was he up to?

He looked over his shoulder as a car went by. I ducked so he wouldn't see me at the little window. When I looked again, he was not on the steps. The doors of Brother Rice were closed and no lights were on inside the school. I went back to my bedroom and watched from the window, hoping to see him leave the school, cross Bonaventure and come back home to 44. What a relief it would be to see him retrace his steps, hear him at the front door then scuffing through the house, kicking books aside as he always did on the way to his room.

But there was no sign of him. I watched for perhaps fifteen minutes. I decided to go across the street myself and try to get into the school. For the sake of appearances, so as not to look absurdly conspicuous, I put on a jacket over my pyjamas and exchanged my slippers for a pair of boots. I crept from my room to the front door, all the while watching the door of my mother's room, listening for the sound of her getting up or lighting a cigarette. I opened the inner door of the vestibule, closed it behind me, opened the outer door. There was not even the faintest glow of morning in the sky. Seeing no traffic the entire length of Bonaventure, I left the front yard and began to run across the street. The lights of a car that was far exceeding the speed limit appeared on the Curve of Bonaventure. I jumped onto the traffic island just in time to avoid the car, which didn't brake, though someone in it, a young man, stared blankly at me.

I watched the car until it dipped below the hill, then resumed my way across the street, running faster when I reached the walkway that led up to the lobby steps of Brother Rice. I tried the door. It swung open easily and I stepped inside. I was sweating and out of breath, and had to wait awhile until I was certain that the school was silent. There was a faint smell of cleaning liquid, but the marble floors were dry, so I assumed that the cleaners had long since left. I climbed the inner steps. The glass front wall of McHugh's office was dark, though I could dimly make out the shapes of filing shelves and furniture inside.

There was just a small window criss-crossed with wire in the door of the lab, but I faintly saw the dim glow of a single ceiling lamp inside. I pulled on the handle, and when the door didn't open I thought it must be locked. Then I pushed and the door opened inward quite easily, barely making a sound. As the door swung to the right, I noted that the lab looked exactly as it had when Pops first took me there ten years ago.

At the desk, in his lab coat, the coat and his face eerily white in contrast to the all but unlit lab, was Pops. Spread out on the desk in front of him were a small brown bottle made of glass that bore a skull and crossbones on the label, the black rubber stopper of the bottle, a beaker half full of what might have been milk, a tiny lab spoon. There was also a piece of paper with two pens laid on it as if to keep it in place. Pops sat there in the dark lab, his hands in the pockets of his coat, thumbs outside, hooked on the pockets.

My mind raced, imagining what must have happened, Pops unlocking the door of the chemistry lab, closing it behind him and, without turning on the lights, making up his concoction, drinking it, sitting down at his desk on the dais, the blackboard behind him, the empty lab barely visible in front of him. How long had he sat there, overlooking the unmanned stations of the lab, goaded by my words into such a state of mind, picturing the scene I had described, the woman he thought of as *his* Penelope, his and no one else's, not even Jim Joyce's, in bed with Medina, *Medina*, the very person whom, above all others, he loathed, his unrelenting tormentor and detractor whom he had hoped, however foolishly, that he and Penelope were secretly in league against? How long had he sat there, wondering how it had come about that he had been undone by the words of a mere boy who knew what *he* had been too stupid, too self-absorbed, to surmise, the *real* secret of 44, the fact that he and not Medina was the butt of the ongoing joke of the house? If not for me, he might forever have persisted in his ignorance, might never have guessed the sort of cuckold the three of us knew him to be.

"Pops," I said, shaking his shoulder, praying that what I was witnessing for the first time was someone passed out drunk from drinking, praying for that even though his eyes were partway open, motionless, seemingly covered with glassy film, and only appeared to be looking at me. I ran my fingers through his hair, something I had never done before. It was sticky and smelled of lotion.

"Pops," I whispered, and began to cry.

I took the beaker and the spoon, dumped the contents of the beaker into the nearest lab sink, rinsed out the beaker and put it on a shelf with rows of others. I washed the spoon under the tap and put it in the nearest drawer. I stoppered the bottle. What to do with it I had no idea, until, looking around, I saw a small security safe high atop the cupboards to the left of Pops. Its door was open and inside it were dozens of other small glass bottles, green, brown, black. I found a chair and, standing on it, was just able to replace the bottle in the safe. I closed the door of the safe and, as I had seen someone do on TV, turned the numbered dial several times until it clicked. I replaced the chair, washed my hands, was about to take the pens and piece of paper from the desk when Pops grabbed one of my wrists. I gasped as if I'd fallen into ice-cold water. "I didn't do it, Percy," he said. "I thought about it, but I didn't do it. Afraid to, I suppose." He let go of my wrist.

I was so relieved, I wrapped my arms around his neck and hugged him. He gently pushed me back, to give himself room to stand, I thought, but he stayed in the chair.

"I put everything away," I said.

"Did you wash your hands?" he said. "There was enough in that glass to put me ten times under."

"I washed them," I said. "I was careful."

"Good boy. Good Little Percy Joyce."

"Let's go home, Pops," I said. "McHugh might find us here."

"McHugh is asleep, if he ever sleeps. It's three in the morning."

"It's almost four," I said. "Let's go home before Mom notices we're gone."

"I'm sorry I hit you, Percy. But everything is ruined. One way or the other, I have lost her. I almost wish the two of them could still go to jail for this. But they don't put them in jail anymore. They pretend to think they're only sick and put them in the Mental. Not even that, I'll bet. But they'll take you from your mother, and her days of working for Uncle Paddy or anyone else will be over. She'll end up begging on the streets, her and the other one. Maybe, wherever you go, you'll be better off without them. Small wonder your father went away. Where would the two of you be if not for me? I can't believe it. She was almost married to a man once. She had a child by him. Isn't that her true nature? That other one must have seduced her. But I can't help thinking of what you said, that your mother must have felt like throwing up every night after she left my room. The very thought of me must have disgusted her. The other one is jealous of me, always has been, I see that. And now I am jealous of her. You know, Percy, I carried that ring box around with me, carried it in the pockets of my lab coat, turned it about in my fingers while I was teaching class. I have gone home when I knew there would be no one there but your mother, and three times, as I watched her at her typewriter, interrupted her and took out the ring. Once burned, twice shy, I thought, but she'll come around. My Paynelope will come around. But the truth is that I have for fourteen years been little more than a piece of human camouflage, an alibi, a decoy for the two of them. As you have been in a way, Percy. I don't know what I shall do about this. Something must be done, of course, this sort of thing going on right under my nose. I had hopes. But I'm just the punchline to a joke about the Joyce women. The worst imaginable kind of cuckold, the deluded fool who doted on a woman who was thought to be holding out hope that her husband would come back, doted on her, waiting for the day she removed the engagement ring, the signal that she'd be receptive if I proposed again."

"Everything will be the same if we don't say a word," I said. "Almost everything."

"Will it, Percy?" His eyes brimming over with tears, he made a washing motion of his face with his hands—something I had done as a child, fancying that, when I took my hands away, my face would be like that of other boys, clean, healed, wholly normal.

"It *will*. The wedding will go ahead—"

"But I'll always *know*. Medina will always be there, always in the same bed as your mother. It will drive me mad."

"Medina always knew about you and Mom. It didn't drive *her* mad."

"It nearly did. Something nearly did."

"Shhh. You should let them think they still have a secret," I said. "But we'll be the ones with the secret from now on. You and me."

"You and me?"

I nodded.

"Turning the tables?"

"Right."

"Would you put up with such humiliation just to be near someone you love? Would you still love them even though you knew they loved someone else and thought you didn't know?"

"Yes," I said, "I would. I wouldn't mind having visiting hours with a girl from Holy Heart. As long as she liked me. Even if she loved someone else. Even if she thought she was tricking me."

"Even if she was using you for money in a farce of a marriage?"

I shrugged. "Mom likes you," I said. "It's better than a pity fuck. I might not even get a pity fuck from anyone. Ever."

Pops smiled at me. "No one has ever recommended a course of action to me on the grounds that it's better than a pity fuck." He pushed back his chair and stood up slowly, as if it pained him. His hands on his hips, head hung down, he exhaled deeply and cleared his throat. "So. We'll keep our promises, is that it? You won't tell and I won't tell. We'll never say a word."

I nodded.

He looked at me as if my marred face was somehow the measure of his anguish. "It's better than destroying you and your mother. We'll all be destroyed unless the wedding goes ahead."

———•———

Together, we hurriedly left the lab and, seeing no one in the hallway or the lobby, went outside. We stopped at each possible place of discovery, made sure no one saw us, crossed Bonaventure, which this time was truly deserted, let ourselves into the house and snuck back to our rooms.

THE PROPER ORDER
OF CREATION

My heart sank when McHugh told my mother by phone that an extra review of the material we had covered in the catechism, one in addition to the final exam that would take place after she and Pops were married, would be necessary. There were, he said, some catechism questions that we had neglected to review. McHugh proposed that he and I meet in the room at the Basilica the next day after school.

When McHugh arrived about twenty minutes late and without his various catechisms, I assumed he meant to quiz me from memory. He sat opposite me at the table as always. But he already seemed as agitated as he had been by the end of our recent sessions. His elbows on the arms of his chair, he made a cage with his fingers over which he looked at me, lightly tapping his fingertips together, chewing his gum.

"What is Hell?"

"Hell is a state to which the wicked are condemned, and in

which they are deprived of the sight of God for all eternity, and are in dreadful torment. The damned will suffer in both mind and body. The body will be tortured in all its members and senses."

"Why can there be only one true religion?"

"There can be only one true religion because a thing cannot be false and true at the same time, and therefore all religions that contradict the teachings of the One True Church must teach falsehood. If all religions in which men seek to serve God are equally good and true, Christ would not have disturbed the Jewish religion and the Apostles would not have condemned the heretics."

"Very good. You haven't forgotten."

"No, Brother."

"It's wonderful that your mother and Vice-Principal MacDougal are getting married, isn't it?" I nodded and he looked about, as though in search of others who would more fervently agree with him.

"She likes Pops a lot," I said.

McHugh stood abruptly and began to walk around the table with his hands behind his back. "Well, I should hope so," McHugh said. "They are about to be married. I should hope that she *likes* him a lot. I should hope her feelings for him match his for her." It was the first time he had not objected to my use of the name Pops. "*Like* is too weak a word for how *he* feels about *her*. A wife should do more than merely *like* her husband, don't you think?"

"I suppose," I said.

He made a full circuit of the room in silence, stopping just behind his chair, facing me. He folded his arms.

"How do *you* feel about Mr. MacDougal?"

"He's nice."

"He would be a very lonely man if not for you and your mother. And me. I have known him since long before he met your mother. I don't know what would have become of him by now if not for her and me. And you. He speaks of you as if you are his son. I think he wishes you were."

"Really?"

"God knows why, but yes, I think he does."

McHugh took out of the inside upper pocket of his jacket what looked like a tightly rolled-up leather belt. He held it straight out in front of him and, grasping the open end with his thumb and forefinger, let it unravel until it hung, swaying at arm's length like a snake that he had expertly captured.

"Do you know what this is?" he asked.

"No." But I did know. It was narrow and longer but thicker than a belt, half an inch thick perhaps. He folded it once in half so that it no longer swayed in front of him. He raised it above his head and, snapping it like a whip, brought it down on the table with such force that the nearest ashtray jumped and wobbled about until he stopped it with his hand.

"This is the Strop," he said. "Its edges are like those of the many straight razors that have been sharpened on it. A barber gave it to me. I only use it on the boys who misbehave the most. The hard cases, the ones who otherwise would never learn. Half a dozen strops will cut your hands to pieces. The last boy I stropped was Stevie Coffin. He deserved it, didn't he?"

I was so terrified, I couldn't speak.

"He never did come back to school."

Nothing had ever scared me more than the sight of that strop. I pushed back my chair and ran to the door that opened on the vestibule. I turned the knob and thrust my shoulder against the door, but it didn't open.

"You have to know how to open it," McHugh said. "You don't need much strength, but it takes a certain knack. You'll never manage it with those monkey hands of yours."

I ran the length of the room to the door by which McHugh came and went. It too would not open. I hammered on it with my fist and shouted, "Help, please, open the door."

"Calm *down*, Joyce," McHugh said. I turned around and looked at him. There was no sign of the Strop. He patted his breast pocket. "I just wanted you to see it. I just wanted you to know what it would be like for you if not for Uncle Paddy. I'm sure you won't tell anyone I called him that, will you?"

"No, Brother."

"Actually, tell anyone you like. They won't believe you. Now sit down."

I went back to my chair but didn't sit down.

"Fine," he said. "Stand. Stand on your head if you like. Either way, that face of yours will look the same." He began slowly to make his way around the table, touching the back of each chair as he passed it. He moved clockwise, so I started moving clockwise too.

"You don't have to run away from me, Joyce. You'll never see the Strop again, I promise."

"I'll stop if you stop," I said. He stopped directly across the table from me.

"I know what you know," he said. He put on his close-mouthed, gum-chewing smile as if all such previous smiles had been leading up to this one. "Crimes against the Order of Creation. Crimes of the sort for which Sodom and Gomorrah were destroyed have been taking place for years across the street from where I live, across the street from where the Christian Brothers of the Mount live and eat and sleep and pray, where the children of the Mount go to school."

"No, Brother."

"Yes, Brother. Your mother and your aunt by blood."

"I don't know what you mean." Could Pops have broken his word after all? Pops who thought of me as his son?

"There must be a reckoning when the proper Order of Creation is disturbed. THERE MUST."

He shouted so loudly that I closed my eyes and opened them just in time to see him complete a lunging crawl across the table. He grabbed me with one hand by the collars of my blazer and my shirt and, as he climbed down from the table, removed the Strop from his jacket with his other hand, let it unravel, then folded it in half against his leg. One hand fisting my collars, he raised the Strop high above his shoulder.

"Hands," he roared.

I held out my hands and started to cry.

"You're not the Coffin boy, are you?" he said. "You're not that tough."

I shook my head.

"Tell me," he rasped, his face so close to mine I smelled the fruity gum that he was chewing. "Tell me what Penelope and Medina do when others on the Mount are sound asleep."

"I don't know," I sobbed.

"If you tell me what they do, Uncle Paddy will see to it that they do you no more harm. You will have the best of everything."

I shook my head.

"Close your eyes," he said.

I shut them as tightly as I could and waited for the first blow of the Strop, but he loosened his grip on my collars.

"Open your eyes," he said.

I opened them to find that once again the Strop was gone. He put the thumb and index finger of his free hand into his mouth, took hold of his gum and withdrew it. He tore it in half, pressed one half into my left palm and the other into my right.

"What should we do, Pen?" Medina said when, crying and still shaking with fright, I told them what had happened at catechism, what McHugh had said and done. She paced, arms folded, puffing rapidly on a cigarette, unmindful of the ashes that fell from it onto her sweater and the floor.

My mother, sitting at the kitchen table, said she wasn't sure. What if McHugh took me from her? she wondered. She had all my life been reckless and indiscreet—"If discretion is a virtue,

Percy, your mother *is* a whore." She had thereby inspired so many rumours about everyone at 44 that there was no telling what sort of trumped-up charge McHugh might convince Uncle Paddy to quietly convey to those members of his congregation who had the power to do his bidding without discovery and with impunity. If I was taken from her, if she and Medina were cast out and vilified for life, and Pops was fired and left without hope of ever again earning a salary, all four of us would be destroyed.

"Jesus, you're the one who's been telling us not to panic," Medina said.

"I'm still doing that," my mother protested. "I'm just thinking out loud, letting off steam. McHugh is *trying* to panic us. I bet he hoped that, when Perse told us what happened today, we'd run. But if he had anything more he could try to flush us out with, he wouldn't have held it back. Not with the wedding so close." But she didn't look or sound entirely sure of herself. She stared off into space as if trying to anticipate McHugh's next move, or as if, in spite of what she'd said, she was spellbound by some vision of catastrophe.

"Paynelope, His Grace has generously suggested that the diocese pay for a modest reception."

"Suggested?"

"McHugh said 'stipulated.'"

"Has a honeymoon been arranged, Pops? How many other of *my* stipulations have you and McHugh vetoed without my knowledge? Not unless I'm kidnapped will I join you on a honeymoon. If the airplane or cruise tickets have already been bought, I hope that you and McHugh will have a wonderful time."

"It's just a reception," Pops said. "A modest, harmless party. Where's the problem in that?"

"The problem is you keep on tricking us," Medina said.

"Us?" Pops was furious. "At first, you didn't even want to be there."

"I told you, Pops," my mother said, "she's a member of the family."

"A member of the family who said she was boycotting the wedding and will therefore not be attending the reception."

"Yes, she will," my mother said.

"Believe me," Medina said, "if it wasn't for Pen, I would tell you to shove all your invitations up your arse."

"You're jealous. You'll be losing your partner in spinsterhood to me."

"He's exactly right," Medina said. "I'm jealous of Pen because she landed you, because you chose her instead of me. I've longed for you all these years, Pops. Loved you secretly, hopelessly. Wished that engagement ring of yours was meant for me. Every moment with you was a torment. But it would seem that Penny has won you with her wiles and good looks and you have let yourself be blinded to the more important things I have to offer. Oh Pops, don't you see? It's still not too late to change your mind. Choose me, Pops, choose me. Even if you don't, I will come by as often as possible just to be near you."

This monologue was delivered in a deadpan monotone, Medina looking at neither Pops nor my mother yet speaking coldly to the latter, telling her in a kind of code, right in front of Pops, how hurt and confused she was. My mother didn't laugh. Pops gave Medina a dismissive wave, went to his room and closed the door.

"What next, Pen?" Medina whispered, tears in her eyes. "Which of the stipulations will be the next to go? Separate beds? Once-a-month visits? No children? Bit by bit you're giving them what they want, Uncle Paddy, McHugh and Pops."

My mother shook her head. "No more," she said. "This is all they get. This is where I draw the line, I promise."

Later, when my mother went out to the grocery store with Medina, Pops called me to the sunroom. He sat in his chair, looking morose. He said he'd been thinking—thinking that, someday soon, after they were married, he would tell my mother that he had guessed the truth about her and Medina. He would leave me out of it and convince her he would never tell McHugh. Everyone on the Mount assumed that, once they were married, there would be an empty bed, an extra room, at 44, now that he was sleeping with Penelope. So why not make things simple, spare everyone in the house the humiliation of sneaking around and pretending to look the other way and feigning ignorance—such a sad charade that would be. He would suggest to my mother that Medina move in with us, ostensibly to occupy the "empty" room but really to occupy the empty space in one half of my mother's bed, the bed that my mother would leave, once a month, to come to *his* room and *his* bed. Time would tell if Medina could endure a succession of once-a-month nights alone in my mother's bed, knowing where my mother was, with whom and for what reason.

THE TEENY-WEENY WEDDING

THE teeny-weeny wedding at the teeny-weeny church, as Medina called the Brother Rice chapel, went ahead as planned. All things considered, Medina said, it would be just as appropriate if *Pops* wore white. He could, she said, wear his lab coat, which at least was off-white. Perhaps, she said, he might even wear his safety goggles, for she had never seen him with them on.

Because it was considered bad luck for the bride and groom to see each other on their wedding day before they were married, Pops got up very early on Saturday morning and went across the street to Brother Rice, where he stayed in McHugh's office by himself until he was joined there in the afternoon by the best man, Mr. Linnegar, and later by me. I brought him his newly bought suit, black with blue pinstripes, his new white shirt and gleaming black shoes, and his boutonniere. But I spent most of the day at 44 with my mother and Medina. Medina, who had been picking at

Pops for days, sat in silence at the kitchen table, morosely nursing a beer and a cigarette. She had teased Pops for not having a bachelor party and lamented that I had lost Vivian, whom I could otherwise have lent him for the night before the wedding. "One last night of freedom, Pops," she said. "One last night without the old ball and chain. Everything's about to change—no more notches on your bedpost. No more breaking hearts. The word is out among the single women of St. John's: Pops is off the market." Pops said that if Medina ever got engaged, the Vatican would send to St. John's a team of miracle authenticators.

Brother McHugh had offered to walk my mother down the aisle, but she had declined, saying that I was quite able to give her away.

Pops insisted on hiring a limousine to drive my mother from 44 to Brother Rice, a distance of about a hundred feet. He said it would be "unseemly" for her to dash across Bonaventure in her wedding dress. The dress was tight-fitting, showing as much cleavage as the Church would allow when she was engaged to Jim Joyce, not that the rules had since been relaxed. It trailed slightly on the ground behind her, covering her white high heels. It had a veil, which she wore pinned to the back of her hair. Pops' colour had risen to scarlet every time she mentioned the dress. He imagined her, thus attired, standing on the traffic island, waiting for a break in the cars. "A bride should go to and depart from her wedding in style," he said. The limousine would wait outside during the wedding and reception to carry all of us back to 44. Pops and I would make only the return journey in the car, as I would have to be at Brother Rice long before my mother.

When my mother and Medina entered the chapel by the rear doors, I was there to meet them. They were laughing about the absurdly brief journey my mother had just made by limousine from 44, and about Medina, who, refusing to get in the car, had walked across the street and arrived at Brother Rice before my mother did. Although Pops had asked her not to drink any beer before the wedding, my mother smelled of it as much as Medina did. "How else could I get through this?" she whispered, looking guiltily at me.

My mother and I waited, holding hands beneath the little organ loft at the back of the chapel, until the Wedding March began to play, my mother's face fully veiled, as I wished mine was. Medina, wearing her best clothes, a green blouse, brown skirt and brown high heels, held a bouquet of flowers in her hands onto which tears pattered like drops of rain.

"I'm getting married, Perse," my mother said under her breath. "Can you believe it?"

"You're not really getting married," Medina whispered.

"I know," my mother whispered back. "Thirty seconds in a limousine didn't make me fall in love with Pops."

The congregation consisted exclusively of the Mount's nuns, Brothers, lay faculty and spouses. The only students were the altar boys from Brother Rice. I walked my mother down the aisle as if she really was "mine" to give to Pops, unable to resist getting caught up in the moment, even as I realized that I was as much a part of the farce as anyone from 44. The McHugh-appointed best man did little more than stand beside Pops during the ceremony. Medina had to watch as Pops raised my mother's veil and kissed her on the lips. My mother said "I do" after she and Medina shed what I think were mistaken by many as tears of joy during the exchange of vows and rings. My mother, in her fourteen-year-old, never-before-worn wedding dress, made sure her bouquet landed nowhere near Medina. No one even bothered to pretend to try to catch it. Then we moved on to the small, alcohol-free reception in the gym, at which tea and biscuits were to be served.

Pops, my mother, me, Medina and the best man, Mr. Linnegar, formed a receiving line just inside the doors to the gym, barely twenty feet from the chemistry lab where I'd found Pops with what had looked like a glass of milk in front of him. We received perfunctory congratulations from the entire faculty of the Mount, all of whom looked resentful at having to give up their Saturday afternoon.

To the accompaniment of a record player, my mother danced with Pops as "their" song was played—"I Only Have Eyes for You," the last of Pops' surprises—while everyone, Medina included, watched.

It was an odd sight, my beautiful mother in her bridal gown moving slowly around the floor of the gym at Brother Rice, Pops with one hand on her waist, the other in *her* hand, the two of them dancing with each other for the first and possibly last time in their lives. I thought of my mother and Medina dancing late at night at 44, asking me to join them, the three of us moving dreamily around the room.

The reception lasted half an hour, during which the wedding party of five stuck together and were followed about by McHugh, who, solemn-faced, made many introductions in which he referred to Medina as Miss Joyce, my mother as Mrs. MacDougal, Pops as Vice-Principal MacDougal, and me, simply, noncommittally, as Percy.

Finally, he loudly announced, "The wedding party has to leave, so please join me in a round of applause." During the muted ovation, Pops walked arm in arm with my mother; Medina and I walked arm in arm behind them. Mr. Linnegar remained standing beside McHugh. We went out through the doors of the gym, down the marble steps and out the school doors, where Pops motioned to the waiting limousine parked by the curb. Attached to the trunk was a display of flowers that spelled "Just Married." My mother pulled her arm from Pops', Medina pulled hers from mine, the two of them removed their shoes and they ran down the outer steps and across the street to 44, my mother hiking her gown to her knees, Medina gleefully holding aloft both pairs of shoes as if she had just stolen them from a shop in Brother Rice. Cars stopped in both directions, their occupants looking perplexed as my arrayed-for-the-bridal mother and Medina in a hat that looked like blue meringue staged their token public protest and ran up the drive-way while Pops and I watched. Pops angrily motioned for the lim-ousine driver to leave, took my arm and led me across the street.

"Jesus, I'm glad that's over," Medina was saying as we walked in. My mother flashed her a look that Pops pretended not to notice.

"It wouldn't have killed you to ride back in the car with me, Paynelope," Pops said. "I suppose you didn't want to let this one walk back by herself."

"Tell me the truth, Pops," my mother said. "You were planning to have that driver take us around town honking his horn while you waved to everyone we met, weren't you?"

"Nothing wrong with a little victory lap," Pops said.

"I knew it!" my mother said. "We foiled your plot, Pops."

Medina cackled as he frowned at her.

"Put her there, Percy," he said, extending his hand to me and smiling. "The men always have the last laugh, don't they?" I grinned and we fervently shook hands.

"Another day, another wedding," Medina said, feigning a yawn.

We all changed back into our house clothes. My mother ordered in a large quantity of fish and chips, most of which I ate. The three of them began drinking beer. Pops stayed at the kitchen table even though Medina kept telling him he'd like it more in the sunroom, where he could look at his new haircut in the window. "To the loving couple," Medina said, and clinked glasses with my mother.

Pops said nothing but, time after time, drank deeply from his bottle of beer. Finally, he stood up, pushing his chair backward unsteadily. "It was not the most conventional of weddings, was it?" he said, hooking his thumbs into the pockets of his lab coat. He walked slowly back and forth as if addressing a classroom of students. "The maid of honour is the sister of the bride's former fiancé who jilted her and ran off when she was pregnant. The bride is given away by her born-out-of-wedlock son who is soon to be thrice anointed by the Archbishop and has all his life gone by his father's last name even though his parents never married. The bride who long ago changed *her* last name to that of the man who jilted her attaches to the terms of a Catholic marriage such a mass of stipulations not recognized by the Church that the groom will need catechistic instruction to remember half of them. The groom's best man didn't know the groom's first name until an hour and a half before the wedding. The bride proposed to the groom who, in spite of all the stipulations, in spite of knowing that he is the bride's mortgage-paying cash cow and puppet, has never been happier in his life to pay for sex and doesn't give a good goddamn about what the never-to-be-married maid of honour thinks of him or of anyone who ever has been or ever will be born."

Medina mock-applauded. "Nothing to say, Perse?" my mother asked.

I shook my head.

"Fewer words were never spoken," she said.

A few days after the wedding, as I was leaving the grounds of St. Bon's late one afternoon, I saw a woman wearing a ragged-looking half-length duffle coat, hood up, going past the fire station, headed down Bonaventure toward the crossing just above the steep part of the hill. The imitation-fur fringe of her coat was grey with age, the once-white coat itself almost as grey. Beneath the coat she wore an incongruously pristine-looking pleated black dress with a pattern of rosettes and stitching that glittered even in what little light of day was left. On her feet she wore black, red-toed wellingtons that flopped about as if they were several sizes too big.

I briefly continued up Bonaventure, then crossed over to the woman's side of the street. Walking slowly so as not to overtake her, I began to follow her. She crossed Military Road and descended the steps that led to the boardwalk of Garrison Hill, disappearing from my view. I traced her route to the top of the steps, from which she was nowhere to be seen.

Knowing she could not have made it that quickly to even the first house on the hill, let alone have had time to go inside and close the door behind her, I walked slowly down the steps, scanning the horizontally parked cars on the hill, thinking she might be hiding among them or even inside one. Unable to spot her, I turned to go back up, only to be confronted by her as she came out from beneath the steps, where she must have been hiding.

Her hands in her duffle coat pockets, she looked down at me. "Why are you following *me*, Percy Joyce?" she said.

It was, as I'd suspected, Sister Mary Aggie, my benefactress, the source of my Saint Drogo Mass cards, whose statement to my mother that "it takes one to know two," made ten years ago, I only now understood. I'd recognized her by her slow, scuffing walk and her round-shouldered posture.

"I wasn't following you," I said. I told her it was easy for people to recognize me but I hadn't been sure it was her after all these years. I lied that I no longer lived where I used to, my mother having got married and the two of us having moved downtown to a smaller, less expensive house from which my mother was running a candy store that got a lot of business from people going to the Paramount Theatre on Harvey Road.

"Lies, all lies, boy," Sister Mary Aggie said, pushing back her hood to get a better look at me. I had never seen her without her nun's cowl. "Lies that work are plain and simple because the truth is plain and simple," she said. "No details. The Devil is in the details." Her mid-length hair was grey but thick and faintly tinted yellow, as if she'd been smoking or living among smokers since I had seen her last. Her face was red from the cold, especially her nose, which was sharper than when I had last met her. But her brown eyes were clear and focused, not darting about as before.

"I've been a long time in the Mental," she said, "but that face of yours still looks the same."

"It is," I said, "but I might have an operation on it soon that might fix it."

"And I might soon be the Queen of Sheba," she said. "I've been out long enough to know what's up. Percy Joyce's big day is coming soon. The Big Do at the Big B, that's what I hear they're calling it. Sounds very grand. And your mother married Pops MacDougal." She laughed, then glanced back at the birdlike facade of the Basilica as if to indicate where they'd been married.

"I still have my Saint Drogo Mass cards," I said. "They're taped to the wall above my bunk."

"You still owe me fifteen cents. Or was it thirty?"

I told her I'd come by with thirty cents for her tomorrow.

"I had an operation of my own, Percy Joyce," she said, tapping her forehead. "Two actually. One upstairs, one downstairs. Some things I can't remember. No chance of little Mary Aggies since I was your mother's age."

"How come you're not dressed up like a nun?" I said.

"Not allowed to anymore. The Presentation will report me. Then it's back to the Mental for me. I'm almost sixty. They'll never let me out if I go back. Don't say you saw Sister Mary Aggie. They'll think I'm up to my old tricks."

"Okay."

"Your mother and that other one never liked me very much. They knew I knew. Nothing's changed, I'm sure. That never changes. Once a lizzie. I should know. Don't mention me to them."

"Okay."

"What did you follow me for?"

I shrugged.

"Would you like some tea and some crackers and jam?"

I nodded.

"I would too," she said. "Could you get me some?"

"I should go home," I said.

"Come visit anyway. I live right there. Same as before. The downstairs half of number three." A row of flat-roofed houses lined the eastern side of Garrison Hill like a steep set of gigantic steps. "You stay here until I close the door, then walk down the hill. It might not look above board, Sister Mary Aggie taking Percy Joyce into her house." She pulled up her hood and scuffed down the hill to number three, opened the unlocked door and went inside.

I did as she told me, walked down the hill, eyes straight ahead, hands in my pockets. I had all but passed number three when the door came slightly open and Sister Mary Aggie grabbed me by the collar, dragged me over the single block of concrete that served as her front step and yanked me inside so forcefully I sprawled across the stairs that led up to the second floor. She opened another unlocked door to our right, waved me inside and shut the door behind us. It was so dark I could see nothing but a vertical crease of light between the drapes on what I took to be her front window, a large one that, if not for the drapes, would have allowed passersby to peer into her house with their faces pressed against the glass.

"Don't move," she said. "You might trip over something priceless. I walk around here in the dark all the time. There's one room and one light bulb in one lamp. I'm on welfare and I don't sell Mass cards anymore." I heard what sounded like the pulling of a lamp chain, but no light came on. "It takes a while," she said. I heard her remove her duffle coat. It sounded as though she threw it on the floor.

In a few seconds I saw, across the room, a dim red glow, then made out a standing lamp with a dark red shade that had a fringe of long red beads.

"I like the room red," said Sister Mary Aggie, sitting on a kitchen chair beneath the lamp. She was the only thing in the room that wasn't red. "Your face looks the same in this light as it did outdoors," she said. "It looks like a baboon's arse. There's only this one chair, but you can sit on the daybed if you want." On a countertop behind her was a small icebox, a two-burner hot plate and a wooden canister without a lid. Along the wall opposite her was a low daybed, no more than a few inches from the floor. The room was otherwise bare. There were no coverings on the wooden floor, which was warped and cracked, no wall hangings, and no other window but the one whose drapes were drawn.

I sat on the bed, my hands in my pockets. "Prosperity is just around the corner," she said. In the normal light of the lone bulb, she stood out like a sculpture on display in a museum. She closed her eyes and folded her hands in her lap. I wondered if she was saying a prayer. She opened her eyes and stared at me.

"What did you do with your nun's habit?" I asked.

"They took it away. Got rid of it. Burnt it, something, I don't know. Don't care, either." She told me that, not long after she gave me the Mass cards, she had thrown a rock through one of the windows in the Presentation Convent and the "nutty nun" was back in the Mental. "It got me a place to live for ten years. More food than I have now."

"I could bring you some food."

"I don't want food from your mother. What did you follow me for, Percy Joyce?"

"Are you a whore?" I said.

"No, I'm not a whore, you carbuncled little bastard. I never was a whore."

"That's good."

"Is that supposed to make my day, your high opinion of me?" She squinted at me as if, accustomed to being able to read minds, she could not account for my inscrutability. "You followed me," she said. "You didn't come to visit me when I was in the Mental—but why should you? You followed me just now. You're not the nice little boy you were ten years ago. You look like you're up to something. Spit it out."

I spat it out. All of it. I broke the promise I'd made to my mother; I spoke of our secret outside the walls of 44. I broke the code of 44. I convinced myself that Sister Mary Aggie, being even more of an outcast than me, didn't count. I told her about my mother lust and "give me myth or give me death," and the Apology of Percy Joyce and all three versions of Francine. It must have taken half an hour. I was almost bawling by the end of it. I confessed to Sister Mary Aggie what, on the day of the Big Do at the Big B, I would not confess to Uncle Paddy and had managed to withhold from McHugh. It was a relief to speak of it all to someone not related to me, someone who had no stake in the family conspiracy. I confessed, but not because I felt sorry for any of it or because I wanted her advice. It was a first step toward something, though exactly what I couldn't say.

She stared at me. "You're an odder duck than me, Percy Joyce," she said. "I never asked *my* mother for a pity fuck." She fell silent. Her head drooped as if she were asleep.

I stood up, intending to leave, but she raised her head and motioned me back down with her hand.

"I never *gave* anyone a pity fuck before either," she said. "No one ever asked for one. The men at the Mental didn't ask. They took, but they didn't ask."

I nodded.

"And," she said, "I'm not giving you one either. I'd be in the Mental or in prison for life if I did and you told on me. You might, too."

"I wouldn't want a pity fuck from you," I said, but I smiled.

"Too old for you, am I?" I nodded, still smiling. "Go away and don't come back," she said. "You've made your confession. For your penance, pretend you don't know me if you see me on the street.

Good luck getting your mother into bed. It might help if you wore a wig."

I got up from the bed and moved to the door as she turned off the lamp. It must have gotten dark outside; there wasn't even that slit of light between the drapes. There was only the sound of Sister Mary Aggie's voice as she went on talking as if someone had taken my place on the bed.

I heard the rustle of her dress, the one with the red rosettes, as she crossed to the daybed, the squeaking of the bedsprings as she lay down.

"Goodbye," I said, but she didn't answer.

I left her there, alone, two unlocked doors away from the world she thought was better than the Mental.

THE CITY OF PERCY JOYCE

THAT evening, not long after leaving Sister Mary Aggie's, I went for my birthday walk. It wasn't my fifteenth birthday yet, but I doubted that I would have time for walking after the Big Do at the Big B.

I was starting to think it might just suit me, this city of obscurity and occasional renown. Surely, in this mecca of misfits, there was a place for me.

The Discovered City. The Adopted City. The city from which no traveller returns. The city of those who roam the earth in search of a place in which to start again.

The City of Homebodies. Of people who had nothing to compare it to.

The city whose people sounded like no one else on earth. The parochial, universal city.

Might not this little city stand as well as any for all the other cities of the world?

The City of Vivacity. The City of Soul-Reviving Laughter. The City of Knee-Weakening Beauty and Stomach-Turning Ugliness. The City of Saucy Crackies. The City Whose Dead Could Do No Wrong.

Its people were descended from a priest-ridden race. Its forgotten souls still walked the streets.

I saw ragged flags, faded flags and flagless flagpoles, all of them the work of the wind.

I went down to the harbour, which smelled of European cigarettes. Dressed in white undershirts and black pants, foreign fishermen played soccer while puffing on pink cigarettes. "*Olá*, Percy," they shouted. Even they knew my name.

"*Olá*," I shouted back.

I spied out, often hid from, priest-driven, window-tinted Cadillacs that cruised the streets like unmarked cars.

The Pretty City. The Eyesore City. The City of Cod.

There were those who thought they owned the place and others who had nothing to their name.

I passed innumerable bars and wondered if, when I was old enough, I would ever go to one. My mother had once said that St. John's was full of captivating alcoholics and clean-living windbags.

The City of Piety and Blasphemy.

I could work outdoors at night, be a cab driver whose fares could see nothing but the back of my head. I could be a mural-painting vandal or one who drew graffiti on the undersides of overpasses.

My mother had told me I needed a profession that would engage my mind, but I knew from her example that an avocation of that sort would do.

I imagined going home to her at night after days of eking out a living as a salesman, mine the front-line face of the latest version of the vacuum cleaner.

I wondered what Pops would want with me if I were not the son of the woman he adored. Pops would have sung the praises of Vlad the Impaler if he was related to my mother. What about Medina? Illiteracy was the profoundest form of world disdain that she could think of, short of suicide. No point boning up on a world in which a nun who beat her bloody with a stick got off scot-free. But she had never volunteered to help the other "challenged" of St. John's. And my mother? She, too, was happy to let the other freaks go on fending for themselves; would she have given me the time of day if I were not her son? Bloody-minded but irresistible questions.

Saint Drogo, I realized, didn't hide himself away to spare other people; he did it to excuse himself from a life he knew he couldn't stand to live. He didn't beatify or canonize himself—the Vatican did that.

I had to do something. I knew what I wanted. I wanted what everyone wants at the end. I wanted my mother. My mommy, you might be thinking.

Would I live out my days as a grudge-holding hermit? Would I find a place in this city whose every other soul was an artist for all seasons, poet/painter/singer/sculptor/actor and musician? Would I swell by one the number of failed prodigies, or achieve an unforeseen success? Perhaps I would become a creepy frequenter of tree-shrouded cemeteries, narrow, pee-reeking alleyways, empty, summer, twilit playgrounds.

No. Heading back on the bus to 44, I felt the distant stir and surge of something great in what I could find no name for but my soul. Percy Joyce. Something was soon to be let loose that nets and flags and prison walls could not hold back from flight.

THE LAST SUITOR OF PENELOPE

T HE night before the Big Do at the Big B, I felt that I had been deep in sleep for hours and that it must therefore be very late or even on the verge of morning. There was a thin slant of light across the bottom right-hand corner of my bunk. I thought my door, which never shut firmly, might have slipped open by itself or have come open in the faint breeze that was always created when someone entered or left the house by the back door. But then the slant of light was interrupted by a shadow. Someone was standing in the doorway, peering in at me through the slight opening. I hadn't moved and it was too dark for the person in the doorway to have seen my face, so I partly closed my eyes and watched.

Because of the height of my bunk, I saw only the upper part of the doorway, but I thought I could make out my mother's silhouette, her hair backlit by the wall lamp in the hallway. She stood there a long time as if she was pondering some decision, looking at

me as I lay there, seemingly sound asleep. I wondered if an encore
of the Great Unveiling might be imminent, or if she might even
be considering granting me my ultimate wish, if she had come
to beckon me from my bed into hers. And as I was lying on my
back atop the blankets, I worried for a moment that she would see
the bulge in my pyjamas, but then realized it was so dark in the
room that she wasn't really watching me, only staring toward me,
perhaps listening for any sound I might make, my breath perhaps,
which I'd been all but holding since I woke up.

Medina had said, "This can't go on." Perhaps she had subse-
quently made an even bolder declaration, told my mother they
were through, that she was never coming back to 44 except to visit
me, or that she was never coming back at all. I wondered suddenly
if it might be Medina who was "looking" at me through the inch
or so of space between the door frame and the door. Medina come
to say a last goodbye to her lover's son, her brother's son, wondering if she should wake me to tell me we would never meet again,
that she was leaving as Jim Joyce had left to begin a new life somewhere far from where my mother lived. Or might the person in the
doorway be Pops, come to make his first-ever visit to my room, to
reconsider what to do about Medina and my mother, or to tell me
that he had told McHugh what McHugh had long suspected was
the truth? My heart pounded and it seemed impossible that the
person in the doorway couldn't hear it.

The door opened farther, the slant of light a foot wide now,
and I could tell for certain that it was my mother. She pushed
the door fully open, closed and locked it behind her, and padded
quietly into the room, coming round to the open side of the bunk
beds. She struck a match, the light from which lit up my pictures
of Saint Drogo, the patron saint of self-denial, self-abhorrence,
self-disgust, who, I newly fancied, hadn't spent his life hidden and
confined for others' sake but for his own, hadn't really believed
that his misshapen body would make those who beheld it less able

to resist the Evil One but had been unable to endure the eyes in which he saw himself reflected. I wondered if I had long known this, long known that his sainthood was absurd, even if it hadn't made me love him any less.

My mother lit a candle that she'd been holding in her hand like a baton. She was fully in the light and I saw that she was not wearing pyjamas but only what looked like a man's shirt, through the side slits of which I saw the full curves of her hips. I smelled her perfume, but there was no hint of the other smell I had noticed the night she hugged me in the basement not long after I happened on her and Medina. A man's shirt. One of Pops' perhaps. She might have gone to "visit" him after Medina left the house. Or it might even be one of Jim Joyce's shirts, a secret keepsake she had never worn in front of me before. And facing the possibly permanent absence of Medina, and with Pops passed out in his room after his return from the East End Club, had she come to me at last, not only because I needed her, but because she needed me, needed the comfort and reassurance of her ever-ardent, ever-faithful son?

"What are you doing?" I managed to say as I scrambled to pull up the blankets past my waist.

She smiled in the light of the candle "I think you want me even more than Medina does," she said. "You want me even more than the men and boys who hardly know me do. I don't know why."

"You *do*."

"I know *what* you want. You saw Medina's face when I was touching her. That's what you want. But most people never feel like that. I can't say for certain that I have."

"I *want* to."

I felt like telling her that I'd be happy to accept an exhaustive list of stipulations as soon as she had the time to type them up but couldn't we just get on with it, with the first time right away, now, since she was already in my room, had already locked the door, and I, after five minutes of looking at her in that shirt that slid up and down with every shrug of her shoulders or movement of her arms, was already *ready*. She kept running her fingers through her wet hair, sending drops of water flying over her shoulder and pattering against the wall behind her as if this was but another way of conferring benediction on the house. Droplets slowly formed on, fell from, her earlobes. She was flushed from the heat of a bath, flushed as only a Black Mick could be, her dark complexion further darkened, deepened almost to the colour of her eyes. How good her wet hair looked in the candlelight, hanging heavy down her back, dampening her shirt, that blackest of black hair that matched the robe which was somewhere else tonight and the V of hair that, on the night of the Great Unveiling, I had tried so hard to see in the shadowed space between her legs. I wished the day was not far removed when she would forbid me none of her, when I could bury my face in that thick, wet moss of hair, hide it there so that we could both pretend I looked like any other boy my age, or that my face would be transformed in that wet nest and would, when I withdrew it, have been healed. I looked at her free hand, her fingers that, without a cigarette to keep them occupied, were fidgeting, playing with each other, the very ones that, on Medina night, worked their magic in Medina as I hoped they would with me, dim though my notion was of what that meant, what special dexterity and slow coaxing my unmarred body might require from them in the dark.

She said we wouldn't call it pity fucking. We wouldn't think of it like that. We might not call it anything, and we wouldn't think of it as incest. We would *never* use that word. It wouldn't be like visiting hours and it wouldn't be like Medina night. It would never be the subject of a give me myth or give me death instalment. It would have to be *our* secret, as solemn a secret as the one about her and Medina, but we couldn't even tell Medina. Maybe. She wasn't sure about that. She was worried not about Medina disapproving but about Medina being jealous. She wouldn't want Medina treating me the way she treated Pops, or anything close to it. She didn't *think* Medina would turn against me, but you could never tell about some things—you could never tell how Medina might regard me years from now when I was no longer a boy who needed all the help that he could get. Pops, of course, must *never* know. NEVER. Our house would fall apart at the seams if Pops found out. She didn't think that even she could cajole him into keeping such a thing to himself or allowing it to continue under what he had some reason to think of as *his* roof.

I could barely breathe. "You're saying yes?" I managed to say. She nodded.

She had been thinking, a lot. She had been trying to imagine how my life would change as I got older. It might turn out that I was right, that I would never have a girlfriend or get married, or even have a one-night stand. What point were reassurances about those things if they were hollow? She had been reassuring me for her sake, not for mine. She wished that people were better than, in my fifteen years on the Mount, they had shown themselves to be, wished that she could tell me of some place where people didn't care or even notice how they looked. I was smart, very smart. I would go to college if I wanted to and, if given the chance, accomplish great things after that. I might make true, lifelong friends. Lots of things that the odds were heavily against *might* happen. It was, sadly, more likely that, whatever my accomplishments, I would spend my life, if not exactly alone, then without someone who wanted me in the way she knew she would always want Medina.

I told her that I *had* found someone, that it was just my luck that that someone was my mother. I told her I would want her no matter what I looked like, no matter if I was normal and it was *Penny* Joyce who looked the way I did. Though I shouldn't have told her I would want her no matter what she looked like, because I didn't know if it was true.

She was barely listening, though. She kept talking. She couldn't stand the thought of me having to endure a life of that sort of loneliness, or of being barred arbitrarily from beauty. There were details that would have to be worked out. Logistics. Precautions. She hoped she wasn't giving in to me simply out of guilt for the fact that, however unintentionally and unavoidably, she had made me as I was; issued me from her body with a warrant of scorn plastered like a WANTED poster on my head. She hoped that by giving in to my seduction, she wouldn't harm me in some way, psychologically damage me or spoil me for any woman who, in the future, *might*, however big the "might" might be, want me just the way I was, a woman who, to my eye, was as beautiful or more beautiful than her. She couldn't tell the future. It might turn out that I would be the first man to break things off with her. It might turn out that our affair would go on to the limits of life or the onset of any of an infinite number of circumstances that no one could foresee.

She said there was a certain symmetry to it. The ménage à quatre at 44 would soon be complete. She knew that my life so far had been nothing to write home about. I hadn't had much, and not all that I'd missed was owing to my "unusual" appearance. There were an infinite number of unforeseeable things that could deprive two people of each other. She might be wrong about Jim Joyce. It had only been fifteen years. He might return at any time and demand I go with him. People changed their minds, or had a change of heart, for reasons they could not explain. And lives could randomly diverge. Given what went on at 44, given my circumstances and hers and Medina's and those of "poor hapless Pops," we were even more susceptible than most to hazard and happenstance. But if we were somehow parted without her having given me the one thing I had ever asked her for, the one thing no one else could or would give, because she didn't understand why it meant so much to me, she'd have a lifetime of regrets; if, at the end of her life, she had still withheld from me, out of propriety of the sort she had always flouted, even scorned, she would have regrets that would break her heart. She believed, foolishly, in defiance of the odds, that someday I would join my heart to another's the way hers was joined to Medina's. But she knew I didn't believe it. Most people took it for granted as their birthright that they would find a person who was meant by Fate for them, but most people were wrong about most things.

She breathed out with a kind of gasp and the candle flame flickered.

"What we've talked about tonight we'll never need to talk about again, will we?"

"No."

"Good. I'm sleeping in the bottom bunk tonight."

"Good."

She blew out the candle.

I stayed awake for the balance of the night, but she fell asleep almost instantly. I listened to her breathe and drew in all I could of her perfume. I looked at Saint Drogo in the hope that he would keep at bay my curiosity about what, if anything, my mother was wearing besides that shirt. There might be nothing more between us than a few buttons that I could easily undo without even waking her. Maybe she was waiting for me to simply *take* what I wanted— climb down the ladder of my bunk bed and get on top of her while she pretended to be so surprised it would be too late by the time she put up a token protest or a struggle. She had *shown* herself to me. Now she had told me that, soon, she would *give* herself to me. She was sleeping in the bottom bunk wearing next to nothing. *What we've talked about tonight we'll never need to talk about again, will we?* Which one of us had she been trying to convince? I turned away from Saint Drogo and peered over the edge of my bunk. In the darkness, I could barely make her out. She had pulled the blankets right up to her chin and was lying on her side, facing away from the wall. I couldn't tell if her eyes were open, if she was looking at me. But she seemed more childlike than otherwise, huddled beneath the blankets as if they were all she had to keep the world at bay.

It was strange to think of it, the three of us feeding off her beauty, each of us taking our turn when the other two were unaware. If she didn't tell Medina, ours would be the secret affair, *our* affair, unknown to others, unmocked and unbegrudged by others, the only *truly* illicit affair of 44. I wondered if, once we began, I would become envious of Pops and Medina, so much more envious than I had ever been that I couldn't stand it. I had worn her down as surely as McHugh and Pops had worn her down, as surely as Uncle Paddy had.

PART III

ST. JOHN'S DAY, JUNE 24: THE BIG DO AT THE BIG B

M Y mother pinned on me or hung around my neck all the holy medals, "talismans" she called them, that she and Medina could find, most of them left over from my mother's school days and not worn since, medals of Saint Anne, scapular medals, the dog tag–like pair of Confirmation medals she had worn but once in her life when she was twelve and had never known the meaning of.

"He can't wear those," Medina said. "He hasn't been confirmed."

"I'll put them inside his clothes then," my mother replied. "You never know. They might help in some way. We're fighting fire with fire."

She fixed light blue Blessed Virgin Mary ribbons to the sleeves of my blazer and red Sacred Heart ribbons to my lapels, prompting Pops to protest that I was not a Christmas tree and Medina to observe that Pops was not my father.

My hair had been shaven the day before to brush-cut length—the stain on my scalp showed through far more than usual. McHugh was not able to find what he called "willing and suitable" godparents for me in time for my baptism but said that, sometime in the near future, he would find two people and they would be installed by Father Bill in a private ceremony at the chapel.

McHugh decided that, to make sure we were on time and I was presentable no matter what the weather, a car would be sent to 44 to take the four of us to the Basilica. Two hours before the service was to begin, a black limousine drew up outside 44. It was driven by a deacon, one of the newfangled married kind, though he was dressed in black and said not a word from the time he opened the car doors to let us in to the time he opened them to let us out. Pops sat in front with him and wondered aloud why Medina was willing to ride in this car but not in any others.

"It's an experiment to see if I can keep from getting sick," Medina said.

"Not exactly the perfect time for *that* experiment," Pops said, looking worriedly at me as I sat between my mother and Medina.

"Don't get accustomed to going to church in this style, Perse," my mother said. "There'll only ever be one Big Do at the Big B."

People were already entering the basilica parking lot through what was known as St. John's Arch, a small Roman archway. We were met there by a trim, white-haired, anxious-seeming priest I didn't recognize. He introduced himself to us as Father Hamlyn, "one of the pastoral assistants to His Grace." Scurrying ahead, he had us follow him to a side door by the main entrance. It led to a waiting room where he left us and told us not to budge until he came back. The room was ringed with dark green leather sofas. A massive, expansive coffee table stood on an oval rug in the middle of the room. The walls, the same colour as the sofas, were cluttered with drawings and photographs of the various stages of construction of the Basilica.

"How did we end up here, Pen?" Medina whispered, suddenly starting to cry.

"Everything's fine," my mother said. "It's just a necessary bit of fraternizing with the enemy. But the walls may have ears and eyes, so be careful. How are you doing, Perse? Nervous?" I nodded. I could hear my stomach rumbling, in part from hunger because, having fasted for Holy Communion, I'd had nothing to eat since midnight—almost fourteen hours ago—and in part from dread of what I knew was waiting for me.

"There's no need to think of anyone as the enemy," Pops said to me. "Being baptized will do you no harm even if you decide someday that you don't believe in it."

"Baptism can't be annulled, can it?" my mother asked, looking at me as though at an expert in such matters.

I shrugged.

"Excommunication is the only way, I think," Pops said.

I realized, when I heard the tramping of footsteps overhead, that we were just beneath the main floor. Judging by the sheer number of footsteps, the students were filing in to fill the pews of the Basilica. I had never heard such a prolonged silence from so many students of the Mount. I would have liked to see them, solemn-faced, not even whispering as, watched over by the Brothers and the nuns, guided by them to various parts of the Basilica, they shuffled along self-consciously in the echoing vault of the great cathedral that I had yet to see.

"It sounds like the whole city was invited," Medina said, as if the size of the congregation held some sinister implications for the three of us.

"There aren't going to be many parishioners," my mother said. "Just some of the more prominent ones, bigwigs who couldn't stand to be excluded from something called the Big Do at the Big B. I saw a television van out front."

Under the scrutiny of so many skeptical students, who would surely not be fooled by a display of piety from anyone, under the gaze of McHugh and Sister Celestine, under the glare of television lights and the all-recording eye of the camera, how would I get away with it? As if I had posed the question out loud, my mother said, "We wouldn't have got this far if they could read our minds."

Pops looked about to object, but my mother raised her finger to him. "No more stepfatherly advice from you," she said. "For your money and your ring, you get me once a month. You do not get a say in how Percy should be raised."

"The walls have eyes and ears, remember?" Pops said.

The sound of footsteps from above abated gradually, giving way to sporadic, nervous coughs that rang out in the silence of the church like rifle shots.

"The balconies must be full," my mother said, just as the pipe organ started up, music blaring from it at such a volume that everything in the room began to shake.

"It's like an earthquake," Medina said, plugging her ears with her fingers. A choir that sounded as if it numbered in the hundreds began to sing "Come, Holy Ghost, Creator Blest."

Father Hamlyn returned with warm, just-printed programmes for the three of us. "Let's go over this," he said. "It's short and sweet. A lot is left out because we didn't want to confuse Percy." He looked at me and rattled the one-page programme. "Follow this to the letter," he said. "But otherwise, just listen to what the grown-ups tell you to do."

I took my one-sheet programme but as he went over it, I tuned out his voice. My mother, Medina and Pops appeared to be listening. Medina was staring at the programme as if she could read it.

Father Hamlyn left.

I wondered how many girls were waiting silently for me to arrive, watching to see what door I would emerge from; Percy Joyce with his port wine-stained face and swollen lips and oversized hands and feet that would disgust them just as much no matter how nicely he might be dressed or how recently his hair had been cut or how scrubbed and polished the rest of him might look. The girls

of Mercy and Presentation and Belvedere and Holy Heart, especially Francine, would all be watching. The Big B could hold three
thousand as long as the fire marshal wasn't one of them. I thought
of the girls from the bay on all the buses I had blessed, of Vivian in
flagrante on the wall beside the leering Saint Drogo, Patron Saint
of Unattractive People. Whenever I'd dreamed of doing it with a
girl, I'd thought of doing it from behind so she wouldn't see my
face. I thought now of doing it that way with Francine—Francine
willing and wanton and glad beyond words to have been chosen by
His Grace to be my friend, Francine making noises like the ones
Medina had made because she so liked what my mother's hands
and mouth were doing.

So then I thought of doing it that way with my mother.

To my horror, the front of my slacks bulged with a hard-on.
What if I came, or even just leaked enough to make a wet spot on
the outside of my slacks? I tried not to think of girls or women,
especially my mother, I tried not to think at all, but that didn't
work. My hard-on grew bigger. I felt it pulsing in my pants. I
nudged my mother and pointed at my slacks. "Oh, sweet Jesus,"
she said. "It's because of you," I whispered, "because of what you
said last night." "Do you have to pee?" she whispered back. I shook
my head. Medina and Pops stared. Medina covered her hand with
her mouth and Pops looked mortified.

"Can't you make it go away?" my mother asked.

I shook my head.

"Why not?" she said, enlarging her eyes as a warning that I
should not allude again, even in a whisper, to last night.

"I don't know. I was thinking about girls, but now I'm not and
it's still— I think I might—"

"Oh sweet, sweet Jesus," my mother said.

The door opened and Father Hamlyn burst in. "What are you
waiting for?" he said. "Didn't you read the programme? You were
supposed to come out when the choir started the second hymn."

"Sorry," my mother said. She put her lips to my ear. "Keep the programme in front of your pants. Once you get out there, you'll be too distracted—"

"*Please*," Father Hamlyn cried. "You're keeping the Archbishop waiting. Come on, come on. You, Percy, you go first."

Holding the one-page programme at crotch level, all but pressing it against me, I left the room and turned right, toward the baptistery, which was just inside the two large doors of the vestibule. I looked down the middle aisle at the sanctuary on the high altar that enclosed the tabernacle. I started down the middle aisle, but two hands that I somehow knew were McHugh's all but closed around my neck and turned me about. I couldn't hear a sound above the organ and the choir.

At one of our catechism sessions, McHugh had had me memorize the prayer that was said by the Archbishop on the occasion of the elevation of the cathedral: "May the demons flee and the angels of peace enter as we, Thy humble servants, go inside. Behold the Sign of the Cross, let all the evil spirits flee. Give us salvation from our enemies and from the hand of those who hate us." It seemed that those prayers had been composed and spoken specifically to ward off the Joyces, me foremost among them. The prayer had failed, for here we were, not just entering the Basilica but being escorted into it by a priest acting on the orders of the very archbishop who had spoken the exorcizing prayer. Me, the Hunchback of Notre-Dame, I thought. The Bastard, Mother-Banging Boy of the Basilica. The Rapist of the Baptist. The Ugly Mother-Lusting Lad of the Basilica.

Thus I set eyes at last on the inside of the Basilica. I had never walked beneath a ceiling even one-tenth as high and wide before. It seemed as if a many-floored structure had had its floors removed, had been hollowed out in the process of its transformation from a cathedral into this massive cavern. It seemed absurd that something so immense could be described as minor. Everything in it seemed oversized—the statues in the recessed Roman arches that lined the walls between the windows, the finely detailed, etched-in-wood stations of the cross, the width of the centre aisle and even the side aisles, the length of the centre aisle that led up to an altar as expansive as the parking lot of Holy Heart. At the rear of the high altar, which was flanked by lance-like candleholders, was the eight-columned sanctuary McHugh had described to me that protectively housed a tabernacle the size of a small car, a gleaming silver globe atop two golden doors. Looming above the tabernacle, stretching more than halfway to the ceiling, was a tapestry of the risen Christ with an infant in his arms. Arching over all of it was a frescoed ceiling whose images I could not have made out unless I had stopped walking and craned my neck to look straight up.

Nothing in my line of vision bore the slightest blemish. Luridly coloured depictions of Christ's gauntlet of agony on his way to Calvary were everywhere. Through panels of stained glass the height of hydro poles, sunlight shone in upon the congregation, each shaft of it teeming with motes of dust, while the walls between the windows shadowed the intervening pews, light and dark alternating from the base of the choir loft to the far-distant enclave of the altar.

I felt overpowered, my blasphemous irreverence shouted down by the earnest enormity of what lay in front of me, the evidence of money spent, of countless hours of mass labour, the imperial seriousness of whoever had designed the place, the force of the unyielding faith and conviction of its framers, its leaders and its congregants. Could so much have been done by so many in error, in vanity, pomposity, unfounded fear and worship of an entity that did not exist, that mere humans had come up with out of self-delusion or hypocrisy, come up with as a means of amassing wealth, acquiring and wielding power, quelling fear and justifying hatred, commanding adoration for which they pretended to be mere conduits for the omnipotent Creator of All Things, humbly insignificant servants of God in comparison with whom the very universe was "minor"?

I looked up at my mother and squeezed her hand. She seemed to be as much in awe as I was, seemed not to notice my appeal for a reassuring glance, a wink, a smile, something, anything to show that, in spite of everything, our conspiracy was still intact. But the very sight of her inspired in me such a resurgence of desire that I was soon concerned again with the matter that, had I been free to, I could have taken care of swiftly with one hand. My hard-on wrapped in paper, I was suddenly facing a phalanx of bishops, all variously attired in layers of vestments. They simultaneously blessed me, making the sign of the cross with their outstretched right arms. I saw a portly, white-haired one wince when I looked him in the eye; for him, for all of them who lived outside the city, it was their first sight of me. Then it occurred to me that it might not be my face he was wincing at. I nodded to him and he tried to smile.

Percy Joyce. The clerics from around the bay had heard of me, had seen my picture in the *Monitor* in black-and-white, but were not, it was apparent by the way they looked at me, prepared for what they saw. So this was the Archbishop's pet, his heart-rending afflicted favourite. For this boy the great occasion had been organized, the boy on whom, and on whose mother, so much misfortune had befallen. The hands on the base of my neck increased their grip, pushing me slowly forward as the bishops parted to let us through into the baptistery.

In spite of McHugh's assertion that my baptism would be the least of the reasons for this gathering, the Archbishop seemed to have done his utmost to make it the "theme" of the Mass. Because there, beside an enormous porcelain bowl, was the Archbishop, Uncle Paddy himself, mitred and holding his bejewelled, ornate shepherd's staff. Thin, bespectacled, hawk-faced, his nose as prominent as Pope Paul's, he smiled, but not in the way his Christmas card greetings had led me to imagine he would when at last we met again. He looked as though McHugh had apprised him of everything he knew or suspected about the Joyces. He came toward me and placed his free hand on my head.

"Little Percy," he whispered. "You're not so little anymore, are you?"

"No, Your Grace," I managed to say. He smiled again and, as he turned away from me, I saw a fully lit TV camera in the open doorway of the church, aimed at me. Of the man who was aiming it, I saw only the hands. At an emphatic signal from Father Hamlyn, who raised his own hands in traffic-cop fashion, the camera was shut off. McHugh stood in front of me.

"Hand me that piece of paper," he said. I let go of the programme with one hand and motioned for him to lower himself to my height, all the while biting my lip to keep from thinking of anything related to girls and to distract myself from the sensation of my underwear rubbing the head of my dick each time I even slightly moved. McHugh crouched down, put his hands on my shoulders and stared into my eyes with undisguised menace.

I cupped my hand and whispered in his ear. "I peed in my pants a little bit," I said. McHugh abruptly stood, looked about and motioned to an altar boy who was holding an incense-steaming thurible.

"Give that to Dawe," he said. The altar boy gave the thurible to the boy beside him and was soon standing by McHugh. "Take off that surplice," he said. The boy removed his surplice and, holding it in his hands, stood there wearing nothing but his red soutane. "Go to the sacristy and get another surplice for yourself," McHugh told him.

As the boy set off, McHugh, without a word of instruction to me, swiftly placed the surplice over my head and inserted my arms into it until the lacy garment came down past my waist. I still held the programme in one hand; I had had to take it away from my crotch when McHugh raised my arms, but, judging by the faces of everyone around me, no one noticed the bulge in my slacks. I looked down and saw that, although my hard-on showed faintly through the surplice, it was mostly disguised and, in all likelihood, would be mistaken by others for a mere bunching of the cloth.

Five Christian Brothers, one on each arm and each leg and one with his hands supporting me from underneath, lifted me and dipped me backward over the bowl. I was splayed out supine, eyes focused on the frescoed ceiling of the Basilica, cradled by five Christian Brothers who, if not for the surplice, surely would have seen my bulging crotch. There were two hands on my lower right leg, the bare part where my slacks pulled up. I recognized the grip as McHugh's. Throughout the baptism, those hands gave me what the boys at school called an "Indian burn"—one hand twisting the skin on my leg one way, the other twisting it the other way, as if McHugh were wringing blood from my leg like water from a towel. I clenched my teeth to keep from howling, but not even the pain made me feel any less as though I was on the verge of coming. Using a barely concave silver cup, the Archbishop three times scooped warm chrism oil—olive oil, balm and water—and poured it over my forehead. I felt the crawling flood of it as he said: "I baptize thee in the name of the Father, and of the Son, and of the Holy Ghost." The Brothers raised me to a standing position.

I looked up at the choir loft and saw a girl dressed in a light blue blouse and a brown tunic. She looked down at me and smiled as no girl had ever done before. I wondered why, wondered what she was thinking. Was I somehow out of bounds, now, rendered harmless by my baptism—or perhaps made more appealing? I smiled back and she looked away. I felt a faint heraldic spasm, followed by enough seepage to turn the fly of my underwear wet and slick. I clenched to pre-empt a further spasm and wondered if, in the confessional, when I had to speak, I'd be able to without spouting over.

The Archbishop gave me a small lump of what he said was salt, "To signify the wisdom imparted by Faith," he said, and instructed me to put it in my mouth and let it melt. I did as he said. He gave me a foot-long, lit candle and whispered, "Follow me."

Behind His Grace, I proceeded up the middle aisle of the Basilica, throughout the whole of which our footsteps echoed. An entire row of girls from Holy Heart turned all at once to face me as if in response to some command. I remembered lurking outside Mercy, watching the girls come down the steps, their bare legs pink, goose-pimpled from the cold. Look at the Archbishop, I told myself, look at his vestments trailing on the floor behind him, look at his shoulders that, even layered in gold-woven cloth, seem so thin and bony.

Instead, the memory of how the chrism oil had felt came to mind, the slow, warm crawl of it across my forehead, as did the thought of how it might feel if I applied it elsewhere, or if my mother did, her hand slick with it. I recalled the night of the Great Unveiling, her tits upright and nipple-crowned. I felt another spasm, a near shudder that I fought back with a clench so tight I wondered if, inside, I might be bleeding. I focused again on the Archbishop, who, in this very church, eleven years ago, had preached a Sermon on the Mount for Percy Joyce. On the mount.

The smoke from the incense-piping thuribles made my eyes water; tears that may have been mistaken for sheer joy ran down my face. I went where I was told to go, did what I was told to do, was steered, guided, pushed every which way by hands that sometimes were McHugh's and sometimes others. I attended to urgent instructions from a dozen unfamiliar voices. I heard my name spoken next to my ear, over and over, by men I was certain I had never met but who said "Percy" as if they had known me all my life. "Follow me, Percy. Don't walk too fast, Percy. Be careful, Percy, you're stepping on His Grace's vestments." Blood pounded in my pants as if my dick had traded places with my heart. "Light this candle from this candle. Don't let the wax drip on the floor. Read these words out loud. Speak louder, Percy, but don't shout."

It occurred to me that my mother and Pops were surely being scrutinized themselves. The unlikely winner of the Penelope Joyce sweepstakes was Pops, never mind how much his ticket cost, the boys of the Mount appraising my mother out of wonder that she let Pops have his way with her, may have let him have it all and then some just last night.

His Grace and I each opened a door of one of the wall-side confessionals, His Grace handing his ceremonial staff to an assisting priest. I stepped into that little phone booth–like compartment for the first time in my life and, with beads of sweat dripping down my face, knelt and leaned my forehead against the screen and considered letting go, letting it happen in here where no one would notice the changes in my posture and expression, where no one would hear if I moaned louder than I ever had.

"Bless me, Your Grace, for I have sinned, this is my first confession." Someone said it, it must have been me. It was not until I was in the musty darkness of the confessional, no longer conspicuously on display, that I felt truly afraid for my soul, in whose existence I did not believe. Just seconds after a soul-cleansing baptism, I was, in the words of the catechism, about to bring upon myself "the dreadful torments of body and mind" that, as a punishment for mortal sin, would eternally endure. "The body will be tortured in all its members and senses." I was about to make a confession that was not humble, not entire, not sincere just after I had received the first and greatest of all the sacraments while in a state of faithlessness and tumescence, which was surely the most mortal of all mortal sins.

I recited, by way of "confessing," my apology of months before verbatim to His Grace, who forgave me without hesitation and assigned me a lengthy penance that consisted of many prayers I had learned from the catechism. I rose to leave, but he wasn't finished with me.

"You have had a difficult childhood, Percy," Uncle Paddy said. I saw him in shadow, sitting side on to the screen, to which his ear was almost pressed. "You have already endured more than most will endure in a lifetime. And, being but a child, you have yet to endure the greatest of the sufferings that will come your way. I believe that you have a vocation, Percy. Offer up your suffering to God. Devote your life to Him and become a priest of God. I say this as much for the sake of others as for you. You can do great good, Percy. You were made as you are for a purpose. Do you believe me?"

I quelled the strongest shudder yet, grabbed my crotch with both hands and squeezed my dick as if in the hope of wringing from it an answer to Uncle Paddy's question.

"Yes, Your Grace," I gasped.

"Are you feeling well, Percy?"

"Yes, Your Grace."

"Will you reflect on this matter of your vocation? Will you pray to the Holy Ghost for guidance?"

"Yes, Your Grace, I will."

"You are a brilliant young man, Percy. It is often those who, as children, are most troublesome who turn out to have true charisma, the gift of the very breath of the Holy Spirit. The charismatic are born to lead, Percy, born to be followed down the road to heavenly salvation. Do you understand me?"

"Yes, Your Grace."

"Who knows, Percy, what God may have in mind for you. Who knows to what height, with His guidance, you may rise in the Church. I am as certain, today, that God directed me to watch over you as I was the first day I saw you, when you were but a child, sitting by yourself on the doorstep of your house."

"Yes, Your Grace."

"May God bless you, Percy Joyce."

I removed my hands from the surplice, which was crumpled and wrinkled. I left the confessional and walked alone, head bowed, to the altar rail, where I knelt, hands palm to palm, and pretended to recite my penance to myself as occasional coughs rang out in the

Basilica like the rebukes of hecklers who knew that I was faking it. When, my penance finished, I blessed myself and stood up, my mother came forward from the front row. I thought she meant to rescue me, but all she did was tug on the sleeves of my blazer. "How are you?" she whispered. Her face had the trace of a smile. Over her shoulder, surrounding my strange little family and filling the first few pews, I saw the clerics, arranged in order of rank, one of the bishops just behind Medina. I smelled my mother's perfume and turned away from her and the swollen bosom of her dress. She returned to the front row and sat beside Medina, next to whom Pops was sitting as if she and not my mother were his new bride.

I knelt alone at the altar rail, forced to keep my dick in check with nothing but my sphincter muscle and forced to look serene while doing so. My hard-on pointed, however well-disguised, at Uncle Paddy and the sacred vessels, the tabernacle, the very place of repose of the body of the Son of God.

At last, His Grace administered First Holy Communion to me. But not even this near sight of old Uncle Paddy could reverse or stall the flood inside me. I looked him in the eye to see the effect on him of my parted swollen lips, my quivering tongue, my oversized clasped hands, but I detected nothing. I knew you were some- how supposed to swallow the wafer without chewing it between your molars like a wad of gum, but I thought of McHugh's gum and the Host wound up lodged in a cavity on the right side of my mouth, from which I would later have to pry it loose with a toothpick, washing down the drain of our bathroom what many believed was the literal and certain flesh of Christ, transubstanti- ated by a priest who, before he drank it, turned wine the colour of my face into His blood.

Then the Archbishop went to the centre of the altar and spoke into a microphone. "I wish to tell you that Percy has made it known to me that it is his wish to one day be ordained by me as a priest of God."

Applause that did not seem spontaneous burst out among the priests, bishops and monsignors, and spread from them to the lesser clerics and the congregation, all of whom, it sounded like, were soon on their feet in a stamping, clapping, cheering ovation that shook the floor beneath my feet. My mother, Medina and Pops may well have been the only ones in the Basilica who were still sitting. My mother came forward, took my hand and, squeezing it tightly, smiled, leaned toward me and shouted in my ear, "Don't worry, Perse. Don't say a word. Don't look around. Just smile and look at His Grace." I saw that Pops and Medina had come up behind her. I did as she said. I smiled at His Grace, who smiled at me and extended his hands, palms upward, in my direction. My mother, Medina, Pops and I faced the congregation; I would not have been surprised if, all together, we had bowed in acknowledgement of the applause. We turned and faced His Grace again.

Making a downward motion with his hands, he instructed everyone to resume their seats. I realized in despair that he had more to say. "I ask you all to pray for Percy and his mother, Penelope. The life of a priest is a glorious but difficult one. Holy orders is the most exacting of all the sacraments. Percy faces many obstacles, more, perhaps, than most of the chosen few who are called to a life in the Church, so please remember him in your thoughts and in your prayers on this, the first day of his life in the One True Holy Apostolic and Universal Church."

Uncle Paddy wanted me to believe that, unless I dedicated my life to the Church, I'd forever be an outcast; only in the Church would I fit in. I should offer up my disfigurements to God and live among the only people who would accept me as deserving of their love and fellowship as any child of God. I'd be seen by my congregation as the cleric who had joined just to cut his losses. I would be confirmed by the Archbishop not long from now, and one day, he would ordain me as a priest. He might—who knew what the future would bring?—administer extreme unction to me, an old mentor giving last rites to his protégé, a sacramental grand slam, Percy Joyce blessed by His Grace with all six sacraments a priest could receive. This was the only ending possible to the story of Percy Joyce, the only one, he thought, that people would accept. The boy who, at birth, seemed to have been cursed by God, the boy who had blasphemed and incited to blasphemy the other children of the Mount, the boy who had seemed least likely to be the One, the chosen one, must turn out to *be* the one, the one in whom all but His Grace had ceased to believe. He would become a priest of God whose outer ugliness was the measure of his inner grace.

I turned around and surveyed the Basilica, the Big B, the labour of decades, the great dome of the ceiling, the regiments of students. I wondered how long I could exploit the patronage of the Archbishop, and when the day would come to tell him that the plot of his, my, story was about to take a sudden, unexpected twist. On that day, I would make of him as prodigious an enemy as he had been an ally. But so far he had won every battle. I turned back again.

His Grace left the altar and a pair of hands guided me into step behind him. Now, as we moved away together, I looked up. I had never seen so many girls gathered in one place before, factions of hundreds in like-coloured uniforms spread out like a patchwork quilt of blue and green, assembled in formation for *me*, gazing at me in wonder that I had come to merit an occasion such as this, that the Archbishop's patronage of me had not merely been for "show," not merely meant as an example for the laity to follow, but had been motivated by something he had spied out in me when I was but an infant, something they couldn't—and never would— see. There were some girls who stood out from the others; they seemed to be members of some upper, super order of girls, the Seraphs of the Mount. I saw Francine, her red hair and freckled face, her eyes the only ones not fixed on me but downcast. Sullen-faced, she looked as if she thought that she alone, of all who were assembled there, knew who and what I really was. I thought of my father, Jim Joyce, and wondered what he'd think of me if he could see me now. Why blame anything on someone I had never even seen? My mother and Medina and Pops might as well have made me, and I realized that was fine with me.

"This is your day, Perse, not theirs, remember that," my mother whispered. Yes, I might never have another day like this, one when I and only I was sincerely, unironically celebrated. I tried not to think if the night to come might be my night, my first night with *her*, the first night she made good on her promise.

I had never spontaneously come, except in the wet dreams of a boy's sleep, had never come without the help of my hand, the slick ring I made of my index finger and my thumb and a dab of Vaseline. Now, unable to summon an image of something more repugnant than myself, I called to mind my first memory of look-ing in the mirror: it had set me off into a bawling fit of fright and taken six months of coaxing by my mother before I looked again. But the memory had no effect in heading off the next subsur-face shudder. This was the longest I had ever spent on the verge of coming. I wondered if it would seep straight through the lacy surplice, a glistening spot, a pearl that no one who saw it would be able to explain away unless they construed it as a miracle— the miraculous, literal issuance from me of original sin, induced by baptism, the physical purgation of that ancient guilt, a shining symbol of the long-delayed banishment from Percy Joyce of the first rough beast that had slithered into Eden out of Hell.

Lines, phrases from one of my mother's favourite poems filled my mind: "A shudder in the loins engenders there. . . ." And the title of another, "The Second Coming." The Second Coming of Christ preempted by that of the "rough beast" that would take His place. What rougher beast could there be than Percy Joyce in full arousal? What "rougher," cruder thing would they ever see than the going off of Percy Joyce in the most inappropriate of places, an involuntary blasphemy that would be taken as a sign of the base corruption of my soul?

"Fuck you, old man," I thought, unable to credit the words that were running through my mind as I looked at Uncle Paddy. "I'll still be getting off when you croak out the last breath of your unlived life."

"Fuck you," I thought at almost every face. "I turned fifteen today. I'll bluster past anyone who can't bear the sight of me." I said it to the primping chorus line of bishops, to the lively ranks of misbehaving altar boys, to the rows and rows of skylarking girls, to the choir with their roundly open mouths, their heaving chests beneath the colourful androgyny of robes, the nuns who long ago were lusted-after girls, the Brothers and the priests who long ago were lusty boys and some of whom even now were lusting after just such boys as they had one time been.

A silent swell of exiting students moved me toward the doors. Hands beneath my arms lifted me clear of the floor, but I still stood upright, a head above the other boys. I felt as though I were levitating, gliding in mid-air.

I thought of my young mother, my Maker, languorous, eyes closed, lips parted as she lay stretched out in a steaming tub of water. I thought of my mother, my mother, her long dark wet hair fanned out across my belly, warm water dripping from it onto my skin as her head moved slowly up and down.

I could hold out no longer. Still inside the church, going past the baptistery, I came as I never had before, flooding my underwear, my slacks, the river running warm down my belly onto my inner thighs. I let loose a groan that was drowned out by the roaring of the celebrants and the Basilica's great bell that bonged as if in tribute.

Still stained, twice stained, thrice stained, by my face, by chrism and by come, I was hoisted onto many shoulders. Facing skyward, I lay flat on my back, made an X of my arms across my chest and closed my eyes as if I had been borne outside minus the casket I would soon be buried in.

I was swarmed by throngs of screaming students, many of them girls who had had to wait outside for my emergence as they might have waited for a sight of the newly chosen Pope. McHugh stood just inside the doorway, applauding with the others, not smiling or chewing gum, wearing an expression that clearly conveyed he had always known. There were so many people crowding the doorway and so many standing on chairs on either side of it to get a glimpse of me that we barely squeezed through, barely made it out into the open air. I saw my mother and Medina and Pops, already outside, descending the steps, my mother and Medina with arms linked in the innocent manner of best friends. My mother and Medina and Pops might as well have made me. I might live with them all their days. I might live with them all *my* days. That was fine with me and I knew they wouldn't mind.

"Here he comes," a girl shouted, her voice as sweetly pitched as any I had ever heard.

"Here he comes."

Yes, I thought, my heart going like mad. Yes, I will. I will, again. Yes. Yes.

ACKNOWLEDGEMENTS

Many thanks to: my editors at Random House Canada/Knopf Canada: the indefatigable Louise Dennys, and Amanda Lewis, both "brilliant" as Kevin's niece, Kate O'Dwyer, would say; to Sharon Klein, my publicist; to the wrangler, Deirdre Molina; to Marion Garner of Vintage Canada; to Terri Nimmo, for remembering that the book is a thing in itself; to John Sweet and Sarah Moscovitch, copyeditor and proofreader; to my agent at Rogers, Coleridge and White, Peter Straus; to the Kitchen Islanders, some of whom are: Lynda Lou Anderson, Heather Hase, Anna Mantua, Cathy Moorehead, Kathie Howes, John Lennox, Caitie Hase, Amy Hase, Todd Lefever, Paul Burrows, Robin Hunter, Sonya Skinner and Gabrielle Genovese, Pat Thome, Peter Ciglenec, Brantz Myers, Jim Perretta, Trish Crema, Roseanne Luckevich, Ann Hoy, Nate Simpson and Tara Postnikoff, Alexandra (Ali) Marin, Diane Timperley, Chris Hartmann, Indira Dass, Chris Marshall and Janice Okada, Rita Botelho, Simonida Simonovic, and any I might be forgetting who know who they are and will be glad to provide me with their names; a special thanks to three women, Pat Wilding, Laura English and Cass Shannahan; and to Rose who said "Yes."

WAYNE JOHNSTON was born and raised in the St. John's area of Newfoundland. His #1 nationally bestselling novels include *The Divine Ryans*, *A World Elsewhere*, *The Custodian of Paradise*, *The Navigator of New York* and *The Colony of Unrequited Dreams*, which will be made into a film. Johnston is also the author of an award-winning and bestselling memoir, *Baltimore's Mansion*. He lives in Toronto.